The Viper and the Storm

The Viper and the Storm

Tom Morris

A Journey of Growth

Book Three

Walid and the Mysteries of Phi

Wisdom/Works
Published by Wisdom Works
TomVMorris.com

Published 2017

Printed in the United States of America

Set in Adobe Garamond Pro
Designed by Abigail Chiaramonte
Cover Concept by Sara Morris

To MTM.

CONTENTS

I

The Poisoned Poet

Egypt. Many years ago.

To be more precise, it was around the middle of the fourth decade in the twentieth century. Exciting things were happening throughout the nineteen-thirties here in the land of the ancient pyramids. And these events would have been equally noteworthy at any time or place.

It was a morning of good things. The air was fresh and clean. A soft breeze was blowing through the open French doors of the royal sitting room. King Ali Fancoom Shabeezar was well ensconced on his most comfortable sofa, sipping tea and reading the daily newspaper in preparation for a busy morning of official duties and meetings. In the anteroom to his private quarters, the head butler was at his desk, busy going over the formal schedule for the day and making any annotations that would be helpful to the king.

Prince Walid walked through the door of the butler's reception area, and a huge grin suddenly appeared on his face. "Kular! You're back!"

"Yes, Prince, I've returned." The butler had a big smile as well, at the sight of Walid. "This will be my first day back on the job, after the nice long vacation your uncle gave me."

"How are you feeling?"

"Very well. Wonderful, actually."

"I'm so glad to hear it! We've all been a little worried about whether you'd be able to recover a hundred percent from that terrible poisoning you went through, and get back to your old self."

"Thank you, Your Highness. I'm happy to report that I'm actually much better than a hundred percent, and vastly improved over my old self. I'm really like a better version of my young self!"

Walid laughed. "Good! That's great. But I have to ask: How can this be?"

"The king let me keep The Stone of Giza in my possession for the entirety of my month-long break from work. I'll have to say that the results have been marvelous—even miraculous."

Walid was intensely curious about how much truth there might be in all the lore about the ancient emerald that was first discovered, it was said, at the foot of the Sphinx, buried deep in the sand. The legend was that anyone in possession of this beautiful jewel would have his or her deepest characteristics, abilities, and inclinations revealed and strengthened, however unknown they previously might have been. An apparently mild mannered man might become a courageous leader, as a hidden part of his character was brought to light and amplified. A secretly greedy person would become more openly and extremely avaricious in his conduct. Hardly suspected talents could appear in full bloom, or long concealed flaws might suddenly surface for all to see. You never knew what the stone would uncover and magnify. And it also carried great healing power for the physical body. At least, that was the myth. So Walid couldn't help but ask, "What exactly have you experienced from having it with you all this time?"

Kular replied with great enthusiasm. "Having it for the entire month away has been quite extraordinary. Within a week, I felt the energy of a young man again. My wife was very surprised, and quite pleased, I might add. I even began engaging in daily exercises once more. I haven't done those for years. And the oddest and most wonderful things started happening."

"Like what?"

"Well, early on, I began writing poetry. And it seems like good poetry. It simply comes into my head and then flows onto the page. Often, I have to write as fast as I can just to get the words down on paper. Then I started drawing, and I even went out and bought some paints. I have a canvas going at all times now. I'm a painter! Who knew it was even possible?"

"Really?"

"Yes! I'm doing some wonderful abstract works. I'm in love with color and form and even with the process of creating such art. It's so much fun! And, the strangest thing of all has been the most satisfying."

"What's that?"

"I can play the piano like I know what I'm doing."

Walid laughed. "You can? Did you ever play before?"

"When I was a small boy, my mother gave me some lessons. And I played now and then for years. But I haven't touched the instrument in more than half a century. Then, suddenly, just this past month, I began playing a bit at the home of a neighbor. At first, I'd just sit and tentatively explore the keyboard. But I seemed to get better every time I messed around with it."

"Really?"

"Yes. Sometimes I'd play for a few minutes, and then occasionally, thanks to the gracious hospitality of my neighbor, I'd be able to sit and play for hours. I mentioned this new experience to the king one day when he visited, and he sent me a beautiful piano for my own home! I couldn't believe it! Now, I sit for a little while each day and play. It's such an amazing emotional release! There's nothing like music to calm you down, or to lift you up for the day."

"Wow."

Kular suddenly looked very serious. "They say music reflects the mathematical structure of the universe and penetrates deep within our brains and bodies. It moves our souls. Some even claim it's the language of the angels."

"This is all pretty wild," Walid said, and then he paused for a moment. "I've never even heard of anything like that."

"It's certainly new to me."

"Let me ask you this: When you first sat down at the neighbor's piano and started messing around, were you playing what you had learned as a boy?"

"At first, I think so, yes, but then I just seemed to be able to play more and more pieces. I somehow played things I had only heard before, and I could read music on sight and play what I was seeing! My fingers just magically knew what to do. It had to be the stone."

"Do you still have it with you?"

"No. Not now. I returned it to the king with immense gratitude this morning when I came back for work. It's much safer with him. He was so gracious to let me hold on to it as long as I might need it, to heal completely from the terrible poison. But the time was right to return it."

"And how do you feel without it?"

"So far, so good. I have to admit that, at first, I was a little concerned. So, right after I gave it to the king, I walked down to the music room, and at quite a jaunty stride, I should tell you. I sat down at the piano there, and I was able to play just as well as I did at home with the stone in my pocket. I actually composed a song quickly, on the spot, and with lyrics. You should have heard me singing!"

"Really?"

"Yes! So, the poetry still comes to me. And I already have an itch to paint later today. Perhaps an abstract piece inspired by the pyramids at sunset." Kular had a grin on his face. "I even did some sit-ups on the carpet right here, earlier this morning."

Walid laughed again. "Good! Maybe the stone's effects are permanent, or at least, long-lasting."

"I certainly hope they are. And I'm sure my wife does too! I'm getting so much done around the house. I don't just sit around after work like a tired old man any more. And, you know, now that I think about it, she's also been much more energetic since we've had the stone in the house. She seems even youthful and lively. It's as if we've both suddenly shed some of the less desirable elements of aging." Kular paused and said, "I might even take her out to a club tonight and do a little dancing."

Walid laughed again. "It's really great to hear all this, Kular. It's so good to have you back, and especially at what sounds like four-hundred percent!"

Kular also laughed and said, "Yes, thank you, Prince, that may be about right—I'm now the four-hundred percent man!"

"It's just amazing that such a horrible thing as the poisoning could lead to all this."

"Yes, it is. And we should always remember that lesson. Bad things can open the door to very good things."

"You sound like the king. That's the sort of wisdom he's been intent on teaching me recently."

Kular nodded and said, "Life unfolds in unexpected and often wonderful ways. It leaves us wondering at all the hidden forces that must be at work under the surface and behind the scenes."

"You're right. That's what I'm learning, as well."

Just then, Mafulla came through the door with a football. "Kular!"

"Hello there, Mr. Mafulla!"

"You're back!" Mafulla sat the ball down on Kular's desk and stepped around it to give him a big hug. Then he said, "Wait! Are those new muscles in your arm?"

Kular laughed and replied, "Yes, I'm delighted to say."

"It's the stone," Walid explained.

"What?"

The prince turned to his friend with a big smile and said, "It's the magic of the stone."

"Really?"

"Yeah. Having The Stone of Giza in his pocket for a month didn't just help Kular heal from the poison, it also gave him back the strength of his youth, and a new experience of several artistic abilities—to draw and paint, write poetry, and play the piano."

"No way." Mafulla looked at his friend and then back at Kular.

"Yes, there's apparently a way," Kular said with a big smile. "Pretty soon, I'll be working out with you two and Masoon, and later writing a song about it. Who knows?"

Mafulla laughed out loud and said, "Awesome. That's just amazing."

Walid went on. "And he gave the king back the stone this morning, but he still has all his new talents and strengths, so apparently, what the stone brings out in a person is either permanent or at least keeps going, maybe as long as you keep using it, or cultivating it, or whatever."

"Jeepers."

"At least, that's my best guess right now." By explaining all this to Mafulla, Walid was trying himself to absorb how the stone might work, or at least what the expected duration of its effects might be. It was all so fascinating and full of mystery.

"Ok, then." Mafulla was clearly thinking it all through as well. He looked at Walid and said, "We have to ask the king if he'll let the two of us borrow the stone for a while. I want to make sure that the deal is sealed with the lovely Hasina."

"You're hilarious."

"No, really. It's important in such matters that there's no doubt. The stone of legend should take care of that. I mean, I understand that my normal animal magnetism is likely more than enough, but then again, you can't be too careful. I'd also vastly prefer to be able to do homework in minutes rather than hours. And then I'd like to invent a telephone that you can carry around in your pocket, so I can talk to Hasina all the time, and you of course, and then maybe I'll discover the cures for a few bad diseases and perhaps even get some world peace going on—at least, later in the day. But, probably it would have to be in that order. Hasina comes first. And then she'll like the phone and the cures and the world peace … you know, the stuff that comes shortly afterwards."

"All thanks to the emerald," Walid said.

"All thanks to the emerald," Mafulla replied. And then he added, "The rest of the world will just have to be appropriately green with envy, but in such a way, of course, that it doesn't at all disturb the blissful peace I will have established."

"Ha!" Walid shook his head, then turned to Kular and said, "I get to listen to such things all the time."

"You're very blessed with continual entertainment, then."

"Yes, I'd have to agree. But I was almost forgetting why I'm here. Could we slip in to see the king for a minute?"

"Certainly. Let me check on him and announce your presence."

While the old but now young-seeming butler went in to tell the king that the boys were there, Mafulla picked up his ball and said, "I'm pretty impressed with all that's happened to our friend."

"Yeah, it's wild," Walid answered.

"I wondered if maybe the legends were just stories, you know, nothing more than entertaining myths made up long ago for entertainment, but with no connection to reality."

"Yeah, I was curious, too. The other stories we've heard about the stone could all have been the results of some sort of coincidence—I mean, if anything is really just a coincidence. But this is way too much for that, and it all seems pretty real."

"True. Kular suddenly has some major arm muscles under those sleeves—quite impressive triceps and biceps. As soon as I grabbed his arm to hug him, I thought, Whoa! What's this?"

At that moment, their favorite butler returned and said, "Boys, the king will see you now, but he has only a short time available before his scheduled meetings begin."

"Thanks, Kular, that's fine," Walid said. "We need only five minutes."

The prince opened the door and held it for Mafulla. Ali was looking up already and said, "Mafulla, good morning to you."

"Good morning, Your Majesty," he said in reply.

"And Walid, a happy morning to you as well."

"A wonderful morning to you, My Royal and Favorite Uncle."

"I am, of course, your only uncle."

"Yes, and so your exalted status will never be challenged."

The king laughed. "I needed a witty spark this morning to start up my brain. I have too much work today, after too little sleep last night."

Walid explained, "We won't keep you from the work long. I just wanted to come by early to check on a rumor I heard late yesterday."

"What did you hear? It wasn't about my dancing lessons, was it?"

The prince laughed. "No. I have in fact, though, heard someone say that you seem quite graceful these days. But the rumor I wanted to check on is different. I was coming back from the library late and I overheard two palace guards talking about Farouk al-Khoum."

"Oh, yes. There is indeed some news."

"Can you share it with us?"

"Surely. I was planning to do so, soon. Recent, confirmed reports from trustworthy sources tell us that Farouk al-Khoum is not just in hiding but that he definitely has left the kingdom, along with his brother Faraj and their close associates, including that man, Tau. His several business ventures here continue to operate, though."

"But, how?"

"There are no laws on the books that would allow us to shut them down or take them over without setting a bad precedent. There are layers of ownership and management that are legitimate and seem to involve citizens who are in no way criminal. But, meanwhile, we're monitoring all the enterprises that we've identified."

"You mean, we can't shut down his companies from simply knowing that he poisoned Kular in an effort to steal stuff from the palace?"

"I'm afraid not. We know with certainty only that his brother Faraj poisoned Kular, and that it's he who sought our treasures. We, as of yet, have no direct way to prove that he was doing so at the direction of Farouk, or even in close league with him. That's obviously how things look, to be sure, but without more proof, we can't move that dramatically against Farouk. Plus, there are the other complications."

"But we're also pursuing Faraj?"

"Yes, at this point, we're equally seeking them both."

"Where did they go?"

"We're not yet sure. There are reasons to believe Farouk left by boat on the Nile, the very day that Faraj poisoned our friend and took the fake treasures, but we're currently unsure of his destination. At this point, he knows we're looking for him. But, remember, he most likely thinks he succeeded in taking from us the powerful weapons he wanted for the schemes he plans, and that mistaken belief on his part will make him both more and less dangerous to us."

"What do you mean?"

"His belief will certainly embolden him to act against us. But, as long as my trick works and he doesn't discover that the items Faraj stole from us are forgeries, we have a great advantage over him. He won't know that the things he'll depend on at a crucial time will inevitably fail him. And that's good. But, in any case,

I'm sure we haven't heard the last from him. He remains a serious danger to the kingdom."

"Yeah, I guess so," Mafulla said. "Since he's a former Phi and everything."

The king continued, "Remember, the only reasons that a man like him could have wanted The Book of Phi and The Ring of Phi would be to identify all the chief adversaries he'll have to fight in an attempt on the kingdom, and learn any of their vulnerabilities, and, of course, to have in his possession the power of that mystical ring, in case he might need dramatic help beyond what's otherwise available."

"What about the stone?" Mafulla asked. "I never got clear on why he wanted that."

"Well, he did own it for a while, and perhaps has no idea what it truly is, and just wanted it back, as an expensive and quite valuable item. But more could be at stake. Who knows? He could be involved in dancing lessons, too, and hoping the stone could bring out some hidden talent that he's never yet manifested." The boys both smiled and nodded.

Walid asked, "Is there anything we can do to help pursue him, or to see to it that he can't gather strength abroad and return to pull off the revolution he clearly wants?"

"We're tasking some of the men on this and will be pursuing all leads. But for now, I'm fairly certain that we don't need to be concerned about any imminent danger from him or any of his associates."

"That guy really worried me," Mafulla said. "Well, he still does."

"Why the worry, my friend?"

"I should have used the word 'concern.' I try not to worry, but you know, it's all the stuff about being the one bad Phi, and about the powers he may have—all the abilities that could make him a pretty scary opponent."

"You're correct in thinking that we've not yet been able to take his full measure as a threat to the kingdom. He's been out of our circles for far too long. There are many things we're yet to learn about him. But we persist. And I'm confident we'll succeed against him. His track record for action against us, so far, isn't great. But he could be saving his strengths to spring something big on us all at once. And yet, we have a unique team in place here, possibly even the strongest the palace has ever seen."

Mafulla nodded his agreement. "I guess you're right, Your Majesty. I shouldn't worry about the guy, or even be that concerned. After all, Walid and I were able to block his plans a couple of times, and you pretty well neutralized his best effort yet to get what he wanted."

"Yes. And as long as he believes that he's finally been triumphant over us in acquiring the things he's sought since we came into power, he'll be inclined to underestimate us. And that gives us an extra edge."

"I hadn't thought of it like that. And now we know what he's after."

"At least, for the most part. I'm sure we don't know all his plans. Yet, we know enough to be able to make general preparations for a next move on his part. As long as we retain the genuine Book of Phi, the real Ring of Phi, and the authentic Stone of Giza, we have all the legendary items that he's presumably convinced he needs in order to prevail over us. So, nothing's really changed except that he's much more vulnerable than when he was working in secret, and especially now that he wrongly thinks he owns the most important tools for his future goals."

The king looked down at his beautiful rose gold Reverso watch and said, "Oh, my, how the time passes when I'm talking with you two! I have a first meeting shortly, and one that you'd find quite boring—a dispute over mining rights that I need to settle, and it should be quite tedious—or I'd invite you to sit in, before you have to go to class."

"That's Ok, Your Majesty, we were thinking about going out to play some ball with the other guys before school."

"Good. But, you know, I do have one meeting today that you might want to attend."

"What's that?" Mafulla asked.

"Rolls Royce is delivering some new cars to us."

"Oh! Great!"

Walid asked, "What time?"

"Right after your class is out, or perhaps about a half an hour after Khalid should be dismissing you."

"We can come to see the cars?"

"Yes. You're cordially invited. Go around to the palace garage and the stable area, out back."

"We'll be there!" Mafulla had a big grin on his face again.

Across town, Anwar the merchant was closing up his store back at the far end of the marketplace. He had decided to take a long mid-day lunch break to rest and had sent off his sole employee to go do the same, even though it was still just the middle of the morning. But already, this early, two petty thieves had brought in valuable merchandise for him to sell, back-to-back, and moments after they left, he had made a very big sale, roughly equivalent to the total income from two normal days. That was enough, he thought. It was his prerogative as the owner of the shop to take some time off whenever he felt like it, and he planned to enjoy a nice meal at his home nearby, followed by a well-earned nap.

He was out front at the corner of the building picking up a sign that he kept inside whenever the shop was closed. Suddenly, a voice whispered loudly from down and across the alley. "Anwar!"

He stopped for a moment and listened but, looking around, didn't see anyone. Maybe it was just the wind.

"Anwar!" There it was again, and a bit louder. "Over here!" A short distance farther down the dirt alley from where he stood and across the narrow path, behind the building next door, he could see someone in the shadows, but couldn't make out who it was.

The voice got a bit louder still. "Anwar, my friend, I need to speak with you. I have something for you."

This got his attention at a new level. The merchant put down his sign and stepped carefully across the dusty path, looking up and down its length to make sure he wasn't being watched by anyone.

"Who is it? What do you want?" He spoke also in a loud whisper and with hesitation. He didn't dare walk all the way to where the shadow loomed. He had enemies.

"It's me." The man stepped partially out of the shadows.

"What? How can it be? What are you doing here?"

"I'm back. I just got back into town."

"But I thought all your men were dead and that you were next, and surely gone by now, meeting your maker in the next world."

"No, no, I'm fine. And not all my men were … eliminated. Just a few were taken, and now I have new men. The coward who betrayed me and removed my former associates would not come to face me himself. He showed that he couldn't stand up to me."

"But I thought it was you who left town in fear of him."

"No. I left only to confuse him and give me a chance to fortify my operation. He had plenty of time to come to where I was and fight me like a man, but no one came."

"Why are you here? It's dangerous for me to be talking to you."

"No, I can assure you. There's no danger, not anymore. I'm back with a new enterprise and a plan that will make you a rich man."

"But don't you understand? I could be killed for speaking to you."

"Don't make me laugh. He's a fraud. Fraud al-Khoum. And he's the one who's now left town. He's fled the entire kingdom."

"What?"

"He's on the run. I've been told. I have sources. He's a large bloated old dog who can still bark plenty, but has very little bite left in him."

"He bit your men to death."

"He got lucky. But against me, he wouldn't dare try a thing, I tell you."

"Still."

"I spit on him. He is a man of appearance with very little that's real."

"But he's rich and powerful. He was your boss, your employer."

"He thought so. But it was only for a while. I took his money, and plenty of it. He's a fool."

"Why did he leave?"

"No one really knows. But I've heard he was trying to get some stone, some jewel, from the king and that, suddenly, he just ran away with his close associates. They're cowards. That's all they are. They're nothing."

"If it's as you say, then why are you in the shadows?"

"I have other reasons. I have plans that need to remain secret."

"What are your plans?"

"I can't say. But I can tell you something. Now that the one we've just spoken of is out of the way and not causing me trouble, I've decided to return to run all the activities in the kingdom that can flourish outside the bounds of our antiquated laws, just like before. I'll soon have some special opportunities for you, my friend."

"Well, that's good, very good, and I appreciate your trust, but only if you're sure he's gone."

"He's gone. I know it as a fact. If you doubt me, go by the Grand Hotel where he's always stayed in town, and ask about him. They'll tell you. He's not here."

"Ok, I believe you. But what does this have to do with me?"

"I wanted you to know I'm back. My brother or one of the men will be in touch with you soon about an item, or a group of items I may want to sell, a sale that could bring you an enormous profit as my agent."

"What is it that you have in mind?"

"The less I say about it now, the better. What I'm speaking about is not yet in my possession, but soon will be. I'll let you know what to expect and when to expect it, when my plans are complete. I'll make you immensely wealthy."

"That sounds good."

"You'll be able to buy yourself a big new home with a pool and servants, I tell you."

"I'm more than ready for that."

"Good. But, meanwhile, we can still do some small bits of business that will be mutually beneficial. I'll be in touch again soon."

With these words, the man who for a very long time had been widely regarded as a master of criminal activity throughout the kingdom, and even in their entire region of the world, simply walked away, back into the shadows.

Ari Falma had returned, and nothing good could come of it.

2

A Surge in Crime

"Did anyone read this morning's paper?" Khalid often liked to start class with a question. The boys just sat and looked at him.

"Have any of you even seen today's paper?" Jabari, Malik, and Set slowly raised their hands.

"This is not a trick question. There's no need for such guarded reticence. Jabari, did you notice any of the headlines?"

"Yes, a few of them."

"Do you remember one?"

"Crime is up in the city and the kingdom."

"Correct. This is the big news story of the day. Crime is suddenly up. Did you notice what sort of crime?"

Set said, "I heard my parents talking about it. They mentioned theft, robbery, assault, and some indication there's an organized protection racket in the city, whatever that means."

Khalid responded, "A protection racket is a criminal enterprise that physically threatens merchants and their property, mainly, then offers them a guarantee of protection against the threat of violence for a price each week, or each month."

"Really?" Set said.

"Yes. It's a big source of income for criminal organizations around the world."

"So, in a protection racket, people pay the bad guys not to do bad things to them?"

"Yes."

"Why don't they just tell the police?"

"Because the bad guys threaten that if they go to the authorities, much worse things will happen to their property and to them, and even to their families."

"But why don't they just tell the police all this—I mean, about the extra threats also?"

"Well, people often do, and then they sometimes suffer the threatened consequences. The police aren't always around. And they have to catch someone in the act, or have good evidence that a person has done these things, in order to put him in jail for it."

"So this activity is increasing?" Walid asked.

"Yes. And other forms of crime are up. The strange thing is that, throughout the city, criminal activity has been quite low for months. But suddenly, we have this spike. Now, the next question: Does anyone know what normally causes an increase in property crime and physical assault?"

"Bad social conditions, unemployment, a big gap between rich and poor that creates resentment and a sense of helplessness. And too many people between the ages of twelve and twenty-five with too much time on their hands and not enough guidance." Everyone turned toward Mafulla, who had just given what sounded like the answer of a sociologist.

"That's well said, Doctor Mafulla," Khalid replied with a smile.

Malik spoke up. "But we really don't have any of those things going on in the city or the kingdom right now, do we?" He had a puzzled look on his face and had directed his question to Khalid, but then glanced over at Mafulla.

"What do you think?" Khalid asked the rest of the boys.

"People are pretty happy wherever I go, or maybe the word is content," Jabari said. "I mean—there are always a few troubled souls around, but not enough to start a crime wave."

"The economy seems to be doing well. Most people who want jobs have jobs, I think," Mafulla offered. "My dad says that business is basically very good."

"So, Khalid, what's the answer?" Walid asked.

He shrugged. "No one seems to know. And that's why I brought it to your attention this morning. There are many questions to which we have no immediate answers. In such matters, we must allow ourselves to realize that we simply don't know. But then, when the question's important, we continue searching for an answer. We keep our minds open and active in pursuit of more information. Not everything is like math class where, for every question, there's a clear answer, often easily available in the back of the book. There are many questions to which we have no sure answers, or at least no answers that everyone knows to be true. People may have opinions. But there's a big difference between opinion and knowledge."

"Could you give an example?" Set asked.

"Of what?"

"Questions to which we have no sure answers."

"Certainly. Some things, we just don't know. There will always be an element of mystery around us. For instance: Why is there anything in existence at all? What, if anything, was happening nine hundred billion years ago and why? What exactly is time? Is the overall cosmic realm of physical being infinite or limited? What really is matter? What is mind? There are many such questions. And some are of vital concern. For example: What, precisely, happens after a person's death?"

"Normally a funeral, some crying, and then a nice buffet," Mafulla said with a straight face and serious tone.

"Very funny," Khalid replied. And then he went on to say,

"Some mysteries can be solved fairly quickly; others, over time; and a few, perhaps, not at all."

"You mean there are some things we'll never know?" Bafur asked.

"Our minds have great power," Khalid responded. "But they have limits, too. We can contemplate eternal matters and ponder infinity, but our brains are finite and temporal things with limitations, despite their truly, amazingly immense reach."

"Ok, our brains are finite and temporal, located in space and time, but could our minds, in their core, be infinite and eternal?" Mafulla asked.

"Ah, that's a deep one, and an issue on which people can disagree. I have an opinion. But do I have knowledge? Or do I, at this point in my life, have limits that prohibit such knowledge, at least for now?"

Walid said, "How do we know exactly where our limits are?"

"By pushing, always pushing and expanding what we do know. Then we can begin to have a clue as to what our ultimate limits, if any, might be. But in principle, I suspect, they are mostly far away from the ordinary, mundane matters of practical living—except of course, for logical limits, like it's being impossible to waste all your time later today completely and yet also to use it well, all at once. And, there may be other exceptions where our ultimate limitations are nearer to us."

"Like, maybe, where understanding girls is involved," Haji said.

"Yes, perhaps, like that," Khalid agreed, and a number of the boys smiled with knowing expressions.

Mafulla raised his hand and Khalid nodded. He said, "Sometimes, we think we have limits that we don't actually have."

"You're right," Khalid responded. "And, if we don't try to go beyond the perceived limit, we'll never know what our true power might be, or where the real limits are."

Their teacher paused for a moment and then remarked, a bit

enigmatically, "We embody both nobility and humility— exalted power and limits. In fact, I believe that we have at the same time unimaginably great power and real, inviolable limits on how that power properly can be used. We do possess the power to break through artificial limits. Some breakthroughs are fast, and yet others are slow. There may even be real limits on how fast we can get beyond our false limits. We need to respect both our true power and our genuine limits. A failure of that respect always leads to trouble. That's the human condition."

The class sat in complete silence for almost ten seconds. Then, Khalid said, "And, speaking of the human condition … I believe the condition of the young men at this particular location within the vastness of the cosmos and at this point in the potentially infinite flow of time, is that you have written assignments to turn in, right now."

A few comments, groans, and a shuffling of papers began to break the philosophical spell that Khalid often created in the classroom, only then to bring his students suddenly back down to earth and to whatever task at hand their ongoing educations required, from a practical point of view. Walid was just glad he didn't announce a pop test, as he often would do after moments of philosophical reflection. It was always hard to switch gears from contemplating fundamental truths and paradoxes to writing out Greek vocabulary definitions, proving theorems, or identifying important dates in history.

As the prince pondered these things, he then began to wonder about some of his own questions, like when he'd be able to see Khalid's daughter Kissa again. It had been a few days, due to an unusually busy schedule. It occurred to him that maybe he could ask her after school to go with him to see the new cars that were being delivered to the king. Mafulla could also invite Hasina to come along. The king surely wouldn't mind. Why would he? Ali was always glad to see the girls. At the break, Walid would have to mention this to Mafulla. And maybe they should talk about the recent crime stuff, too. He began to have a strange feeling that something was going on beyond what the newspaper had reported, and that it somehow would eventually involve him, and most likely, his best friend.

The big grocery stand that was down a few storefronts from the Adi shop was always a popular spot in the market. This morning, the fruit and vegetables shined brightly and even seemed to glow in the warmth of the sun. The grocer had just been out to spray them with clean, cool water. Everything looked delicious. Shapur Adi was glad that his wife Shamilar had asked him to go down and get a few things she could use in her preparations later on for dinner. He loved smelling the fresh fruit and squeezing whatever could legitimately be squeezed in his quest for the perfect degree of ripeness.

At the moment, he was gazing at some particularly bright vegetables, lost in thought. "Hello, Shapur. How are you on this fine day?" Badar Sakat suddenly stood beside him, carefully making selections for a mid-day salad that he would share with his brother Mumar at their shop later.

"Oh, Badar! I didn't see you there. Good day to you. I'm doing well on this new morning. Thank you for asking. Business is already brisk."

"Excellent. That's nice to hear. Of course, if you see anyone with shoddy sandals, send them over to my shop for a quick repair. So far, there have been very few feet though the door this morning."

"I always recommend you and Mumar. You have by far the finest leathers in town, and you do a magnificent job of both making and repairing sandals. I've never been so comfortable on my feet in my entire life as I have since you two moved in and set up shop across the way."

"Thank you for the kind compliment. I'll pass it on to my brother."

Shapur then said, "Have you, by the way, seen any of this crime wave they're talking about in the paper?"

"Yes, I'm sorry to tell you," Badar replied right away. "I've witnessed two muggings and some petty theft in the past week, right here in the marketplace."

"Oh, my. That's too bad. I'm sorry to hear it."

"Yes. It's a shame. One potential theft I was able to break up, and the criminal ran away, but I have to be careful what I do, as you know. It can be a bit frustrating at times, but my main job is important, as I think you'd agree, and it requires a good measure of caution, care, and discretion," he confided in a low, hushed tone.

"Your job is very much appreciated, I can assure you."

"Thank you."

Badar and his brother Mumar were military men, assigned by the king right after the revolution to the task of watching over the Adi shop and protecting the family from harm. Since Mafulla had moved in to the palace as the best friend of Prince Walid, his family had been targeted a couple of times by enemies of the monarchy, led by the notorious crime lord, Ari Falma, a man who had disappeared from the city and the kingdom after a number of his men were killed. They had met their end while holding some of Mafulla's family as kidnap victims, in pursuit of something Falma wanted. And even though he had left town months earlier and had not been heard from since, the Sakat brothers still kept a close vigil over the family's store.

Just then, a man appeared in the doorway of the grocery, looking straight at Shapur. He walked right up to him, approaching him from behind. And as he reached out to take his arm, Badar, standing no more than four feet away and seeing the shadow of his movement, tensed a bit, ready to act quickly in the next moment.

"Brother, how are you?" The man spoke up, still unseen.

Adi spun around as Badar also turned, and the one who had been addressed replied, "Reela! When did you get back in town?"

"Just now. I went to the shop to see you, but they told me you were down here, so I came to greet you and snag a bag of figs."

"Ha! Good. You know Badar Sakat don't you? The fellow who runs the sandal shop with his own brother across the street from me?"

"Yes, Badar!" Reela looked over and said, "It's nice to see you."

Badar smiled and said, "It's good to see you, as well. I know we just met months ago, but I've always had a strange feeling that I knew you in the past, or knew of you. I seemed to recognize you when we were recently introduced."

"I've never been in the sandal or leather trades, and I must admit that I hadn't had the good fortune to be one of your customers until we met, some months ago."

"I had a feeling it was from long before that. But my memory's not putting it into context. What's your work?"

"I'm a consultant to companies doing international business."

"Hmm. That's not it."

"I used to work for the kingdom, in diplomacy," Reela said.

Shapur leaned over and whispered, "He was a spy."

Reela smiled and said, "I was in the diplomatic corps. I worked on matters of international information gathering and analysis."

"He was a spy, and a good one, as our enemies could attest," Shapur explained with pride.

"Oh?"

"Ok," Reela laughed, "I was a spy."

"That's why I remembered you. In part of my early career I recall hearing of many good things you had done for the kingdom."

"Ah, yes, thanks—it was a pharaoh's age ago. I had my share of success along the way. But it's not a business for a man of my years now, so I retired some time ago."

"You seem to be in excellent shape."

"I try. But I'm sure my reflexes aren't quite what they once were."

Badar quickly tossed a pomegranate right at him and he caught it, mid-air, and smiled.

"Sorry, I couldn't help myself," Badar laughed. "If that's slow, I would hate to see fast." Reela laughed also and nodded, as he gently handed the fruit back to the younger man.

"Badar, I know of your present work, and appreciate your diligence. My brother has confided in me, for reasons you might imagine. I would like a minute of your time, and Shapur's, if you both could join me out front, whenever it's convenient."

Shapur was curious and said to Badar, "Let me have your bag. The proprietor here of course knows me well. He'll hold our selections for us until we come back in." Taking it in hand, he motioned over to an older man who was arranging fruit in the back and set both the bags down on a nearby counter. Then, picking up a pen that was lying there, he marked one 'S' and the other 'A' and turned to walk outside.

Reela was already there with Badar. As Shapur drew near, Reela said, "We need to stand close and speak in low voices."

"What is it, my brother?"

"There's no cause for alarm, but I have reliable reports that Ari Falma is back in the city with a newly expanded band of men, and they've already organized several extensive criminal operations that are now active around town."

"Oh, that's terrible news," Shapur said.

"I don't think he'll bother you or the family again," Reela reassured him. "I think he's had enough bad luck with you not to get involved with the family any more. He's a superstitious man. But, still, I thought it would be good for me to pass on this information to you both, first thing."

"Thank you for this," Badar said. "May I ask the source of the news?"

"I was in Morocco for business. I still keep in touch with old friends there, and they, in turn, with their old friends. The resulting networks of information span our part of the world, as well as Europe and even America. A reliable source there told me of this development. There were at first some purchases from arms dealers, then a few rumors of recruiting. Falma was apparently in Libya for a time and was in touch with our previous king. They're bound on continuing the collaborative efforts that were so lucrative for both of them when Rasul was in power. My sources don't know whether their intent at this stage is entirely criminal, or if there are royal ambitions in the mix."

"Oh, my."

"I need to tell King Ali about all of it. But I suspect very strongly that the king doesn't know of my previous work for the kingdom—unless, Shapur, you've had occasion to mention it."

"No, no, until today, with Badar just now, I haven't told anyone. I was tempted to share your work history with the king when I first met him, to reinforce the ties between our family and the monarchy, but because of who was in power when you served, I wasn't sure it was a good thing to bring up at a first meeting."

"It was quite sensible not to introduce the topic at that point."

"I mean, you had absolutely nothing to do with that regime's corruption and served simply out of a sense of patriotic duty to our land, but I didn't want to bring all this into the mix of the relationships that were just beginning to be built because of the wonderful and unexpected friendship of the prince and Mafulla."

"You were wise to allow the past to be past, and the present to be present. But in the very near future, perhaps a friendly introduction would allow me to warn the king about all that I know."

"Yes, that's a good idea, and something to do right away."

Reela suddenly caught a glimpse of someone at a distance, and it surprised him. He said, in the low voice he had been using, "Please, both of you, and this is important … if you could continue to stand just where you are, and don't look around at all, for the moment, and let's continue to talk, about anything."

"What do you mean?" Shapur asked, puzzled.

"Badar, you can tell me about your business."

"Ok. The business is going well, and yet is a bit quiet today. But I must ask you what's going on."

"I think I recognize a man down the street coming this way and, if I do, his presence here could be bad news of a different sort for all of us. He's just now stopped to look into a shop window."

"Is there an imminent threat?" Badar asked, as he instinctively repositioned his right hand nearer to his concealed weapon.

"No, you won't need that," Reela said to Badar, looking him in the eyes. "At least, not now." Badar nodded slightly, and his body relaxed a bit.

"What?" Shapur asked, with a puzzled look. Reela held up his hand as if to signal silence or restraint, or that the question could wait.

A few seconds passed. "I'm very surprised at this."

"Who is it?" Badar said.

"I'm not yet quite sure that my eyes aren't playing tricks on me," Reela confessed. "But as he gets a bit closer, it confirms to me that an old adversary of mine is unexpectedly here, and his presence in the kingdom right now is something I don't take to be a positive sign."

"And this is?" Badar again sought more information.

"A man named … Kinkaid. At least, that's what I think his name is. He's assumed many aliases over the decades. And he's a very bad character. Under the guise of the British diplomatic corps, he did many things that would horrify his countrymen, if they only knew."

"Are you sure that's the man you see?" Badar allowed himself a quick glance up to the side.

"Yes, now, I just caught a fuller glimpse of him, and … I'm certain it's the man. Wait. Ok, good, he just turned down a side street with someone and didn't likely see me at all. I need to tell the king about him, right away, and find out why he's here."

"We can go to the palace now," Shapur offered. "The shop will be fine. Kaza can take care of everything for me."

"That would be a good idea," Reela said.

Badar made a suggestion. "I can call into the communications office at the palace, tell them you're coming, and ask someone to do a background check on this Kinkaid. Reela, what's his given name?"

"Harvey. Also, if you could ask them to find out where he's staying, that would be nice to know, as well. I'd suspect, from his past habits, that it's the Grand Hotel. But, double-check. And if you can, find out how long he plans to be here."

Shapur turned to his brother. "Do you think this has anything to do with Ari Falma being back?" He couldn't shake from his mind the way he had once been deceived by Falma, who under the pretense of kingdom business had for a short time set up a hotbed of criminal activity in the back of his shop and used the space to store things that had been stolen, some of them from the palace. Then, later, there had been the assault and violent kidnapping. To all in the Adi family, Ari Falma was bad news, and the possibility that he was in alliance with an old enemy of Reela's was just too unsettling to contemplate.

Reela said, "I don't know if Kinkaid and Falma might be linked or not. It's really impossible to say at this point. It may just be a bad coincidence, or something more might be going on. I think we need to get to the bottom of it all, though, as soon as we can. Whether they're working together, or are in the city on separate business, we'll likely very soon have problems on our hands, and perhaps trouble of major proportions. We need to be prepared for the worst."

What Reela, Badar, and Shapur could not know was that, at least in the current context of kingdom life, the first seeds of what Reela referred to as "the worst" had already been planted and they were beginning to sprout up, just barely peeking out of the soil.

3

Unexpected Developments

Hoda knew it was time to summarize the discussion her class had been having. She began drawing some conclusions by saying, "So, there has to be a proper balance in life between freedom and order."

But there was one more point to make. She said, "The United States of America is the biggest experiment we've had in the democratic realization of these ideas and their healthy balance, despite an early scourge of slavery in parts of their land." She paused.

"The nation we know there today was initially settled and developed, beyond the local and regional presence of the Native Americans who were largely tribal, by means of a vast immigration of people coming from mostly European monarchies. These settlers arrived in their new land imbued with lifelong habits of political order, but also typically had felt that the ordered structures in which they'd lived had gone too far and had become oppressive. So, after arduous journeys across the ocean, they arrived on the new continent with a burning desire for freedom, or liberty, in both the areas of religious and political expression, as well as in several other matters of life choice. A past presumption of order and a new passion for freedom was the heady mix that launched the process of self-rule on a national scale that much of the world at present either admires and seeks to emulate, or else fears and even resents."

Kissa said, "I guess it's always hard to get the freedom and order balance right, even in your personal life."

"Yes it is," Hoda replied. "And that's well said. Too much order can be repression or stagnation. Too little order can create chaos and confusion. Whether people live in a monarchy or in a representative democracy, they need a dynamic balance of freedom and order."

"Are they really just opposites?" Bakat asked.

"I was about to ask the same thing," Cabar said.

Hoda answered, "That's a good question to raise. We do often think of them as opposites, these two qualities, but the truth about them is much deeper."

"What do you mean?" Bakat seemed to be intensely interested.

"Well, let's see. How can I best say it?" Hoda thought for a second and then said, "I believe that each exists for the purpose of bringing about the right measure of the other."

"Ok. I don't understand that at all," Ara laughed. "Can you explain it?"

"I'll try." She smiled and continued, "We have freedom for the purpose of creating the proper forms of order in our lives at the right times. We have order to provide a safe structure within which to exercise freedom in healthy and fulfilling ways. We need both. Each helps with the other. Neither should become a thing unto itself, apart from its paradoxical partner. And we should all remember what Kissa said. This insight applies just as much to an individual life as it does to a kingdom or to a democratic nation."

Hasina then spoke up and added a thought that had just popped into her head. "So, it's sort of like a Yin and Yang thing."

"What?" Khata voiced her perplexity as she looked over at Hasina with a puzzled expression on her face.

"Yin and Yang. You know, the two ultimate things we read about in that essay on Chinese culture—the complementary polarities that need each other."

Khata smiled and said, "Yes, those complementary polarities. Hasina, where do you get these words?"

"I think I've been spending too much time around Mafulla." At that, everyone laughed.

Kissa looked at her best friend and said, "No. There's a better explanation. You're just independently precocious."

"Hoda! Please, a little vocabulary time?" Khata asked with an imploring tone.

Hoda smiled again at Khata, but interrupted the silliness to say, "Actually, Hasina's right. It's very much like Yin and Yang. Too many people take an Either-Or attitude about everything, and yet sometimes, it's crucial to have a Both-And perspective. Many of the most important things in life involve a dynamic tension between apparent opposites, a paradoxical partnership that cannot and will not be resolved into a One-or-the-Other type of scenario, without something profoundly important being lost."

Hasina said, "It's still amazing to me how we can start off talking politics or economics and almost always end up with philosophy."

"Everything is related to everything else in deep and wonderful ways," Hoda replied. "To see how, you often have to step back and take a bigger view. And whenever we do that, and especially when we go deep, we're always somehow getting philosophical."

She smiled at all her girls and concluded by saying, "But now, I can tell that we're getting late with my effort to end class. So, once more, let me thank you all for your attention and participation in the day's subjects. I hope you've had a fruitful time together today, in your own estimation. We certainly have, in mine. Remember your assignments, and I'll see you tomorrow."

Several voices murmured, "Thanks, Hoda" and "Have a nice evening, and "See you tomorrow."

The girls picked up their things and most headed for the door. Bakat, Cabar and Kit lingered a few minutes to ask their teacher about one or another topic that had come up earlier in the day. And, just as Kissa and Hasina were about to walk toward the door, Walid and Mafulla popped their heads around the doorframe.

Walid spoke first. "Hi, ladies. Is it safe for a couple of guys to come in now?"

"Which guys?" Hasina asked.

"The crème of the crop," Mafulla answered, as he appeared.

"Yes, I'd love to meet them," Hasina said.

"Hardee, har," Mafulla replied. "It's just us."

"I don't think anyone will run you out, given your extremely exalted palace credentials, but I can't promise that it's safe in every possible way," Kissa said and gave Walid a big smile. "And yet, I do have to ask: To what do we owe the unusual, rare honor of this unexpected visit?"

Walid looked a little sheepish and said, "I've been … We've been wanting to come by and say hello for the last couple of days, but something happens and we get dragged into stuff—good stuff, but stuff that takes longer than we thought."

"Is that so?"

"Really. We've been trying hard to stop by and say hi."

"You don't have to explain, silly. I know that being the prince brings responsibilities. I'm just kidding with you."

"Oh! Good. That's a relief." Walid grinned.

Throughout this, Mafulla had just been smiling at Hasina, who smiled back, then looked a little self-conscious and glanced over at Hoda. Walid said, "Mafulla has something to ask you both."

Kissa looked skeptical and said to Mafulla, "You do?"

Hasina then gazed back up at Mafulla, who said, "Yes. I do." He cleared his throat dramatically and continued, "Actually, I was wondering … we were wondering … whether you ladies would like to accompany us to what may be in some ways the most important event of the year, happening this very afternoon a few short minutes from now, outside the palace on the lovely and spacious palace grounds. It will take only a little time and it promises to be an amazing experience. The king will be there, and has invited us, and he said he thinks we'll love it."

Hasina smiled and replied, "This sounds absolutely delightful, for what's still a complete mystery. What sort of event or experience are we talking about?"

"Well, perhaps my friend would like to take over here," Mafulla said, and gestured toward the prince.

Walid immediately jumped in, looking at both Kissa and Hasina, back and forth, as he said, "The king himself has planned this special event for some time. He's invited us to be part of a very small group that will see something of great beauty, something exciting that will be arriving at the palace today. The two of us were to be the first of our age group to have access. But we couldn't even think of enjoying such an opportunity without sharing the experience with both of you."

"Well, that's sweet," Kissa commented.

Walid continued. "The king will indeed be there—he set up the whole thing—and he's promised that it'll be great fun and even memorable for all who attend."

"This mystery, you mean."

"Well, yes. But a little mystery is nice sometimes, isn't it?"

Kissa and Hasina looked at each other, and then back at Walid, and then at Mafulla, who, of course, belatedly punctuated his friend's well-crafted statement, dramatically ending and reinforcing it, while bringing it to the rhetorical crescendo it deserved, with his famous double eyebrow jump. Hasina laughed and Kissa said, "You two are doing a fine job with being elusive about this, and I think that, as a result, you've piqued my curiosity." She then turned to Hasina. "Hassi? This is just too strange and intriguing. Can you go?"

"Sure, I mean, I think so. As long as Hoda says it's Ok. It sounds like it might be fun. And I'm with you. I want to see what it's all about."

"Let me go ask mom."

Kissa walked up to the desk where the other girls had just gotten all their questions answered and spoke quietly to her mother about the invitation. They both then walked over to the boys and Hasina.

Hoda said, "Gentlemen, it sounds like you have a nice mystery event cooked up for the girls. And so I grant permission. They can go. Just try to have them back to my office within two hours. I'll be here working. Does that sound acceptable to you?"

"Yes! Excellent," Mafulla replied. "Thank you."

"Very nice," Walid chipped in and added, "We'll have them back as requested, and as good as new."

Mafulla grinned. "I completely concur with what my friend just said, whatever it means. We'll get them back at the right place, at the right time, and … as good as new!"

"Great, now go enjoy yourselves," Hoda said with a smile.

Walking out the door, Mafulla again repeated the phrase slowly and with his eyebrows both raised high, "As good as new."

Walid replied, "It's an old saying."

"That means?"

"Basically: Everything's going to be fine. Don't worry. So, don't worry about it."

"Hey, I'm fine. No worries. I'm … as good as new."

"Ha!" Walid just shook his head after the laugh.

"What?"

"I just never quite know when to expect these little linguistic investigations."

The street was busy outside the front gate of the palace. Two men walked up to the main gate. "Yes? How can I help you?" The palace guard was cordial but businesslike.

"Shapur Adi and my brother Reela to see the king, if it's possible. We have some important business."

"Is the king expecting you?"

"I hope so. My friend Badar Sakat said he would radio in that we were coming." The guard looked skeptical. Shapur explained, "My son lives in the palace as the best friend to the prince, at the king's invitation, and I have important information His Majesty needs to hear as soon as possible."

"Oh, wait, you're Mafulla's father! You're Mr. Adi. I'm so sorry. We haven't met before." The guard reached out to shake hands with Shapur, and said, "Some papers were just delivered here in the gatehouse a few minutes ago. Let me go look." The guard walked over to a table and thumbed through some documents. He returned, carrying one of them. "Here it is, the note from Sakat, and there's an indication that the message has also been relayed directly to the king. You're all set. I'm sure he's expecting you now. Please come in. I assume you know your way to the king's quarters?" He waved and two men opened the large iron gates.

"Yes, thank you very much. We can indeed find our way."

Shapur led Reela through the gates, now ready for their entrance, and up the long walk toward the front of the golden palace, where more guards greeted them and pulled open one of the large doors. Inside, two other guards were standing, talking, and one of them recognized Shapur right away. "Mr. Adi! Have you come to visit Mafulla?"

"Hello, hello, my friend! Good to see you!"

"It's good to see you, as well."

"Actually, I do hope to see Mafulla, but my brother and I need to speak with the king briefly, and I think he's expecting us."

"Oh, certainly, that's fine. You probably know the way as well as I do."

Shapur smiled and said, "Well, I've been honored to see the

king in his private quarters on a couple of occasions, and I do remember the way up. "

"Good! Welcome to you both! Please have a nice visit."

"Thank you." The two Adi brothers walked up the long flight of wide marble stairs and then went down a hallway toward the reception area for the king's private visitors.

When they arrived, Shapur gently knocked on an open door and immediately saw a familiar face. "Kular! Greetings! It's so good to see you back at work after the unfortunate turn of events you had to go through not long ago."

"Hello, Mr. Adi! I thank you. It's nice to see you as well, and great to be back at work."

"How do you feel?"

"Very good. Back to normal, and even better!"

"That's so nice to hear."

"Thank you for asking," Kular replied, and said, "I just received your radio message from the communications room, and the king is expecting you. He's supposed to be outside at the stables and garage area in a bit. But I know he's eager to see you first." The head butler then led them to the inner door and, opening it, announced their arrival, and invited them into the king's sitting area.

"Shapur! Reela! Good to see you both again!" The king was standing by the window. He smiled and gestured to them. "Please come over and have a seat, anywhere you'd like."

"Thank you, Your Majesty," Shapur said. "It's always good to see you. And you remember my brother, Reela!"

"Yes, from your visit right before Mafulla was able to move into the palace."

"You have a good memory, Your Majesty," Reela said.

"I keep waiting for it to begin to weaken, as always happens with age at some point, but so far it seems to remain strong—or else, it's become, like my eyes, very good at tricking me!"

"From what I've heard, there's nothing about you that's not

strong," Reela responded with a smile. The king nodded his appreciation for this gracious remark.

"Thank you for seeing us on such short notice," Shapur said. "My brother has some news that you'll want to hear, and I'm afraid it's not good."

"Ah. Well. Good news often depends on taking what seems like bad news and doing the right thing with it," the king replied. "I welcome any important information you might have for me."

Reela said, "Well, I've been traveling on business recently. I consult with companies doing international trade, often on security matters, and still use a network of acquaintances I built up over the years while I was serving the kingdom in a diplomatic role, decades ago."

"He was the best spy we had," Shapur said with pride.

"Oh? I didn't know that."

"I was not a political man, Your Majesty. I didn't at all approve of how the kingdom was being run. I kept my distance from all that. And, of course, I absolutely deplored the events long ago that removed your father from power. I grew up hearing everyone in my family praise his reign and long for more ethical rulers than those terrible men who replaced him. I was always hoping you'd return and restore lawful order to the kingdom. I served in the intelligence capacity for our nation only to benefit the good people of the kingdom, and I learned a great deal in the process."

"I deeply appreciate your service," the king said.

"Thank you. I'm just back from Morocco and heard there about our own Ari Falma."

"Oh?"

"Yes. I was told that he's been seen with known arms dealers who work in Libya, Morocco, and Algeria. He's even thought to have been recruiting men in recent months to join his personal organization."

The king nodded and said, "I'm not at all surprised. He left town suddenly and disappeared from the kingdom months ago after futile attempts to steal valuables from the palace. They were things that could be used for the purpose of political revolution. But that actually didn't seem at all like him. It didn't fit his normal pattern of interest or operation. He's not a revolutionary. He's just a criminal focused on making money. We suspect strongly that he was working for someone else, and have recently come to believe that it might have been Farouk al-Khoum, the industrialist and investor."

"That's interesting," Reela said. "I heard one report that Falma fears Farouk now with an almost paranoid concern. He seems to have come to think that al-Khoum killed many of his men, and is now set on eliminating him, as well."

"I didn't know that," the king responded. "So, if you can trust your sources, it looks like Farouk may have employed Falma for a time, Falma failed him, and then, when a number of his men were killed, Falma assumed that was Farouk's punitive anger at work. But, as a matter of fact, in a raid to save Shapur's wife and young children, as I'm sure you know, Masoon and Hamid and their men had to put down a number of Falma's associates in the warehouse where they were keeping the family. And that was shortly before Falma disappeared. He likely thought that Masoon's work was actually done by al-Khoum, and then fled the kingdom to avoid that fate himself."

"I see," Reela said.

The king continued. "And of course, in fleeing, he abandoned his assignment for Farouk, who must have been truly furious at his sudden disappearance, since Falma failed him and left with no explanations—in the midst, presumably, of his ongoing employment. Since then, Farouk has probably wanted to do to Falma and his men exactly what the criminal believes he already had begun to do."

"That seems like a sensible hypothesis," Reela responded.

"So, now Falma, out in the cold and on the run, has been gathering men and arms, but for what purpose? Merely for his self protection?"

"I don't think so," Reela said. "I'm reporting to you only the things I've heard from the most reliable sources, people I've known for a long time and trust. I was told that Falma's been seen meeting with the usurper king you recently dethroned and mercifully put on a boat down the Nile with warnings that he should never come back."

Ali said, "Ah, the rascal, Rasul Appolonium. It's been a while since I've heard anyone mention him at all. I thought we were rid of him for good. Do you suppose the previous king or, I should say, the previous pretender to the throne, is now homesick?"

Reela replied, "Yes, that may be exactly what's going on. Falma might have convinced him that, with the right men and weapons, he can have a glorious homecoming. Or the disgraced former monarch himself may have already harbored those desires, and is now opportunistically using Falma to help make them happen. Falma does have a lot of connections in the kingdom. Perhaps Appolonium has promised him protection against al-Khoum as part of a deal. After all, from what I've heard, Farouk rose to business prominence only because of the corruption and assistance of the previous regime."

"I see."

"And Falma's back in town."

"He is?"

"Yes, that's what I've been told. I've heard he just recently arrived back, within the last week or two with a few men, and that he's up to something—but no one knows precisely what it is."

Shapur said, "Perhaps this is why the paper reported that crime is suddenly up in the kingdom and the city again, and without any normal explanation that anyone can offer."

"You may be right," the king replied, nodding his head. And

then he said, "This is definitely vital information to have, and news I need to act on right away." He looked down at his watch and said, "Oh, my. The time's later than I thought. We're having a major delivery of new automobiles to the palace, and a ceremony in less than half an hour. I've promised to be present for the official unveiling. I need to go down to the stable area and meet the man from Rolls Royce who is now head of this region, a fellow by the name of Kinkaid."

"Oh, my goodness," Reela said. "Harvey Kinkaid?"

"Sir Harvey, now," I'm told.

"Well then, if it's at all possible, we very badly need to talk more, later today." Reela had a serious expression of concern darkening his face. "I knew of Kinkaid during my intelligence years."

"You did?"

"Yes. He was in the British diplomatic corps, but used his position to satisfy his own tremendous greed and seemingly endless needs. He was responsible for several heinous deeds that must be known to no one in the current government or he would never have been knighted, if indeed that's true. He wouldn't even be walking around as a free man. He's bad business, indeed."

"I had no idea," the king said. "He hides his nature well."

"Yes, he always has." Reela thought for a second and said, "Shapur and I saw him earlier in the marketplace today and I was concerned. That's part of what I wanted to tell you. I would be greatly surprised if it's a coincidence that Falma and Kinkaid are in our fair city at the same time without there being something that they're both embroiled in, something far beyond the delivery of luxury automobiles."

"Well, I must thank you again for this important information. Can you and Shapur stay a while? I can get away and be back within about an hour, I would imagine. And if you can accommodate me, I'd very much like to have Naqid Bustani, the director of our palace guards, and Masoon Afah, the head of our military, come in and speak with you about all these things while I'm out. You can bring them up to date with the information you've just shared."

"I know of both these men and their sterling reputations. It would be my pleasure to brief them, Your Majesty." He turned to his brother and said, "Can you stay as well, Shapur?"

"Yes, I'm sure Shamilar won't be worried unless I'm too very late."

The king said, "Where is she now?"

"Actually, at the shop."

"Well, good, I'll have Bancom send a message to the Sakats for her."

"That would be very kind of you, if it's not too much trouble."

"Not at all. I greatly appreciate your good friendship and help, Shapur."

"It's my honor, Your Majesty."

"I need to be on my way now to meet Kinkaid, but it will be a more guarded meeting than I had anticipated, and in more than one sense of the term. I'll keep a careful watch on him in all ways, and will have a team of capable men around to make sure that nothing unexpectedly unpleasant takes place on the grounds, here."

"That's wise," Reela responded. "I have no idea what Kinkaid's up to, but it will be prudent to watch him closely at all times. Rolls Royce can be trusted. Kinkaid can't."

4

That New Car Smell

Walid, Mafulla, Kissa, and Hasina all made their way down the stairs, across a broad entryway, and out the side palace doors. From there, they walked along a beautiful path around the back of the building and over to the far side, where a few of the king's stables and garages were located. A larger stable area was out on the edge of town, but this smaller facility was perfect for keeping a few of the royal horses in proximity to the palace, easily available whenever they might be needed for ceremonial purposes. There were also several cars parked in a spacious garage building for the use of the king and his top advisors.

"Now, what do you have cooked up for us?" Kissa asked.

"You'll see in a minute," Walid said with a big smile on his face.

"I'm just glad this didn't involve blindfolds and earplugs, as secretive as you two are being about it," Hasina commented.

Mafulla said, "Oh, we trust you to close your eyes and keep them closed, starting now." He touched her arm and stopped walking. She looked surprised and he grinned and said, "Just kidding," and then nudged her forward, as they continued to walk toward the far outer buildings.

Behind the stables, there was an open area where the horses and a few donkeys could be exercised. It had been cordoned off today and a wall of dark blue canvas twenty feet high blocked any view of it from the palace area or the outbuildings. Several gentlemen in western business attire stood at the corner of the stable, and they seemed to be engaged in a lively conversation.

Walid looked around but didn't yet see the king. However, he spotted in the group of men Sir Harvey Kinkaid. He started to wave, but Sir Harvey was standing with his side to Walid and just then turned toward the field, with his back to the young people. A man near Kinkaid noticed the four friends and walked quickly toward them, holding up his hand and saying, in a distinct British accent, "I'm sorry, this area's closed off today. No visitors can be accommodated."

The four stopped in their tracks but Walid just smiled and said, "Oh. Hello. Don't worry, we're not visitors. This is actually my back yard. I'm Prince Walid."

The look on the man's face over the next second or two was by itself worth the price of admission. Shocked, stunned, briefly panicked, and instantly obsequious might capture the swirl of unconscious expressions that appeared in rapid-fire succession. "Oh! I'm so sorry! Prince! I had no idea! Please forgive my terribly unfortunate clumsiness! I'm mortified! I do apologize!" The man had his hand over his heart and was bowing and backing up as he spoke.

"It's fine. You're just doing your job, I'm sure."

"Yes, yes, thank you. Indeed, it's my task today to keep the area clear of any curious gawkers or uninvited parties so that any member of the royal family and their entourage, meaning of course, you and your friends, can enjoy the upcoming presentation with an unencumbered view and in the peace and quiet appropriate to full enjoyment. It's for your convenience and comfort that I'm here."

"We appreciate it. Now, where should we go in order to be able to have the best view?"

"Oh, there's a group of viewing chairs right over here on a slightly raised platform." He gestured and said, "Please, make yourselves comfortable. I believe that one chair is marked for the king and any others would be available. Oh, there's His Majesty now!"

Everyone turned to see the king, flanked by six palace guards, striding across the lawn. There were another ten or more guards off to one side, and a roughly equal number approaching from around the other corner of the building. And this was not expected. The men were fully armed. Kinkaid, O'Connor, and the two other members of their group each felt the same thing at that moment, an instant chill and tingle of uncertainty at the sight of all these guards converging around them. There's an old adage: "The wicked seek to flee, even when no one pursues." Inner guilt has a way of making a person prone to panic. But then, the majority of the men stopped twenty yards away and took up security positions encircling the proceedings. Still, Kinkaid worried, and Walid wondered what was going on.

The king moved forward, approaching the small group assembled there with only two of the guards and said, "Sir Harvey, thank you for following through so well on your promises and being here today."

Kinkaid took a sharp breath, bowed, and said, "It's my great honor, Your Majesty. It's good to see you. I must say, the sight of your large security detail gave me pause for a moment. I hope there's nothing wrong. It's quite a crowd of unexpected greeters to … welcome us."

"It's just the security I like to have available for certain special occasions and visitors such as yourself," the king replied with a smile. "I can assure you that all the guards, including the snipers you may not see, up on the rooftops, will be on their very best behavior."

"Oh! Good! Well, then, so shall we!" Sir Harvey coughed a couple of times and said, "Pardon me, Your Majesty. Would you like to have a seat? We have a special chair of honor reserved for you."

"That would be good. I see the prince is here already with his friends. I'll take my seat and, if you have a few words to say, that will be an appropriate time to begin."

"Certainly, Your Majesty." Sir Harvey bowed again and took a step back. The king walked over to the young men and their lady friends, who stood immediately in greeting. He smiled and said a word to each and then they were all seated.

Walid whispered, "What's up with the men?"

"Nothing to worry about at the moment. I'll fill you in later."

"Good. That's good."

The king then gestured and nodded at Kinkaid, who walked over to a spot in front of them. "King Ali. Prince Walid. Distinguished guests. Ladies and Gentlemen: It's truly a banner day when one of the world's great kingdoms and one of its great automobile companies can come together in partnership for a bright and productive future." Sir Harvey began his prepared remarks quite auspiciously. It was clear that he had done this before, and he was good at it. He spoke of technology, craftsmanship, car travel, the human community, and the future. He talked of royalty and quality and excellence. He quoted several statesmen of the past, including King Ali's father, the late King Malik Shabeezar, and he even had a couple of humorous lines that evoked chuckles from the overall audience of perhaps forty-five people—but this number included the nearby guards who, as a policy, do almost no chuckling while on special duty.

The presentation went on for less than ten minutes, and then there was the great unveiling. One of Sir Harvey's assistants pulled a cord, and the twenty-foot wall of blue canvas dropped neatly to the ground, revealing four spectacular automobiles parked together at a jaunty angle and spaced apart for the best viewing. They were all well waxed, fully buffed, and brightly glistening in the sunlight. An audible murmur ran through the crowd and then there was a hearty round of applause. Mafulla turned to Walid with a beatific look on his face and said, "They're all red—a deep and majestic red!" Then he said to Hasina, "Nice, huh?"

"Very nice!"

Walid leaned over to Kissa and asked, "What do you think?"

"Pretty impressive. It's a great surprise. I've never seen such cars as these, even in magazines."

There were two incredible hard top sedans and two extraordinary convertibles sitting there, each of them a masterpiece, painted a beautiful distinctive dark red and with incredible, deep tan interiors. Even the tires shone darkly with polish. Sir Harvey grinned, gestured grandly like a carnival barker, and shouted, "It's time to examine your magnificent new cars! Please come forward as you will, and go over each of the vehicles that have been customized for your use and enjoyment." He then said in a lower voice, "It will be my pleasure to answer any questions you might have. And my associates, all automotive experts, will gladly help, as well."

The king rose, as then did everyone else who had been seated, acting in his honor and following his lead. He immediately turned and said to Walid and Mafulla, "You young people go ahead of me and scrutinize our new transportation."

Mafulla said, "You don't have to ask me twice!" He touched Hasina's arm, smiled at her, and led her straight out over the field to the closest convertible that was gloriously inviting, with its top down and interior open to the air. He stopped at first some five feet away to take it all in, gestured with outstretched arms, and said, "I can't believe it. The perfect Mafullamobile! Greatest of all possible Adimobiles!" This, of course, got the double eyebrow jump times two and a big laugh from Hasina. Then he walked up and leaned over the side, took a deep breath and exclaimed, "That new car smell is amazing!" He turned to Hasina and said, "You've got to take in the aroma of the leather and look at the deep glow of the finish. It's just incredible."

"It's pretty amazing," she replied.

Smiling broadly at her, he opened the front passenger door and urged her to "Sit, sit, and take it all in." When she was settled in and comfortably supported by the supple leather of the seat, he gently closed the door with a satisfying thud and jogged around to the driver's side, where he opened that door and practically dove into the seat. With his right hand on the wheel, he double-jumped his eyebrows again and said, "Where would you like to go, young lady?"

Hasina had to laugh. She said, "We don't even know there's any gas in these cars!"

"Ah, but, then, how did they get here?" he asked, as if proving his point.

"On the backs of trucks, maybe?"

"Hmm. I hadn't thought of that."

"That's my guess," She said.

"I see. And, given the complete absence of any speck of dirt on any of them, you may actually be right." Mafulla sighed. "Oh, well. I guess we won't be scratching off any time soon and leaving the others in our dust."

That very second, as he was looking down at the carpet, he heard a loud noise and turned around quickly to see … Walid opening his door and Kissa the other. Both of them squeezed behind the front seats and landed in the back, at once, laughing. They had separately opened the two doors on cue and slipped into the car so quickly that Mafulla didn't even know what was happening until "Ta Da!"—as Walid merrily announced—there they were, on their respective seats in the back.

"Where are we going?" Kissa asked.

"Nowhere fast," Mafulla answered.

"My favorite destination," Walid offered. "I go there often."

Mafulla explained, "I was going to drive away across the grounds and out the gate, but the lovely Hasina just pointed out that there might not even be any gas in the cars yet."

"Well, then how did they get here?" Walid asked.

"You see?" Mafulla said, looking at Hasina. "It's the question any normal genius would ask."

"It's apparently the question the two of you would ask," Hasina replied.

"Trucks," Kissa said.

"Ha!" Hasina loved it that her very smart friend had made the exact same suggestion. "That's what I said."

"But," Kissa added, "first of all, of course, from their original location, different trucks, and then a ship, and maybe a train, and last of all, trucks again."

"You see?" Hasina said to Mafulla, mocking his tone. "Your next Genius Project is to figure out how girls know so much more about the world than boys. But then again, you'll probably need our help to come up with a good answer," she added, laughing.

"Yes, undeniably—in fact, indubitably," Kissa said.

Hasina turned to look at her and said, "You sound like you've been spending too much time around this one." She pointed at Mafulla.

And, of course, that made them all laugh. "Too much perambulating in the proximity of his prolixity," Kissa said.

At that, Walid laughed so hard he snorted and said, "Hasina, would you check the glove compartment and see if these things come with dictionaries?"

As Hasina popped that compartment open and pretended to look, Kissa teasingly said, "You know what those words mean, silly man!" She then sighed and explained. "I was just telling Hassi earlier that she's quite a precocious girl. I guess it's a burden we both have to bear."

Hasina laughed and said, "Yes! You're clearly as precocious as I, and as far as such things go, very likely, much more so!"

Walid looked at Kissa and said, "Well, the velocity of your own precocity just now made me go blank."

"Yikes. I think this car is turning everyone into poets," Mafulla said with his eyebrows high up.

"It's just the open convertible nature of it," Walid replied. "There's nothing impermeable between our brains and the heights of inspiration. It converts us into bards."

"Is that it?"

"Yes. Definitely. The roofs of regular sedans, like the tops of buildings, must cut off the eternal, ethereal cosmic vibrations before we can soak them all in." Walid then cleared his throat, and in a dramatic voice, said:

"Open,
the drop top
won't stop
the crop
of poetry
that daily
develops
in me."

And, instantly, the female voice from the backseat said,

"But what
if you flop
and produce
only slop,
which would be,
you see,
a real tragedy?"

For the next two seconds, there was total silence, in which the two young people in the front seats looked at each other, eyebrows raised, and then at both their friends in the back seat. Mafulla suddenly began to fumble with nobs and switches on the dashboard, left and right and said, "Does anybody know how to get the lid up on this thing, and fast?"

That comment made everyone laugh again. But Mafulla and Hasina were both secretly admiring their best friends and their astonishingly quick cleverness. Kissa was, in turn, smitten anew by Walid's silly rhyme, and her fast retort had the same effect on him, in addition to just impressing him tremendously at her instant wit, a sign of extreme intelligence, as he said to himself. And amid all these thoughts, the four of them had no idea they were about to get another big surprise.

Ali walked up and said, "My friends: Darwishi, the head palace driver and chief chauffeur, wants to take one of the cars out for a spin, a sort of test drive or short excursion. He's chosen the stretch sedan and says it has plenty of room in the back to accommodate at least four passengers. He's just had it fueled up. Would any of you happen to know anyone who might like to go along for the ride?"

Mafulla said, "Are you kidding me? I mean, Your Majesty? I mean, absolutely! I know just the right guinea pigs for the test drive."

"Guinea pigs?" Hasina said.

"A phrase. A saying. You know, like lab rats, chimpanzees, early experimental users—volunteers!" Mafulla's enthusiasm was, as usual, quite a thing to see.

"Rats? Chimpanzees?"

He looked over at Hasina and said, "Cute and charming versions of such early adopters, of course. Darling little things! Yes?"

She said, "Sure, Ok, certainly, Mr. Guinea Pig, as long as we're not gone too long."

Walid looked expectantly at Kissa, and she said, "Consider me an eager little piggy, too."

"Good!" Walid said, "Let's go!" Slipping out of the convertible, he looked up at the king and said, "Which car was it, again?"

Ali pointed in the direction of the three other cars and said, "The red one."

That made Walid and Mafulla laugh. Then the king said, "The sedan on the far end. Dar's there already standing beside it and waiting for his special passengers."

"Just us?"

"Just you."

"Very nice."

"I've asked him to have you back within thirty minutes."

"That's perfect," Kissa said.

The four students walked eagerly across the field to the car at the end. The chauffeur greeted them all and opened the doors and then invited them into the automobile in the order dictated by palace etiquette, first the prince, then his personal guest, then Hasina, and finally the top automobile aficionado present, Mr. Adi. There were forward and also backward facing seats behind the driver's compartment, in the manner of a limousine for this particular car, the largest of the four. But the outer size of the vehicle was not that much longer than the other big sedan, one that had only a forward facing back seat and a vast amount of leg room.

As they settled in, the driver said to Walid, "Your Highness, I have for the four of you, in a central compartment back there, a corked bottle of cool water and four glasses, in case you get thirsty. There's also a small bag of freshly baked cookies in the compartment. Please feel free to help yourselves, all of you."

"Thank you so much, Darwishi."

"You're quite welcome, Prince."

Mafulla looked around and said, "This is nice."

"Especially for guinea pigs," Hasina said, and Mafulla just grinned.

Darwishi announced, "Now, if you're all settled in, I'll start the car and pull slowly over to the drive, then out to the side gate. We'll do a short tour of this part of town, and finally, make our way back."

"That sounds good," Walid said. "We're all ready." The engine started with a muffled roar and then a quiet, faint rumble could barely be heard. It was indeed much quieter than they had expected, far more insulated against noise than an ordinary car, even one that might have been quite luxurious. As the driver put it into gear, it began to roll smoothly forward over the uneven ground. And then, once it was on the driveway, riding in it was almost like sitting on the sofa back in the king's private quarters. Walid suddenly realized that he and his friends all had big smiles on their faces.

Mafulla spoke again, as he felt the leather of the seat. "This is pretty great."

Hasina said, "Yeah, I can't believe how comfortable it is."

Kissa said, "The ride's so smooth."

Mafulla dramatically added, "And, the leather's incredible. Plus, I have to say, that new car smell is just intoxicating."

Walid replied, "I won't ask how you would know that."

"What do you mean how I'd know it? Smell for yourself!"

"No, I mean the appropriateness of your descriptive term, the one that rhymes with … incriminating."

"Oh. Oh. I know in fully legitimate and completely proper ways, my friend, from my extensive reading and listening to the older people around us who have come from many nations, and then extrapolating in creative ways from all that I've heard."

"I see."

"Plus, I may not be able to produce a rhyme as quickly as some people, but I do have the soul of a poet, you know."

"The poor poet," Walid said. "How did you get his soul?" At that, they all laughed.

"I promise, he gave it up willingly," Mafulla protested, playing along. "Wise man that he was, he realized the superior packaging it would have, if properly housed in my well-honed physique."

"You boys are just too silly for words," Hasina said.

Mafulla replied, "And yet words are all I have—in addition to my princely friend and, of course, my distinctive good looks and charming personality, but I should stop."

"Ha!" Walid did a fake, and also, a sort of real, laugh.

Mafulla, undaunted, continued. "I should point out, by the way, that this young man, the prince, and I spur each other on to greatness, verbal and otherwise, many times a day."

"You do?" Hasina replied.

"Yes, most definitely! There's an ancient book of proverbs that explains this well when it says, 'Like iron sharpens iron, so one man sharpens another.' And it's true."

"Of you two?"

"Of course, as you can clearly see. We're as sharp as two tacks, back-to-back. In fact, if humility would allow me for a second the further elaboration, I would have to say that through our interactions, we've become quite superior, edgy wits, knit together, who constantly improve each other's game."

"So, you're saying you're both nit-wits ... on-the-edge. That sounds about right." Hasina deadpanned her words, with no expression on her face whatsoever. And that made Kissa laugh again, while Mafulla displayed a very convincing expression of mock shock.

Walid happened to look out the window at that moment, and he noticed a famous shop up ahead, one that sold various handcrafted items of a luxurious nature, including clothes and jewels and ladies' bags and travel accessories, plus fresh cut flowers that were brought in a couple of times a week. He suddenly had a strong urge to stop. He said to the driver, "Darwishi? Could you pull over up ahead, near the next lamp post?"

"Certainly, Your Highness."

"The one on this side of the beige building. Mafulla and I need to jump out for something. You can take the ladies around the block and pick us up in about four or five minutes." He looked at Kissa and said, "Is that Ok? I just realized there's something quick we have to do."

"I guess so, Mr. Mystery," Kissa answered, with a look of some surprise.

Mafulla was altogether as puzzled but didn't say anything, playing along that he knew what Walid had just remembered. He simply nodded at Hasina and, as the car pulled over slowly to the sidewalk, he said, "We'll be back in a flash. As always, there's palace business of the highest order. I'm glad Walid remembered. Dar will give you a nice drive around the block. We'll see you in a minute."

Walid and Mafulla got out and started to walk toward the shop. Walid said, "Dar," drawing out the word.

"Yeah, our new buddy, Dar, the man with the car. But hey, what's this all about?" Mafulla asked Walid quietly, as soon as they were more than a few steps away.

"I want to get flowers for the girls, for them to remember their drive with us."

"Oh! Wow. Excellent. You really surprise me sometimes. This will be a bright red cherry on the top of the experience for both ladies."

They walked up to the open door and through it. The store was large, and they seemed to be the only customers at the moment. But then, back in the far corner, they could see two men as they walked farther in. But neither of the men saw them enter. They appeared to be in a loud and heated conversation of some sort. Walid pulled Mafulla behind a tall display of ladies' clothing.

"You've cleaned out my cash register! Just leave! You have what you want!"

"No, I want the money in your safe."

"There is no safe."

"You think I'm a fool? I know there is."

"You don't need to wave that big knife around. I have a family, please."

Walid whispered, "Do you have your mask?'

"No."

"Your guard-whistle?"

"No."

"Wristband?"

"Always."

"Ok, then take this." Walid pulled a tan scarf off the display of clothing and handed it to Mafulla. He took down a yellow one for himself, tying it around his head to cover most of his face except his eyes. He quietly flipped his watchcase—click—and slid his wristband over his Reverso, and once he saw that Mafulla had done the same, he said, "Very quietly … I'll go high, you go low. There's a knife. Disarm, down, detain."

Mafulla nodded. Walid, crouching low, peered around the clothing to get a better look at where the criminal was and what was happening. He then saw another man, lying on the floor face down, not moving. He whispered, "Man down, right side."

Mafulla squeezed Walid's arm to signal understanding and readiness. At that moment, the two of them slid their sandals off and began to sneak across the shop silently, from the clothing rack to a flower display, to a handbag counter, staying very low and getting as close as they could behind the robber, without being heard or seen. More words had been exchanged in the back. The shop owner pleaded, "If you'll just put the knife away, I'll get you what you want."

"Empty your entire safe into the bag. Everything! Do it now!"

A loud rustle, which was the sound of the boys suddenly rushing the man, made him begin to turn around to see what the noise was. But halfway through his turn, Walid shoved him violently forward into the waist-high, marble-top counter and slammed his right arm onto the countertop, breaking his grip on the knife. And just then, Mafulla, still crouching low, swung his fist with all his strength up into the man's crotch from behind, dealing him a blow of excruciating, paralyzing pain that flooded his brain with what seemed like a searing flash of lightning. The sharp agony shot through his whole body in an instant, with a wave of nausea close behind it that made him go completely limp, losing control. The knife fell off the counter onto the floor behind it and the proprietor, as shocked as he could be, still found the presence of mind to reach down and grab it, and then he protectively stepped back to take in the unexpected scene.

"Give me your belt," Walid yelled to the man. By this time, he had the now unconscious thief on the floor, flat on his stomach. And within seconds, he was wrapping his hands up with the belt, securing it so that he couldn't wiggle out of it.

"Storm, get his feet."

Mafulla found a nearby long scarf and began wrapping it and tying it around the man's ankles. The other individual who had been unconscious on the floor started waking up. "What … what's happened?"

The shopkeeper bent down and said, "Brother, you were hit from behind by a thief and now these two men have knocked him down."

He just groaned. "Oh."

"Are you Ok?"

The man slowly sat up, rubbing his head. "I think so." He looked up at Walid and said, "Who are you?"

Walid, checking again the security of the thief's hands and feet, said, "I'm called The Golden Viper and this is Windstorm. We fight crime."

"I've heard of you." The man still seemed a bit groggy.

"We came into the shop to buy something and saw what was happening, and we just took action."

The proprietor behind the counter spoke up again and said, "Thank you so much! Thank you both so much! It was terrible." He had a look of astonishment on his face, and then he turned to the other man, who was now slowly getting to his feet.

"Are you all right?"

"Yes. I think so."

"Can you walk?"

"Yes."

"Ok, then, please go call the police, now, as quickly as you can. Use the phone two buildings down. But on your way out, tell the new shopkeeper next door that I need help." The man spoke quickly and then turned to the boys and said, "Viper and Storm, how can I show you my appreciation for your heroic action?"

"Well, we just came in to get two small bunches of flowers for our lady friends," Mafulla said from behind his improvised mask. "I mean, before we noticed all this going on."

"My treat to you!" The shopkeeper said. "Please!" He reached down behind the counter and produced two big bunches of roses that were fresh and of many colors. "These just came in, and I haven't even put them out yet. They're the finest flowers in the shop. Please take them, with my eternal thanks."

"We thank you!" Walid said as he took both bouquets, giving one to Mafulla. "And now we need to go." Then they turned and walked quickly toward the door, but right at it, Walid whispered, "Scarves!" They both jerked off their impromptu masks, tossing them onto a nearby counter right before they turned into the doorway and walked through it out to the street. Seeing the car down the road slowly coming their way, Walid began to jog toward it, and Mafulla followed close behind him. The prince made a gesture as if to direct Darwishi to pull over where he was.

The driver caught sight of them and parked the car right away, a few establishments up the street from where he had let them out. The boys quickly opened the back door before he could even start to get out, and Walid said, "Thanks, so much! To the palace, if you please!"

"What in the world is going on?" Kissa asked.

"We wanted to get you ladies these flowers," Walid replied. And both boys handed their favorite girls the bright and striking bouquets.

"It's important for you to have a special memento of our test drive," Mafulla added, and then he said, "Beautiful flowers for our beautiful passengers."

"Yes, beauty to acknowledge beauty, inside and out!" Walid echoed.

The girls responded with big smiles. "These are amazing! Thank you so much!" Kissa said. "You didn't have to do this!"

"Yeah, really! This is so, so sweet"! Hasina exclaimed.

"You guys are full of surprises!" Kissa said. "As if a ride in a new Rolls Royce wasn't enough by itself for us to remember forever!"

"That's for sure!" Hasina said. "We take back everything we've ever said about either of you," she added, with a serious look, and made them all laugh.

"Hey," Kissa said. "What's with the cloth fabric over your watches, all of a sudden?"

Walid and Mafulla both looked down at their arms where the cotton bands covered their watches. Mafulla thought to himself, "Uh, oh."

"Oh, that." Walid said.

Mafulla quickly explained, "When … we … were shopping for you, we knew we had only a few minutes but we wanted to just stop the clock and take our time to get you the best flowers we could find, and since we couldn't do that—only you ladies seem capable of bringing time to a halt—we … simply … covered it up instead."

"Good try," Hasina said, laughing. "Creative. Almost, but not quite, impressive." She glanced over at Kissa with her best here-we-go-again expression.

Mafulla quickly took another stab. "Actually, we hoped they'd protect our nice watchbands against any thorns the roses might have, but then, those seem to have been cut off already."

"Better, but still not quite plausible," Hasina said.

The boys looked at each other. "Well, it's a long story," Walid commented.

"Oh?"

"It's like a game we have, but it can't be explained properly quite yet, in all its requisite detail."

"Really?" Kissa said.

"Yes. But remind me later to tell you both the whole story. I promise you'll find the full explanation interesting and totally plausible. But, if we told you now, it would … cover too much time."

"Ha! That's good," Mafulla said.

"The Mystery Man, indeed!" Kissa responded. "Well, as long as the mysteries you guys deal with end up getting us rides in cars like this and producing gorgeous flowers, we'll be content to wait for everything to be revealed in its proper time."

"Waiting is good for the soul," Mafulla said.

"Yeah, that poor poet is still waiting to get his back," Walid replied.

"Very funny," Mafulla said. "You see?"

"What?" Hasina asked.

"Iron sharpening iron. And I was worried about him getting rusty."

The girls looked at each other, smiled, and just shook their heads.

5

Books and Trips

Khalid looked up at his wife, who was sitting near him, and watched her for a few seconds. He said, "You've been living in that book today."

"I'm sorry. What?"

"You and that book. What is it that has you so entranced? What's the book about?"

"It's about family."

"Family?"

"Long ago family." Hoda smiled and said, "Cleopatra."

Khalid laughed. "I thought you already knew everything there is to know about your worthy predecessor, the former Queen of the Nile."

"Well, I know most of the things that have been written about her, I'd guess, and a few other secrets in addition—the really good stuff. But I was just rereading this particular account of her trips on the Nile and it was sparking my imagination in a new way."

"In what way is that?"

"All right. How about this? Tell me what you think. We should take our classes on a road trip together down to Memphis for a look at the spiritual past of the kingdom. We'll introduce the kids to the priestly traditions and their important role in the history of our people. And, of course, we'd have to hit Giza, too. You know, to ponder the pyramids and speculate on the Sphinx. Then we could all get on a royal barge and come back on the Nile, like Cleopatra did."

"Really?"

"Yes!" She went on, "We'd combine serious study with a big party. I think it would be very educational for the students and also a lot of fun. And that combination seems to reflect the spirit of Greatest Grandmother Cleo. I'm not sure that any of our students has ever seen Memphis or Giza, and they have such importance in our history, along with Alexandria, which we could do another time, since it's in the opposite direction."

Khalid nodded with an approving expression, but said, "How would we get the students there?"

"We could ask the king to provide transportation and, of course, security for the trip."

"Good idea. It makes sense. Actually, I think it's a great idea. Did I ever say anything to you in the past about such a trip?"

"No, why?"

"Well, it's far too good an idea for me not to be able to get any credit at all for it."

"Hey, mister, you can get plenty of credit for helping to make it happen. I'll even let you do extra work for extra credit."

"I figured you might. But what sort of work do you have in mind?"

"You know, carrying large books and suitcases, for example—the big, awkward stuff."

"I'm afraid my back isn't what it used to be."

"Your front isn't, either."

"I set myself up for that one, didn't I?"

"It was actually too easy for me to really enjoy it. And, of course, I'm just kidding."

"You are?"

"Yes, definitely. Front and back, you're my favorite Greek god in all of Egypt."

"I sound a bit out of place."

"It may explain why you have so few worshippers."

"I need only you."

She sighed. "Ok, that was perfectly played. You win."

Khalid smiled and said, "Good. Winning feels nice for a change. But I really do think you have a great idea. Should I pitch it to the king?"

"Would you?"

"Yes. Right away. I know how much he cares about education and the wisdom that comes from the deeper things in life. And he's a true believer in fun as well. I think he'll be thrilled with the prospect of such a trip. He'll probably want to come along himself."

"You think so?"

"I do."

"Well, then, why not invite him?"

Khalid thought for a few seconds and said, "Indeed, why not?"

"Let me put together something like a rough possible itinerary, laying out the things we could do, and in what order. I'll outline all that the students would learn and emphasize how much fun it would be. You can show it to the king when you ask him about supporting the trip."

"How long will it take you to write that up?"

"I could have it by tomorrow."

"Ok, that sounds great. Let's do it."

"I'll get started later today."

Khalid paused and said, "Where are the girls, by the way?"

"They're actually with Walid and Mafulla and the king right now at some sort of ceremony that's happening this afternoon on the palace grounds."

"Oh, Ok. When are they going to be finished?"

"Soon, I think."

Not long afterwards, in the palace, upstairs, Kular knocked on the king's door and stuck his head into the room. "Your Majesty, the boys are back from their excursion in the new car."

"Excellent. Send them in."

Walid and Mafulla walked into the room sporting big smiles. The king asked, "Did you have a nice drive?"

"Your Majesty, it was unbelievable. Those cars are the best. I've never had such an experience," Mafulla said.

"It was great in every way," Walid added.

"Good, Good. Sit and tell me more."

As Walid sat down, he said, "Well, something interesting happened when we were a couple of miles away and really enjoying the car. It's amazingly roomy, by the way, and the leather on the seats is so thick and soft. Thanks for the water and snacks, too. They were great."

"I thought you might appreciate those little touches at the end of the school day."

"We really needed the cool water, and the cookies were perfect."

"Good." The king nodded with a smile of his own.

Walid glanced over at Mafulla, and then continued, "So, a couple of miles from here, I saw a shop up ahead of us that I'd heard mom talking about not long ago, a luxury ladies' shop that also has flowers for sale. I suddenly remembered her mentioning that. And right then, I asked Darwishi to pull over and stop so Maffie and I could run an errand, but without saying what it was. We told the girls we'd be quick, and we jumped out and asked Dar to circle the block with them and pick us up in about four or five minutes. We got the girls the most beautiful bouquets of roses as a memento of the trip, and they were so excited about the flowers."

"What an excellent idea!" The king said, "That was very considerate."

"Your nephew understands the ladies," Mafulla said with real admiration.

"But, here's the unexpected side of it. While we were in the shop, we had a chance to stop a crime that was in progress."

"You're not joking?"

"No sir, Your Majesty. We walked into the place and heard a guy threatening the shop owner. He had a knife he had pulled on the poor man, and so we grabbed scarves from a clothing rack, covered our faces, and took care of business. When we left, the bad guy was out cold and tied up, hands and feet, awaiting the arrival of the police. We got out to the car with our flowers, and the girls and Darwishi never knew anything had happened but a quick shopping expedition."

"Did either of you get hurt at all?"

"No, sir, only the bad guy. And he went down pretty hard." Walid smiled, but with a touch of trepidation underneath it.

"Good," the king said. "Did the shopkeeper see the car?"

"No, I don't think so. When we left, we caught sight of it pretty far up the street and jogged up to it so that Darwishi wouldn't bring it any closer at that point. I'm pretty sure we got away clean."

"Incredible. But in another sense, it's not at all a surprise. You seem to have uncanny instincts for when and where things are happening that need to be stopped."

"It sure looks that way," Walid said. "I mean, on a conscious level, I just had the idea to stop and get flowers. But maybe on an unconscious level, I was in touch with more that was going on."

Mafulla added, "Yeah, it's really strange how often we happen to be in the right place at the right time, and especially in ways that most people would consider the wrong place at the wrong time."

"The mind works in its own mysterious ways," the king said. "We may indeed feel promptings we don't understand, and yet we rationalize these urges with things we do understand, to make sense to ourselves about why we're doing what we feel compelled to do. Sometimes, the rationalizations are just wrong. But at other times, they make perfect sense on their own terms. Walid, you may have felt the shopkeeper's fear and his need, in a level of your mind that you can't fully access to conscious awareness. You had an urge to stop and go into that shop. You knew they sell flowers, and so that suggested to you the great idea of getting flowers for the girls."

"That's wild," Walid said. "It's sure strange, but it makes sense."

"And here's something else to add another twist to it," the king suggested. "Darwishi, your driver, chose the route to travel. Why then did things play out so that you got into the car at the precise moment you did, and he pulled away at the time he did, and then you were on the right road at the right moment for you to enter that shop exactly when your assistance was needed and could be so effective?"

"Wow. Yeah," Mafulla said. "Good questions."

The king continued. "Five minutes earlier or later, and I imagine it would all have been very different. Plus, the timing of your arrival at that shop depended on not only Darwishi's decisions, but on when we got to the viewing area to see the cars, when we took our seats, when Kinkaid started his remarks, and how long he went on. Then, there was the matter of the stretch of time that you were in the convertible just looking and talking, and then the timing of when I approached you with the suggestion that you should have a ride in one of the cars, along with how fast or slowly you walked to the right one and how long it took you to settle in and drive away."

"It's all a little overwhelming when you consider all that," Mafulla said.

The king concluded, "Yes, when you first begin to think like this, it is. But when you ponder it enough, it can become deeply empowering. We aren't in this world to do some good alone and without help. If your presence was needed at that shop, and all these events had to fall into place at just the right times and in just the right ways in order to make it happen, well, that gives you a sense of how much more is really going on around us than we normally realize—behind the scenes, beneath appearances, and beyond what we know. Some would dismiss things like this as mere coincidence. But that seems to me far too easy, and even preposterous. Chance is not purposive, and your presence served a needed purpose. An invisible tug of sorts brought you to where you needed to be. Sometimes, the things we can't see are the most important things of all. It is in many ways a matter of overwhelming fascination to me, my friends."

Walid said, "It's pretty incredible, for sure. It's hard to get my thoughts around it completely. I guess we're sometimes like characters in a play, where the things going on backstage and offstage are just as important as our actions onstage, and help to bring them about."

The king thought for a couple of seconds and added, "Yes. That's a good image, properly understood. Here's what I think. We're all participants in a great drama that encompasses us in space and time. We're chosen to help move it forward, but we never have to depend on just our own abilities to do so. We're free, but we're also deeply supported and guided. Let that build your confidence, your faith, and your hope in the future. Great things are afoot. And we're among the foot soldiers of destiny."

The boys just sat there for a moment trying to take this all in. "Wow," Mafulla responded.

"You've said a lot," Walid replied. "I mean, I think we've both felt inklings of what you've just said, but you've put it so well and brought it to a new level of understanding for me."

"For me, too," Mafulla added.

"Good," the king said. "Very good. But, now, back from the cosmos to the car, and to the ride itself. It was indeed nice? You really like the new automobile?"

"Absolutely," Walid answered. "The entire ride was super-great, we loved the car, and the girls enjoyed everything about it. And I do think the flowers will help them remember it for a long time."

"That little gift, along with the ride, will likely get us major points," Mafulla said. "But to your question, Your Majesty, everything about the car is pretty spectacular." He went on. "Every detail. Even the car log Rolls Royce gave our driver is in this beautiful dark red leather that matches the exterior color of the car."

The king said, "Oh? I haven't heard about that. What's the car log?"

Walid jumped in and said, "It's this great looking leather book, sort of a notebook or a diary that the driver's supposed to write in every time he takes a car out. Actually, Darwishi said there was a separate book for each car. Sir Harvey gave them to him, told him what to write in them, and said he should instruct the other drivers to do the same."

"What's he supposed to write?"

"Well, I asked him that myself. As we were getting ready to leave, Dar was already opening the book for our car to write down something. I was just curious. He said Sir Harvey told him that for each trip, he should record the date and time of departure, the destination, the road conditions, the performance of the car, the number and names of the passengers, and the purpose of the trip. He should also log in at the end the full route, the distance traveled, and the time of arrival back at the palace."

"He requested all that information?"

"That's right. Sir Harvey said that every couple of months, Rolls Royce would send one of their regional representatives to study the book and make sure the cars are performing as needed. He explained that they want to make certain no changes are required—of the cars, or of the types of car being used, or with the features and equipment of the particular vehicles themselves."

"That sounds more than a bit odd," the king replied. "I've never heard of such a thing—not with all those details, and especially the exact times and names of the passengers and the purpose of each trip. What would it matter to the maker who was in the car and what time it arrived back at the palace, or the reason for which it was taken out?"

"It seemed a little strange to me, too," Walid said. "At first, it sort of made sense on one level, you know, as a top customer service thing. But the more I thought about all the information the drivers are supposed to include, the more I started to wonder. Something just didn't seem right. I mean, why indeed would the carmaker need to know the destination of each trip, or the exact roads used, or the precise timing? What would that matter? And the purpose of the trip seems completely irrelevant."

"Precisely," the king said. The questions are far too intrusive, and unrelated to automotive performance. I'd wager that no other Rolls owner has been asked to keep such a log, or to have his driver keep one. I have a strong suspicion, bordering on certainty, that these questions come from Kinkaid, and not from his employer."

Mafulla now spoke up. "But why would he want to know such things?"

"I have no definite idea, Mafulla. But your father and uncle Reela visited me this afternoon to share with me some information that might shed light on the situation."

"Dad and Reela came to see you?"

"Yes, they did. And we spoke some more right before you came in—a few minutes ago."

"They were just here?"

"They were. They came to see me with some information they had, and initially got here right before the car delivery ceremony. We spoke briefly and they stayed around to talk more with some others while I was busy out back."

"What was going on?"

"Well, first of all, your father told me things about your uncle that I didn't know. Did you realize that he had served in the diplomatic corps for a good long time?"

"Yes sir, Your Majesty, we're all really proud of him. Dad always said he was the best spy in the kingdom, but that was his little joke."

"Actually, it turns out to be no joke at all, but true."

"What do you mean?"

The king nodded and said, "It seems that, while serving officially in the diplomatic corps, Reela was secretly engaged in intelligence gathering and data analysis, as well as doing field agent work for our Special Service."

"I didn't know anything about that!"

"After their visit, I spoke with Masoon about it all and he was able to give me more details. Your uncle has always been extremely loyal to the people of the kingdom and has done many great things for us. We should honor his service."

"Wow."

"He came to me today with some news he thought I should hear."

"Can we ask what it was?" Walid said.

"Yes. Ari Falma is apparently back here, in town."

"Oh, no."

"He's believed to have been associating with known arms dealers in a couple of other nations near us over the past few months, and he's thought to have been recruiting new men to work with him. The recent rise in crime reported by the paper is most likely his personal handiwork, first from afar, perhaps, and now up close."

"What's he doing?"

"No one quite knows."

"At all?"

"Well, Reela's heard reports that Falma has also been seen meeting with the former king of our nation, the man we deposed. They may have formed some kind of alliance."

"Why?"

"We have no certain idea. But it's rather doubtful that the previous king wants to work with Falma as just an ordinary criminal and a potential partner in crime. Most likely, he'll be helping Falma reestablish his criminal kingdom here, and Falma, in turn, will be helping him retake what he may think of as his political kingdom."

"Oh, gee. That's bad news."

"There's more. Reela saw Kinkaid in the market today, before the ceremony. He recognized him from his years as an operative for us. He said that the man worked in British intelligence as a spy, too, but that he was a rogue with his own agenda, and he did terrible things that London never found out about."

"Man."

"Reela explained that he's a bad guy to the core, despite his cultivated exterior and friendly demeanor. He thinks that the presence of Falma and Kinkaid in our city at the same time is no mere coincidence."

"Does Uncle Reela think they're working together?" Mafulla asked.

"Oddly, he seems to think they may be adversaries in whatever they're doing, but that they themselves might not even know each other, and so may not yet be clear about their oppositional situation."

"Really?" Walid said.

"Yes. It appears that, unknown to each other, they're very likely working independently and at cross purposes for the same thing—to help another man get what he wants, in order really to get what they want. Falma would be doing such a thing in service to the former king, and Kinkaid perhaps in collaboration with our nemesis, Farouk al-Khoum. We now know that Kinkaid and al-Khoum have, on at least one occasion, met together."

"Oh, gee. I can easily imagine the one thing that Falma and Kinkaid are both seeking for these other guys." Mafulla said.

"Yes. Farouk and the former king, it seems, each want to rule our land. Farouk has Kinkaid doing some intelligence gathering for him, and probably other things. The former king has Falma perhaps doing the same, plus raising funds, arms, and followers through his normal enterprise of crime. I would guess that the few top, corrupt officials we sent down the river months ago have reorganized any of their own networks that are still in the kingdom to help Falma, who will then, in turn, be able to help them. So, Falma is an agent for the previous king, and Kinkaid is serving that role for al-Khoum."

"Let me make sure I get this straight," Walid said. "How's Falma supposed to be able to help the previous regime?"

"With the money and men that he can get through his criminal activities," the king said. "In fact, this sheds some new light on your crime stopping activity today at that luxury shop."

"It does?"

"You blocked a theft of money that would most likely have gone to these enemies of the kingdom. I happen to have heard, in a meeting on kingdom and city economic activity, that the shop you visited had just received major payments for their biggest sale of the year and perhaps in their history. It would have taken an Ari Falma type of organization to know about that and plan a theft on the day before they were to transfer all the funds from their own safe to a much more secure bank. One of our officials is friends with their accountant, and was telling me about their great windfall of profits just yesterday, as an example of local business success, while we were talking about trends in recent economic activity."

"Wow. We had no idea. We just thought we were helping the shopkeeper," Mafulla said. "We didn't know we were stopping the act of a major criminal conspiracy."

"You likely were," the king said.

"We are now officially international men of intrigue." Mafulla raised his eyebrows, with a serious look.

"How you can joke at a time like this is pretty impressive," Walid pointed out.

"I'm as nervous about all this as you are, but as you know, that just kicks my wit into the Full-On Position," Mafulla explained. Walid nodded, and responded with a weak smile.

Mafulla turned back to the king and said, "I understand why Falma would go to those former monarchy guys, and why they would work with him, but why would Farouk work with a Rolls Royce car guy?"

"Well, first, remember that he's not really just a Rolls Royce car guy, but a dangerous secret agent. He's all about serving himself and his perceived self-interest, regardless of any consequences to others. He's using Rolls as a cover, just like he once used the British diplomatic service, and even their intelligence division. And with Rolls, he has access to us and to the palace. That's likely a part of what attracted the ambitious industrialist to the new car guy, but there may be something extra that Farouk found especially useful about Kinkaid. Perhaps it's another aspect of his connection to Rolls Royce in particular. You see—they do make magnificent cars, as you both have experienced, but they also manufacture armored vehicles, the type needed for a revolution, or a war."

"Oh, wow." Mafulla looked quite concerned.

"So," Walid said. "Let me make sure I get this. We're surrounded right now by two separate enemies, or groups of enemies, both involving powerful individuals, and we likely may have to fight them on two fronts—but, hopefully, not at exactly the same time."

"Or perhaps it's we who surround them," the king said.

"What do you mean?"

"Remember, they're in a crucial sense among us, in our kingdom now, and so on our playing field. Plus, we know what they're up to, or at least strongly suspect it, and they have no idea that we know what we do. That puts us at a tremendous advantage. Knowledge is power. We'll be constantly vigilant and suspicious, watching for everything. They won't be quite so much on the alert concerning us."

"Why is that?" Walid asked.

"They think they have the element of surprise on their side. We know that we have surprise on our side. And, as a result, we have by far the stronger position."

"This is all so interesting—a little scary, but interesting," Mafulla said.

"Plus, and forgive me, Walid, for saying this, but they think we're basically a bunch of country bumpkins—simple, naïve souls from the hinterlands of the kingdom, small village thinkers who have no idea of the sophisticated enemies we might face."

"That's pretty interesting," Walid said. "And it's about as far from the truth as can be imagined."

"Yes it is. And it's a sign of arrogance, which is always a marker of weakness, not of strength," the king responded.

They were all quiet for a few moments and then the king said, "They have other weaknesses that we can depend on, too."

"What are the extra weaknesses?" Walid asked.

"When Faraj, Farouk's brother, came here and poisoned Kular in the attempt to get The Book of Phi, The Ring of Phi, and The Stone of Giza, I asked for whom he was working. Without naming names, he said that his brother Farouk thinks he's working for him but that he, Faraj, prefers to think that it's Farouk who's working for him. He also added that, of course, they can't both be right, and he thinks that he himself is the one who is. He meant it as a bit of a joke, but some important truth came through his remarks. The two of those brothers pretend to be unified and to have each other's interests at heart, but they are each deep down so selfish, so exclusively self-interested, and perhaps jealous of each other, that they represent a house divided against itself, which is something that cannot stand."

"We can exploit that weakness, I would guess," Walid said.

"Yes. And Kinkaid is just as exclusively self-interested. Their alliances are, because of this, all uneasy and fragile, despite any rhetoric to the contrary with each other and the world. And they know in their bones that they could never actually trust each other. The same is true of Falma and the former regime. The famous crime lord is no servant to anyone else. We know that. And the previous king should, as well. A veneer of shared goals and mutual support can't cover up the reality that they would just as easily slit each other's throats as give help and support. And they must both at some level realize that, if they aren't completely deluded. If in fact they do have that basic mistrust, we can use it, and even if they don't and are totally blind to the realities of their situation, we can also exploit that in different ways. In either case, they have much more to worry about in the future than we do, if we continue to be wise and wary."

Mafulla said, "Your Majesty, you're teaching us well to be completely logical in thinking through situations like this. Something that can appear very bad and even scary on the surface, when it's thought through thoroughly, can look really different."

The king said, "That's correct, and it's important to remember. We need logic and intuition working together. Neither alone will do the entire job. Sometimes intuition will guide us better than anything else can. At other times, it's only by also using the best of logic that we'll find our way forward, in the right direction, and with sure footing."

Walid ruminated for a few seconds and said, "What do you think we should do now, Uncle, in light of all this new information?"

"Well, we should keep on our guard and deal with problems as they confront us. First, we have to handle the car log matter and, using it, we can begin to lay a little trap for our enemies. Presumably, it's meant to be a trap for us. And we can just turn that around."

"I love how your mind works," Walid said with a smile. "I also love what Masoon has always called a turnaround, a paradoxical inversion of what your adversary is attempting and expecting."

"I do, too," the king said with a smile of his own. "There's something so … completely satisfying about it. You give your opponent an appearance of something he wants so that you can get what you really need."

"How do you think they were planning to use the car logs against us?" Mafulla asked.

"Well, they obviously want to track our movements away from the palace in every detail, most likely to be able to strike us in some way at what they believe to be a point of vulnerability, perhaps in order to begin their attempt to take over the palace and then the kingdom. It could be that they think a kidnapping or two would allow them to rid themselves of us in a minimally troubling way. Or they could have something else planned, like selective assassination, or a direct assault. And there are other possibilities."

"That's pretty scary. What should we do about all that?"

"We have to set them up. We must seem to be going along with what Kinkaid has requested, but we'll instead create a false record showing not what we have done, trips we've actually taken, but what we want them to believe we've done—something that would suggest to them points of vulnerability that will actually be points of strength."

"Oh."

"We only have to take care to coordinate our creativity with the odometers on the cars. We may be able to get our adversaries to intercept one of the vehicles they think to be alone and carrying members of the royal family when it's actually carrying Phi warriors and is, at a short distance, easily surrounded by many more men, poised to intercept and defeat our attackers."

"Wow. That's a good plan," Mafulla said.

"I hope so. It, of course, depends on total secrecy. So I'll ask that from both of you. Without surprise, the plan will never work. Given what our enemies have tried in the past, we can reasonably infer that if we give them what they believe to be a chance to kidnap or harm a member of the royal family, they'll try that—for whatever particular purpose they may have in mind. Farouk already thinks he has the three things he most wants, in order to prevail against us. But he surely has other desires as well, involving our comings and goings, as the existence of the car log proves. So, as long as we're tight-lipped about what's really going on, we should be able to gain a significant advantage here. Remember, though, that this plan requires complete surprise and thus absolute secrecy."

"Our lips are sealed," Walid said.

"What plan?" Mafulla said, with a look of utter puzzlement. "I can't recall anything about a plan."

"Good!" The king smiled. "Then, of course, there will be many more things to do before all of this goes away. And some of our actions may involve you two, either as yourselves or as your … alter egos, Mr. Viper and Mr. Storm." The boys both smiled. And then the king added, "But, first things first." He paused for a moment and called for the butler. "Kular!"

Within two seconds, he appeared at the door and said, "Yes, Your Majesty?"

"Could you get Naqid to bring up the four palace drivers as soon as possible? I need to speak to all of them together about a matter of great importance."

"Absolutely. I'll get to it immediately."

"Oh, and if Masoon or Hamid might still be in the palace, I'd love for one or both of them to be present as well."

"I'll track them down."

"That's not at all as urgent, but would still be good."

"Certainly, Your Majesty. I'll see what I can do."

6

Surprising News

Walid stared at his watch, as if he wanted it to tell him something more than the time. He said, "They should be here any minute."

Mafulla glanced once more over the table and admired everything he saw. Four linen place mats, sparkling crystal glasses of ice water, the monarchy's best morning china plates with red edging and a red crown outlined in real gold sitting in the center against a sandy, almost lightly golden background, paired with beautiful matching tea cups on saucers, all flanked by highly polished silver utensils.

A large arrangement of multicolored flowers stood tall in the middle of the table, brightening the entire room. A long narrow service table along the wall sat heavy-laden with all the best breakfast goodies. Sweet and savory pastries from the palace bakery were accompanied by a wide array of fresh fruit. There were nuts and small bowls of hummus and sauces. To make it even more perfect, lightly scented candles created an atmosphere that was especially welcoming at such an early hour.

Suddenly, Kissa appeared in the doorway with Hasina right behind her. Walid spotted them first. "There you are! Welcome to a royal breakfast! Come in! Come in! Chef Mafulla and I have a splendid repast set out for you!"

"Oh, my goodness!" Kissa said, as she slowly stepped through the open door. "Look at all this!"

"This is just amazing," Hasina added. "Do you guys eat breakfast like this every day?"

"No, no, no, not at all. This is the room, but to be honest," Mafulla said with a smile, "we normally have a small, humble meal with no table settings, using simple plates and with a quick coffee or tea from any cup we can find."

"Oh! Well, then, this is special, indeed."

"Yes! For you two, only an extravaganza of elegance and an overwhelming abundance of delights will do!"

The girls both laughed. "We're certainly honored, kind sirs," Hasina said, right away.

Walid explained, "It's not exactly like they normally just throw us scraps from the kitchen and we eat on the floor like a couple of stray dogs … I mean, it's always nice. And compared to how most people eat breakfast, I guess it's fit for a king. But we decided to really do it up first class for the two of you today!" He had a big smile as he added, "We do hope you'll like it."

"We love it already," Kissa replied.

Mafulla said, "Good! Good! So, here are the plates, and you can help yourself at the service table. This is all for us, so have anything you'd like, and as much as you'd like." He then added with his characteristic enthusiasm, "Remember that, according to some philosopher whose name I forget—Professor Fava Bean, or something: 'You are what you eat.' So, eat well!"

"Feuerbach, not Fava Bean," Walid said with a grin.

"What?"

"He's the German philosopher who said you are what you eat."

"Oh, Ok. You're right. I remember now. That's the guy who was … what he ate."

"Yes. And I guess his philosophy implies that it's too bad for you, my friend, that there's no … ham on the table."

"Ah, but for you, dear friend, we should have them bring in some silly goose. And fortunately, we have plenty of bread here, I see, that's cheesy," Mafulla replied, drawing the word out extra long.

"Here we go," Kissa said with a laugh.

"Yeah," Hasina agreed.

"Whatever could you mean? We're just our normal, affable selves." Mafulla handed both the girls their plates and urged them to go first at the buffet table. He then grabbed a plate for Walid and one for himself.

"Try the warm hummus on the toasted pita, it's always good," he said, leaning over and watching Hasina put things on her plate.

"I love a man who loves his food," Hasina said.

Walid laughed and said, "Then, you'll certainly swoon for this guy."

"Oh, yeah?"

"Yes, indeed. He practically does a happy dance every time he sees a meal set out for us. And I don't know if I've ever heard him actually read a menu—he always sings it."

Then, as if on cue, Mafulla instantly broke into song, in the mock dramatic voice of a star from musical theater.

"Don't be a fool, Madame,
Just have the fooll mudammes,
And then between you and me
I'd definitely try the tea."

The three others just looked at him as he spread his arms in a final gesticulation accompanying his little rhyme, and at the end they all put down their plates and clapped, with Walid weakly going, "Yaaaay."

"Thank you, thank you. Your applause sweetens the repast. I'm honored by your most appropriate reactions."

"You see what I mean?" Walid said.

"Yeah," Kissa answered.

The prince explained, "He never fails to impress me with new forms of Mafoolery, but built around common themes."

"An uncommon twist on the common—that's me," Mafulla admitted. "It's what I'm all about."

Hasina, looking at Walid, said, "And I thought Kissa and you were the only ones who could spout poetry, instantly."

"Well, you sort of did, too, just now. Nice ending—poetry, instantly."

Mafulla looked at Walid and then at Hasina and said,

"Ahhh, the geometry
of a rhyme-to-be
is a thing to see,
auditory-ally."

"Well then," Hasina said. "That's also impressive."

He grinned and suggested, "Let's finish serving our plates, and sit down before I fully break into song and you ladies truly regret coming here this morning."

"Good idea," Kissa replied, "If we can be absolutely sure the early entertainment portion of our time together is over."

"Over and done," Mafulla said.

She took one more biscuit before moving over to the seat where her name was inscribed in calligraphy on a folded card. Walid pulled out her chair, saying, "Allow me."

"A true gentleman, who can find?"

"Something you need when you're in a bind," Walid could not help but add. But then he said, "Sorry."

"It's like we're still in the musical, the breakfast scene," Hasina said, as she stood and looked at Mafulla, then at her chair, and then back at Mafulla, with eyebrows high, and then again at her chair.

"Oh! Yes! Please, allow me, gentle lady," He said as he nearly dove into the chair, and then recovered enough to slowly pull it back for her with a look, and the body language, of exaggerated, courtly attention.

"Now, you said that you both had something important to talk with us about," Kissa commented, redirecting their attention and getting them down to business.

"Yes, definitely," Walid replied.

"Most definitely," Mafulla agreed, nodding his head.

"Well?" Kissa said.

"That's a deep subject." Walid commented.

"And a joke as old as water. But not as fresh as what we have to drink this morning," Mafulla remarked.

Kissa looked at Walid and said, "Ok, what is it, silly? Or should I say, Mr. Mystery Man?"

"So, here's the deal." Walid didn't quite know where to start. He just then realized that maybe he should have rehearsed this part.

While he was momentarily stuck in place, Mafulla simply blurted out, "We just wanted to let you know that it looks like we're still sort of going to be active as the city's superhero masked crime fighters, in our spare time—the best new hope of the kingdom in these challenging and troubled days, and all that. Could someone pass the fig preserves?"

Hasina and Kissa looked from one boy to the other and then at each other. "You're serious?" Hasina was the first to speak, as she put down her fork.

"Yeah. Crime that needs to be stopped insists on coming our way," Walid replied. "Things keep happening, and Maffie and I have had to keep responding."

"I had no idea," Kissa said. "I sort of assumed that it was, you know, a short-term, passing thing."

"Yeah, I know," Walid confessed. "I did too, sort of. And now it's like maybe that's part of what we're supposed to do, at least for now, like its even a mission or something."

"Really?"

"Yeah. We wanted to share with you both that maybe it wasn't just the one or two-time fluke we might initially have thought. The masked crime fighters have had to continue to strike and stop bad stuff in its tracks."

This was met by a moment of silence. The girls looked at each other. "You're not just kidding around with us, right?" Kissa said. "I mean, after being really proud of you, we both sort of hoped you'd stop doing such dangerous stuff."

"Nope, this is the real thing," Mafulla interjected. "Would anyone like more hummus? It's really extra good today."

Kissa looked at Walid and said, "So, what's been going on?"

Walid took a deep breath. "Ok. If you don't mind, let me backtrack for just a minute to get it all in view. Perspective is everything in stuff like this."

"Like what?"

"I'll get to it all in just a minute. I promise."

"Ok."

"So, here's the story. Remember, months ago, when we first told you about this, I mean, about how we came up with crime fighter names?"

"I do," Kissa said. "It all started when there was that criminal gang operating out of the back of the store owned by Mafulla's dad, and Mr. Adi didn't know who the guys really were."

"That's right," Walid replied. "They told him they represented the king and were doing some politically sensitive things and needed his extra space for their work. So, Mr. Adi cooperated, thinking they were good guys. And then that day when Maffie and I were in the marketplace not far from the shop, and we found out what was really going on, and minutes later, Maffie learned that his mother and the little ones were on their way to the shop right then and might be in danger, and he took off running to get there and I followed him."

"Yes, I remember all that," Kissa said.

"Me, too," Hasina added.

"Ok. I figured you would, but I just thought I should do a basic review quickly here to get us all up to speed."

"Ok." Kissa said. "Unless you're just burning time, putting off what you really need to say."

"No, no, not at all. Stick with me here. There's a reason."

"Go on."

"So, back to the criminals: we were able to help stop those guys—but it was really a bad scene with guns and whips and knives and lots of dangerous men in a foul mood—and they sort of tried to kill us, but we ended up helping to get them arrested."

Kissa looked shocked. "I don't think you ever said anything about whips and knives, or guns, or that your life was in clear danger."

"Yeah, I may have left that out. I thought you might freak out about it. Sorry. You were sort of worried enough for us, anyway."

"I was."

"But then, later on, after all that, remember we told you that we were talking about how it's too bad that the criminals all saw our faces and knew who we are, because when you try to stop crime, you're going to make some people pretty mad. And then they or their gangs might later try to get revenge on you or your family, or your friends. So, we were saying that it would make sense for crime fighters outside the normal police force to wear masks and have secret identity names. And, just for fun, we each made up a name."

"Yes," said Kissa, who still looked like she didn't have any idea why Walid was repeating all this.

Hasina said, "We know. You became The Golden Viper," and she turned to Mafulla and said, "and Windstorm."

"Yeah. They're really cool names, right?"

"Yes, they are."

"Thanks. And, remember, we never thought we'd use them. We just initially made them up for fun, like Walid said," Mafulla assured her.

"I remember," Hasina said.

Walid then went on. "We were really just messing around, having a good time, thinking it all through. But then, when we asked the king one day if it was Ok for us to go to the marketplace just to hang out and look around, he said sure but he wanted us to wear those face scarves that some people have been wearing to protect against blowing sand, at least since we've had all the high winds in town."

"You see plenty of people wearing them, recently," Kissa commented.

"Yeah. Well, the king thought if we wore them outside the palace, people would be less likely to recognize us, and we'd fit in to the crowds better and be safer."

"We know. We remember."

"Good. And so, we said Ok and went to the market with the scarves on, and, remember also, we saw that lady being attacked by the man stealing her bag, and he ran off and we chased him."

"Yes, of course, we remember that too," Kissa said.

Mafulla, caught up in the retelling, jumped in and said, "Well, Walid chased the guy. I didn't even see him at first, but when my friend here went running out of the store we were in, I ran after him and at first I didn't know why, and then I saw the lady on the ground in the middle of the street and this scruffy looking older guy with a nice bag running away down an alley." Mafulla then looked back to Walid to pick the story back up.

"So, we caught up with him, and I tackled him," Walid said. "And the bag flew out of his hands, and he got up with a knife and said he was going to cut us. But then Mafulla ran up to him and kicked the knife out of his hand and it bounced off a building and the guy panicked and ran like crazy just to get away from us. Then we gave back the lady's bag and she asked our names, and we said the made up names, and it got into the newspaper story that you both saw, as the first report of the exploits of The Golden Viper and Windstorm."

"And we were really proud of you, but we also hoped that such stuff wouldn't have to continue, for the sake of your safety," Kissa said.

"Yeah. I remember."

"Ok, you've given us some new details in your retelling of everything, but I know the basic story well," Kissa said. "I mean, this is about you guys and we're not going to forget dramatic stuff like this."

"Well then, you may also recall that it was on the front page, but under the fold," Mafulla added. "And they spelled my name wrong, as two words rather than one."

Walid said, "Yeah, they spelled his name wrong, and now journalists all over the world have a bad precedent that we're both hoping they can overcome."

"At least, before the movie comes out," Mafulla said, with a serious expression. Then he sighed. "I'll be lucky if they ever get it right."

"You're funny," Hasina said. "Look, I don't want to just repeat what Kissa's been saying, but we're still not sure why you're telling us all this again and in such detail. I mean, it's interesting to hear it again and see your enthusiasm for it, but … truly, what's up?"

Walid smiled and said, "Give me just half a minute more for the review. You're right. It's going somewhere. But, where was I? Oh, yeah, after the article came out, the king told us he had figured out it was us, and talked to us about it all."

"And he approved."

"Yeah. He actually approved, but he said he always wanted us to share such things with him and not keep them secret, so he can help. He really thought we maybe do have a mission here, at least part time, to help out in this way."

"Oh?" Kissa said. "You never mentioned that part."

"Yeah. I must have forgotten to tell you that."

"A mission."

"Yes."

Mafulla jumped in, saying, "And, you know, he wanted us to tell our parents what we were doing, so we wouldn't be keeping a big secret from them. And then he suggested we bring in Masoon and Hamid, and we thought that would be the total group of people who knew—at least, for a while. But then, when the two of you had those crazy dreams about the emerald, and you dreamed about a viper, Kissa, and a windstorm, Hasina, and we felt like we had to tell you about it all, and our made up names. We thought it probably wouldn't ever happen again—the crime fighting, I mean. We really did, sort of. I mean, at the time."

"He's right," Walid said.

"Yeah, it's the total truth," Mafulla emphasized.

Walid then picked up the thread at this point again and said: "But then, yesterday, when we were on that nice drive in the new car, we got out to get flowers for you both and when we got back into the car, you noticed that we suddenly had wristbands on and asked about them and we said we'd tell you later."

"After making up some lame stories," Kissa said.

"Well."

"And now you're going to tell us what was really going on?" Kissa said with a suspicious look on her face.

"The thing is that, you know, we have these really eye-catching watches, our Reversos, thanks to the king."

"Yes. They're beautiful."

"Thanks. And we had suddenly realized one day that if we were ever in a crime fighting situation again, and I promise that we actually had no real plans to go out and do it again, ever, but if it happened

… then we'd need a way to cover these watches, because not many people have them, and likely nobody else our age. And so there's a really good chance we'd be recognized for sure with them on. And we couldn't be always taking off the watches, so we had the wristbands made up. And we usually keep them on us, like in a pocket or something—just in case. But we weren't ever going to wear them unless we had to stop a crime as the Viper and the Storm."

"Wait. You both had them on when you got back into the car."

"Yeah."

"So that means …"

"We had to stop a crime in the shop."

"What?"

Reaching for a piece of pita, Mafulla said, "When we went into that really nice shop to get you both flowers, it was being robbed."

"It was being robbed?" Kissa said, looking over at him.

"Yeah, it was."

"How did you know?"

Walid jumped back in and said, "One man had been knocked out and was lying on the floor unconscious and a bad guy with a big knife was in the back threatening the shop owner and demanding his money."

"A big knife?" Hasina said.

Walid explained, "Yeah, it was big. That's why I reviewed so much just now, before getting to this part. I wanted you to know that we've faced knives and worse before, and successfully. Ok?"

"Ok," she said, dubiously.

Then he continued on. "The guys we saw in the back didn't see us come in—either of them. They were too busy robbing or being robbed, or in the case of the other, third guy, he was too busy being unconscious to notice. And it's a big store. We hid behind a clothing display as soon as we realized what was happening. We didn't have our normal wind scarves, so we took two regular scarves off a display and wrapped them around our faces, and then realized that we did in fact both have our wristbands, so we put them on and pulled them up over our watches and snuck up on the thief from behind, and took him down, big time."

"Boom!!! He didn't know what hit him," Mafulla couldn't help but add.

"Wait. You two stopped another armed robber?" Kissa said.

Hasina added, "Yesterday in the shop, while we were circling the block in the car?"

"Yeah, he got bit by the Viper and slammed by the Storm," Mafulla grinned. "The guy was on the floor out cold before he knew what hit him."

"What did you do?" Hasina asked.

Walid answered, "We just did our thing and then tied him up and the shopkeeper sent his brother, the guy who had been knocked in the head and just then woke up, to call for the police. So then we got the flowers we had gone in to buy for both of you, and we took off the scarves, but forgot about the wristbands. And so when we got back into the car, we had just broken up a major crime and had hardly broken a sweat."

"Yeah, it was sweet," Mafulla reported, still chewing.

"I don't know what to say," Kissa responded.

"I don't, either," Hasina added.

"But then, later," Walid went on, "we found out that it wasn't just a simple robbery, but an effort of organized crime to fund a political revolution here in the kingdom that would have major international implications, in addition of course, to the consequences for us."

"Really?"

Mafulla smiled and said, "Yeah. So now, the Viper and the Storm are guardians of the peace, the kingdom, and the stability of the worldwide political structure."

Both girls were shaking their heads. "Unbelievable," Kissa said. "Completely, totally, absolutely, and without a doubt unbelievable. You got into the car like nothing unusual had been going on. And you had just been through all that?"

"Yeah, smooth, huh?" Walid had to say.

"Are you guys Ok? Did you get hurt?" Hasina asked.

"We're totally Ok, which is more than we can say for world politics generally—and no, we didn't get hurt, but you should have seen the bad guy. He's certainly had better days," Mafulla said, and laughed loudly. "Sorry, but he deserved it, pulling a nasty looking giant knife on that nice shopkeeper."

"This is just too much," Kissa said. "You mean, you got back into the car and gave us those beautiful flowers maybe a minute after a major fight with a grown man who's a professional criminal and who had a big knife?"

Mafulla said, "Well, he didn't have the knife for long after we got going, and it wasn't much of a fight, actually. He hardly knew what hit him. We had him down in about two seconds, and when we left, he was still out. But, yeah, that was about a minute before we were back in the car with your flowers."

"How can you do something like that?"

"What do you mean?"

"I mean, how do you even begin to know how to do something like that? You're our age. People our age don't go around stopping grownup professional criminals in the act of committing a crime."

"Well, fortunately, we do know how," Walid explained. "It's all from our training with Masoon."

"Already? This early on in the process?" Kissa said.

"Yeah. He's sort of supercharged our lessons. He's amazing, and he's preparing us for nearly anything."

Mafulla added, "Most bad guys have no idea how to defend themselves against skilled adversaries like us who really know what we're doing. We don't just go into a situation like that and hope for the best. We know ahead of time exactly what we can do, and even what to fall back to, if that goes wrong. Walid went high and I went low, and as a result that guy, I promise you, likely wishes he had never gone into that particular store, for any reason whatsoever. I doubt he'll ever go there again."

"But." Kissa got out the one word.

Walid said, "We have really specific actions planned for stuff like that, and we back up each other. I mean, we're not Masoon—no one else is, either—but we can already handle most of the situations we could ever face like that. And it seems like these things just continue to come our way. We're really getting experienced, at this point."

"Still," Kissa said.

Walid continued, "We wanted you both to know that, now, it looks like, maybe, it's an ongoing deal and not just the fluke we thought. But we're being very careful and everything—super careful. I wanted to review everything before telling you about this recent situation so you'd know that we've faced really serious adversaries with knives and guns and stuff before, and we were just fine. We didn't want you to be shocked about this new incident, or worried or mad or anything." They all sat in silence for about three seconds.

"I have to admit that I'm sort of speechless," Kissa said. A knot started to form in Walid's gut. But then she added, "I mean, you guys are … heroes. You really are. You're actually doing something about the bad things in the world and not just talking about how bad they are. But, you're right—we had no idea that this had become an ongoing thing. Are you sure it's safe for you to do this?"

"Well, not completely sure," Walid conceded. "But the king seems to think we're safe enough, given what we know and can do."

"Yeah, he seems fine with it," Mafulla said. "And he's always reminding us how to be cautious whenever we have to take action."

Walid continued, "And he's offered us all the backup we need if we ever anticipate something like this. But, so far, all the crime-fighter-in-disguise situations have been sort of spontaneous."

"Yeah, we never knew they were going to happen."

"We just came across something going on, or someone who needed help, and we took action."

"You guys are pretty incredible," Hasina said. "Just incredible. I'm really, really proud of both of you."

"Me, too," Kissa said. "I mean, we're also getting some great training, as you know, but I think you guys are way ahead of us at this point."

Walid smiled big, but then got a very serious look on his face. He said, "We just got a head start."

"Still."

"You'll end up just as prepared as we are."

"Maybe."

"No, for sure. And, well, we're telling the two of you right now about this ongoing stuff because we totally trust you. I mean, totally. Remember, it has to be kept a complete secret, just like the larger club we're in, but this one's even smaller. That's why we couldn't mention it in front of Darwishi, even a trustworthy guy like that."

Mafulla jumped in and said, "We'd prefer it if even your parents didn't hear about this. But we know your moms are Phi, so if they ever ask, it's Ok to tell them, I guess, but then also as something confidential, totally, one hundred percent confidential."

"I understand," Kissa said.

"Me, too," Hasina assured them.

"We were going to tell you, eventually," Mafulla said. "I mean, about what happened during the car ride and about our sense that this is sort of an ongoing now-and-then job for us, a continuing kind of thing. But there's a way in which knowing about it could possibly put you at some sort of at least minor risk. So, we were a little hesitant to tell you anytime soon."

Walid added, "But then again, you saw the wristbands and we didn't want to lie to you about them so we needed to have this conversation as soon as we could."

Hasina looked at Mafulla and said, "I guess the wild fib about wanting to stop time and instead just covering it up doesn't really count, since it was so lame—creative and sweet, for sure, but transparently lame." Mafulla did a fake grimace.

Hasina then continued, "The bit about the thorns was better, but not by much."

Walid added, "Yeah, we were going to have to tell you the real story sooner or later. I mean, we actually want you to know everything, plus, we may need your help."

"Really?" Kissa said this with great feeling.

"Yeah, really. You're Phi. You're strong. You both know things that most people don't know. You can already do lots of things that most people can't do. We want you at the center of the circle."

"You've got us," Kissa said. "Hassi?"

"Yeah! You've got us, for sure. We can be your semi-superhero backup team."

"Really?" This time it was Walid who was amazed and pleased.

"Yes!" They both said at the same time.

Kissa reached over to touch Walid's arm. "We believe in you."

Hasina did the same thing to Mafulla. "And we believe you'll be careful, and honest with us about it all the time."

"Well, this is even better than the warm hummus on crisply toasted pita," Mafulla said. "And that, of course, is very good indeed."

Just then, Kular came to the door and knocked and said, "Please excuse me, everyone. Today's papers are in. May I drop off copies?"

"Sure thanks, Kular," Walid answered.

"*The Kingdom Daily News* and two others," Kular said, as he put the papers down on a table close to the door. "I hope you're enjoying your breakfast."

"It's wonderful," Kissa said. "Thank you so very much!"

Mafulla couldn't take his eyes off the stack of papers. After about three seconds, he got up from the table, walked over without saying a word, and picked up *The Kingdom Daily.* He unfolded it, and there under the fold on the first page, was the headline he had almost expected to see. And he read it aloud, in a slow and dramatic tone of voice: "Masked Crime Fighters Strike Again!"

"No way!" Walid said.

"Let's see! Let's see!" Hasina exclaimed.

Mafulla brought it over to the table and spread it out so all could see it. He continued to read aloud. "The Golden Viper and Wind Storm—jeez, two words again—stopped an armed theft in progress yesterday at the Kingdom Luxury Goods Shop on Nile Avenue. The proprietor, a Mr. Ali Arumbar, said that an armed assailant came into his shop and hit his brother from behind, rendering him unconscious and dropping him to the floor. The man then demanded all the money in the cash box and everything in the store safe. The owner said he tried to reason with the man, but to no avail. Just as he was about to empty out his safe for the dangerous scoundrel, two masked men appeared from nowhere and attacked the criminal so quickly and effectively that he crumpled up onto the floor, completely unconscious. The masked crime fighters tied him up tightly while someone went to get the police. The men were as polite as they were powerful, the relieved shopkeeper said, and they left as quickly as they had arrived, but this time, they crossed the threshold of the shop with gifts from the owner, a token of his gratitude that he insisted the heroes take. The good people of the kingdom hope that The Golden Viper and Wind Storm will continue their patrols and keep the kingdom safe from such vermin and thugs. Long live the kingdom's new heroes!"

"Well, that was some story!" Walid said. "Well told."

"Front page again!" Hasina said.

"Yeah," Kissa commented in a strange tone.

"They pretty much got it all right, except, of course, for my name being just one word, not two," Mafulla commented. "I can't believe it. I really can't believe it."

"I'm glad they didn't describe in detail exactly what we did. That's our secret," Walid added.

"They probably couldn't have," Mafulla explained. "We were too lightning fast for the proprietor to even see what we were doing. And he was probably in shock or something anyway."

There was silence for a second, and then Kissa said, "So, and let me make sure I get this right." She paused and went on, "The flowers you gave us were gifts to you from the store owner."

"Well."

"You didn't actually buy us flowers at all, but they were given to you to show the owner's appreciation for what you had done. Then, you got into the car and were all romantic about the bouquets you had specially selected for us."

Walid and Mafulla both grimaced, and the prince quickly said, "That doesn't sound quite accurate in all respects."

"Oh?"

"Ok. I mean, we originally stopped the car just to buy you flowers. That was the whole reason we stopped and got out. We were talking about it as we walked to the store. We wanted to make the trip really special for you."

"He's right. I was there," Mafulla said.

"And?"

"And we did all the other stuff because we had to. And then the guy asked what he could do for us. And it just came to me why we were there in the first place. So I mentioned that we had come in for flowers and all of a sudden he was handing us the most beautiful ones in the whole entire store, bouquets he hadn't even put out yet."

"So … we were really lucky to be able to get you the best," Mafulla interrupted and said with a pleading smile.

"The very, very best," Walid said.

"Better than anything else in the store, maybe in the whole town, and who knows, maybe the entire kingdom," Mafulla emphasized.

Kissa started laughing, and so did Hasina. She said, "They were, and are, the very best. The very, very best in the whole world."

Then everyone laughed, and the boys did so with great relief.

7

An Announcement

Ari Falma waited. His left leg shook and bounced with pent up nervous energy. He was in a small office at the back of a building in a part of town rarely visited by police. Three men sat outside the office in a slightly darker area, lit only by high transoms through which the early morning sun was shining.

Another small thin man who looked a bit like Ari walked into the room. He stopped and exclaimed in a loud and disgusted voice, "He was arrested."

"What? What's this announcement you're making?"

"Sebak was arrested." The man practically spat out the words in anger.

"How? What do you mean?"

"The story I heard was that two men burst into the shop and attacked him, knocking him out and tying him up while he was waiting for the money in the safe. They wore masks and told the owner their names were The Golden Viper and Windstorm."

"Are you kidding me?"

"Do I look like I'm joking?"

"This is terrible. This can't be happening."

"I know. We needed that money. You promised the real king."

"There was over a hundred thousand dollars in that safe."

"Yes. And it was ours to take."

"When we missed grabbing the jewels the shop sold, I knew we could get the cash before it also went away."

"Yes. It was a good plan."

"Is Sebak naming us?"

"I don't know. I have no access to him now."

"He's your man. You know him well. Will he rat on us?"

"No, I don't think so. He understands how things are. He has to take his medicine for now. He knows we'll free him soon."

"I can't believe he was stopped!"

"I feel the same way. It makes no sense. We had it all planned out in every detail."

"Who could have guessed that we were going to rob The Luxury Shop? It's mostly just clothes and bags and leather goods and flowers! Almost nobody knows they also at times sell fine jewels on consignment for big money. And after the huge sale this week, the biggest sale they've ever made, there was likely more cash in that safe than ever before. I bet there was a lot more than a hundred thousand! It was crucial for funding everything!"

"I know."

"This town is cursed."

The other man let out a long breath and calmed down a bit and said, "We've had a few setbacks. Everybody has setbacks. We've just had a few more than our share. But luck changes. It's fickle."

"Who are these Golden Vipers and Storms?"

"The Golden Viper and Windstorm."

"Yeah. Fine. Who are they?"

"No one knows."

"How can no one know? What do they look like?"

"I asked around. Not even the owner of the store knows."

"How can he not know? He was right there."

"Well, each of them wore a mask over his face."

"Were they tall or short, fat or skinny, old or young?"

"He didn't now any of that. I tell you, no one could answer these questions."

"Did they take the money we were after?"

"No, they just stopped Sebak and left the building. They appeared and then disappeared. The whole thing apparently took place in little more than a minute."

"Sebak is strong. How did they overpower him so quickly?"

"No one knows."

"This is idiocy. We should have sent two or three men."

"But how could we have known that? Sebak is a bull."

"Listen. Tell me this: How did they know he was there? How did they figure out when it was going to happen?"

"I have no idea."

"We must have a leak."

"What?"

"Someone in our organization is speaking about our business. How else could these vipers know where and when we were going to strike?"

"You're talking about my men."

"I know I am, and I'm talking about my money. When we divided up our duties and I gave you the job of raising the men and took for myself the task of raising the money, I expected you to do a good job of checking people out to make sure we'd have no weaklings or weasels in our midst."

"We have no such men! Don't you insult my work or my men! You have no right, I tell you!"

"You're in no position to tell me anything. You're now insulting me! If you like your throat the way it is, you'll close your mouth and listen to me with respect."

"All I ever do is listen to you."

"Of course you do! I'm your superior! I'm your older brother. I was in the world when you weren't even a dream—a bad dream! You can do nothing without me! I make it all possible."

The two men glowered at each other. Ari went on, "There has to be a leak. There's no other way anyone could have known where and when we were going to strike. Draw up a list of anybody who was told in advance about the theft. We'll question each man and learn who's been talking."

"I can do that. But I can't imagine it was deliberately leaked."

"You say Sebak was arrested."

"Yes."

"Was it right there? On the spot?"

"That's what I was told."

"Who arrested him? These vipers and storms?"

"No, they're not police, apparently, or government."

"Well, what happened?"

"They knocked him out and tied him up, and someone else went for the police."

"But who are they?"

"No one knows, I tell you, no one."

"Someone knows. Someone has to know. Get to the bottom of it. Find out. Learn this as soon as you can. We have to stop anyone who tries to stop us. We need to be rid of these obstacles. Remember what I told you: It's all about money and men. Without the money we need, we can't get the men we need. Without the men we need, we can't get the money we need. We have a problem now with the money and it comes back to a problem with the men. This is not just me telling you; this is simple logic talking."

Up on the second floor of the palace, Khalid walked into class with a big smile. He put down his bag and stood in the front of the room and just grinned at the boys.

"What is it?" Mafulla asked. He thought for a second and said, "Wait. You've finally concluded that we are the smartest and best looking class you've ever taught and … you're very happy about that and you have an award for us."

"Or maybe, a relative you never really liked that much anyway just left you lots of money in his will," Jabari suggested.

"Anyone else?" Khalid asked, still grinning. The boys darted glances at each other. Now, many of them were smiling as well.

"What is it?" somebody said.

"You're going to announce that there will be no school for the rest of the week," Malik suggested. "We're sufficiently educated for now."

"No. Excellent try. But I do have an announcement."

"What's the announcement?" Walid could not help but say it aloud. "We're all ears—or, at least Jabari is." He grinned and looked over at the small boy he had spontaneously decided to rib on this occasion, instead of Mafulla. And, indeed, the young man's ears were more impressive than Mafulla's, and especially relative to his overall size.

"Hey," Jabari said, "Very funny. I hear things that others don't even suspect. I can hear what you're thinking." And with that, he flashed a smile back at Walid. The prince knew that the boy was proud of his protuberant audio receivers, or he never would have made a little joke like that in front of the others.

Khalid looked back and forth across the room and said, "The king himself has approved and funded a request Hoda and I made that both this class and her class be allowed to go on a field trip together out of town."

"Really?" Mafulla responded. "Where are we going?"

"The king will provide us with a train car that will take us to the nearby ruins of the famous ancient city of Memphis, the primary spiritual center of Egypt in the time of the pharaohs. We'll also visit Giza nearby and tour the pyramids and the Sphinx. And then, like the rulers did in Cleopatra's day, we'll get on a Royal Barge and float home down the Nile River."

Bafur said, "We're going to see ruins?"

"Yes."

Mafulla could not resist saying, "You know, I've heard that Memphis was once a really great place, but it's been … ruined."

Bafur laughed and said, "And we're going to ride on a barge?"

"A barge," said Khalid.

"Will it be a large barge?" Mafulla had to ask, over-articulating the words, of course.

"Yes, a very large barge, as long as I'm in charge," Khalid answered in a similar tone.

"Ha!" Mafulla said. "Good answer."

Khalid nodded at Mafulla and added, "The goal of the trip is two-fold. We'll learn some important new things, and we'll have a big party."

"A party?" Haji suddenly seemed excited as well.

"A big party on the river," Khalid replied.

"We'll party hardy?" Mafulla jokingly asked.

"If you don't mind using an adjective as an adverb, then, I suppose the answer is yes," Khalid responded.

"I like to be a bit adjectively wild with my modifiers now and then—it's a part of my hardy party spirit," he answered, and then paused. "Class goal: To adjectively smile on the Nile all the while, in style, and for each and every mile." He turned to Walid and gave him the ultimate signal of Mafoolery, the now famous double eyebrow jump.

Set laughed loudly and then turned back and said to Khalid, "Isn't Memphis pretty close by?"

"Yes, only about twelve miles or so outside of town, to the south."

"How long will it take us to get there?"

"Well, once we're all on the train, I'd estimate about half an hour, maybe a little more, depending on whether there are any local goats on the track."

Mafulla had to comment. "I do hope someone's keeping the local goats on track; they tend to lose focus so easily on whatever the task might be, and just wander about aimlessly." Walid and three others rolled their eyes.

"So, it's a short trip." Set said, and seemed pleased.

"Well, it's a very short trip in space, but we'll be going back over four thousand years in time."

"Oooooooo," Jabari made what he thought of as a ghostly sound.

Walid, ever the practical thinker, asked, "How are we going to get from Memphis to Giza?"

"It's not far from Memphis—just a few miles. The king will be sending extra transportation for that part of the route, some military trucks I think, and then after our time with the pyramids and the Sphinx, they'll take us a few miles back east over to the Nile, where we'll then embark on the barge for our return home."

"Good security?" Walid asked.

"Yes, very good," Khalid replied.

"When do we go?" Mafulla asked seriously, raising the one remaining question that all the students now had on their minds.

"One week from today," Khalid said. "It takes a lot to set up such a trip. Now, speaking of a lot, we've got a lot to do today, so everyone take out a notebook."

At about the same time, Hoda was breaking the good news to her class. The girls were very excited. No one was making silly jokes like the boys. They were just very enthusiastic about the prospect of getting out of their normal classroom and seeing something new and exotic. And they immediately liked the fact that both classes would go together. A couple of the girls looked at each other and smiled.

They all started asking questions right away about Memphis and Giza and the pharaohs. Hoda began a little impromptu lesson, putting the trip into a solid historical context. They learned all the latest theories about the building of the pyramids, whose idea it was, how many workers it likely took, how long the project went on, and what the whole purpose was intended to be. Every one of her students, of course, knew various parts of the story already, but Hoda did a good job of helping to make the puzzle pieces fit together. Then Cabar raised her hand.

"Yes, Cabar?" Hoda said, acknowledging her.

She had a serious look on her face, almost of perplexity, and said, "So, Memphis was a spiritual place for thousands of years?

"Yes it was, and actually it still is," Hoda replied.

"But what makes a place spiritual? I always thought that only people could be described as spiritual."

"That's a good question. There have always been special places around the earth in different countries—some in the mountains, a few in the desert, others near a river or by the ocean. These have been areas or locations where people have felt a deeper connection to something-greater-than-themselves. In these places, they've felt awe and wonder, or peace and inspiration."

Hoda went on, "Pilgrims and other visitors to these places often later claim that they experienced something very special there, as if their minds and hearts and souls were more open to insight and wisdom, and even love. Meditation is reported to be easier and quicker, and often deeper. If you go there with a problem, you may return with a solution. Occasionally, there have been reports of physical healings from a disease or disability. Attitudes alter. Emotions change. New adventures are launched with a sense of mission and purpose."

"Wow," Ara said.

"But no one is sure how to separate the myths and legends from the realities. We know with certainty only that these stories are so persistent, and many are told by such otherwise reliable sources that there must be some sort of underlying truth behind them. What it is that makes these particular spots so special, no one really knows."

"Where are these places you're talking about?" Bakat asked.

"Well, in addition to our ancient Memphis, there are sites I know of in locales like Israel, Saudi Arabia, Tibet, France, India, and other nations. I've heard of at least four in the United States."

"Where in the U.S.?" Khata suddenly asked. "You know, I've always wanted to go there."

"Yeah. You talk about it all the time," Cabar commented with a smile.

Hoda answered, "There's one I know of in the state of Arizona, one in New Mexico, one in California, and another on the southern part of the coast in the state of North Carolina, on a small barrier island. There may be more."

"Really?" Ara said.

"Four spiritual places or more in one country?" Khata seemed impressed.

"Yes, and there are likely more."

Cabar spoke up again. "Why does the U.S. have so many?"

"Well, there are several other countries with multiple spiritual places, as well. India is one. Great Britain is another. I just happen to know of these in America from my time there. And what's particularly interesting about the U.S. is that the ones I'm aware of in California, Arizona, and North Carolina are on or close to about the same latitude, the 34th parallel north. It's a latitude, or swath of geography, that circumscribes the earth and that's been said in many other places, along extensive stretches, to be a ring of the planet that's unstable or poor, desolate or tumultuous, and in certain spots unusually violent."

"Really?" Bakat seemed surprised to hear this.

"Yes. But in those few sacred places along its span, it's said to be quite different."

"How so?"

"In those locations, it's extraordinarily peaceful, tranquil, beautiful, and elevating to the spirit."

"That's strange," Cabar said. "What are the countries that the 34th parallel north runs cross?"

"Let's see: Morocco, Algeria, Tunisia, Lebanon, Syria, Iraq, Iran, Afghanistan, Pakistan, India, China, Korea, Japan, and the United States. I hope I'm not leaving out any."

"That's a lot," Bakat said. "And you said there are violent places along this band?"

"Yes. Violence and difficulty have, unfortunately, always been a part of the human condition in various ways, and in almost every part of the earth. But in some of these countries along the 34th parallel north, they've had a particularly powerful history of difficulty. And yet, out of this ring of fire, it may be that great things can arise."

She thought for a second more and then said more. "There have been various prophecies about the coming future on and near this latitude that are deeply unsettling. One sagacious mystic in a deep meditative trance has seen a place in Asia close to this parallel and, in his vision, there was a blinding flash of severe destruction in an intensity and variety never before witnessed, as he reported later to some of his colleagues and students. I mention this only by way of contrast with those especially peaceful, spiritual spots along the same line that encircles the earth."

"But the spirit is an inner thing, right? And geographical places are outer things, aren't they?"

"Kit, that's a very good question. A person can have a spirit, in both metaphorical and metaphysical senses—but can a place?" Hoda looked carefully at each of the girls.

"Meta-what?" Khata said.

Hoda smiled, "You know about metaphor."

"Yes. A metaphor is a strange and wonderful mirror that can produce or convey insight. It's an imaginative reflection of something in a sort of poetical way."

"Right."

"But what was the other word?"

"Metaphysical."

"Yes. What does that mean?"

"It means having to do with fundamental being or reality. The ultimate nature of things is a metaphysical question. Whether you have a soul in addition to your body is a metaphysical question. It goes above or beyond physics to questions that probe even deeper than science can. Where did the basic particles or forces of the universe ultimately come from? We live in a vast cosmos—so why is there something rather than nothing? Why does anything exist? Is there a dimension beyond the physical, or many such dimensions and realities? Is there a God? And, if so, what's God like? Is there life after death? What is free will? Is the mental fundamentally different from the material? And if so, then how do minds manage to act in the physical world?"

"That's a lot," Khata said.

"Yes it is. And there's more. Metaphysics is the branch of classical philosophy that deals with ultimate questions like these."

"Are there answers to all these questions?" Kit then asked.

"Yes, to many of these questions, answers have been suggested and widely debated for a very long time. But even the top experts find it hard to agree among themselves on all the answers. That's part of our condition as human beings. We can ask beyond what we can prove—or at least beyond what we can prove to the satisfaction of all sincere inquirers. And yet, the truth is surely still out there. Answers in principle exist. It's part of our challenge to find the right ones."

"Do you think we'll get some answers in Memphis?" Khata wondered.

"We'll certainly talk about the questions that have been asked and the answers that have been given there for many thousands of years. But, more importantly, we'll stand and also sit at the spiritual center of our kingdom, a location that's been a special place in our history since before anyone ever wrote any of it down. And the extraordinary things that have happened in that neighborhood have produced monuments on a scale and of a nature that's unique in the world. We'll open ourselves up and let those monuments, or the secrets behind them, speak to us." She smiled.

"So, will they answer our questions?" Kit was half joking, but only half.

Hoda said, "Possibly. They may ask us questions. Or they could give us hints about ours. They might spark in us thoughts that we've never before had. So you'd better take a special bucket with you to collect and bring home whatever new insights may come your way."

"A what?" Kit looked puzzled.

Hoda smiled again. "The king often talks about having a good wisdom bucket with us at all times, and I like his metaphor."

Khata also looked perplexed and asked, "What's a wisdom bucket?"

"His Majesty has a nice way of putting this. He says that, every now and then, it's almost as if a big invisible hole opens in the sky and wisdom falls down on us like rain. It comes suddenly and can be refreshing or bracing and just what we need. For these times in our lives, we should have something like an inner bucket available to catch the wonderful shower of insight and allow us to keep it and carry it away to have available later when we may need it, and so we can also share it with others who might drink of its benefits as well."

"But what does it really mean to have such a bucket?" Kit asked.

"It means carrying in your heart a readiness and a willingness, an open spirit, an available container in the soul that can capture new wisdom when it comes and keep it ready for use. It means paying attention when insight breaks into your heart and mind, and it requires remembering the wisdom that's come your way."

"I like this image and the idea," Kit said.

"I do, too." Khata looked at Kit and then back at Hoda.

"So, when we go to Memphis and Giza and boat on the Nile, let's all take wisdom buckets with us, buckets that will allow us to catch and bring back any new insight that falls into our lives while we're there."

"I'm preparing my bucket already," Hasina said with a smile.

"Me, too," Kissa added.

"Good! So, class, a show of hands: Who here plans to take a

wisdom bucket with you on the trip?" Hoda looked around the room as she would if she had asked an academic question. "Ah, good, all hands are up. Very good! And so will I! Together, we can be The Girls' Class Bucket Brigade!" Some of the girls laughed and even clapped.

"Remember, though, that you don't need to go to a special place in order to nourish your spirit or connect with something deeper, or to gain real wisdom. Those are things you can do wherever you are, whenever you open up your heart and mind and allow yourself to be spoken to, and choose to listen. You can fill your wisdom bucket at almost any place and nearly any time. So always have it ready. If your spirit is truly thirsty, refreshing waters will appear."

Hoda smiled at all of her students, and then looked down at her desk for a moment. "Now, I must remind myself that we have a lot of scheduled work to get done today. I'm glad everyone's excited about our trip, and I'm pleased to say that it will happen in about a week. I'll give you plenty of advance notice on what day. But for now, let's all turn our attention to some of the homework you did last night. We have a lot to cover before this afternoon."

"Not a problem," Hasina said. "I've brought my Random Academic Information Memory Bucket with me to class today, like usual. So I'm all ready." At that, all the girls laughed, and the planned work of the day commenced.

8

In The King's Quarters

It wasn't often that the king and prince got to spend time together alone these days. They had enjoyed a lot of private time to talk on their trek across the desert months ago, although it now often seemed like that trip was years in the past. When they did have a little one-on-one time, big ideas often took the opportunity to arise.

They had been together now for almost an hour, just the two of them, talking. The king stood at the window and looked out over the city. He sighed, and said, "Too much of world politics has been nothing more than an exercise in greed—an unseemly and endless quest for money and power, and all the trappings of both."

"Money and power." Walid repeated the words and then said, "These two things? Both of them?"

"Yes," the king responded. And then, after a moment, he went on to say, "But when you understand money, it's just another form of power. It's the power to gain, have, and do. It's the power of options, or of possibilities." The king reached over to the nearby table and picked up his cup of tea, but continued to speak as he turned around, took a few steps, and sat back down in his favorite chair.

"There was an Italian philosopher hundreds of years ago, a Nicolo Machiavelli—not a particularly accomplished man, and in fact perhaps the most moderately successful individual ever to become a widely renowned advisor on worldly success. But he was a shrewd observer of human conduct and wrote an influential little book called *The Prince*, specifically to give guidance to people in high political positions. It contains some great insight and some equally terrible advice. There's a copy of it over on my desk. I was reviewing it this morning with some notes I had written in the margins years ago."

"I've heard someone speak of the book, but I've never seen it before," Walid commented.

The king took a sip of his tea and then went on to say, "Part of the book's problem is that its focus is simply on power—getting it and keeping it. There's no thought that the whole purpose of power is to serve higher ends."

Walid said, "It sounds like Machiavelli was describing people like the previous king and Ari Falma, and Farouk al-Khoum, and Farouk's brother, and maybe Harvey Kinkaid as well."

"Yes, indeed."

"From pretty much everything I've heard, they seem to be all about greed and power, and nothing higher."

"Unfortunately, you're right. Whenever politics is corrupted, it always becomes almost exclusively about power—grabs for power, efforts to retain power at all costs, and schemes to expand it beyond reason. It devolves into something very ugly. And this can be as true in democratic nations as in monarchies or dictatorships. Whenever an attitude and practice of power-politics takes over, a morally empty gamesmanship replaces statesmanship and everyone suffers."

Walid thought for a moment and said, "I've been curious about the best way to understand our enemies right now. It's almost like they know nothing about history—that their way of behaving can have, at most, very temporary results; and that those who live by the sword, usually die by the sword."

"You're right again. That's the thing about greed, or any exclusively self-serving attitude: It becomes a blinding and deafening force, and a distorting filter for everything. People dominated by greed can't think straight. Otherwise, they'd realize that their course is ultimately, over the long run, guaranteed to be self-defeating."

Walid wondered aloud, "Can we ever create a society where greed never gets out of control or prevails, and the practice of power politics won't dominate government—where, instead, people will govern themselves rationally, reasonably, and with an eye toward every form of greater good?"

"It's a noble ideal, my friend. And I believe that we can move toward at least a rough approximation of it. But we have to be realists. We come into this world with self-interest built into our souls and operative at a high level of functioning. No baby ever cries just to get another baby's diaper changed."

Walid laughed. "I never thought about that, but I guess you're right."

"No young infant fusses for someone to bring milk to another child. Self-interest is instinctive. It's the first mindset we ever have, and it remains well embedded in us throughout life. And there's nothing wrong with self-interest, as long as it's not our only interest."

"That makes sense."

"Self-interest is the foundation for self-care. And that's important in life. But when self-interest gains an exclusive sway over the adult soul, then it becomes the overall mindset that undergirds power politics. It can never see beyond itself. More people need to realize that to rise above an exclusive concern for the self and a personal greed for power, we're not forced to abandon self-interest at all, just to see what the most enlightened self-interest requires—that it's properly embedded into a web of many other interests as well, including a healthy interest in the good of others."

Walid said, "From what you've told me before about monarchy and democracy, it's our role to educate and prepare the people generally for the demands and joys of self-rule, and that's going to require a broader set of interests on the part of most people."

"Yes, we have to educate everyone in the real requirements of citizenship and self-rule. And, as you've often heard me say, our success will eventually consist in putting ourselves out of a job. But that's nothing to worry about, because then we can take on a new job, gratified with the success we will already have had, and confident of the future that can be provided only by a sufficiently enlightened and active citizenry."

"How long will that take?"

"It's hard to say. It depends on many things. How much of our energy will we have to use fighting unnecessary battles? How well will the reforms work that we've already put into place? How quickly can we improve education in the kingdom? How successful will we be in getting people to think beyond the confines of family, tribe, and village, to be concerned also with the good of the entire nation and beyond it, the world? All these things matter, and they will each contribute to the ultimate answer as to how long it will take us to reach our goal."

"It sounds to me like it's not a quick process."

"No, such things take time. It will potentially be your role to see it to completion if we do our jobs well, and not mine. Or it could take even longer. But there will come one day a true springtime for our people, when the seeds of democracy and enlightened self-rule will begin to sprout and blossom. There will always be weeds as well, and many times of drought and blight and flood—all the forces that will oppose this growth. But, nurtured appropriately, the growth of that spring season can yield great and long-lasting benefits, results of which you can be justly proud."

Just then, Mafulla stuck his head in the door. "Excuse me, my favorite royal friends. Who wants hot scones, fresh from the oven?"

"My dear boy! Come in! Are you now a baker, in addition to all your other many talents?"

"No, I wish! Kular just got these from the kitchen. He said he thought you might like a bite or two. And I volunteered to bring them in."

"Good man."

Mafulla walked over to the king, did a little bow, and placed the plate of delicious looking pastries on a table between him and prince. He smiled at Walid and then glancing at them both said, "Your Majesty, and Your Also Elevated Though-Not-Quite-Majestic Highness, please: Enjoy your snack."

"Thank you, but sit," the king said. "You're to enjoy this as well."

"Yes, sir! I'll never pass up a hot scone—and rarely a cold one. I have a personal policy."

"What's that?"

"Never leave a scone alone."

"Good! Then, help yourself."

As they now reached for the pastries, Walid asked his friend, "Are you all packed up for the trip?"

"Yep. I actually finished a few minutes ago. You?"

"Yeah, me too. I got up extra early this morning to make sure I had plenty of time to eat. Did you have something already?"

"Just now, a while ago. A little. I packed first."

"Well then, make sure you're not shy with the scones," The king instructed.

"Yes, sir, as you wish!" Mafulla took a bite and said, "Oh! Goodness! Crunchy deliciousness to a nearly mystical degree!"

"I wholeheartedly concur! They're extremely tasty," Ali offered.

But then Walid suddenly looked down at his watch and said: "Yikes."

"What?"

"Khalid's expecting us in just thirty minutes."

"Yeah, I know. I'm excited."

"This should be a great little trip," the king remarked. "Have you heard that I plan to join you for a portion of it?"

"No!" Walid exclaimed. "No one's mentioned that at all!"

"Oh. Maybe it's supposed to be a secret, and I just now messed it up," the king joked.

"The secret's safe with us," Mafulla replied.

Then Walid asked, "When will you be coming?"

"I plan to join you at the end of the trip for the boat ride back. I couldn't miss a floating party like that. My mother told me that I once participated in such an event as a small child, but I was too young to remember it in later years. This should be fun."

"Well, that's great. I had no idea." Walid smiled.

"When you're in Memphis and Giza before I join the group, make sure you give yourselves some quiet time within the expanse of your minds, to just be open to insight and new thought."

"Yes, sir," Walid said. "Kissa and Hasina told us all about the spiritual history of these places, or at least what they already know. I'm eager to see first-hand what they're like."

"Yeah," Mafulla added as he munched. "It's so interesting to hear about what people call spiritual places. The whole idea is new to me."

The king said, "A special connection, a flow of the spirit, seems to have come down to us at Memphis, and then to have broadcast out to the world from Giza through the pyramids and the Sphinx and all they represent. We have such a special history here. We may have been, at one point, the first monotheists in recorded history, acknowledging and worshipping one and only one ultimate God. And yet, we have a weave of various spiritual traditions here as well. There has always been a creative tension in matters of the spirit—a unifying force and a diversifying impulse, but the aspiration of unity is in the end uppermost, and it weaves together the various skeins of experience and belief to be found in our land. And it's quite useful for us to know of and understand them all."

Mafulla said, "I've been doing some extra reading about it. I'm looking forward to getting there and seeing and even feeling the places."

Ali replied, "One thing to remember at all times, though, is that the most spiritual place we have is within us. That's the place where we're always able to receive and give of the spirit. You've heard me speak of the oasis within us, a place of peace and power."

"Yes, sir," Walid answered as Mafulla nodded.

"It's the most sacred and holy place of all, and is to be enjoyed every day." He then smiled and said, "But enough talk of things spiritual. It's time for you to get your bags for the trip and go off to start this new adventure. Make sure that you're a few minutes early to the doors near the classrooms, where I believe you'll be departing."

"Sure thing, Your Majesty," Mafulla said.

And then Walid added, "Oh, I almost forgot. I've asked Khalid about security on the trip. I'm sure you have that well in hand." The prince was cautious and always wanted to know what he could about issues of safety, but especially now, since Kissa and Hasina and the other girls would be going on the trip. The thought had crossed his mind just the previous evening that his presence with this group of friends outside the palace could in some way, theoretically at least, place them all in jeopardy. His being a target could indirectly make them targets as well, and this thought deeply bothered him.

The king said, "Yes, definitely. You'll have excellent security with your old friend Omari, along with Hamid, on the trip, as the two Phi leading a small group of highly trusted military men personally selected by Naqid and Masoon, six in total, well armed. Paki wanted to go, but he might not be fully enough recovered from the injuries he received in the basement explosion, and even

Amon expressed a wish to join the travel. He's already stronger than most, but again not yet completely healed. They'll sit out this trip. But you'll be quite well guarded."

"That sounds good. With Hamid and Omari there, I won't worry."

"A good thing to avoid, in any case," The king said with a smile.

"You're right, of course."

"Oh, and you should know this," the king said. "The soldiers all officially report to Hamid. But you're next in command. As with any school function, you're technically under the authority of your teachers on this trip but, of course, you're the prince and, as such, you're officially in command of the military, including the guards, and they all know this. So, if you need them for anything and Hamid happens to be busy elsewhere or doing something else, you shouldn't hesitate to issue direct orders. They're all prepared to respond properly."

"Oh, Ok. Thanks, Uncle. It's easy sometimes to forget my overall role in the big picture here, at least when it goes beyond the most normal day-to-day things."

Across the palace grounds, the morning light was coming through a small window at the back of the royal palace garage office. A figure suddenly appeared in the doorway and said, "Darwishi, my good fellow! A fine morning to you! What's going on today?"

"Oh! Sir Harvey! What a surprise to see you. I had completely forgotten that you were scheduled for a visit. We're getting ready for a short trip." The head driver arose from his chair.

"It looks like you're preparing several cars at once."

"Yes, five in all."

"What's the occasion? I see you're using only one of the cars I recently delivered."

"We're employing mostly the older cars for this highly informal excursion. Two of the classes from the palace school are going on a field trip."

"Oh, how many are traveling?"

"I think that, including drivers, we have thirty people going out today."

"Where, may I ask, are they off to? Field trips are such a good idea."

"Well, we're just taking them to the train station in the cars. Their teachers wanted them to have the experience of a short trip by rail down to Memphis, and we'll then pick them up there with some trucks so that, after they've toured the ruins, we can take them over to Giza for a bit, then on over to the Nile for a fun boat trip back."

"It sounds like a marvelous journey, a real adventure!"

"Yes, I think it will be." Darwishi suddenly worried that he had told the man too much, given the king's concerns about him. But then, it was just a school trip and wasn't the sort of thing that would be repeated on any regular basis, and the king had said that Kinkaid was likely looking for regular patterns in royal travel. Still, he regretted saying quite so much. Then after these thoughts, he remarked aloud, "I'm sorry that it's slipped my mind, but to what do we owe the honor of your visit today?"

"I just wanted to take a first look at the trip logs, to make sure all the information was being entered that we need in order to serve you at the highest possible level and, of course, to field any questions you might have. Your specific needs are important to everyone at Rolls Royce. I was in Algeria for a part of the week and thought I'd stop in and check on the cars and their logs. The king even had two guards waiting at the gate to escort me over to your office here, and then back when I finish. So I suppose I should get on with the purpose of my visit. How are the new cars performing for you?"

"They're marvelous, truly wonderful."

"Good. No problems?"

"None whatsoever."

"None to be expected, of course, but I always like to ask."

Kinkaid looked around quickly and added, "Do you have the car logs available for me this morning?"

"Yes, yes I do. I have one right here from the vehicle we've used the most, so far."

"Excellent."

"Let me get the rest of them for you, as well. Would you like to have a seat here in the office? There's tea, and some bread and jam, if you'd like a bite."

"Oh, that would be very nice, very kind of you. Thank you so much. I'll happily sit and relax here, as you suggest, while I begin to peruse the first of the books." Darwishi handed Kinkaid one of the logbooks, which he then took over to the desk to scrutinize during his brief wait for the others. And as he began to read the entries, he smiled. This would be every bit as effective a little tactic as he had hoped, and perhaps even more so. He could already discern some patterns that could be exploited, regularities of royal travel that could be used by his good customer, and the future king, Farouk al-Khoum.

A few minutes later, the head driver returned and said, "Sir Harvey, here are the rest of the travel logs. I hope they contain all the information you need. I've checked with all the men to make sure they're faithful in making their entries for each and every trip, as you suggested. And they've assured me they are."

"Good, and yes, from the look of this first log, everything's well in order."

"I'm glad."

"You're doing a fine job already of using this important tool in our relationship. You know, it's been the practice of Rolls Royce Motorcars throughout the world to maintain a meticulous oversight of our automobiles and make sure they're of superior service in every way. I'll be sending our area representatives around soon to begin to check in with you on a regular basis. They're not all automotive mechanics or engineers, but they're very well trained in getting us the information we need in order to provide you with the assistance you can use."

Kinkaid had already made contact with a few local men who would pose as Rolls Royce representatives, for a fee, and feed him all the information he personally needed. He would then, of course, pass on to the automotive headquarters any real problems relevant to the cars. But his focus, as always, was on his own concerns and plans.

Darwishi replied, "I'll make sure your men have all the access that you would enjoy, whenever they visit. We'll be honored to have them as our guests, any time their schedules bring them here." He was as friendly as could be and was playing his role well, just as the king had instructed.

"Sir Harvey! What brings you here today?" Khalid El-Bay stood in the door of Darwishi's office with a look of surprise. Kinkaid stood up and greeted Khalid with a broad smile.

"Oh, Khalid! Good to see you! I'm here on a visit to the garage to check over the car logbooks we left the drivers, to make sure our automobiles, the ones we just delivered, are performing well and up to expectations. Darwishi tells me there's a school trip today."

"Yes, it should be great fun. Our young scholars will be arriving any minute now."

"You're going, as well?"

"Yes, indeed."

"That reminds me," Kinkaid said, "My son sent something along for your friend, the prince."

"Oh?"

Sir Harvey opened up his brief case and pulled out a book. He explained, "It's the nearly unreadable new treatise by that fellow Wittgenstein that we discussed some time ago in the dining room of the Grand Hotel."

"Really?"

"Yes. I told my son of the interest the prince had expressed in the man, and he got him a copy, just to show him the strange things that are going on in British philosophy at the moment."

Kinkaid handed him the book, and Khalid said, "That was so nice of Lyle! I'm sure Prince Walid will be thrilled with the gift." He then turned it open and saw an inscription on the title page in black ink: "To Prince Walid. Good Wishes. Yours. L. Wittgenstein." Khalid looked up and said, "He signed it? You got the new prince of philosophers to autograph his book?"

"Well, I wish I could take credit for it, but that was Lyle's idea. For whatever reason, this fellow's indeed the new guru among academic philosophers, and the new king, perhaps. So Lyle thought it might be of value for the prince to have a signed copy. Wittgenstein apparently won't often do such a thing, but when he learned it was for fellow royalty, Lyle said, he seemed eager to comply." Sir Harvey chuckled.

"Very nice. Very nice indeed," Khalid replied.

A woman's voice could then be heard. "Khalid? Khalid!" It was coming from somewhere outside the office.

"Oh, gentlemen, I'm sorry, I have to run. I hear my wife calling for me. I should get back to the business of welcoming our students and assigning them to the cars, as we discussed, Darwishi." He looked at the head driver and then turned back to their guest. "Sir Harvey, it was good to see you. And again thank you for bringing the book. Please also thank Lyle for me, and for the prince. I'm sure Walid will be writing his own note of appreciation. I'll be able to give him the book in just a few minutes, I would imagine."

"Think nothing of it. My pleasure indeed," Kinkaid said, with a very convincing look and tone of graciousness. As Khalid left the small office, Sir Harvey turned to Darwishi and said, "So, the prince is on this field trip today?"

"I'm not sure exactly who's among the students going," the head driver said with some consternation, adding quickly, "Whenever the prince is going on a school trip, there's usually a large military detail involved, and I haven't been aware of any such activity today."

"Oh, I see."

"I'm so glad to be able to speak with you, Sir Harvey, and if there's anything else I can do to be of help, please let me know. But at present, I'm a bit late getting to some work that I simply must do prior to the cars leaving in just a few minutes. I'm sure you'll understand."

"Yes, indeed. You've been generous with your time. I think I've seen enough already today to know you're doing a splendid job with the car logs. I'll have one of my representatives drop by soon for a more thorough reading and compilation of data."

"That'll be fine. I look forward to his visit," Darwishi said, feeling a bit of pressure to usher the guest out of his office and the garage itself. "May I see you out?"

"That won't be necessary. My official escorts will accompany me. But I thank you for the offer. Good day to you, sir."

"Good day, Sir Harvey."

A short time later, Idi Falma was sitting at a back table in the Tower Café. His hair had been cut and he had a new beard, so as not to be so easily recognizable. A short, stocky man weaving through the tables came up to him and took a seat without a word. He looked around first and then said, in a low voice, "I've had a request just now. And there's big money on the line."

"What is it?"

"A man needs a team to do an operation for him."

"What do you mean?"

"He needs us to put together some men. They're to travel this morning, very soon, just a few miles south of the city."

"Why?"

"A group of school kids from the palace is going out to Memphis on a class trip or something. Our potential client wants us to intercept them and snatch one or more of the kids."

"Yeah?"

"And like I said, the money will be very good."

"Tell me more."

"The kids are taking a train later this morning, so we need to get something in motion fast. Their plan is to be in Memphis for the day, camping there tonight, and tomorrow they'll go on to Giza, and—get this—then they're all coming home down the river on a barge. The prince is likely in the group, along with his best friend."

"Those two little rats ruined an operation I had going on not long ago, something that was very profitable. They cost me a lot of money and got me tossed in the can and made me look stupid to my brother. I'd love a chance to get even."

"Well, the guy I'm talking about wants someone to see if those two are on this trip, and if they are, he's interested in having one or both of them grabbed, I think just to see if he can get some major dough out of it."

"I don't know. My brother tried that with the family of the kid who lives with the prince, and it ended pretty badly."

"But that was Farouk's doing, right?"

"Yeah. We think so."

"He's gone."

"So it seems."

"Well, then, what's to stop us? I'm telling you, this guy will pay big."

"How big?"

"It could make up for a lot of the cash we recently lost."

Idi thought for a few seconds. He took out a pen and scribbled a note. "Ok, go here and ask for this man. He's just a few blocks away. Tell him to take any help he needs. He may be able to snatch one or both of the kids, and we can play it from there. Even if the prince and his friend aren't in the group, but it's a palace class, then there should be somebody to grab for a ransom. We could likely make some serious cash for your friend, or at least ourselves, in either case."

"Will do."

"By the way, who's this guy that wants it done?"

"Some big deal Brit."

"What's his beef with the prince?"

"I have no idea. He just seems to have it in for the kid."

"You know, I could really show my brother something, if I could produce the prince, or even his best friend, bound and gagged." Idi smiled big and had a look of supreme satisfaction on his face.

"The guy said to me, even if this ends up as just surveillance, that would be fine, too. He'll pay for it, however it turns out. He'll pay lots more for a kidnap, but he'll pay plenty just for information. He seems like a real money-bag."

"Well, if the prince is in the group, there's not going to be just surveillance going on from us. Let's get him. Go straight to my man here and tell him we've got a job for him. Offer to pay him double the usual, half up front, if he'll take off right away for Memphis. Tell him his methods are up to him. And like I say, he can take along anyone he might need. It's a school field trip. Explain it all to him, and the itinerary. There's likely going to be some security, maybe a lot. So, he can figure out how to get around that. And tell him to bring back to the warehouse anyone he's able to snatch, preferably the prince—today, tomorrow, whenever it happens. I'll be ready to lock up anybody we can get. Then, we'll turn him over to the Brit, or who knows? Maybe we'll go it alone at that point. I mean, why take good money when you can get great money?"

The stocky man said, "But then, again, why take more risk than you need to?"

"That's a good point, usually."

"We can squeeze a lot from the Brit. I'm sure of that."

"I'll think about it," Idi said, and added, "But, either way, the prince or somebody is going to have a pretty bad day. And we're getting ready to have a very good one."

"Sounds great."

9

Fine Autos and Train Cars

For most of the students, it was going to be their first train trip. The king wanted it to be special from the start. That's why he was having them driven to the station in palace cars. The drivers would come back to the palace after dropping them off, and military transport trucks would be used for the transfer to their destination in Memphis, and then on to Giza and then over to a dock on the Nile River. That would also be a new experience for the students. The king wanted the whole adventure to begin in style.

Outside the royal garage, seven boys, seven girls, two teachers, one historical expert, two security detail leaders, six palace guards, and five drivers were ready for their car assignments. Darwishi read out names for car one, car two, and so on, through car five. The baggage was loaded up, the drivers opened the car doors, the passengers all got in, and everyone felt a peak of excitement about the trip.

Mafulla had brought along a pack of cards decorated with four colors, thirteen of them with a red block on the face, the same number with green, and likewise for blue and yellow. Before the engines started up, he was telling Ara how to play the game. He said, "Ok. When I pick a card and look at it, seeing the color and thinking the color, you tell me what color I've picked."

"But you'll already know, right?"

"Well, yeah. Sure. The game is to see if you can guess it."

"Oh."

"You have to say the first thing that comes into your head. Ok?"

"Ok. Kitty cats. Orange cats."

"What?"

"You said I should say the first thing that comes into my head. It was a bunch of orange cats."

"No, no, no."

"What? That's the color they were."

"I mean, when we get started with the card-guessing game."

"Oh."

"I pick a card and look at it and you say the first color—the first relevant color like blue, green, red, or yellow—that comes into your head."

"Oh. Ok. I got it. No orange cats."

"No orange cats. Ready?"

"Yeah. I guess."

"Here goes." He picked a card. "What is it?"

"I was going to say 'a card' just to be funny, but maybe I shouldn't."

"No, you shouldn't. Leave any silliness to me."

"Imitation is the highest form of flattery—my mom says that a lot."

"I'm flattered. And I'm sure she would be too if she were here. Now, what's the color, in case we still remember what we're doing here?"

"Green."

"That's right! Very good! Next."

"Blue."

"Nope."

"Ok, wait. Yellow?"

"No again. Sorry. It's red. Was blue the first thought that came into your head?"

"Yeah. Well, sort of—or maybe alternating with yellow, I guess."

"Hmm. Ok."

"I mean, I thought I saw blue and then maybe I thought I saw yellow. Then I sort of saw Kissa's dog Shibby. In my head, I mean."

"Ok, that's strange. What was Shibby doing in your head?"

Ara said, "Just sitting there?"

Mafulla couldn't help but have a big grin at this point. He said, "A dog sitting in your head. Man, that's … rough." He pronounced the word, of course, to mimic the sound of a dog barking.

Walid looked over at him and said, "Ok, no cornball dog humor this early in the morning."

At that moment, the driver started passing around small maps for the trip. Mafulla put away the cards and promised more scintillating games later. He then began to look over his map. Walid leaned over and said, "How are you at reading maps?"

"Me? I'm an advanced amateur cartographer, especially adept at scanning maps created by others, however accurate … or … rough."

"You're not still doing the exact same bad dog humor, are you?"

"Of course not. I've decided to put all that on … paws, and everything it en-tails. I pre-fur to be serious now. I'm not that much of a … wag."

"Ugh."

"Doggone it, I've got an itch."

"What?" Walid said. And then Mafulla then started scratching his chest in imitation of how a dog would do it, and panting. The prince sighed. "Here we go. I wonder if there's room in another car."

"Don't … flea. Please. Stay! Good boy."

"Wait. I thought you were being the cur here."

"Yap. I was kidding. I just want you to know that, in fact, in a sense, like a great natural hunting dog, I myself am almost like a walking map. I have an internal guidance system that's uncanny, when it's totally … unleashed."

"Jeez."

"Follow me wherever I point."

"If you ever have a point."

"Good one."

"Good what?"

"Point."

"Ok then, Rover, you can be our guide-dog if we ever get lost today."

"I tell you this, you have nothing to fear, my friend. I don't get lost."

"Never?"

"Nope."

"Not even when someone tells you to?"

"Hardee, har."

"You're serious?"

"Have you ever seen me lost?"

"In thought. And in a self-made maze of bad jokes."

"Well, that's different, isn't it? In the great outdoors, I'm an acute three-dimensional thinker with uncanny instincts. My mind stores directions and landmarks like you would not believe. So, when in doubt, follow me."

With a very serious look, Walid said, "A leader of men."

"Yes," Mafulla replied. "A leader of men—and so long as we don't leave out the ladies, I like the sound of that."

And at the sound of the word 'sound,' they all heard the sound of the engines starting up. Then, the cars began to move forward and take them through the back area of the palace toward the side gate and through it, and then down the adjacent city street in the direction of the train station. The great class trip was officially underway.

It didn't take long before they had arrived at their first destination. At the station, a locomotive was hooked up to a royal rail car, a second car, and a caboose. The students and chaperones all alighted from their special palace transportation, thanked the drivers, and carried their baggage to the platform at the side of the train.

Walid set his bag down and said to Mafulla, "I can't believe your uncle Reela got invited to come along. I'm really glad."

"Yeah, I had no idea that he was some sort of top expert on the history of Memphis and Giza. I just remember hearing him tell stories about both places when I was younger, and when I mentioned that to Khalid, he told me that Reela was widely recognized as one of the three most respected experts on the spiritual history of the kingdom."

"Who are the other two?"

"Some professor, I think, is one of them, and the other is maybe some … spirit."

"Funny man. Then, Khalid personally invited Reela to come along?"

"Yeah. And I'm glad. I mean, it's great to have him with us, even though it does sort of cramp my style a little bit in the Hasina department."

"I know what you mean. But with Khalid and Hoda all around anyway, and Hamid and Omari along, it wasn't like this was going to be one long private, candlelight dinner in the desert, anyway."

"True. And I'm sure that I'll get some serious extra credit in Khalid's mind just for having an uncle like Reela. It speaks to the depth of intellect in the Adi family."

Walid grinned and said, "Despite any appearances to the contrary."

"Yeah, despite any of those."

The conductor and an assistant started coming around and directing everyone as to where they should get on the train and put their bags. Porters were loading what looked like folded tents and supplies into the second train car. Reela, Omari, and Hamid were assigned to join Khalid and Hoda with the students in the first car, the luxurious royal passenger car that was configured with several tables and leather chairs in addition to normal rows of seats separated by a wide aisle. The accompanying soldiers were to split up for the ride—one in the engine, one in the caboose, and four in the second passenger car with all the extra baggage, food supplies, and camping gear. The girls boarded first, so when Walid and Mafulla got on, they saw Kissa and Hasina already at a game table, sitting in two of four available seats.

"May we join you two ladies for the journey?" Mafulla asked.

"Certainly, dear sir," Hasina replied. The boys took their seats and saw smiles from some of the other guys as they in turn got on and walked by. Haji pinched Walid gently on the arm as he passed.

Malik gave them a big grin as he ambled by, and Jabari actually stopped for a moment and said, "No disorderly conduct on the voyage. Anyone who violates this rule will be let off in the desert."

"We're all going to be let off in the desert," Mafulla replied.

"We're such trouble makers, that comes as no surprise. They've anticipated our tendencies," Jabari quickly retorted and walked away to choose a seat.

Mafulla turned around, and as Jabari walked away said to him, "Hey, what's in the backpack?"

"Just … some stuff," The small boy looked back and said with a strange expression of mock surprise. "We all need stuff."

"True," Mafulla responded and turned back to Hasina.

Ara, Cabar, Kit and Khata were all together at another table, talking low and giggling about something. Hoda was standing and having a lively conversation with Bakat, who was on an aisle seat next to Set, who was already reading a book. He was going through a Persian Poetry Phase, and couldn't get enough. Today it was a book by the great mystic poet Rumi, in honor of whom Walid's father had been named. Bafur and Reela were already in a big conversation as well. Bafur was keen to ask the older man about the history of the palace, and how he came to know so much kingdom history, generally. And Reela, a natural teacher, was explaining something about the location of the palace and how it was selected long ago. As he recounted some of the more interesting facts, his eager student was peppering him with more questions.

The conductor appeared at the back of the car and, walking toward the front, began to speak. "Excuse me, everyone, if I may have your attention for just a moment, we'll be pulling out of the station any minute now. The porters have some snacks for you and will begin bringing those around momentarily. It should be a very short ride down to Memphis today. If there's anything you need, just ask me, or one of my associates. There's a lavatory in the back of the car. Feel free to use it and just lock the door from the inside while in it."

Mafulla whipped out his cards again and explained the procedure to Hasina, who looked mildly interested. He shuffled the deck well and put it face down, lifting up the first card and holding it so he could see its featured color but she couldn't. He gazed expectantly at her and she spoke.

"Yellow."

"Correct." He drew another card and looked at it.

"Red."

"Correct again. Two in a row." He picked another one.

"Red again."

"Yep. You're on a streak."

"Green."

"Yes."

"Blue."

"How did you know?"

"I just did. Next."

"Ok then."

"Yellow."

Mafulla smiled really big. He went through twenty more cards, and Hasina got them all right, every single one, with no misses at all. "Ok, have you done this before?"

"No."

"Is there a shiny surface behind me, like a mirror? Or is someone around here signaling you?"

"Nope."

"Then, my friend, there's no mistake about it. You have a spooky skill. There's no point in playing card games of any sort against you."

"I do tend to win," Hasina humbly replied with a smile. "So, you'd do well to keep any money off the table."

"I'd do well to keep any money, period."

With the smallest lurch, the train slowly began to pull away from the station. The view out the windows was great. And the comfort of their club chairs was amazing. It was like being in a room back at the palace, only moving. Mafulla had now gone on to showing his friends a new card trick he had just learned. And, of course, he was also making them laugh, pretending to fumble through it.

Within three or four minutes, two young porters in uniform appeared with baskets of snack items—fruit, nuts, breads, cheeses, and even a few candies. The students were not shy about sampling what was offered. Both Bafur and the ever-skinny Jabari took a double serving of nearly everything. Bafur was a big guy and loved to eat more than anyone else, but Jabari, Mafulla thought, must have an even greater ability to burn calories than his own. He always ate well, and right now seemed to be proving himself a total snack maniac.

In a small bare office a mile or more away from the train station where this class trip had begun, Ari Falma sat behind his desk as three men emptied out bags on the surface in front of him. Paper money, gold, and jewelry fell out onto the desktop. "Good, good. But much more would be better," he said.

One of the men explained, "All my guys are a little worried about those mystery men, the Viper and the Storm, and because of that, they aren't getting as many straight robberies as usual."

"Is that right?"

"Yeah. Even pickpocket stuff is down. The protection is still coming in well and, as you know, the other stuff is Ok, but the extras are a little harder to get when the guys are always looking over their shoulders. I mean, these masked crime busters just appear out of nowhere and somebody gets hurt. It's spooky. Nobody's feeling confident like normal."

Falma frowned. "Look, we're working on this Viper and Storm stuff. We'll take care of them soon enough. Meanwhile, tell your guys not to worry. The mystery men haven't interfered with anybody since the big mess-up at The Luxury Shop, and we think there's a special explanation for that trouble. I've even staged a few purse snatchings in the marketplace to lure these guys out when we had backup available that could take care of it, but so far, no luck. They're just not around."

"What? You think they're gone?"

"Yeah. Maybe they're just gone. It could have been a fluke. And we can't let a few wild stories stop us from the work we need to be doing. I mean, do you like your cut of what you're bringing in to me now?"

"No," another of the men said, "Not at all."

"I didn't think so."

"We all want the normal amount we're used to getting. Our part of what's coming in now is so crummy, it's hardly worth the trouble."

Falma leaned back in his chair and said, "So let's get it back up to where it needs to be. We've got the manpower. We've got the organization. Tell the guys to forget the stupid Viper and Storm stuff and get to work. Nothing else bad is gonna happen."

"That's what you think?"

"That's what I know. I'm going to make sure we have no more trouble."

"Ok, boss. We'll be motivators." The man grinned and showed his gold tooth to Falma.

"I depend on you guys."

'We'll get it done."

"Good. So, get out of here and get back to work." The men took their now empty bags and shuffled out the door of the office just as another man entered at a quick walk.

"What?" Falma said to him.

"Idi sent me."

"I wouldn't brag about that if I were you."

"I know who I work for. Don't worry about that."

"Good. So, do you bring some sort of a message from my brother?"

"Yeah, we questioned all the bosses and they questioned all their guys, and nobody knows anything."

"How sure are you?"

"Pretty sure."

"Well, I guess we need to set up whoever's talking."

"What do you mean?"

"I don't know. Maybe we need to fake some plans for a big heist, like what we had going for real with The Luxury Shop. We get all the men together here and explain the plan. It has to be something that's going to happen not a long time after the meeting, like within a day or so. We tell the men we're going to all keep off the streets and stay together, preparing for the score and laying low until it happens. Then, we see who tries to leave. If anybody ducks out, whatever the excuse, that's likely our leak."

"So," Falma's guy said, to make sure he had the plan right, "we follow anybody who tries to leave. I mean, we let him leave, and then we tail him to see if he goes to spill the beans."

"Yeah, that's it. This way we find out who our traitor is, and we locate the Viper and Storm guys—a twofer. If we can, we grab 'em right then, but if we can't for some reason, then when the famous crime stoppers show up to prevent the fake heist, we get them both there and we get rid of 'em for good."

"You're the boss for a reason, boss. If I had half your smarts, my head would be too small for all the brains."

"You saying that I got a big head?"

"No, no, not at all. Just that you're the smarts around here, for sure."

"Tell my moron brother that, the next time you see him."

"I will."

"Or just smack him in the face and say it's a present from me."

"You're funny, boss."

"You know, the name 'Idi' is just short for 'Idiot.'"

"Ha! That's too good. You're definitely the funniest guy I know."

Ari Falma smiled at that point and said, "It's a sign of my high intelligence, which is just another reason my slow brother never gets my quick wit. I'm glad to have some sharp guys like you around."

On the train, the students had been watching the city go by outside the windows. Old people stopped and stared. Little children waved. The clickety clack of their steel wheels on the tracks provided a rhythm for the movie unfolding in front of them in slow motion. Every now and then, they saw a car or a truck pass by, or glimpsed one sitting, stopped at a crossing. There were many more donkey carts, though, than gas powered vehicles. As they approached a couple of crossings, the whistle blew and goats and sheep scattered away from the rails. And then, they had clearly left the buildings and city behind.

The boys were moving freely through the car, talking with different people, and so were a couple of the girls. Most of them were at any particular time facing forward, or looking out the side windows. There was a door at the back end of the car, but it had no window in it, for the privacy of the royal party. And there was no corresponding door at the front of the car. So no one could easily see ahead of the train, or behind it, except at a curve. But that didn't matter to anyone, since those who wanted a view were just absorbed in the passing spectacle as it was visible out the side windows of the car.

The security detail at this stage of the journey was fairly relaxed. The four men in the following train car were enjoying themselves by playing cards. The soldier posted in the caboose was reading a news magazine he found there when he first entered and looked around. The armed guard in the engine was in a pleasant conversation with the engineer. In the luxury parlor car with the students, Hamid and Omari were talking together about something they had both just read. Everyone was enjoying the morning's travel, as short as it would be.

At some point away from the city, something quite unexpected happened, but at first in a nearly undetectable way. Hardly anyone noticed a soft clunk under and behind the parlor car, a sound that was quite muffled. Those who did hear or feel it thought it was just another ordinary track noise. And there were plenty of little sounds like that along the way, with louder ones, now and then. The train gained a bit of speed, but again, there was nothing very noticeable about that. And they were still moving at what would be considered a slow, measured pace, for the leisurely enjoyment of the passengers. No one saw the two men who had jumped up onto the small platforms whose connectors joined together the parlor car and the second coach car. And because of the various general clickety-clak rail sounds and softer groans of the train's undercarriage that were a nearly constant cascade of background noise, no one recognized the sound of the second coach car being uncoupled and released.

As the unhooked baggage car and the caboose behind it continued their forward movement, for now just coasting over the flat elevation, the engine and the parlor car gradually began to outpace them and leave them behind, a fact that was also unnoticed by anyone at this point. Up ahead, quite a distance away and farther down the track than anyone could now see, there was a very large herd of goats spread out across the tracks and at a standstill. There was also a truck parked on a small road that crossed the tracks at the closest all the goats. The royal train car was just now passing another truck that looked like a delivery vehicle, broken down on the side of the road near the tracks. But it was merely another of the many sights the passengers might see if they looked up and out the windows.

"Kissa?" Hasina spoke softly to her friend, but with a tone of something almost like urgency. The boys were both in the back talking to Khalid and Reela.

Kissa turned and looked at her friend. "What's wrong, Hassi?"

"I don't know. But something is. I just got a funny feeling."

Kissa turned around and caught sight of Hoda a few seats back. "Maybe I should ask mom if she could come up here for a minute."

"That's a good idea."

Just then, the train whistled three times and began to slow. The engineer could now see the flock up ahead, beyond the crossing where the truck sat. And the animals weren't moving. The vehicle looked like it had crossed the tracks and stopped about twenty feet away, and was simply parked there, for whatever reason. A man dressed like a goat herder was standing near it. And then he moved toward the track, waving a white cloth at the train and motioning like he wanted the engineer to stop. They were still a few miles away from Memphis and in a desolate area. It was fairly unusual to see two different trucks so relatively close together sitting near the tracks this far from town. But no one except the engineer would know that.

Omari opened a window on one side of the car and stuck his head out to see up ahead of the train. He then pulled it closed and sat back down next to Hamid. "What is it?" The older man spoke first.

"Goats on the track. Some goat herder is waving at the train, I think, just to let us know there's a big group of them up ahead."

Hamid nodded. At the same time, he noticed that they had slowed now almost to a stop. He instinctively got up from his chair just as the train creaked and groaned and then did come to a full stop. He could hear the brakes expelling air, as there was the slightest rock of the cars forward, and then back.

That same instant, there was a sudden loud noise as an armed man burst through the back door and into the parlor car, followed by three others with their own weapons out. They were rapidly scanning the faces in the train, up and down both sides of the aisle. One yelled out, "Everybody freeze! Nobody moves! Look down at the floor! No one speaks!" There were quick gasps and muted exclamations from many of the students as they sat, stunned, and some began to lower their heads, as commanded. Omari started to move, but Hamid put his hand on the younger man's arm to signal him to wait before acting.

Two of the men rushed toward the front of the car, while they were covered by the other two in back. It was all happening so quickly and altogether unexpectedly that there was no time for any other reaction on the part of any of the passengers, except of course that all the students and more than one of the adults felt a jolt in their gut and a shiver of fear run through their bodies as their minds struggled in that moment to make sense of what was going on. It was all so sudden and developing so fast that no one could quite grasp what was taking place.

"Wait," Khalid said, to protest, but without knowing what he would say next. Hamid and Omari were focused and watching to see what the full situation might be, before they attempted any form of action. The last thing they wanted was a gunfight in a train car full of students.

It was then in the next few seconds that the most unexpected thing of all happened in a flash.

10

Going Bananas

The first man who ran down the aisle of the train car two or three feet ahead of his partner, gun raised and now momentarily silent, was about to have the surprise of his life. He got to the position he wanted toward the front and turned around to yell, in a loud, forceful, rude and guttural voice, "You will do what we say! And you will do it NOW!"

That was a bad mistake. In a split second, Jabari's backpack in the open overhead bin stirred, as if under its own power, right next to the man, and then it stirred again. The flap on top of it then flew open and a small blur of fur and bones, teeth, and nails suddenly leapt forward onto the man's head, screeching at a volume not to be believed from a creature its size. It seized his hair and pulled with all its might while screaming like an entire jungle full of animals in battle. As its claws then dug in hard, deep into the flesh underneath it, the man yelled out wildly in pain, which made the now clearly visible small monkey bite into his ear with a viciousness not to be believed. He was shaking the ear like he was determined to rip it from the man's head. The stunned individual under attack reflexively dropped his gun as he spun around and bent over, now himself screaming at full power, grabbing and flapping his arms in a panic, trying to shake this storm of excruciating pain from his head.

The other armed man standing right next to him was so shocked by what was happening two feet from his own head that he didn't even notice Mafulla grabbing the loose gun off the floor while Walid simultaneously lashed out at him with a fast and extremely well aimed blow to dislodge his weapon. As the prince hit the most vulnerable spot in this second man's wrist, he yelled out and spun around, first dropping his gun and then falling to the floor from a violent kick to the knee that Walid had also expertly just administered. And with one fluid motion, the young Phi scooped that loose gun off the floor as well. The other two men at the back of the train had no time to react to what they were seeing up front. And in part, this was because they had no clear idea what had just happened.

This completely unexpected whirlwind of activity toward the front of the train car, with its thunderously loud shrieks and screams and confusing jumble of actions, drew the shocked and puzzled attention of the two assailants at the back long enough for Hamid and Omari to lunge forward toward them. Just then, the small monkey swung down into a lower position and began to attack his victim straight in the face. Mafulla was able to aim a blow, using the grip of the gun he now held, right at the back of the man's skull, knocking him out cold on the spot, and mercifully saving him from any further pain and facial disfigurement. Walid applied a hold to his own adversary's neck that also took him out in about four seconds, while the monkey, in the middle of all this, continued to screech and spin around, but was no longer attacking his victim, now bloody and unconscious on the floor.

As Omari and Hamid forcefully disarmed the two remaining men, one of the attackers suddenly yelled out in pain and grabbed his head, which neither of the Phi had touched, and instantly fell to his knees. His gun had just flipped into the air because of a powerful blow to the arm delivered by Omari. Reela, a couple of feet away at this point, reached out and caught it midair and instantly aimed it at its owner. The other man had crumpled under Hamid's assault and was out in about three seconds. Gripped by Omari, the remaining assailant lasted only a few more seconds before he joined all his comrades flat on the floor, immobile and without awareness. Before anyone could quite register all of what had just happened, Reela had the two closest men tied up tightly and was moving down to the third and fourth to do the same.

Hamid suddenly said, "The soldiers." And with those words, he grabbed a loose gun to augment what he was carrying and headed toward the back door of the car. Omari was close behind and also now doubly armed. Mafulla looked at Walid, and the prince said, simply, "Yeah," as the two of them, with their newly borrowed revolvers, also ran the length of the car, passing by their stunned schoolmates, to the door at the end.

"Boys!" Khalid called out, but the two students seemed not to hear, and they quickly reached the door behind Hamid and Omari.

The bandits who had descended on the train in what they had thought was a well-planned way had no idea that the second train car carried four fully armed kingdom soldiers, with a fifth close behind in the caboose. When they uncoupled those two cars from the parlor car and engine, they had just been following an age-old adage to "Divide and Conquer," figuring that whoever was in each car, they were best off splitting them away from each other and dealing separately with whatever opportunities or challenges the two different cars might hold. That's why they had unhooked them in such a way that they would become separated by a stretch of track.

As Hamid slowly opened the door and looked back, he could see the second car maybe fifty to seventy five yards or more back down the tracks. A second group of bandits had never made it inside. As the soldiers felt themselves slowing down, they became aware that they were no longer attached to the engine and first car, and warily took up defensive positions. When they then slowed nearly to a stop, one of the men jumped out of the train on the side opposite to where the first truck was parked and the bandits were waiting. He dropped down to the ground to hide next to the slightly raised track bed until he could tell what was going to happen.

When the five waiting attackers approached the second car to board it, they immediately and unexpectedly took heavy fire from the occupants inside, as well as from the man next to the track, now behind the cars. Overwhelmed in a way they had never expected, they fell back from the train, sloppily and desperately seeking cover while haphazardly returning fire, in near total shock from the fierce resistance they were meeting. They hadn't anticipated anything even remotely like this. It was supposed to be a quick, simple operation.

The five soldiers on board these back two cars were all seasoned sharpshooters and one was a highly trained sniper, as was the lone sentry up ahead in the engine. When he heard the first shots and jumped down from the engine, he had physically taken down the man disguised as a goat herder, and then picked off at a distance one of the other men who had been shooting into the second car. At that moment, Hamid, Omari, Walid, and Mafulla now all stepped from their own car, firing at the remaining adversaries. And the thieves, at this point completely outgunned from three directions, took off like crazy men, running wildly toward their waiting truck while sustaining various nonlethal wounds along the way. None made it to their destination.

"Separate them from the weapons!" Hamid shouted as they ran toward the now prostrate men, sprawled in various positions across the sand and the road next to the tracks. Two were barely crawling forward. At that point, all the soldiers were outside, swarming over the downed shooters and patting them down for hidden weapons. Walid and Mafulla stopped at the feet of a large man being searched by Hamid. Their hearts were pounding and their breathing was labored. But the realization that they were now apparently out of danger gradually brought a sense of exhilaration to them both.

Walid turned to Mafulla, grabbed his arm, and said, "Good work, man."

"You, too," Mafulla huffed out, and then added, "Geez, that was pretty dicey in the train car. I almost shot at one of the guys in the back, but then Hamid and Omari got too close and I was worried about a bullet bouncing around in the car."

"What about that monkey?" Walid said with a slight smile, as he bent over to catch his breath.

"A-Plus. But who knew there was a monkey on board? Good thing we didn't have one of those signs on the train."

"What signs?"

"You know, 'Monkey on Board.' It would have ruined the surprise."

Walid laughed and said, "We gotta tell Jabari that his totally peeved pet saved the day for sure. Did you see that little guy go crazy?"

"Yeah!"

"It was a show!"

"I knew Jabari had a monkey at home, but I had no idea he was going to bring him on the trip."

"And who knew he could go totally bananas like that?"

Mafulla laughed and said, "That was who was eating all the extra snacks Jabari took! He probably attacked the guy with the gun, thinking he was there to steal his food. I mean, from a monkey's point of view, you've got a gun, you've come for my grub."

"You crack me up." Walid shook his head. "But you're likely right. Remind me to stay clear of the monkey at snack time."

"Yeah. Good plan."

By now, all the attackers had been tied up and were being watched by the soldiers. Omari dashed back into the parlor car to let everyone know that the danger was over, and all the unwelcome visitors had been subdued.

"Are the boys all right?" Khalid and Hoda both asked, right away.

"Untouched and fine," Omari said. "They helped us take down a group of men who were attacking the second car and the caboose."

"They did?" Hasina said aloud.

"Yes, and they're still standing guard as Hamid checks out the wounded ones and tends to their injuries."

"You're patching up the guys you just shot?" Set spoke up on hearing this.

"Yeah. We're tough on criminals, but we're humane, as well."

"Really?"

"Yes. We'll never sink to their level. We shoot to stop and not to kill, in a situation like this. We believe in the value of human life. It's a big part of what separates us from them."

"That's pretty impressive," Set replied. And Hamid just nodded.

Reela, with Khalid's assistance, was watching over the formerly armed attackers in their own car, laid out wherever along the aisle they had fallen. They had come back to consciousness by now, and were all in major pain. But they had been tied so tightly they couldn't move, except to rock back and forth on the floor. Their mouths were also gagged, so they couldn't talk or yell out. Omari announced that he was going to have the engineer back up the engine to recouple with the separated cars, and that everyone should expect a small jolt.

Reela said, "First, could we get these unpleasant fellows off the car? Out of sight, out of mind, and all that."

"Yes, yes, indeed. Good idea. Sorry I didn't think of it already," Omari replied. He and Reela then set to work pulling the guy closest to the back out the door, onto the platform, and down to the ground next to the tracks. When they went back to get the second man, they saw that Khalid and Haji were already dragging the third one the length of the car, and that Set and Malik were doing the same with the fourth assailant.

"Some guys," Jabari said loudly, "don't know when the party's over. They have to be shown the door." At that, several people smiled or laughed. And within about two minutes, they had the car cleared of their captives. Everyone felt better right away.

"Those guys were scary!" Khata said to Cabar.

"Yeah, but Jabari's monkey was even scarier," Cabar replied.

"Who knew a monkey could save the day?" Bakat said.

They all three looked over, and the monkey in question was sitting calmly on his owner's shoulder, eating a piece of bread. At this point, Jabari had a long skinny leash hooked up to his bright red collar.

"I think Jabari's monkey deserves a round of applause," Kit said.

"And Jabari, too," Ara added, "for bringing the fierce little guy on board."

"Hip, Hip, Hooray! Hip, Hip, Hooray!" Kissa and Hasina led the cheer, as everyone started to clap for the two smallest members of their entourage, the two who had, indeed, saved the day. Just then, as the monkey twirled around and let out a happy screech, Khalid came back into the car and saw everyone clapping. He smiled at their resilience and experienced a major sense of relief. Not many people could bounce back from such a frightening experience so quickly.

"Manni and I thank you," Jabari said, with a big smile and a waving gesture of his hand. He then looked at Khalid and said in a loud voice, "I guess maybe now I won't get in too much trouble for bringing my friend along?"

"None whatsoever. We'll even go on the hunt for some special tasty bananas and other tropical snacks," Khalid replied. "Manni's now officially our smallest and toughest hero."

"There's no business like monkey business," Jabari said, and he got a few additional laughs that helped everyone even more in the emotional transition they were all experiencing. Jangled nerves were just now starting to settle down, as the earlier shock and fear began to give way to relief, surprise, and even a sense of celebration.

Within a short time, Hamid had come back into the parlor car and he told everyone that they would get underway once more in just a few minutes, after the train cars were recoupled and ready. He also explained that the bandits had all been secured in the second passenger car and were going to be transported, along with the class, the rest of the way to Memphis. They were already being questioned and would be turned over to a second contingent of guards awaiting the train's arrival at the Memphis station, where the king had already set up a temporary radio communications tent. When they got there, they would alert the king to send prisoner transport and would then be able to get these assailants to jail without using any of the men on the current security detail, and so without compromising any ongoing security needs the group might have.

Ara said to Cabar, "I didn't know we even had any security needs."

Cabar replied, "Well, I guess it's obvious now that we do."

"Yeah, I suppose you're right."

Cabar added, "I imagine that, you know, anywhere the prince goes, security goes, but especially with the rest of us also on this trip. I mean, all our parents are connected to the palace, and so I suppose our little group could sort of represent the monarchy to its friends and its enemies, whoever they might be. I bet the king just wants to be extra careful whenever we leave the palace as a group."

"Yeah, that makes a lot of sense," Ara said.

At the same time that Ara and Cabar were having this conversation, Kissa turned to Hasina and said, "I wonder if these guys attacked us because of who we are—you know, because we're from the palace and have the prince on board, or if it was maybe just some random, unrelated thing."

"I don't know," Hasina said. "It could have been a politically motivated attack, or something, but I sort of feel like it was more random. It's not like these guys tried to grab Walid or shoot him or anything. It looked like nothing but a robbery to me—not that I know from personal experience or anything what a robbery looks like, but it just happened the way I think a robbery attempt would."

"Of course," Kissa said, "the monkey didn't actually give them much of a chance even to spot Walid. Maybe they were going to grab him but just didn't have time to get to it. They didn't say it was a robbery and that we should give them our money."

"True, but it could be that Manni acted so fast they didn't even have time for that, either. Who knows? Maybe he freaked out because he thought they were monkey thieves."

"Good point. I never thought of that," Kissa said and laughed, "Monkey thieves." And then she added, "You know, I was pretty amazed at the guys and what they did to stop the bandits, or the mean monkey-nappers. I was worried for a second, but they really did look like they knew what they were doing." She leaned over and whispered, "That makes me feel a lot better about the Viper and Storm stuff, a lot better."

"I so agree. I feel the same way. Mafulla grabbed that guy's gun before I could even think, and then Walid moved so fast. And for them to leave the train and walk out into a very uncertain and dangerous situation with all the shooting going on—that was pretty incredible too. I was scared for them, but somehow confident at the same time, if that makes any sense."

Kissa nodded. "It does make sense, at least to me. I didn't get any deeper negative feelings at all about it. And that really surprised me. And mom would have called them back if she had any warnings or sense that it was wrong."

Hasina then made a funny face and said, "I've got to ask you one thing. Did you do anything to that guy in the back?"

Kissa lowered her voice again and said, "Yeah, I did, I guess. I don't really know how to say this, but I sort of poured energy at his head. I sent some sort of force of energy to stop him. I mean—I aimed all my thoughts and all my focus at the middle of his head. I didn't actually know what I was doing, but I felt like I was supposed to do it. It was just spontaneous and, I've got to admit, pretty strange."

Hasina lowered her voice as well and bent in closer to her friend, to say, "This is amazing. I did the exact same thing."

"No!"

"Yeah. It was crazy. I didn't really know what I was doing, either, but just like you, I felt like I was supposed to do it, and then the man went down right away, holding his head, looking like he was in wild pain, and letting out that strange noise."

"That's really weird that we felt the same thing and did the same thing."

"Yeah, for sure."

"I was so surprised when I saw him make that agony face, grab his head, and fall down."

"Me too. It was pretty awesome. I was as shocked as I was glad. I wonder if your mom was also somehow zapping the guy."

"We'll have to ask her later," Kissa said. "She and I talked about it once, after that time she sort of mentioned it in training."

"Really?"

"Just for a minute. I think she's going to teach us about it soon. I mean—we sort of knew it was possible, I guess, at least in a way, because of what she had said about causing pain through the power of the mind, but I sure didn't know how to do it, or even how to try."

"You're right. But it just came naturally, even though I had no clue what I was doing."

"Yeah, for me too. But mom may not have been doing it."

"Why?"

"She told me she's really careful about it and won't even try it in front of people if she thinks there's another way. Maybe it would just be too obvious, you know because of her amount of power and skill."

"Oh."

"Yeah. Remember, we have to keep this you-know-what stuff as quiet as we can."

"True. And you know you can count on me not to say anything to anyone else, other than the boys. I've just never done anything like that before, and I still don't know how I did it, or how we did, I mean."

Kissa looked around quickly and said, "I've heard mom say that what comes before how pretty often in life. Just because we don't understand how something works doesn't mean it isn't real."

"Well, we got the what, girl, that's for sure!" Hasina said.

"And how!" Kissa added.

In Cairo, Ari Falma scowled at his lunch. He was sitting at a small table in a rented house that was not up to his standards. It was nowhere close to luxurious. It wasn't even that clean. And he was feeling a keen bout of irritation, so as not to experience the much worse emotion of discouragement. He took a bite of food, chewed for a couple of seconds, and said, "I'm tired of all this sneaking around. I'm sick of living in shadows. It's time for a change. We'd better be able to move along with our plans quickly. I'm losing patience."

The stocky man sitting with him said, "Yeah, I totally understand what you're saying. It's definitely your time to shine. It's time to be out of the shadows, all shadows—and everyone else's shadow. It's time to take your rightful place in the order of things around here. You deserve it, boss. Your brain needs room to shine bright."

Falma nodded in agreement. "It's just taken far too long to get to this point, and to finally have some sort of real power almost in my reach."

"Good things take time."

"I suppose so. But it still stinks."

The other man popped a fig into his mouth and said, "Ari, I hate to bring this up, with you already in a little bit of a mood today, and I sure understand it, but there's something worrying me and it relates to what you're saying."

"What is it now?"

"Your brother, Idi."

"What about my brother?"

"I'm a little worried about him."

"What's the worry?"

"I'm not sure he's really working for you and your interests. I'm concerned that he's secretly working just for himself. It's some stuff he's done and said recently."

"What do you mean?"

"I don't know. Like I said, it's your time to shine. And I don't think he realizes the difference between you and him. I'm suspicious that he thinks it's his time to shine. And that could create problems."

"I can crush him like a worm."

"Yeah, I know that, and most people who know you know that, but does he know that? Or is he maybe a little mixed up about who he is and who you are, and what this is all about?"

"You think he has his own agenda?"

"I don't know. But I'm worried about it."

"I think he just wants to win my respect, and everybody else's respect. And good luck to him with that. But at least it motivates him."

"Yeah, you could be right, but there might be more. He wouldn't be so mouthy to you so often if he didn't have his own itch to scratch."

Falma sat quietly for a few seconds and then replied. "Well, I get what you're saying. I don't always have the feeling that he's working in my best interest, or even in our mutual best interest, to be generous about it. Too often, I feel like I'm having to force him into line, like he'd drift into his own little idiotic world of arrogance and Idi-illusion if I didn't remind him all the time of what I'll do to him if he crosses me."

"That's how it seems."

"Look, I'll be the first to admit that he's got a little fantasy life going, a distorted, pathetic little idi-ology." Falma smiled as he made his little word play joke and then added, "But I'm sure he knows that if he really crosses me, it's the end for him."

The stocky man nodded and then with a small gesture of his hands said, "It's hard to control people through fear, for the long run."

"Yeah, but what's the option with that guy?"

"Maybe kill him with kindness, or just plain and simple kill him, I don't know."

"What?"

"Give him a chance to be lured into thinking you want to make him great, promise him the platform he craves to do great things, make him feel like you appreciate him and need him. That stuff can win a guy over and turn him into your slave. You make his delusions serve you. Then he has a real commitment to you, thinking you're all about helping him to achieve his own goals. And if that doesn't work, you can just go ahead and get rid of him before he can muck it all up for you and the rest of us."

"Look, I see what you're saying, but coming from anybody other than you, and you know this, I wouldn't tolerate a suggestion like that for even a second."

"I realize that, boss, and I don't mean any disrespect at all."

"I know. I mean, he's still my brother, like it or not—but, such an idea from you, I know it comes from a good place."

"It does. I promise."

"Yeah. And actually, you may be right. Look, I know you've got my back."

"I do. I always do."

"You have my interests in mind."

"Always. You can count on it."

Ari paused and said, "We've worked well together for a long time, my friend. And I know I can trust you. Plus, you know I have great plans for you because of what I think about your mind and your capacity to shine in your own way. Unlike my brother, you're a natural leader."

"Thank you. I appreciate that."

"So I'm going to give careful thought to what you've just said. I really am. I appreciate your boldness in bringing this up, because I know you want our enterprise to succeed, just like I very much wish for you to succeed."

Falma actually knew no such thing, and had no such wish, but he was doing to this associate of his exactly what the man was just suggesting that he do to his brother—or, at least, he was firmly in the mode of using option number one: flattery, kindness, promises, and compliments—and would continue to do so unless it ever became clear that option number two would be a better way to go. Then, he would cut his losses, this guy's throat, and move on.

The fact was that nobody could be friends or true partners with an Ari Falma. He had no room for real concern about anyone else but himself, and he hid that fact as well as he possibly could, as a part of his overall strategy for getting whatever he might want. And sadly, with such a habit deeply ingrained in his soul, it was also impossible for him at this point even to be a friend to himself.

At that same moment in a smaller house about a mile away, the very brother in question, Idi Falma, was also having lunch, but alone. His thoughts on this day were very different from his brother's. He was eagerly anticipating some word on the big operation now underway to impress everyone else in the organization, but especially Ari. He had already prepared a secure place in the house to welcome his soon-to-be-arriving involuntary guest of all guests. But the young man would first be brought to neutral ground down in the old warehouse building, just to make sure that the kidnappers hadn't been followed. He wanted his men to see this great success long before Ari knew anything about it. The thought of how much it would surprise and impress his arrogant older brother brought a big smile to his lips.

And yet, the best of plans can be derailed or complicated. A man working for him suddenly knocked at his door, and entered the room saying, "The train's been delayed."

"What?"

"The palace train didn't arrive when it was supposed to. Something's wrong."

Idi said, "What do you mean?"

"The train with the palace school kids on it didn't arrive in Memphis when it should have. There's something wrong. Our people are there already and they're waiting for it. They're prepared to snatch the prince or one of his friends. They have several plans to do it. But there's no sign of the train. None. They just sent us a message."

"You mean the train's late?"

"So far, there is no train. And it should have been there more than an hour ago, at least. They wanted you to know."

"What could have happened to delay it by that much?"

"We have no idea. It's a short trip. There are no reports of trouble with the tracks. There are no storms, and the dedicated royal engine is always kept in good working order. It's a mystery."

"Have them keep me posted. Nobody had better be messing

with my prince. I don't want to hear that something's happened to him before I could get my hands on him. I need this, and I need it soon."

"Got it, boss. We'll keep on it."

"Good."

"I'll get back to where we got the call."

"And make double sure my brother doesn't hear anything about any of this," Idi added.

"We'll keep it our little surprise," the man said.

"Excellent. It's important."

"Yeah. I know."

"Now, quick, go send a message to Memphis and tell that guy to contact us as soon as they locate the target."

II

A Spiritual Place

The king had been busy all morning doing kingly things, as Mafulla might say. Or, maybe that's misleading. He wasn't walking around in an ermine trimmed robe and a golden crown, or sitting down on an elaborate, raised throne to hear supplicants, or being fed grapes by servants dressed in colorful finery. He wasn't incessantly issuing commands and sending attendants scattering in all directions to satisfy a variety of royal whims and fancies. He was busy doing the things that an enlightened modern executive would do, and lots of them. He was engaged continuously in the sort of activities that would demand the attention of any high government official who was passionately on a mission for the good of his people.

King Ali had read and considered and signed papers to launch a new educational program for the entire kingdom that was meant to enhance literacy, instill practical knowledge, encourage creative thinking, and cultivate all the sensibilities required for active citizenship, including an eagerness to participate in an informed way in the eventual democratic institutions that he was already beginning to encourage and nurture. He had also passed some laws on land ownership that were more equitable than any that had ever been on the books in the kingdom, and he had made a few final decisions about a tax reform that was being prepared since the first week he took power. He had finished more vital business by noon than many sovereigns or top executives could get done in days, and all of these morning accomplishments were things that would make life better for the people of the land.

Ali's head butler Kular had watched him debate and decide the last points for the new tax code, having been invited into the room for this historic occasion. The three men who had been meeting with the king, administrators whose job it was now to implement what had been decreed, left the room and Kular, as he was clearing some cups and saucers from where they had sat, looked up at the king and said, "Your Majesty, do days like this feel exhausting? You've achieved a tremendous amount already and it's not yet lunch time."

The king smiled and said, "It's a real joy to have been doing the work of this morning. It's not just politics or government. It's a spiritual activity. In fact, I believe something very deeply: Every job at its best is spiritual. When I get to do transformative things for the good of the people, this office actually becomes a sacred place. It may sound strange, but I feel a touch of the holy here at times like this."

Kular replied, "Actually, it's not strange at all for me to hear you say that. I sense a spirit here as well, a spirit of good, when you're engaged in this sort of activity. Normally, of course, I'm occupied in my office and don't get to watch you work, at least not for extended periods like this morning. I'm grateful for your invitation to sit in on the proceedings today. It's reminded me of something quite vividly."

"What's that?"

"There's no such thing as an ordinary day when people are doing extraordinary things."

"Well said, my friend. And yes, it's a great blessing for us all," the king replied. "I'm also glad you could join me in here for some of the culminating work this morning. I wanted you to see and enjoy the fruit of your daily labor for the good of the people we serve. I couldn't do all this without your constant help."

"I thank you deeply, Your Majesty, but you seemed to get along without me just fine during the extent of my recent vacation and recovery."

"Ah. I can put on a good front then, I'd have to admit. I was determined not to let you worry about me while you were recovering. I wanted you to be able to rest with no anxiety or stress on your mind at all. So I pretended quite well to be doing fine throughout those weeks. But, the truth is that never was anyone's presence so missed as yours. You're impossible to replace. I hope you know that." Ali smiled and did a little fun salute to Kular.

"You're far too kind, Your Majesty. But my replacement should have been serving you well for that time. Should I speak with him about the quality of his work while I was gone?"

"No, no. His work was just fine, perfectly fine. But no one else will ever be you, Kular. Your mind and heart have no equal. And your work has its own special signature of excellence with kindness. No substitute could ever match up to what we get from you."

"Well, in that case, I promise I'll try my best to avoid future poisonings and the lengthy vacations they seem to necessitate," Kular said with a smile.

"Good!" The king laughed and said, "By the way, how's the music going these days? And the poetry?"

"Never better, Your Majesty. The effects of the stone linger on at what seems to be full strength. My new vigor is undiminished, and I even find myself with a heightened appreciation of all the good things that each day inevitably brings."

"That's so nice to hear, my friend. I was hoping your newfound energy and talents would continue to enhance your life." The king paused for a second and said, "I just had something come to mind and, before I forget about it, could you send a message to Masoon that I'd like to see him at lunch? I do think that, after all the work of the morning, I should be ready for a good but low calorie meal in about half an hour."

"Yes, Your Majesty. As always, it will be my pleasure. I'll set out lunch in thirty minutes and I'll have Masoon here to dine with you."

As Kular left the room, the king took a moment to reflect on what he had felt about the recent events south of town. He didn't know all that had happened, but sensed both the danger and its passing, and as a result, he felt proud of those who had protected the group—and this, of course, prominently included Walid and Mafulla.

The train had been recoupled and was ready to complete its intended short journey to Memphis. Things had pretty much returned to normal, or at least a new normal, in the parlor car where the students were riding. But everyone was still recapping and analyzing what had happened. Right after the train began to roll again down the track toward its destination, Set and Jabari came up to Walid and Mafulla. Set said, "Hey. Listen, Jabari and I just wanted to thank you guys for all that you did to stop those bandits."

Jabari chipped in, "I know Manni confused them and helped a lot, but if you two hadn't acted so fast, it would have just been a temporary distraction and who knows what would have happened next? Somebody may have hurt Manni pretty badly, or worse yet, taken him out of this world and sent him to Banana Heaven. Monkeys don't do well on the wrong side of a gun."

At that, Set added, "Yeah, but I suppose that, for a monkey, either side of a gun is the wrong side."

"True. I should be careful to make sure that the little man never packs heat."

At that, they all laughed. Walid replied, "Thanks a lot for your kind words, guys."

"Yeah, thanks," Mafulla echoed.

Walid continued, "It felt good for both of us to be able to help out. When Mafulla saw Manni act so fast, he had to imitate him and take action himself. You know the old saying."

"What old saying?" Jabari asked.

"Monkey see, monkey do," Walid replied with a completely serious expression. All three of the other boys laughed.

"To quote a great sage, 'birds of a feather stomp bad guys together,' but he did more than me," Mafulla offered, to their further merriment.

"Seriously," Set said, looking at Walid, "I mean, I wish I could trade places with you for a day, man. You seem to have amazing things happen to you all the time and you get to step up and make a difference. The rest of us can only watch and wish. I mean, even our security guys treat you like you're not some kid they have to protect, but more like you're one of them, except for the fact that they all have to do whatever you say."

"Well."

"No. Really. I'd give anything to experience that. So, whenever you feel like it, I'll trade identities with you, you know, to take off some of the prince pressure you've got to be feeling every day. That'll be my present to you, a sort of thank-you gift. And of course, I'll also benefit. And I guess that's true of any gift giving. But it's your call. Whenever you want, we'll switch. I can be you and you can be me for a day."

Walid laughed and said, "You know, that's actually not a bad idea. And Jabari, you and Mafulla could switch for a day, too."

"Good idea, indeed," Mafulla said. "It's sometimes a royal pain being best friends with the top kid in the kingdom."

The prince then suddenly cracked another smile and said, "Why don't we do it now?"

Set and Jabari just laughed. Mafulla thought for a second and said, "Under one condition."

"What?" Walid asked.

"During the new one day scenario, it's the boy named Set who's good friends with Kissa, and the one known as Jabari who's friends with Hasina. An extra little twist."

"I like this better and better," Jabari said.

"Me, too," Set quickly added.

"No, no, no. I think you're missing my very precise point," Mafulla explained. "Right now, in the real world, Walid and Kissa are buddies, and Hasina and I are very good friends. But in the take-a-break, Identity Switch World, the gift-to-us-all world that's about to start, if you accept my condition, you guys will be Walid and Mafulla, but I'm not about to turn over the delightful Hasina to anyone. And I'm sure that Walid feels the same way about Kissa. So, for twenty-four hours, the False Set, or, better, The New Set—played by Walid—will be special friends with the real Kissa. And the False Jabari, The New Jabari—played by yours, truly—will be friends with the real Hasina."

"But what about us?" Jabari looked worried.

"Ah," Mafulla said, "You both get to be very special friends with everybody else. And Jabari, you get to be best friends with the prince for a day—Ok, a pretend prince, but on this one remarkable day, a fully functional one. And Set, even better, as the New Prince Walid you get to be very best friends with The Great and Honorable Mafulla, Man of Mystery, Deputy of Danger, Master of Magic, and of course Lady Magnet to the World. Who knows what could result?"

"So, basically, we don't get the girls," Jabari concluded.

"Yeah, bottom line, you can have all the glory, but not the girls—or, I mean, not those particular girls, but in all likelihood, many others. Perhaps even, all the others. You'll see. Trust me on that."

"Ok, Ok, we accept your condition under friendly protest, but with full empathy and understanding," Set said.

"Who gets the monkey?" Mafulla asked.

"Mafulla does," Jabari said, and at the sight of Mafulla looking quite concerned, he explained, "The new Mafulla, I mean, namely me. That's our one condition, balancing yours." He looked over at Set, who gave him a quick nod.

"Oh, Ok, good," Mafulla said. "I get the girl, you get the impish chimp. Or is he the chimpish imp? Either way, I can live with that."

"This could be a little confusing," Walid remarked, with a look of concentration and concern. "But I have a way to simplify it." He stood up and said to all the rest of the passengers at the same time and in a loud voice, "Excuse me, everyone. Can I have your attention? I have a small announcement—something fun and very different."

Everyone turned to look at the prince, and there were at first lots of murmurings throughout the train, and then quiet. Walid continued. "For the rest of the day, Set and Jabari and Mafulla and I are going to do a little experiment. We're going to change identities, just to see what it feels like to be in each other's sandals, so to speak. So, for the rest of the day, please call me Set and refer to Mafulla as Jabari. The real Set will become Walid and Jabari will be Mafulla. We ask your kind cooperation for this novel effort, but only until this time tomorrow." He looked down at his watch, and then back up again at the students and chaperones. "Will you help us and play along?"

The scenario and the question were greeted at first with surprise, and then smiles and words of affirmation around the train car. And even light applause broke out sporadically. Kissa and Hasina had the standard "Here they go again" look on their faces, but it was Ok because they were also laughing. Khalid turned to Hoda and said, "I truly never know what they'll come up with next."

Mafulla stood up and, pointing at Walid with the second word he was about to utter, said: "Ready, Set, Go!" And with this last word, he raised his hand and pointed index finger to jab the air. More laughs were heard.

The boys' teacher then turned to look down the aisle and said in a loud voice, "Walid, could you come over here for a second?"

The real Walid started to move, but Mafulla stopped him and motioned for the real Set to go ahead. Walid grinned and shrugged. He said to his friend, "Wow, this is harder than I thought."

Set, as the New Walid, stood a little taller and said, "Excuse me, Set and Jabari, we can talk more later." They all laughed—except for Manni, who looked like he disdained the entire game that was being played. People! You just never knew what crazy thing they'd do next.

New Set—the real Walid—walked up to Kissa and said, "So, what do you think of our little experiment?" And as he started to sit next to her, she covered the chair with her hand and said, "I'm sorry Set, but Walid's sitting here."

New Set laughed and said, "Oh! No, no, no. Don't worry! I forgot to mention that we negotiated one condition in our favor for this little switch—or two conditions, if you include the fact that those guys get to keep the monkey."

Kissa looked dubious, or skeptical, or indulgently curious. Walid, or the New Set, couldn't really tell. He explained, "In this twenty-four hour Alternate Identity World, you and Set, namely me, have become especially good friends, and Hasina and the new Jabari are very close. So, actually, as Set, I get to sit here after all, next to my good, good friend, Kissa El-Bay."

"Oh, I'm so sorry, Set," Kissa said, as Hasina just sat there listening with a smile on her face. "You must be confused. My name is Kit, and with my friend Ara here, I'm waiting for our best guy friends, Malik and Haji."

Walid, namely, the New Set, looked completely surprised at first and then laughed and said, "There's no one more clever than you girls. You win the prize. But, I'm afraid you can't identity shift at the same time as we do. It would be far too confusing. Nobody would know who anyone was and pretty soon Hoda would be married to the monkey."

At that, everyone laughed. Kissa gestured and replied, "Ok, Ok, Set, good answer. Have a seat. You too, Jabari." She said this in a very indulgent tone to her friend and to the real Mafulla as he walked up the aisle to join them. "We'll see where this goes."

At about that time, having exchanged a few words with Khalid, the New Walid was sauntering with a touch of regal bearing back down the aisle toward Hamid and Omari, figuring that a prince must saunter, as one of the smaller but still important perks of royalty. There was no need to hurry. He was on Princely Standard Time now and, surely, he need not rush. Stopping casually by Hamid's chair, he said, "Please excuse me, dear sir, but I suppose you heard the announcement about our little game."

"Yes, I did, Prince," the indulgent Hamid replied.

And at that, Set—the New Walid—beamed. He said, "I just wanted to make sure that I understand my full role in the military now, since we never know, as recent events have just demonstrated, when that might come into play."

"Well, Your Highness," Hamid replied, laying it on thick, "I serve at the pleasure of the king and you, of course, in my position as the second highest ranking general of the military, with a specialty in the areas of recruitment, training, fitness, and medicine."

"I see."

"I officially report to General Masoon Afah, and in addition, directly to the king. But if you have any needs, it's also my job to help with those. Likewise, if you as the prince have any urgent use for our soldiers, and I'm not immediately available, they're to obey your direct orders, as well, of course."

"Oh, good. I mean, excellent. Thank you, General. That's all. I mean, please be completely at ease now. As you were." New Walid tried every official sounding phrase that seemed even remotely right in the situation, and then turned with a smile and a nod of his head and began to saunter back toward his seat.

Hamid said, "As you wish, Your Highness." And that, of course, provoked a very big grin from the boy. New Walid had no idea, but Hamid already had a plan to kick this all up a notch, and very soon.

Khalid had watched the exchange and turned to Hoda and said, "For Set and Jabari, I mean, New Walid and New Mafulla, this apparently silly game may end up being as good as a sociology or civics class—maybe even better. They're going to learn a lot."

"I think so, too," Hoda replied. "Even though it's on one level just a goofy amusement the boys have made up, it's also a very good way to turn a natural sort of fantasy into a learning situation."

"Yes."

"Genuine role-playing often has a pedagogical effect far beyond what any amount of lecturing or even discussion can accomplish. It's a unique experience to walk in someone else's shoes and to try, for however short a time, to see the world from their point of view."

"Indeed," Khalid replied. "It's almost a dramatic exercise in empathy and understanding. I wish all our students could have this experience. We'll at least have to get the four boys involved in the switch to meet with their classmates later on and talk about what it was like during this little drama, or comedy, or whatever it actually is."

"That's a good idea," Hoda said. "I'll get the girls to think about it as well."

Khalid pondered it all for a moment more and said, "Maybe the best thing is to have that discussion among all the students while we're still on this trip, with both of the classes together."

"Great idea, my near-genius husband."

"Near-genius?"

"Yes."

"How near?"

"Close enough that your rugged charm closes the gap entirely, as far as I'm concerned."

"Good answer. In fact, I'd have to say: Near-genius," Khalid replied. Hoda couldn't help but smile at that—near-genius, indeed.

Within ten more minutes, the train's whistle blew and they began to slow down. They were approaching the station at Memphis. Kit turned to her friends and said, "It looks like we're here."

"Yeah, that was quick," Ara responded.

"After all the excitement," Kit said.

Khalid stood up and announced, "Ok, everyone, it's time to put your things together. When the train comes to a complete stop and the conductor boards our car with the signal that it's safe for us to get off, please exit the door to the platform at your left and stay close together there until you get directions from Hoda or me." He then turned and began gathering his own stuff, quickly repacking some items he'd taken out during the short trip—a book, a notepad, and a few other things. And then he helped Hoda fetch her large bag down from the overhead storage area.

A moment later he looked up and said, "Oh, Mafulla." Mafulla and Jabari both looked at him.

"I mean New Mafulla of course—not you, New Jabari." He looked at Old Jabari-New Mafulla and said, "Make sure you keep Manni on his leash, Ok?"

"Will do, Khalid," New Mafulla said. "We're tethered like brothers."

"Good. We can't have the royal monkey of the monarchy getting loose." At hearing that, Jabari, which is to say, New Mafulla, did a double eyebrow jump, and that broke up everyone who saw it.

The students made their way down the aisle, out the door, and onto the platform at the station. The soldiers were at this point all in the second car, the six of them, talking with Hamid. But at that moment, four came out and stood on the platform as well, looking about in all directions. There were only a few other people scattered around the old station building at that point. Mostly, the new arrivals were just surrounded by desert-like terrain, with a few scrubby trees and bushes here and there.

Khalid and Hoda made sure everyone was off the train and that all their stuff had been taken off as well, and then they stepped down onto the platform. Raising his voice, Khalid said, "The king has provided transportation locally for us. There will be some trucks on the other side of the station house. Pick any truck as you walk up to them." Then Khalid looked directly at Old Set and said in a loud voice, "Prince Walid, would you join me in leading the way?"

"Yes, certainly," New Walid said with a smile. "It will be my great pleasure."

As he and Khalid approached the four soldiers outside the second passenger car, one shouted out what sounded like "Ten—Shun! The Prince of Egypt!" And they all as a unit snapped briskly to attention, saluting the New Walid as he passed them. The Real Set couldn't believe it. His mouth fell open just a bit. "Man," he thought. "This is awesome. I could get used to this." The few other people in and around the train station who were not in their group stood very still, grew quiet, and all bowed deeply to show their respect for this unexpected appearance of royalty in their midst.

New Mafulla, walking beside New Walid, was speechless to experience even the reflected glow of this royal treatment. Like the Real Mafulla, he was feeling that he had been magically admitted into the sphere of royalty, just by association. The salute of the soldiers and the bows of the other people seemed to take him in as well. "Wow," he thought to himself. "Is this what it's really like?" He forgot for just the slightest moment that the soldiers were all play-acting, and he actually felt a surge of pride swell through him, but pride in what, he didn't quite know. It was almost as if he experienced a twinge of satisfaction for a deep spiritual need, a need for recognition and appreciation and specialness that we all have inside us. It didn't matter that he hadn't done anything to deserve this treatment. Something inside him realized that you don't have to do anything to deserve it. We all deserve something like it, not for what we do, but for who we are. A nobility of the inner spirit, the deepest core of personhood in every one of us is, in a sense, royalty and that gives rise in each of us to a need that's not often met in this world as it is. But when it is met, magic happens.

It was ironic that, stepping into the clean, clear air of a famous spiritual place, two of the students were feeling something touch their spirits that was coming, on one level, not from the place at all but from a fun little game they were playing. Of course, there is a sense in which we're always playing games—not in some frivolous way, but in the assumptions we take up, and in the roles we enter for minutes, hours, days, or even years and, sometimes, for life. And we can't often predict how these games will play out or end. Some are spiritually elevating and tremendously empowering. Others are not. Some end well. And others lead to unexpected challenge and great difficulty.

The rest of the group rounded the station and walked down some wide, weathered wooden steps. There were four large trucks awaiting them, with their drivers standing by the open backs of the vehicles next to where the young people would all step up onto small stools placed on the sand and clamber into the sitting areas where they would perch on long benches, side-by-side and across from each other, like soldiers on their way to war.

That phrase actually came into Kissa's head right then, as she saw some of her fellow students who were already seated. "Like soldiers on their way to war." She then heard it a second time as a sound of words in her mind: "Like soldiers on their way to war." She didn't know exactly what this meant in the context of coming to her now, or why these words were ringing through her head. But she was curious and mildly concerned.

Kissa and Hasina, the real Kissa and Hasina, of course, since they weren't switching identities with anyone, had immediately felt a sense of peace the moment they stepped out of the train and onto the platform in front of the station. With a first breath of the air here, it was as if they sensed that it is indeed a special, spiritual place. There was an almost indescribable sensation of calm that came over them both. There was truly something here.

But then, almost as instantly, they felt something else, something strange—a stirring, a keen alertness, a sensation that was very different, a feeling that was a bit disturbing and even foreboding. And yet, at the same moment, Khalid had made his announcement and then, seconds later, the soldiers did their salute, and both Kissa and Hasina put the odd feeling out of their minds as they switched the focus of their attention and followed everyone else across the platform, around the station house, and down the steps. Now, however, something like a concern was once again rising to the surface of Kissa's mind and steadfastly refusing her effort to ignore it.

She turned to her best friend and spoke in a soft voice. "Hassi."

Hasina took a deep breath and let it out and answered back in a low tone, "Yeah. I know. Me, too."

12

Many Stories

As Khalid was watching their students get into the trucks and take seats for the short ride to their destination, a man holding what looked like a notepad walked up to him and said, "Excuse me, sir."

"Yes?"

"Hi. I'm Shaaban Farghali, of *The Kingdom Daily News*. We're doing a series of reports on tourism in Egypt and a special feature story on visitors to the ruins here at Memphis. I see that you have quite a number of young people with you."

"Indeed, they're the students in two school classes."

"Are they here to see the ruins?"

"Yes, and to learn about the role of Memphis in our Egyptian history."

The man made a note on his pad. "May I ask how long you plan to visit?"

"We'll be here for the day, camping overnight, and then go over to Giza tomorrow for a time with the pyramids and the Sphinx."

"Oh, wonderful. That's perfect. This is just the sort of group that my photographer and I had hoped we'd find. When we saw you getting off the train, I said to him that I bet this is a school group and that, if so, you'd be a marvelous feature for the article."

"You identified us quite well."

"Would you mind if we tagged along, then, and asked a few questions every so often for the article?"

Khalid said, "No, I don't think that would be a problem."

"Great! I certainly appreciate it."

"I'm eager to do anything I can to encourage other teachers to take their classes on informative field trips like this. We'd be happy to include you in any way that would help your article."

"Oh, that's kind of you. Thanks very much. But could I go ahead and ask a first question?"

"Sure."

"There's quite a military presence with the group, which is of course very unusual for a school trip."

"Yes, I would imagine so."

"May I ask why?"

"We have the prince with us, Prince Walid."

"Oh, my, that is very special. Would it be possible for me to interview him while you're here?"

Khalid thought for a moment and said, "Later on, there might be a good time for such an interview. At first, I'd rather have the students just adjust to the setting and focus on their learning."

"Oh, of course, that's very understandable and will be fine with us, fine, indeed. It would be a great privilege to interview the prince and a few of his classmates, whenever it's appropriate. There's no rush at all. We'll shadow the group a bit throughout the day if you don't mind, and later, at your convenience, we can do some special, short interviews."

"That should work. Thank you for your kind understanding," Khalid said.

"We wouldn't ever want to be disruptive or get in the way." The man then paused and said, "Oh! I almost forgot. May I ask your name?"

"Yes—of course. It's Khalid. Khalid El-Bay, spelled 'E, L,

hyphen, B, A, Y' but pronounced as if it were 'B-U-Y.' My wife's name is Hoda and she is the teacher of the girls' class. She's standing right over there." He discreetly nodded in her direction.

"Oh, yes. Oh, I see. Yes, indeed." The man was silent for a moment, and then said, "And you teach the boys?"

"I do."

"Excellent. Well, Mr. El-Bay, we'll be following you today, and discreetly snapping some pictures, but will try mostly to stay out of your way. We'll also be getting other photos of the site, as well."

"It's nice to meet a member of the press who is concerned with education," Khalid said with a smile.

"And it's a great pleasure to meet you, as well," the gentleman said in reply, adding, "I'm sure we'll have plenty of time to talk more, later." He did a quick partial bow and turned to walk off toward another man who was standing at a distance and holding a large camera.

Omari came up to Khalid a minute or so later and said, "All is done. Everyone's loaded."

"Good."

"Who was the man with the notebook?"

"Oh, a journalist from *The Kingdom Daily News* doing a feature article on tourism at our ancient monuments and ruins. He asked if he could shadow us, take some photos, and perhaps interview some of us about our experience here on the field trip."

"How did he know that we're here?"

"He didn't. He said he was just on site with a photographer hoping to find a group of tourists to feature and saw us, and he got excited when he realized that we seemed to be a school group. So he asked my permission to write about our trip."

"Did you see his credentials?"

"Oh. I honestly didn't think to ask. I just saw his notepad and the guy with the camera, and he seems very professional."

"We'll check the credentials later." Omari smiled. "It will be thoroughly in line with the king's new push on education to profile a trip like this and perhaps suggest to other teachers that they also find creative ways of engaging their students in learning our kingdom's history."

"Those were my thoughts exactly," Khalid said.

"Well, shall we get underway?" Omari suggested. "It'll just become hotter, the longer we stand here, although today promises to be a reasonably comfortable temperature."

"Yes. You're right. Let's go." Khalid patted Omari on the back and both men walked over to the trucks and took their respective places. Omari, in the first truck, told the driver to lead the way, and their small caravan began its slow trek down the dusty road leading to the main archeological site in the area. They would set up their encampment right beside it and then have a first lesson about the history and significance of the place.

At a short distance behind the military vehicles, a smaller truck followed. The man with the notebook was driving and enthusiastically reporting his entire conversation with Khalid to the gentleman in the passenger seat who had the large camera on his lap. There were also some other things next to his feet, including a large knife and a coiled length of rope that he had thought he might need later on. Some photographers prefer spontaneity. This man liked to plan his work as well as he could. He sat quietly, nodding his head, as he heard about the nature of the group and the fact that the two of them would be allowed to interview the prince later on, probably tomorrow.

"Which one is he?" The man with the camera asked.

"You were on the platform. Didn't you see?"

"No. I was there when they got off the train, but had to go back to the truck for a minute and didn't see who was being saluted when the soldier shouted, 'The Prince of Egypt!' I heard it from where I was, but couldn't see anything. And by the time I got out of the truck, they were all standing around in a crowd."

"Did you notice a tall boy standing next to a much smaller boy who was holding a monkey on a leash?"

"Yeah, I couldn't really miss that. I mean, who sees a monkey on a leash in the desert?"

"Well, the tall boy is the prince."

"Ok. I've never seen his picture in the paper or anything, so I had no idea."

"I haven't either, but that's the one."

They drove on in silence for a couple of minutes and the cameraman said, "This place feels strange to me. It creeps me out."

"Haven't you been here before?" The driver turned to look at him.

"No. Never. But, of course, I've heard people speak of Memphis and Giza my entire life: The pyramids and the Sphinx. Who cares?"

"Your whole life, you've never been down here?"

"No, why should I? What's the big deal?"

"You've lived a sheltered existence, my friend."

"Yeah, right. I've been plenty busy in the center of town and on trips in other directions. I never had any reason to get out here, and I'm glad, because it just seems odd. There's something strange in the air. I don't like it. It gives me a bad feeling."

"The kings of the past and their priests haunt this place," the driver said. "People report the presence of spirits."

"I doubt it."

"There are stories that would make your hair stand on end, and then keep you up at night."

"Maybe so. But the stories could be nothing more than fairy tales."

"Ah, but it was you who said that the place feels strange."

"I just don't trust it. There's something off about it. And it doesn't have to be ghosts, or spirits from the ancient world."

"Well, it doesn't really matter, though, does it? We have our job to do."

"You're right. I'm going to focus on the job and ignore whatever it is that I'm feeling about the place. I could have just had a bad dinner last night and it's getting to me."

The driver looked at the camera in his passenger's lap and said, "Do you have any film in the camera?"

"I can't believe you're even asking me that. The camera is my . . ."

POP! Thump, thump, thump, thump, thump, thump. They had hit a large whole in the road and the instant they did, the right front tire blew out. The driver was fighting the steering wheel, trying to control the vehicle, and they came to a bumpy stop slightly off the side of the road. Once they realized what had happened, the men got to work and changed the tire, a job that took them nearly an hour in the sun, given the fact that they first had to find and get out the jack and tire iron. And then lifting the truck up even a few inches was difficult, because of its size and weight, along with the softness of the sand on the roadside. No one from the school caravan had noticed their plight, due to the amount of dust the four larger trucks were throwing up behind them. So they faced the task alone. By the time the two of them got the problem fixed and made it down the road to the archeological site, the teachers, soldiers, and students had already pitched their tents and the encampment was complete.

The men parked their truck and walked over to the edge of the group where everyone was sitting, backs to the tents, and facing out over the nearby dig site, as Khalid talked about the history of Memphis.

"The great ancient Egyptian historian, Manetho, tells us of the legend that Memphis was founded by the Pharaoh Menes around three thousand years, BCE, before the Common Era. It had a busy port nearby on the Nile and was a city housing many workshops, factories, and warehouses during those times. It was said to be under the protection of the god Ptah, the patron deity of craftsmen. Ancient theology of the time tells us that Ptah dreamed of the universe, then opened his mouth and called it into being. His name means 'opening,' as of the mouth, and of creation, and of the story of our universe."

Of course, at this, Mafulla had to lean over toward Walid, the real Mafulla and the real Walid, and open his mouth wide and say "Ptah."

His best friend and ever-ready collaborator in such silliness laughed and said in response, in nearly a whisper, "Ya. Ptah, so … Ha!"

Khalid just then went on to say, "An additional item of interest is that the name of the main religious temple here gave us the name of our kingdom, Egypt."

The man holding the camera turned to his associate with the notebook and said, "I didn't know any of that. The whole country is named for a temple?"

"Shhh."

Khalid continued, "In its history of roughly four thousand years, the city itself here had many names. One name meant, 'The White Walls' and another meant 'Everlasting places,' while a third connoted, 'The Life of Two Lands,' referring to the different regions of Upper and Lower Egypt. Then, around 1,500 BCE, we're told that it came to be known as 'Men-nefer' which meant 'Enduring and Beautiful,' and this name was shortened to 'Menfe' in the Coptic language, and then became, in Greek, the name we now use, 'Memphis.'"

Khalid went on to talk about the size of the city in what was known as the Old Kingdom, with its population of thousands of residents, huge at the time, and then he spoke of the siege of the city during the Middle Kingdom, and how it later became the place where royal families were educated, throughout the time of the New Kingdom.

The boys were surprised to hear that Alexander the Great was once crowned pharaoh in the Temple of Ptah right here in Memphis and that, when he died in Babylon, his body was brought back to this place to be embalmed. Khalid went on to explain that even the ruins of Memphis were viewed as themselves magnificent and beautiful as recently, he said—in the Egyptian time frame—as the thirteenth century. But he added that, because of all the ravages of nature and man, there is now far less that's left to see of its glorious past.

Set raised his hand. "Yes, Prince Walid," Khalid said, recalling well his duties for the remainder of the twenty-four hour identity switch.

Set smiled and asked, "If there's so little to see, then why do people still come here to see it? Why did we come?"

"That's a sensible question. We've come to visit because of the overall significance of this place. And that leads me to a philosophical point. A place like this is not just what it may seem at any given moment. Such a remarkable place is, in an important sense, a sum total of all it ever was, all it ever will be, and whatever it's in the process of becoming right now. We may not have a lot left on the physical plane to see, at present, as we survey the horizon here in all directions. But, there's still much to experience and reverence about this place, in its essence, and in its past, present, and future."

Set, or the new Walid, said, "Wow. That makes a lot of sense."

Khalid turned around and looked in the direction that his seated students were facing. For a few seconds he took in the vista in front of them, and then turned back to them and said, "We can't tell what a place really is by just looking at it any more than we can tell what a human being really is just by looking at him or her. But immediate, firsthand experience is still important. Without a good measure of personal presence, direct perception, and immediate contact, there's so much we can't know. We have to abide with a place or with a person through some extended segment of time, in order to get more of a feel for the real identity we confront. That's one reason we're spending this day and tonight here, and some of tomorrow morning."

Bakat spoke up and said, "Hoda told us about how long this has been regarded as a spiritual place."

"Yes, that's a good part of the reason why so many temples and shrines were built here over the centuries," Khalid explained. "And that leads to some questions. What did people find here? What did they experience in this place that they wanted to acknowledge in their buildings and rituals? What made this spot of the earth so special to a person like Alexander the Great? And is it still special now?"

"I felt something as soon as I stepped off the train," Hasina said. "I felt a sense of peace right away."

Before she could say any more, Kissa spoke up and added, "I felt it, too. I think it's still indeed a very special place."

At that moment, the monkey screeched and everyone laughed. Khalid said, "I suppose our closest primate relatives may also feel its mystical distinctiveness." As the laughter died down, a loud CLICK could be heard, the sound of a camera shooting a photo.

"Oh, I almost forgot to tell you something," Khalid explained to the combined classes. "We have with us today, unexpectedly, some guests—a reporter and his associate, a photographer from *The Kingdom Daily News*. They were already here when we arrived, doing research for a story about tourists who visit Memphis and Giza, and have asked permission to follow us around and photograph what we do while we're here." He gestured in their direction. "They'll be interviewing some of you later, so feel free to share your thoughts and feelings about our visit here. We're hoping that our example will help encourage other teachers to take their classes on field trips like this. Please help me make them feel welcome to our little group."

At those words, there was some scattered applause. Khalid smiled and said, "But for the moment, I think it's finally time to show our concern for the body as well as the mind and spirit, so let's have lunch. I'm sorry we're this late getting to it. Our earlier delay has just pushed back everything a bit. Everyone, go help yourselves at the big mess tent."

"How could it be a big mess already? We just got here," the real Mafulla said.

"Ha. You joke; I'll eat," the equally original Walid replied.

"No I'm coming, too. I'm so hungry, I'm about ready to eat my shoes." He then raised his eyebrows extremely high, and with a completely serious look on his face, said, slowly, "Filet of Sole. Get it?" Walid shook his head as he dropped it downward.

Everyone stood up from where they had been sitting and walked over to gather around the kitchen and dining tent for a buffet of food that had been packed up for them in advance. It was quite a layout that the palace chefs had prepared. Khalid and Hoda's older twin sons, Baqid and Shumar, who both worked in the kitchen as chefs, had taken special care to make sure the class trip was equipped with great food at each of their meals. Today, for lunch, it was classic picnic fare, nothing fancy or anything that required heating, but nice, tasty selections that had been prepared expertly in advance.

"Oh, this is good, Set, my friend," Mafulla said, when he took his first bite of a pita sandwich.

"Yes Jabari, my old buddy, it's amazing," Walid agreed as he also picked up one of the sandwiches and dug in. "I wonder if they eat like this in the king's private quarters all the time?"

"I bet they do. I'm so jealous," Mafulla said, and then he asked, "Do you know what's going to happen this afternoon, when we get done with lunch?"

"I think I heard Khalid say that we'd take a rest first, a time for reading or napping in our tents, and then walk over to the dig site."

"Do we get to see some actual ruins there?"

"Yeah, I think so."

"Cool, I can't wait to view the physical rubble in this spiritual bubble that's seen so much … political trouble."

Walid commented, "Good rhyme. Impressively improvised, especially with a mouth full of pita."

"As I eat-a. And I thank you, fearless leat-a."

"Ok, that was a stretch."

"Yeah, I should have quit while I was ahead."

"That's a good policy in general, Jabari, my friend." Walid sat eating for a few seconds and then said, "I think Reela's going to join us at the dig site and talk about this particular location in the Memphis area and its history, and we'll be able to take some notes."

"Good. Ancient history around here can be pretty interesting. Dad now and then gets some really old stuff in his shop and there's always a story that comes with it. In the olden days, somebody was always fighting somebody else for control of the kingdom, and it's just amazing that everything didn't get busted up and broken. I sometimes think it's a miracle that pretty much anything has made it down to us through so many violent centuries."

"Yeah," Walid said, "I guess, in a world of change, some stuff never really changes. You can always count on trouble."

Mafulla nodded as he ate. And then, with a full mouth, did his best to utter the word, "Profound." After some more chewing and a big swallow, he said, "Alert. Royalty on the way."

"What?"

About then, Set walked up, the real Set, and Walid, the real Walid saw him and said, "Prince! Hey, man. We're both already having a great time here. We're learning a lot and the food is really good."

"Yeah, it is good," the new fake prince replied, adding, "I think I ate too much."

"Us, too. And hey, when you get back, would you thank your uncle, the king, for us—first, for making this trip possible and then for supplying all the great grub?"

The boy being addressed barely suppressed a big grin and said,

"Absolutely, Set. I'll be certain to let His Majesty know of your appreciation. I'm sure he'll be delighted to hear it."

Then, just as the Real Set was about to walk on, Khalid came up to the group, and looking at him—the New Walid— he said, "Prince, I'm sorry to interrupt, but when we get back into town, I'd love it if you could secure a place for me on the king's busy schedule. I'd like to talk with him about some innovative ideas I have for the school."

"Why, yes, I'd be quite pleased to help in that way," the day's fake royal said. "I'm happy to do anything to assist with education, which is so important for the kingdom now, and high up on the king's priority list, as it is on all our lists, for that matter. If you'll just remind me a few days after our return, I'm sure I'll be able to get you an audience with my exalted uncle."

"Wonderful," Khalid said. "I'm very appreciative."

The real Set, the temporary pretend prince, then nodded around at everyone, said, "Gentlemen," and walked away, sauntering again, of course. Mafulla muffled a laugh and nearly choked on an olive, coughing vigorously until he recovered.

The time for rest after lunch was needed. Both Walid and Mafulla fell asleep right away—Mafulla, with a book on his chest that he had intended to begin reading. After an hour, he awoke with a start, checked his watch, and realized he had another hour to just laze out and recuperate from the many events of the morning. Walid woke up shortly after that, and they just lay in their tent motionless and quiet, enjoying the down time. "Hey, are you awake?" Walid whispered.

"Yeah, are you?"

"Very funny."

"No, really."

"Stop."

"Ok. I'll take that as a conscious refusal to answer; hence, you're awake, in which case we can talk. So, what's up?"

"Wait. First of all: Hence?"

"Therefore, thusly, and in conclusion, as an inference from what's gone before."

"Ok. Yeah. But … you actually talk like that?"

"Sure. Hence, you clearly should pay more attention. But what's up?"

"I just wondered what you thought about all the action on the train."

"It was wild."

"Yeah, it was like we were in GV and Storm mode, breaking up a bunch of criminals. And, do you realize that those were the biggest odds we've ever faced? I mean: four guys initially, guns out, and with us unarmed."

"Well, yeah, GV, I get what you're saying, but remember, we had a maniac monkey, along with Hamid and Omari and Reela on our side. And Reela was a spy. You don't mess with spies."

"True. You're right. But it's still too bad we couldn't have put on the wind scarves and made it an official masked-crime-fighters-thing."

"Yeah, in front of all our classmates and lots of others."

"That was the problem."

"It's not something we ever want to have happen."

"No, you're right. I was just thinking it would have been cool."

Mafulla said, "It was us in action at our best, I would completely agree. It was certainly done in the spirit of the Viper and the Storm."

"True."

"I seriously think we should count it, even though we weren't masked, and had help."

"Count it?"

"As an official part of the legend, however untold."

"Yeah. Ok. You're right. It's counted. It's hereby a part of the official lore." Walid thought for a second and added, "I'm just glad Kissa and Hasina saw it."

"Me too. I like to show off to friends in the face of danger, especially on those occasions where I also actually live through the situation."

"No, silly, I meant that maybe now they won't worry so much about us and the whole GV and Windy scenario."

"Oh. I hadn't thought of that. Yeah, I guess you're right. They'll know we can handle ourselves. And maybe they'll get us our own monkey."

"Hardee, har. Wait, is that Khalid's voice?"

"Yeah, I wonder if it's time to go." The boys crawled out of their tent and saw that Khalid was mustering everyone for the short walk to the archaeological dig. Within no more than ten minutes, they were all over at the site, which was a lot closer than they had realized.

The session there was great. Reela gave an interesting presentation and was very funny at times, keeping everyone's attention. He was a natural showman and a good teacher. Khalid and Hoda were both impressed. They spent a couple of hours in lecture and discussions before walking around and inspecting everything they could. By the time they got back to the encampment, an early dinner had been put out and was awaiting them, and some announcements were made about the next day's activities.

They ate a wonderful meal again, and afterwards sat around a campfire under the stars. It was pretty spectacular. As always, outdoors and far away from city lights, the stars were totally extraordinary—amazing blazes of distant fire scattered throughout the deep black sky. It was hard to look at them at all without feeling a major sense of wonder at the world and life, and everything.

As the students leaned back and gazed into space, they heard more stories about the past and the great people who had lived here in previous centuries. They also learned where they would go, what they would see, and some of what they would be talking about tomorrow. Khalid, Hoda, and Reela really built up Giza and the Great Pyramid and the Sphinx, and the various mysteries surrounding them. By the time the session around the campfire ended, they were all convinced that there's really no other place on earth like Egypt, and even throughout the endless stretches of space beyond our planet. The history here is unique. The mysteries are special and distinctive. Their future ultimately would be bright.

They all went to bed that night with great excitement and such anticipation about the morning that they could hardly get to sleep. They had no idea what the new day would really bring.

13

A Few Warnings

In Cairo, a man walked into a room and saw his boss with a strange expression on his face. "What is it, Idi?"

"What do you mean?"

"You look worried."

"Oh, it's just that guy, the Brit."

"What about him?"

"He came by an hour ago while I was having breakfast."

"He came here?"

"Yeah. I have no idea how he knew where I was, or that I'd even be up this early."

"I sure didn't tell him."

"Yeah. Well. He just suddenly appeared outside. He called out my name in that accent and scared me to death. I had no clue who it could be. He wasn't on my mind at all."

"I bet. So what happened?"

"He opened the door and came right in and introduced himself, which was good, since I was ready to shoot him. He said, 'I'm your client, Sir Harvey Kinkaid.' Just like that."

"Really? I could not have guessed he was going to show up here. I'm shocked."

"And he was all business. He was very serious and really intense like nobody I've ever seen, not even my brother."

"What did he say?"

"He told me right away that he's the guy who hired us for the big job. And he said he's representing interests involving international politics and powerful people. He was pretty mysterious about it all but said he needs the package we're getting for him because of something important and time-sensitive that he has going on."

"What did you tell him?"

"I told him not to worry, that we had the operation well underway. And then he said again how crucial time is to him, that time is of the essence, in his words, and that we had to do this quickly and let him get off with the object of interest as soon as possible. I think he wants to take the package out of the country."

"I had no clue about all that."

"I didn't either. But it's apparently going to be a part of some big international scheme. I tried not to ask too many questions. I mean, I don't know this guy, for one thing, and second I always need what they call deniability. Plus, I don't want to get too deeply involved in somebody else's mess. That's never a good idea. I just want to snatch the package, deliver it, and get paid."

"Well, earlier you were thinking differently."

"Yeah, I know what I was thinking, but this is simpler and less messy. I don't want this guy or any of his friends as an enemy. Believe me. We do the job and we get paid."

"Good. At this point, we all feel the same way about it. But why are you looking so worried?"

"Well, when this guy was ready to leave, he looks me in the eyes with a steely stare and says: 'This job has to go well. If it doesn't, powerful forces will be mightily angered, and no one will survive the wrath that results.' That's what he said."

"Powerful forces?"

"Yeah. I mean: I have to admit the guy was intense in a way that I've never seen before, and he was more than a little scary."

"Well, we'll do our jobs, and so will the man we hired. He's good. He's really good."

"He'd better be, because I'm warning you, I got the feeling that if he messes up, or if anybody else falls short with this, then we may be in for some big trouble we don't need."

"I'll warn all the other guys that a lot's at stake here."

"Yeah. Do that. And let's hope we get the job done fast."

Miles away in Memphis, everyone had slept well in their tents overnight, but unknown to each other, every single Phi on the trip had experienced a strange dream at some point during their slumber. The dreams varied. But they all involved losing something and looking for it. In her dream, Hoda lost a ring. Kissa lost a scarf. Walid lost a favorite ball. Mafulla misplaced his Reverso watch. That was certainly a dream involving high tension and bad stress for the poor boy. But, he eventually found it, and in the nick of time, at just the last second before he woke up.

In Walid's dream, as in Mafulla's, as well as in Hamid's and Omari's, the lost item was found. The girls each awoke from their respective sleep before any such resolution. But the various dreams weren't so strange or alarming that any of the dreamers thought to mention it to anyone else when they got up, or at any other point during the morning. They all simply put aside their nocturnal narratives, dressed, had a good breakfast, and got ready for the day.

Khalid had built into the schedule a little morning exercise time for anyone who wanted it. And everyone did. Some kicked around a ball, others just jogged on the nearby road, and still others did stretches and floor exercises on large mats that had been brought along. The teachers had also gotten the soldiers to rig up boys' and girls' shower tents on two opposite sides of the camp. That was nice. It was a little cold but refreshing to be able to shower and wash up after the workouts, and before the rest of the day.

Of course, the full twenty-four hour period for the Great Identity Switch Game was still in force for a little more time, so the students were having all sorts of fun with that as they ate, played, goofed around, and did other things together. They'd have a lot to talk about in reflecting on it after the trip.

While all this was going on, Omari wandered over to the tent being used by the reporter and the photographer out on the far edge of the group. They were both sitting outside and having a bite to eat. "Hello, there," the reporter said as Omari walked up. "Good morning to you."

"Good morning to you, as well," Omari replied. "I hope you both had a pleasant evening."

"Yes, thank you. And you?" the reporter replied, as the other man nodded.

"Indeed. I just wanted to stop by briefly for a little chat before everything gets started."

"That's very nice of you."

"First, I should say that I think it will be a great day for what we have planned with the kids. We'll start off here and later go on to Giza, where I'm sure you'll be able to take some fine photos. And sometime later in the day, we'll try to make the first opportunities available for interviews with the teachers and students."

"That will be helpful," the reporter said.

"And I'll snap some shots while they talk," the photographer added.

"Good," Omari responded. "As the second in command of the security detail for the trip, I also wanted to come over this morning and view your official press credentials. It's always something we do for the palace school students and any others involved in the monarchy, or the life of the palace."

"Oh, my," the reporter said, looking worried. "We were just

talking about that. We've been with the paper for only a little over two months and yesterday morning, when we were given the assignment out of the blue to come over here to Memphis and get a story with a tight deadline, we left in a hurry, both of us, without grabbing our *Kingdom Daily* tags. We have those neck lanyards with our passes on them for easy viewing when we're at work on assignment, but we ran out in such a rush, we both left them in the office."

"Oh, I see. That's unfortunate," Omari replied. "The official pass is an important part of the process."

"I'm so sorry," the reporter said, with a feeling of inner panic. "Could we possibly provide them for you on our return to town, as soon as we get back?"

"Well, that's not the usual procedure. Who assigned you to the story?"

"The editor of the regional desk."

"And what's his name?"

"Mr. Razi. He's a tough boss sometimes, and if he finds out we forgot our badges, we could lose them for good!"

"Razi. Razi. Oh, yes, I know the man. I mean, I know of him. He's been there for a long time."

"Yes. That's the man." The reporter explained, "My brother's worked for the paper for years and he warned me that Razi could be a hard boss, and then when I got assigned to him, I was worried, but so far, it's worked out pretty well. We're both still proving ourselves to him, though. So, please, if we could just do our jobs here and then show you our credentials on our return to the city, it would likely save our positions. You see, we're both married, and our wives would be distraught if we lost our incomes over something so small and stupid as our forgetfulness under pressure. It's our own fault, of course, but it can be rectified, I hope!"

"All right," Omari said and nodded. "But, as soon as we return."

"Yes, as soon as we return. Thank you so much!"

When Omari walked away and was well out of earshot, the photographer said, "You handled that well. We're two very lucky newspapermen."

"Yeah, it's a good thing my brother's worked at the paper for so long, and that he gripes about that Razi all the time, and in detail, to the point that I've sometimes wished I'd never heard the name. But today, I'm glad I knew it well."

A bit later in the morning, Khalid sent out word that everyone was to meet where they had the previous day, and that their session would begin in about ten minutes. They all gathered as directed and he explained again the agenda for the day—this time, in detail. They would start with more on Memphis and visit a second cluster of nearby ruins and then, after lunch, pack up and drive over to Giza for the afternoon. It was going to be a full day again.

"But, before we get started on our first presentation of the day," Khalid announced, "Hoda would like us to break up into our two classes. The girls will stay where you are. The boys will come with me over to the other side of the tents. We plan to spend fifteen minutes in silent meditation, to prepare us to absorb everything that this place has to teach us today." In response to this surprising news, there was sudden chatter of comments here and there among the students, as they speculated or voiced questions about why they would be doing this.

Khalid raised his hand and his voice. "Your attention, please! I'm not yet finished." He paused for a moment for the noise to die down and then continued. "In a minute, as you get into position and sit quietly, without speaking or looking around at your neighbors, please seek to make your mind blank, free of the distractions of conscious thought, devoid of words and shifting images. You may choose to fix your mind on one inner or outer image to center yourself, or you could simply focus on your own breathing, as it goes in and out. Just allow yourself to relax into a wordless state of mind that will prepare you to be open and ready to learn. It will help us all to make the most of our time here. Now boys, if you would, please follow me."

Hoda stood up in front of the girls while the boys were walking away with Khalid, and she began leading them gently through the process of preparing for their meditation. She wanted to make sure they were all seated comfortably and in sustainable positions. She then said a few more words about the process of focus they would need in order to clear away the chatter and clutter of their normal consciousness, opening themselves to a deeper level of thought that would allow real insight the space it would need to enter their hearts.

A short distance away, across the encampment and on the other side of the tents, Khalid was soon doing the same thing with his students. But being boys who were full of early morning energy, he was first leading them through some relaxation stretches and explaining the nature and purpose of meditation. For Walid and Mafulla, the real Walid and Mafulla, this was something they were accustomed to, and they knew how to do it well. For some of the other boys, it was all unexplored territory. A couple were skeptical at first, but as they listened, it all made more sense, and in the end all of them were sufficiently open and eager to participate in this part of their sessions.

The two men who had just been introduced by Khalid the previous day as their guests from the newspaper had followed the boys and were also now sitting, side by side, back away from the group a very short distance. And they were also going through the motions that Khalid was suggesting, as they each thought through their own task in this special place. In their business, not everything could be planned. But some aspects could be anticipated in advance, and had to be. The main thing was to be consciously attentive, keenly opportunistic, and open to whatever developed.

Hoda stopped talking and, across the way, a few minutes later, so did Khalid. Each of them was seated cross-legged on the sand, hands in their laps, eyes unmoving, breathing slowly and growing calm. Hoda could go deep very quickly. Within thirty seconds, she was an empty vessel ready to be filled with insight, or else simply by the deep relaxation of a soul at rest. She felt total peace and then a flow, as of air, but within her mind, and then there was a flash, or a momentary vision like a moving picture or short snippet of film, a quick glimpse of a storm filling the air and scattering both things and people. Her emotions wanted to jump to attention and her entire body poised to react with a quick, full alertness, but she wouldn't allow the response to take hold. She merely noted the vision and let it pass, remaining instead calm and open and grounded.

In the big marketplace back home, Hasina's mother Layla was at that very moment visiting the big fruit and vegetable stand near the Adi shop and picking up some fresh produce when she also felt an uneasiness—a first hint that something somewhere was wrong. Her hand rested on soft lettuce, cool and wet from a grocer's recent spray of water. She didn't pick it up as she had intended, but instead let her hand gently lie on it, her entire body momentarily at rest while she experienced her conscious thoughts quiet down, slow in their pace, and gently move aside so that her mind could go deep. There was something, something coming to her or needing her, or reaching through to her. But what was it? There was as of yet no vision, and no words. She knew enough from her life and experience to hold any possible inquisitiveness and reactive emotions in abeyance for now and to simply open her heart and remain attentive in the wide receptive freshness of the moment.

Then, suddenly, there was a voice. "I'm sorry, but are you Hasina's mother?" The sound and the question at first seemed to come from a distance and then grew louder and broke through her process. Layla looked over and up to where the words may have originated. Her full conscious clarity returned in an instant. An attractive and kind looking lady was smiling at her. "I thought I recognized you. I'm Mafulla's mother, Shamilar Adi, and I thought you might be Hasina's mom."

"Yes, yes I am. How nice to meet you, Shamilar. I'm Layla." She was able to put aside completely what she had just been doing, and not worry at all about this interruption of the process of possible discovery that had just been underway. A calm mind is able to adapt.

"I've heard so much about you from my son."

"You have?"

"Yes! He's so fond of Hasina, and often speaks of both her and you. I don't want to embarrass you, but I have to say that you're even more beautiful than I had gathered from Mafulla's enthusiastic descriptions, and from, of course, knowing your lavishly lovely daughter who, as you certainly know, is your very image. It was my son's detailed verbal portrait of you, as well as having met her, that allowed me to recognize you just now."

Layla laughed and said, "That's so nice of you to say, Shamilar. Mafulla is a wonderful boy and he's just too kind to characterize me in what I'm sure are utterly undeserved terms."

"Well, I did recognize you, after all," Shamilar said with a big smile. "And I can reassure you that Mafulla did his best to do you justice in his description, but for some things, as we all learn, words are quite inadequate."

Layla smiled and, tilting her head to one side, said simply, "Thank you, Shamilar. You're very kind."

"Mafulla has been so excited for days about the trip they're all on now," Shamilar said.

"So has Hasina. I think it's a great idea to get both classes out to see the world a bit, even so close to home. I'm sure they're already learning things they never could have gotten just from a book or a classroom lecture."

"I so agree. In fact, Mafulla's experience of living in the palace is clearly the greatest education of his life. There's nothing like direct experience with something new for broadening horizons and deepening thought."

Layla replied, "And with all the dramatic events that have transpired since he came to the palace, I'm sure he's grown more in this short time than during any comparable period in his life."

"Yes, it's been an exciting time for him—far too exciting, from a concerned mother's point of view."

"I know what you mean. Palace life is full of action, for sure."

"It certainly is. But he and Walid are becoming, as a result, the sort of men we need in this new generation to lead the country forward."

"You're right. We'd always prefer to shelter our children from adversity and risk, but it's precisely these things that can make them strong and wise."

"Yes! Well said."

"Thank you. It's one of the great lessons in my own life."

Shamilar nodded. "We all learn the most from the hardest things."

"Yes, we do."

"But it's tough to keep that in mind for our own young ones."

"It is."

"We're also fortunate that the king and Walid's parents, and so many others in the palace, are such good role models for our children."

"We are, indeed," Layla agreed.

"I didn't mean to interrupt your shopping," Shamilar said, "but I simply had to say a quick hello. Our store is just over there," she added, discreetly pointing, "and I was stopping in here for a moment to get a spice I need for tonight's dinner. When I saw you standing here, I just couldn't resist saying something."

"I'm glad you did," Layla said. "I've been wanting to meet you and your husband. It would be great if we could get together some time for a meal with our budding leaders of the future."

"I'd love that," Shamilar said. "Let's look at our calendars and get back in touch soon." She started to reach out her hand to shake Layla's but instead leaned forward and gave her a warm, one-armed hug, holding her bag of spices in the other hand. And then with a small wave and a "See you soon!" she walked back off toward the shop and left Layla to think for a few seconds about their children, and then to wonder what had caused her experience of a few minutes prior. Did it involve them? Could she recapture the connection, whatever it was, that had opened up? Not knowing the answers to these questions, she said a brief prayer, sending her love and energy to Hasina, Hoda, Kissa, and the rest of the girls and boys on the trip.

She had, at the moment, no way of knowing exactly what her good friend Hoda had just experienced, or what it might mean for the next few minutes and hours in the lives of their children. But then, neither did Hoda.

A very bad storm was brewing and it was going to bring with it a difficulty beyond imagining.

14

Sand and More Sand

Ari Falma sat on top of a desk in front of his brother and fifteen other men who were standing in small groups around the room, talking. "Ok. Quiet, everyone! I need your attention. I have something important to tell you." As the men stopped their conversations and looked over at their leader, he said, "We're on the verge of one of the biggest jobs we've ever had. There's a small shop at the edge of the market, a stall run by the man named Anwar. Most of you know him. He's helped us in the past by quickly moving some of our recently acquired merchandise. We've paid him a percentage and he's always given us anonymity and good service. But recently, he's changed. He's become no friend of ours over the months while we were gone. These things happen. He's done some stuff. I won't go into details. But we need revenge. We need justice. I decided early on that no simple retaliation would do. We won't burn his store. We won't visit him in the night. But we will hurt him more deeply than any of that. And to do so, we've had to wait. Now, finally, the wait is over."

He paused a few seconds for dramatic effect and said, "Anwar is going to be engaged today in the biggest sale of his life, moving some jewels for an immensely wealthy man in a neighboring country. For about forty-eight hours, he'll hold an enormous amount of money, as a result, in his safe. His client will come the day after tomorrow, in the morning we think, to take the money and leave his customary fee, and it will be the biggest payday by far that Anwar has ever seen. But before the rich guy arrives with his people, we'll descend on our old friend's place of business and take all the money for ourselves, leaving him at the mercy of the client, who will be suitably enraged, and is known to be brutal in his reaction to sloppy work. But that's not our business. Our job is just to take all the money off Anwar's hands, a pile of loot that, in my estimation, is properly ours as restitution and retribution for several wrongs we've suffered at his hands."

"What's he done to us?" One man asked.

"Don't worry about it at all," Falma said. "It soon won't matter."

"How much dough are we talking about?" One of the other men also made bold to speak.

"Maybe as much as a quarter of a million dollars,," Falma answered. Then he smiled. "Maybe much more."

"In that little shack of a shop?"

"Yes, oddly enough. The small and unfortunate look of Anwar's store has always helped him keep his business outside the concerns of most who would otherwise block his activities or do him harm. Things are not always what they seem. He's a shrewd businessman, and occasionally makes a big score. Like I said, this will be his biggest ever and, with the proper planning, we'll reap the harvest for our own use and make up for the decreased business we've had lately."

"When's all this going down?" Another man asked.

"Soon. We'll take action tomorrow afternoon when we can blend into the crowds."

"Who's gonna do it?"

"I'll need only two of you to actually go into the shop. The rest of you will help prepare for the heist from now until then, and support it."

"Won't Anwar have the place well protected, so that we'd need more than two guys going in?"

"Good question. Most people in his situation would. But that's against his whole philosophy of playing poor, pretending that nothing's going on, and not drawing unfortunate attention to himself. Guards would just announce the presence of something worth stealing. There won't be any guards. It'll be just another day and another night at Anwar's shop. Except for our little visit, of course." Falma smiled. "And you'll all get a good piece of what we take."

"This sounds great," one of the men said.

"Yeah, really," another replied.

"Well. Here's the part you might not like as much as what I've told you so far, but it's also important. And you have to trust me on this. I need you all to lay low, stay off the streets, and stay together here in the building until this happens. We need total secrecy, absolute surprise. No one connected to our victim can see any of us on the street or anywhere in town. The only time you'll leave this place at all between now and the score will be if Idi or I need you to go out for something, or to come with us somewhere. Then you can step out with us. Otherwise, you have to stay put right here."

There were some loud murmurs and grumblings around the room in response to this. Falma saw who had turned to speak to a neighbor or to complain. He quickly added, "But listen to me, listen: You'll be very well paid for this minor inconvenience. I can promise you that. You'll be handsomely rewarded. You'll have the best day ever, if all goes according to the plan." At that, the men quieted down. He spoke again. "So. Do you understand? Nobody leaves here without Idi or me, and that starts now."

"What about my wife?" One guy said. "She'll get worried when I don't come home tonight."

"Yeah, and mine." Another man grumbled.

"Ok. You're the only two married guys. Idi will take a note to your homes saying you're on a big assignment for a couple of days. If anybody else needs something like this, tell us now. This is important."

"Well, I got a lady friend."

"Yeah? Congratulations." Several of the men laughed.

"No. Ari. I mean she'll be worried, too. She needs a note."

"Ok. No problem. Anyone else?" The men now stood silent. "Everyone else is fine? Good."

Idi was thinking how lucky he was that Ari had chosen the warehouse as the place where all of them would have to stay. He knew his brother well enough to know that he would soon go back to his office a few blocks away to get work done during the wait time. And that's when the package Idi was expecting would be delivered to this very place where all the men now would be, to see it happen. The situation could not be better for what he had planned.

Ari resumed talking. He said, "My brother will be assigning you roles for the preparation and the event. Our target time is 4 PM, tomorrow. And again, let me emphasize that this will be our single biggest score ever. A lot turns on it. Like I said, I'll give each of you a percentage of the take, and that will likely amount to real money. Our old king needs some of the cash for his comeback. And we need our own part of it, as well. The failure of the last big heist set us back. The sand of time is running through the hourglass. Our funds are, too. We need this to happen. So, everybody be sharp and get comfortable here, and do your jobs as I assign them, and you'll see a great reward from this."

At the campsite in Memphis, the students and adults were still in their brief meditation time. One of the soldiers came up to Khalid, bent down, touched him on the shoulder and whispered, "Excuse me, sir. There seems to be a big storm on the horizon." Khalid opened his eyes and stood up. The man pointed to an area where, at a distance, the sky was completely darkened. Hamid was already standing and looking in that direction.

Khalid calmly said to the group, "Boys, allow yourselves gently to come out of your meditative state. Stretch your arms, then your legs. And when you stand up in just a moment, I want you to make your way toward our tents, and remove the main pole in each to let it lie flat. Then walk to the trucks. It seems that a bit of a storm may be coming toward us, and the trucks are sturdier than our tents, in case there's a strong wind. There's no reason for alarm. We'll be fine."

Set was seated near Khalid. He spoke up and said, "Aren't sandstorms in the desert pretty dangerous?"

"They can be, but mostly in the center of the kingdom, not here."

"So we should be safe?"

"Yes. So please, just walk at a normal pace over to the tents, lay them flat, and go to the trucks and get inside them. We'll close and tie the back flaps once each truck is full. Storms like this usually pass in no more than a few minutes. Again, there's no reason to worry. Just take the tents down and get into the trucks as quickly as you can, without running to do so. We have a few minutes, most likely."

The boys began to do as Khalid had directed, while he made his way over to Hoda and the girls. He spoke with Hoda, and then said to the girls exactly what he had told his class. "Don't worry at all," He assured them. "Sandstorms come and sandstorms go out here in the open. But they're typically not as bad in a place like this as they are across our main desert areas. In the trucks, we'll all be fine. Then, we can resume our day."

As they all walked over to the tents and got about the work of removing the poles to flatten them, the wind gradually began to rise. At first, it was just a breeze. Then it started to gust and boom. Some of the boys grew more than a little concerned. Getting the tents down took a bit longer than they had expected, and by the time some of them were walking or jogging toward the trucks, sand was blowing hard, at first low in the air, stinging their legs and their arms. "Cover your eyes!" Khalid shouted. "Tell everyone else!"

It's surprising how fast visibility can be compromised out on the open sand when a strong wind whips the sand into the air. The gusts can be disorienting, and especially when you're having to cover your eyes and breathe with a closed mouth, being stung every second by the streams of sharp tiny particles all over your body. Set and his friend Jabari—the real Set and Jabari—had worked on their tent together, but Jabari was having trouble keeping his monkey Manni in the backpack where he'd been put with some figs to enjoy during the meditation time.

Just as they were getting the tent flat, and then turning to walk toward the trucks, a big blast of wind and sand hit Jabari in the face, stinging his eyes badly. He yelled out and that scared Manni, who wriggled and fought and managed to pop out of the newly loosened flap of the pack.

At first, Jabari didn't know what had happened. And then the little monkey took off like a shot, running away across the sand and screeching.

"Manni! Oh, no!" Set saw it happen first and started chasing the little guy, running as fast as he could. Within a split second, Jabari realized what was going on and also took off running in pursuit of his pet. No one else noticed what was happening, since the wind noise had risen considerably and general visibility had dropped further and everyone at that point was just struggling to get to the trucks, heads down and eyes covered, as the storm howled and boomed in their ears. Manni ran away from the four trucks the students had come in, and the two boys continued to give chase, calling his name against the loud noisy wind.

The small animal was in a panic and frantically looking for

cover and safety, heading toward the nearest shadow he saw. As he drew close, a shadow he didn't see descended on him and scooped him up not more than a second or two before Set and Jabari got to the spot. The little guy was too relieved to react with any resistance. "I have your monkey!" a voice called out loudly, even though the boys were mere feet away. "He's Ok!" Arms reached out and handed Manni to Jabari, who grabbed him and wrapped the long leash around his arm.

"Thank you!" Jabari yelled back.

"Yeah, thanks!" Set echoed.

"No problem, Prince," the voice said. "But, I noticed that the trucks you came in are already closed up. They don't know that you and your friend are missing, in all the chaos. My own truck is right here and is actually stronger than the others. If you and your friend and the pet will get into the back, we can close the metal doors tight against the storm and you'll be fine."

"Who are you?"

The man took his hand a bit from his face and said, "I'm Shabaan, the reporter from the paper. My photographer's already in the truck!"

"Oh! Yes!"

"Khalid just said that we're all to drive slowly to the train station where there's better shelter, in case the storm gets worse. Our backs will be to the wind, so we'll be able to see the road well enough, I think. But quickly, we need to jump in and get going before it gets any worse!"

"Sure! Ok!" Set and Jabari simultaneously agreed to the sensible plan and climbed into the back of the truck with Manni. The doors were shut behind them, and they could hear a latching sound. It was much quieter in the back of the truck, and they both breathed out the anxiety that had overtaken them for the last couple of minutes.

"Oh, man!" Jabari said, as he started brushing off his clothes.

"That was total chaos! What a mess! And wow, that sand really hurt."

"Yeah, a storm like this is scary, for sure!" Set replied. "I'm just glad that guy caught Manni and gave us shelter here."

"Me too. And thanks for chasing Manni. If we hadn't come up to the guy right away, my favorite attack monkey would likely have bit him."

"Yeah, I know what you mean. I figure he was so scared at the moment he got snatched that he was glad to have anyone big pick him up!"

"Yeah. I bet you're right."

"Well, at least we're all safe now. But I can't believe the newspaper guys are going to be able to drive in all this."

"Me neither."

"Did you hear Khalid say anything about the train station?"

"No, but we were pretty far from his tent, and then chasing Manni. I'm sure we just missed it."

"Yeah, you're right."

They could feel the truck begin to move and turn around, jerking a bit as it did, stop and go, stop and go. Hamid, Omari, and the soldiers were all busy with the palace trucks, making sure the kids were seated, and securely tying the flaps once they were in, then deploying around the trucks, but especially at the lead truck where Walid and Mafulla were well protected with Kissa, Hasina, and a few other students. Omari had actually joined them inside at the last second to make sure they were Ok.

Because of the thick canvas flaps now closed at the back, these trucks weren't as quiet inside as *The Kingdom Daily News* truck. But the students could still talk in louder voices.

"This is scary," Ara said.

"Yeah," Khata replied.

"Don't worry," Walid said. "I was in one of these storms in the middle of the desert, months ago. We didn't have any protection at all except to lie down next to our camels, away from the source of the wind."

"Wow. Were you afraid?" Ara asked.

"Yeah, at first. Storms like this can get bad, but they don't last that long. And the key is to have a safe place to ride it out. My uncle taught me something important that day."

"What?"

"In the face of something like this, we should just stay calm, move quickly, and use what we have—in this case, these great trucks—and everything can be fine. And we'll learn something from the experience."

The girls nodded. "Thanks, Walid, that helps," Ara said.

"Yeah, thanks," Khata also replied.

Kissa was holding on to Walid's arm, and Hasina was doing the same to Mafulla. "It's actually pretty exciting," Mafulla said to Hasina. "Who knew that we'd come out here and get into this? It's like a movie. I've never felt such a powerful wind."

Walid turned to Mafulla and said, "Bashir must be near."

That cracked Mafulla up completely. Bashir was a man who had crossed the desert with Walid and the king, and was the father of their classmate Bafur, who was on another truck—and the older man was a very large individual known for his love of beans and for the legendary, explosive movements of air they always entailed for him.

The girls looked puzzled. "Never mind," Walid said. "It's just a passing reference." Mafulla laughed again as his friend added, "But we'll explain later, at the tail end of all this."

"Once the feared winds are behind us," Mafulla said, to Walid's private amusement, and further perplexity on the part of the girls.

"Did everyone get into the trucks Ok?" Walid had turned to Omari with this question.

"Yes, Hamid and one of the soldiers did a last minute check of the encampment, and could see no one from the group still outside."

"What about the reporters?"

"They have their own truck. I'm sure they're safe in it, as well."

At that moment, the truck just mentioned was moving away from the encampment, unseen and unheard, and slowly making progress toward a nearby highway. The reporter had been right. Their direction of movement was giving them just barely enough visibility to be able to view the road and make their way forward. There were no windows in the back of the truck, so the boys couldn't see their progress, but they could feel every rut and mound in the road as they bounced along. Jabari said something, addressing Set as "Prince," and that got a laugh from the boy, and then sparked a few more funny remarks. Within less than a minute, they were both talking about their brief identity switch game, and what they'd already learned because of it. It had surprised them both.

Set said, "You know, when Walid agreed to my offer to switch places, I thought it was just going to be a silly fun game for a day, but I've really learned a lot because of what's happened—how people have treated me, and how I've felt about it."

"Definitely, me too," Jabari said. "You go from being a normal person to being something super special, all of a sudden, and it's not because of anything you've done."

"Yeah, it's not like you've won the Olympics, or some battle or anything. People are just recognizing you for who you are."

"I guess that's the way it really is for Walid, too."

"I had never thought of that before."

"It's not like he's had to do a lot to earn whatever special treatment he gets. He was just born into the family where ... he's a prince."

"It's sort of strange," Set reflected. "He does lots of good things, but he's not the prince because of what he does; it's almost like he does what he does because he's the prince. I mean, most of the good stuff he does is just because he's a good guy, but it sometimes seems like he feels a need to live up to the role and the many expectations that come with it."

"Yeah, maybe so. But he acts just like one of us most of the time. And when you really think about it, we all have roles and expectations to live up to. When people think highly of us, it's like we're always trying to justify their esteem, even if we know they're wrong."

"Ha! I guess you're right. But I doubt everybody's like that. I mean, some people rebel against roles and expectations."

"True also, but by doing that, they're just taking up different roles."

"Good point." Set sat quietly for a moment and said, "You think these newspaper guys are going to interview us?"

"Yeah, I suppose so."

"Have you ever been interviewed?"

"No."

"Me, neither."

"Oh, man."

"What?"

"Bad news. These guys think you're the prince and I'm the royal best friend."

"Oh, yeah. I sort of forgot."

"You're Walid and I'm Mafulla, to them. The guy called you 'Prince' before we got into the truck."

"Yeah. You're right. Oh! I get what you're saying."

"If they interview us today, they're going to think they're interviewing the prince and the first pal."

Set said, "I guess we've got to just explain what's going on."

Jabari laughed and said, "You think? Or maybe we should just keep up the game and set off some national or international scandal by what we say."

"Good idea," Set replied, also laughing. "It's our one chance."

Jabari then raised his eyebrows high and said, "You know, we could prank Walid and Mafulla really good on this one, but I think we'd better play it straight and come clean and admit who we really are."

"Yeah, I agree."

"And then later, we can tell them, just for fun, that we did the interview as them and said some crazy things."

"That would be a great joke."

"Yeah, for about a minute while they totally freaked out, but then we'd have to tell them the truth."

"I agree."

"Ow!" That was a big bump!"

"For sure!"

After a few seconds of silence, Jabari said, "Hey, Fake Prince."

"What?"

"Do you think we've been riding longer than we should have to get to the train station?"

"Well, yeah, maybe, Equally Fake Princely Pal, but that could be because we're going much slower in the sand and all."

"It seems like we picked up speed a couple of minutes ago."

"Yeah, it did feel like that."

"Maybe we should knock on the wall here at the back of their cab and see if we can ask the guys where we are. It looks like there's a partition that they could open from their side. I mean, I'm just curious, that's all. And, you know, maybe we could also take the chance to explain who we really are."

"It's a good idea." Set rapped his knuckles gently three times on the place Jabari had pointed out to him, which did look like a metal window slot on the back of the cab that could be opened from the other side, where the newsmen were sitting. There was no response. He rapped gently two more times. Nothing.

"Do it again," Jabari suggested, "a little louder this time. It could be noisy up front. Or they could be talking."

"Yeah. You're right." Set banged much louder, five times, and they both listened. Nothing again. "Hey, guys!" Set yelled out, with his mouth near the cab wall. He then banged even louder, five more times. Still there was no response. The truck continued to bounce along, until just then it lifted slightly up onto a smoother surface, like the pavement of a better road or highway. The bumping stopped and the engine noise went up, and it felt like they were suddenly going much faster.

Jabari said, "There was no paved road between the train station and the ruins, was there?"

Set replied, "I don't remember one. We bounced the whole time."

"Well, we're on a nice paved road now. And we're going much faster."

"Oh, man. I wonder what's going on. I wish we had windows."

"Maybe the guys just had to go way around and take a different route back to the station because of the storm, or maybe the road was blocked or something. Open the back door a bit, and see what you can see."

Set crawled the few feet back to the door and grabbed the handle, to turn it. "It's stuck."

"It's stuck?"

"Yeah. Or, maybe, it's locked."

"Why would they lock it? Try it again."

Set started jerking it back and forth, but it would hardly move. "Maybe they locked it to keep it extra secure from the storm, or to keep it from bouncing open on the bumpy road. It was a pretty rough ride at first."

Jabari said, "Sure, but would they have had to actually lock it?"

"What do you mean?"

"Doors like these close pretty securely without locking, and they close well. I heard the latch click when the doors came together, and then I heard a second metallic sound, but I didn't really think about it at the time. I bet that was the lock."

"Oh, man," Set said.

"What?'

"When you lock a door, you're normally either trying to keep someone out, or keep someone in."

"You mean those guys locked us in here to keep us in here?"

"Yeah, maybe."

"Why?"

"Well, they do think I'm the prince."

"Oh, gee. Uh, oh."

"Yeah, maybe they're rebels or something, and not a news reporter and his camera guy at all." Suddenly, each boy felt a sick sensation in his stomach and a jolt of adrenalin that caused a quick shudder to run through his body.

Jabari said, "Man. We could be in deep, deep trouble."

"Maybe. Maybe."

"We gotta do something."

"What?"

"I don't know. Look around and see if there's anything we could use as a tool. Maybe we can take off the door or the handle and undo the lock."

"And what? Jump out of a fast moving truck onto a hard road surface?"

"You got a better idea, Your Highness?"

"Good point."

"Rebels don't tend to treat royalty very royally, if you know what I mean—in case that's what we're dealing with here."

"Be more optimistic. Maybe we're just being kidnapped for a ransom."

"If that's the most optimistic option you've got, then we are in trouble. They think they have the prince and his best friend, the two kids in the kingdom who are the most important to the king. If we're being kidnapped for a ransom, what are they going to do when they find out we're not the real thing? Take a deeply discounted ransom?"

"Oh. I guess not."

"It's not like they'll be in a mood to run a Special Sale on Kidnapped Commoners. 'Get Two for the Price of One.' They'll probably just cut their losses and our throats and get rid of us."

"Really?" Set was now getting deeply concerned.

Jabari said, "I've read enough relevant history that I don't predict a rosy outcome, if they're in charge of it. We've got to do something, and I don't see anything like a tool or a weapon in this part of the truck so far."

Set looked around really carefully and said, "Wait a minute. Is that a screw in the floor?"

"Let me see. Yeah, it is."

"Does Manni still have on his collar?"

"Yes, of course. I'm keeping it on him now."

"It's got a regular tang buckle, right?"

"Yeah, I guess. It's a regular buckle, but I didn't know it was called a tang."

"Yeah, that's it. Take it off him. I might be able to use the tang, or pin, to undo the screw. If it's shaped right, it can be almost like a little flat head screwdriver."

"Genius. Sheer genius. No wonder you're the fake prince and I'm just the fake best friend." As he said this, Jabari reached into the backpack and stroked Manni sweetly, speaking to him in a low and friendly voice, while removing his collar from around his neck and from the leash. He looped the leash to create a makeshift collar and put it back over Manni's head. He then handed the real collar to Set and said, "Here it is, Your Highness, Hope and Savior of Your People, all one of us, or two, if you count Manni—which you really should."

Set took the collar and examined the pin's shape at the end. "This is good! It's just what I need."

Jabari said, "That looks like a pretty small hole that's going to open, if you can get the screw out. It's not like we're going to be able to squeeze through it and escape."

"No, no, no. That's not the idea at all. This is likely a compartment for the tire jack and any tools they have. If we can get to them, we'll be able to use them as tools for an escape, or even as weapons, if we can't get out."

"Oh. Ok. Good. That's makes sense. But then what?"

"We'll see."

Set was right that they would soon see the next major development in what would be their monumentally dangerous ordeal, an enterprise that was already far further along than he could have imagined. But he also never could have guessed what the two of them would see in the very next minute.

15

More Surprises

Ari Falma's younger brother was sitting alone, going over some papers in an office at the back of the warehouse. A man stepped into the doorway. "Idi! They have them!"

"Who has what?"

"The guy we hired to kidnap the prince, and another man!"

"Keep your voice down! Someone could hear you!"

"Ok, but the guys doing the job, they have the prince and his best friend! They've locked them both in the back of a truck, and they'll be here at the warehouse within fifteen or twenty minutes."

"How do you know this?"

"They stopped on the outskirts of town and found a phone and called some guy who got the message to us just minutes ago."

"My brother doesn't know?"

"No, he's out back or something. He didn't hear the message."

"They have the prince and also his friend?"

"Yeah, both of them."

"How in the world?"

"I have no idea."

"This is even better than I hoped."

"We'll be rich very soon."

"Yes. And that infuriating brother of mine will finally have to admit that I'm smarter than he is. Whether he ever says so or not, he'll know now. He'll know. And the other men will, too. I've done something that not even he could do—not even in his dreams."

"What about the Brit?"

"Who?" Idi faked a surprised look.

"The guy who gave us the information on the whereabouts of the prince—the man who asked us to do this, the one paying for it."

"Oh, him. Yeah, the Brit—I don't know. He promised to pay a lot of money for the prince if we could snag him, correct?"

"Yes, he did."

"But we could get a true fortune in ransom for these boys just by ourselves."

"I'm sure you're right, Idi. But remember, that would involve risks that turning them over to the Brit wouldn't bring on us."

"That's also true."

"And you said yourself that, when he visited you, he was really serious about representing what he called powerful forces."

"True. I suppose I shouldn't let extra profit blind me to that."

"The entire government, the whole military will be hunting for the prince and, if we have him, for us. We're good at avoiding the police, but the entire army? I'm not so sure. If we turn these boys over to the Brit, we give him the worry and just take his money."

"Find out how much, exactly, he'll pay us. Tell him we got the two of them, the two top kids."

"I know how to contact him. I can have the answer within half an hour. But I'll need to leave and we're not supposed to leave."

"It's Ok. I'll tell Ari I need to take a couple of the men, just my men, out on a quick errand. He only needs to be reassured that I'll watch everybody and not let anyone wander off and go have tea with a viper or a storm. Then you can get through to the Brit. Tell him we have the prince and his best friend. Find out how much he'll pay for both the boys. Let him know how hard we had to work and how creative we had to be to snatch them both."

"What do I say? I have no idea what the men did. They didn't reveal anything in their call about their methods or what they had to do."

"You just say we worked very hard and had to be extra creative and that it's a once in a lifetime opportunity that's worth a fortune. See what he offers. Whatever he says, you say: 'Is that the best you can do? We were thinking more.' Then we'll see what he comes up with."

"Ok, boss. But I think first you got to get Ari out of here and back to his office, if you don't want him around when this first happens. He needs to learn about it only when the money's in our hands. And the guys we're waiting for aren't that far away at this point."

At Memphis, as soon as the thundering wind began to die down and the main danger from the storm had passed, the soldiers assigned to security for the field trip began to go truck-to-truck and untie the flaps that had protected the students and adults inside.

"All clear! Everyone out!" The soldiers called into the trucks. "The storm's passed. We're fine." The boys and girls and adults began to climb down from the trucks and brush themselves off in the renewed daylight. There was a rush of excited voices that could be heard from all directions as the students from different trucks called out to each other, and Khalid and Hoda carefully looked them all over.

"Where's Set? Has anyone seen Set—the real, original Set?" Khalid spoke in a loud voice, addressing himself to the students generally.

There were shrugs and negative expressions all around, and

quick mumbles of replies like "No," and "Not since the storm came."

Khalid surveyed the groups that had emerged from all four trucks and said, "How about Jabari?" He looked at the other students, none of whom had a positive answer about either of the boys. It was odd.

Khalid cupped his hands and, turning toward the trucks, shouted, "Set! Jabari!" He then called out again, "Set! Jabari!" Then he walked quickly toward the next truck over, while saying loudly to as many of the students as he could, "Raise your hand if you sat next to Set or Jabari in any of the trucks." No hand went up.

Khalid turned around. "Omari! Have the men search under all the tents."

At that point, Reela walked up. "Are Set and Jabari missing?"

"We can't find them, and no one sat next to them during the storm, which means they weren't in the backs of any of the trucks. We need to check the cabs."

The men instantly went to all the truck cabs, opened the doors, and saw no one inside. "Nobody in the trucks," one of them shouted.

"Where are the newsmen?" Omari said to no one in particular.

"What?" Khalid replied with a look and tone of surprise.

"The newspaper guys," Omari said, "the reporter and the photographer—where are they?"

Khalid said, "I don't know. Why? They had their own truck."

Omari said, "Their truck's gone."

"Gone? What do you mean? It's gone?"

"Yes, it was back there away from our trucks on the other side of the tents, by itself, and it's not there now." Omari turned and pointed to where the other truck had been right before the storm.

"Oh."

Just then Hamid walked up. Omari looked at him and at Reela and said, "Set and Jabari are missing and so is the truck of the news guys, and so are those men, whose credentials we never saw."

Khalid looked puzzled. "Why would they take off with Set and Jabari?"

Walid, overhearing the conversation at this point and walking up, said, "They likely think that Set's me and Jabari's Mafulla."

"What?" Omari was the first to react.

Walid reminded him, "The game of the day, the Great Identity Switch. They likely saw the soldiers salute Set and Jabari yesterday as they would me and Mafulla."

"That's my fault," Hamid said, with a very serious look. "I arranged it to give them a full sense of royalty."

"But also, those guys could have heard anyone call Set 'Prince,' since everybody was doing it. We were all playing along, throughout the afternoon yesterday, and even this morning," Walid offered.

"So, they think they've taken the prince and his best friend," Reela said.

"Yes," Omari replied. "That would seem to be the situation."

"Oh, no." Khalid looked sick. "It's my fault. I trusted that guy," he responded.

"They fooled me, too," Omari said. "I spoke to them about their official credentials this morning, and they made up a story about forgetting them and leaving them at the paper, and I believed it."

Hamid said, "The men sure looked legitimate enough. But that was apparently part of their plan. It doesn't matter now. We have to find the boys."

"Where could they have gone?"

"Not many places out here, and especially in the storm," Reela said. "They probably drove with the wind for better visibility, toward the train station."

"But there's no regularly scheduled train any time soon."

"No," Hamid said, "but there is that road near the station, a paved road, the highway back into town that runs alongside the tracks."

"It also goes south as well," Omari reminded them.

"Yes, but to where?" Hamid reasoned. "There's no place to hide that's anywhere close to us in that direction. The nearest possibilities for concealing a truck and four people would be back in town. And I'm sure they'll want to get out of the open as quickly as they can. They certainly know that we'll be in pursuit."

At that point, Omari called to the soldiers who were standing nearby, and they immediately jogged over to join the conversation. Hoda had also walked up, as had Kissa and Hasina.

"What's going on?" Kissa said.

"It looks like the newspaper guys took Set and Jabari, and I guess Manni," Walid explained.

"But why?"

Omari said, "We never saw their credentials. They're likely frauds who are kidnapping our friends, thinking they've got the prince and his best friend."

"Oh, no."

Hoda spoke up then and said, "I had something like a warning before the storm was spotted, a feeling that something bad was coming. But it was too vague a feeling for me to act on."

"What sort of warning was it?" Hamid asked.

"While we were meditating, I had a quick vision of a storm, a flash of it really, but not of what the storm would make possible."

"I felt something bad, too, mom," Kissa said, "Yesterday, I had a sudden sense, like everyone in the trucks at the train station, or some of them, were going off to war—that's the phrase that came into my head."

"Me, too," Hasina added. "But it wasn't clear. I suddenly felt like some of us were going off to war or to battle or something. But I had that sensation only for a second as we were first getting into the trucks back at the station."

"Why didn't either of you say anything?" Khalid asked.

"It was too vague and strange, Dad. We didn't know what to say."

Hasina said, "I just thought it was a natural association with military trucks, so I forgot about it."

Kissa thought for a second and added, "When we did our meditation, I also felt right away a real sense of peace, and then something disturbing. I had no idea it could be a premonition about the future. I thought it was just some signal from this place and its past."

"I understand. You did nothing wrong by not speaking of it, either of you." Khalid turned to the other men. "What should we do now?"

"We need to send out a rescue party, and quickly," Omari said. "I think Reela and I will be sufficient senior security for the entire group here at this point, given that Walid and Mafulla can handle themselves pretty well, as they amply demonstrated on the train earlier, and so they can also help with the protection of the other students. Plus, those guys think they have the prince and his friend, so they're not likely to come back looking for anyone else any time soon."

"I agree," Reela said.

Omari continued, "I say we release our entire military escort to take two trucks and get on the highway now, heading toward the city. Someone should go to the train station right away and send a telegram to the king, explaining what's happened, and asking if Masoon can launch a major search effort from the palace."

"Good thinking," Reela said, as all of them began to walk toward where the soldiers were. "These are either rebels or criminals or both. And there's a chance they've kidnapped the boys they think are the prince and his best friend for the purpose of demanding a ransom. If they somehow find out that Set and Jabari are not the boys they sought, our friends could be in great danger. And if ransom isn't their game, they could be in even more jeopardy. We need to move fast."

"Wait. I think I have an even better solution," Hamid said, and stopped walking, as did the others.

"What's that?" Reela asked, as Omari also turned toward the senior officer.

"We'll do as you suggest, Omari, but reassign the groups. Let's you and I and Walid and Mafulla go after the boys. Reela can stay here with the soldiers in protection of the remaining students. Reela, you can send one of the men to the station to telegraph or telephone our news in to the king."

Omari said, "Ok. That makes sense. That's a good plan."

Reela just looked puzzled and replied, "I have some worries about the idea. Is it wise to send our boys to find the people who were trying to capture precisely them? And, surely, they're not as prepared as the soldiers for such a mission."

Hamid looked him in the eyes with both kindness and determination and said, "In our company, there's no chance that the real prince can be taken. Plus, they think they have the prince already and won't know who these two are." Hamid then leaned over much closer to Reela and whispered, "We're Phi, and we've made sure that these two are actually now better trained than any of the men we have here. You saw the results on the train. They can do things the soldiers can't do to save the boys who've been taken."

Even without Hamid making clear who he included in the word 'we,' the whispered remark evoked a look of great surprise from Reela. But he then simply nodded his head and said, "I understand. Ok, then. It's a good plan. I'll watch over things here."

In the palace, the call came into Bancom in the communications room. He sent word to Masoon and Paki, and walked quickly to the king's rooms to bring the news in person. He entered the outer office in a hurry, and with a serious expression. "Kular, I need to see the king immediately. It's a matter of great urgency. Two of the boys on the school trip have been kidnapped."

Kular said, "Oh, my. That's terrible. Come right in," as he opened the door to the king's sitting room, where Ali was at a desk going over some reports.

Bancom walked in speaking. "Majesty, I'm sorry to barge in, but there's been an incident. Two men pretending to be a reporter and photographer from *The Kingdom Daily News* have kidnapped two of the boys from Khalid's class—Set and Jabari."

"Why would such a thing happen?"

"The boys apparently were abducted in a case of mistaken identity. The kidnappers wrongly believed they'd taken Walid and Mafulla. It was the prince they were after. During an unexpected sandstorm, they gave the two boys refuge in a truck, locked them in, and drove for ten minutes or more before anyone realized they were gone."

"Do we know anything about where they went?"

"We think they headed toward the train station with the wind at their backs, and took the highway running near the tracks into the city."

"Do we have a description of the truck?"

"Yes, Majesty."

"The men?"

"Also, yes."

"Do we know anything else about the situation that would help in locating the boys?"

"Not much. We have only the reasonable speculation by Reela Adi that these men are either rebels or criminals and are either aiming at a ransom demand, or at eliminating any royalty they believe to stand in their way of controlling the kingdom. In either case, the boys are in great danger. Even if it's a ransom situation, their safety is in doubt, especially if they're discovered not to be the prince and his friend."

"Who from the scene is in pursuit?"

"Hamid and Omari have just reported they've organized a small group and they've left already."

"You've contacted Masoon?"

"Yes, sir, and Paki."

"Good. Get them in here as soon as you can."

"I'll do it, Your Majesty."

As Bancom turned to leave, the king said, "I also want Naqid to be told about this. I feel that a Falma plot may be behind it all. Kinkaid's also a major suspect, of course. We need to locate him immediately. Have Darwishi send him a message that he needs help right away with some questions about the car log for the main vehicle used personally by me. Have some guards also make discreet inquiries at the Grand Hotel and any other establishment that Kinkaid might find suitable as his lodging."

"Yes, Majesty. Right away." As Bancom was leaving the room, Masoon walked in. The king briefed him as quickly as he could about what was happening.

The general said, "Your Majesty, I have one of my officers out in the hall. Let me send him to get some of this operation under way immediately."

The king replied, "Good idea. We have no time to waste." Masoon ducked outside the door, spoke to his man briefly, and returned to the room. A second later, Paki came through the door as well.

"Paki, Masoon, we need a Phi led assault team to help with a hostage rescue situation. Put together a unit of elite performers right away. Masoon, you can fill our friend in on what's happened. Paki, your job will be to assemble the team quickly, with the most appropriate men for an operation on what we should presume is a group of well-armed kidnappers, and even revolutionaries. We're going to be narrowing down possible target locations within the hour. We need a team ready to move at that point, if not sooner."

"Yes, Your Majesty." Paki and Masoon walked over to the side of the room and began talking, with Paki taking notes on some paper that he had found on the table next to them.

Masoon then turned back toward the king and said, "Your Majesty, time is our main adversary right now, unless we make it our stealthy ally. These men will expect to be pursued, but not to be tracked down as quickly as we may be able to find them. I suspect we should invest a few moments of deeper thought into how best to proceed."

"Yes. I agree. Would both of you come over here and please sit?"

Masoon took a chair across from the king's desk and sat very still, looking intently at the monarch. Paki did the same. King Ali said, very quietly, "Center yourself, each of you, my friends. Be at peace. With your open heart, ask for guidance, expectantly. Focus your mind on these good boys, Set and Jabari. They're in a truck. They're moving into the city. They're headed toward a destination. Relax, release, and go deep." Masoon lowered his head and half closed his eyes. The king did the same thing. Paki had his eyes open, but sat motionless as he emptied his mind of all concerns and fleeting thoughts.

Both Masoon and Paki realized how important it was to make this immediate investment in meditative openness. These few minutes could well become their most important time of preparation for what lay ahead. Fast action improperly guided rarely produces anything of value. Paradoxically, it's often in still and quiet that the most and best is accomplished.

The minutes passed. Kular came to the door, saw them sitting in silence, and closed it gently, asking their most recent visitor to wait. He explained what was going on in the sitting room and then inquired as to whether Naqid would like to sit quietly for a few moments himself, before admission to see the king. He agreed and took a seat.

It was well known among all the men in top leadership positions throughout the government that the king believed in the practice of meditation, and ascribed to it many of his best and wisest decisions. Compared to the Phi behind the closed door, Naqid was an amateur in all aspects of this ancient activity, but he knew that bringing himself to a state of rest and peacefulness could sharpen his thoughts and senses for what was to come.

Ten minutes later, the king spoke softly the words, "We can now come back with whatever gifts we may bring. The good far country, nearer to us than our own hearts, is our home, and blesses us whenever we set foot by its welcoming hearth. I thank you men for the time you've invested in this brief sojourn with me just now."

They were all silent for another five seconds. "It's a warehouse," Masoon said quietly. "On the Rue de L'Or, in what's now the old warehouse district. I've seen a street of gold and a building, nearly empty, and a truck making its way there now."

"Paki, how many are there in the palace or nearby that could join a team right away?"

"The three of us and at least three others, if we count Amon, and perhaps a few more."

"Can he be counted yet?"

"Yes, I think he's healed enough from the explosion to be on the team. He can't yet move at his normal speed, but he's strong. And I know he's eager to serve."

"I should stay here," the king said. "I need to coordinate things from this room. Will five or six men be enough?"

"Yes," Masoon said. "The three of us Phi would do just fine, in my view, and two or three trusted and highly skilled others will be plenty."

"Ok, then. Masoon, gather the team and lead them to your recognized destination. Tell Amon he's mostly backup, this time. Follow your heart and then your head, as always. Go in peace and power."

"It's done, Majesty," Masoon said as he and Paki left the room at a brisk walk. When they saw the head of palace guards seated in Kular's anteroom, Masoon said to him, "Naqid, we need a truck at the back entrance, one that doesn't look military and that can hold five or six men. We'll need it within ten to fifteen minutes."

"Done," Naqid said, and followed the men out the door.

In the kidnapper's truck, things had taken a surprising turn. Set and Jabari had felt the vehicle slow, turn, and then stop. They heard a door open and close. Things were quiet for several minutes. Then, the sound of a door again, and the truck was put back into gear, slowly commencing its progress toward what the boys realized would be a very difficult destination unless they did something fast.

Set was now once more looking carefully at the tang buckle on Manni's collar as he held it in his hand. He then bent over and inserted the flat part ever so gently into the slot on the head of the screw they had found on the floor of the truck bed where they were being held captive. The truck continued its forward movement, now making more turns, and with a stop and go motion. "The fit isn't really good, but the screw's loose already," Set said, surprised. "This could be easier than I thought."

"Good. Let me know if you need any help," Jabari answered.

It was a good thing the compartment had been opened the previous day. A flat tire had made the men work hard to loosen the partially rusted screw, and when they got the tire changed and reclosed the compartment for the truck's tools, they just gave the screw one quick twist, in a hurry. They had to catch up with the palace group. And now, as a consequence, the screw easily popped up. Set then quickly dug the buckle's tang into a narrow space or gap that outlined the door of the inner compartment in the floor of the truck bed. He was able to wedge up the metal top without much effort. He then grabbed it with both hands and lifted it loose, sliding it to the side.

"All right, here we go," he said to his friend. They both looked into the space that had been covered.

"Wow. You did it." Jabari felt a moment of relief, even before knowing what might be there that they could use, and how they could use it. As they peered into the hole they had uncovered, they could see a large open space with a deflated old tire, a truck jack and a tire iron, and also a piece of wood under those things. Set moved stuff around and under the wood he could now see a screwdriver, some pliers, a small book of some sort, and down at the side of the compartment, a lumpy old brown burlap bag containing something else, an object that was not immediately identifiable from a first glance.

Set took out the tire and with Jabari's help put it aside, and then the jack and the tire iron. He reached down into the compartment and moved the small piece of wood that had been under those items. Now he could pick up the screwdriver and pliers and hand them over to his friend. The book was an Owner's Manual for the truck.

"What's in the old bag?" Jabari said.

Set reached down into the very bottom of the compartment and lifted out the dirty pouch. He pulled open a drawstring and peered into it.

"No way."

"What?"

"Never assume anything about anything, my friend—unless, as Khalid would say, you have to. And I thought we were in a situation of deep, deep trouble, with a maybe unsolvable problem." He actually smiled, and carefully lifted from the old bag a small black revolver.

"Jeepers." Jabari just stared with his eyes big and his mouth hanging open.

"Yeah, too bad for the bad guys," Set said.

"How did this get here?" Jabari asked.

"I don't know," Set said. "They must have gotten this truck from The Sloppy Criminal Rent-A-Truck lot in downtown Cairo, and either didn't know about, or else forgot about, this little item."

"What idiots! Is it loaded?"

Set responded by carefully checking it. "Yes, indeed it is, I'm pleased to report."

"Do you know how to use it?"

"Since I was about ten, my dad's taken me target shooting."

"Wow. Are you any good?"

"Yeah. Excellent. I have great aim. "

"Oh, man! That's amazing!" Jabari said. "I'm better with screwdrivers and pliers, and nearly anything else. What are we going to do now?"

"Well, first, let's see if we can get the door open using these other tools as quietly as we can. Then, if that doesn't work, I hold in my hand the entire backup plan."

"Ok. Let's see. My dad's pretty handy and he's taught me a lot about how things are put together. I'll get on it right away," Jabari said, and he turned to examine the door handle, along with the hinges that held the door to the truck body. Set gently put down the gun, facing it away from the two of them, and started his own examination of the mechanical challenges and possibilities they faced.

"I think we can get the hinges off," Set said.

"Yeah," Jabari agreed. "I think most truck door hinges are completely on the outside, but these are different."

"Ok." Set looked more closely and said, "We might be able to get the pin out."

"You're right. And I think I can get this handle off, as well," Jabari offered. "If I can, then maybe I can get at the lock and disable it."

Using different tools, they both got to work on the doors that were hinged at the sides and closed in the middle, where they were locked.

"Look, we need to talk about this," Set said, while he kept working. "If we can get one or both doors off, we jump when we can and run and get out of here. The truck seems to be going much slower and it stops now and then, like we're back in the city or something."

"Yeah. I agree."

"We should be able to hop out without getting badly hurt, and maybe just end up a little bruised. And you can probably hold Manni well, and safely, when we jump."

"Ok," Jabari said. "It's better than many alternatives I can think of right now."

"Let's keep on this, hard. We likely don't have long before we'll get to our destination, whatever it is, and have some really bad problems."

The boys worked as fast as they could, but it was difficult. It was hot in the truck and they had to wipe sweat out of their eyes every few seconds. They were trying hard to be quiet, but were forced to make a little more noise than they planned. They both silently hoped that the men up front couldn't hear them. But now, through it all, they were making progress. It would only be a few more minutes and they would be able to open a door and get out.

Just then, the truck slowed a lot and turned, and there was a distinct bump. The boys were thrown off balance for a second. The vehicle rolled a few more feet and then came to a stop. Set and Jabari could hear muffled shouts and then the sounds of what seemed like big metal garage doors being closed behind them. The truck's engine shut off. And then there were more voices, much closer and near the truck. At first, they couldn't hear what the voices were saying. Set whispered something into Jabari's ear and the smaller boy nodded his head in understanding.

"Ok, get 'em outta there," a loud voice commanded. Then, just as the door handle began to turn and jiggle, it fell out of the door, clanging down onto a hard floor. And they could now hear, close to the truck, another voice say, "Whoa! What happened here?"

At that moment, both doors suddenly exploded outward, slamming into the two men at the back of the truck who had moved close to open them. Set and Jabari had managed to get both doors by that point unpinned from their hinges, and the lock disabled, with the handle loose and useless. And so, right after the handle fell out, they had both kicked the doors as hard as they could, outward and toward the men, who yelled, cursed, and stumbled as the heavy metal fell out and hit them, one in the head, knocking them backward, and confusing them badly. From the opening of Jabari's backpack, Manni screamed his loudest jungle scream and, simultaneously, Set fired the gun once toward the first guy he saw. Whether it was a lucky shot or all those target practice days were paying off, he got the guy in the upper leg, and the man yelled as loudly as he could, while collapsing to the floor. It was total chaos. At the thunderous crack of the shot, the two men the doors had hit flattened themselves on the floor of the warehouse in protective positions, and the third man, maybe twenty feet away, the one who had been shot, also lay flat while writhing in pain, hoping not to be hit again.

"Stay where you are! Face down!" Set shouted, as the monkey continued to scream and he and Jabari jumped from the truck. Two other men appeared at an open door about ten yards away, and Set instantly shot a second time at them, hitting the door frame right beside one guy's head, and forcing them back to wherever they had come from. Jabari held the screwdriver like a knife and the two boys with their little monkey friend ran across the warehouse floor toward a door through whose window some light was coming in. Set turned the knob. It was locked. He shook it, and then he kicked it with all his might and it popped open. As he and Jabari went out through it, the two men who had not been shot, but only bruised by the doors, got up and began to run toward that same exit in pursuit of their captives.

"Stop 'em!" one of the men shouted. As soon as the boys cleared the door and got outside the building, they ran down an alley toward the nearest corner of the structure and, as they rounded it, they were suddenly grabbed from behind by two other men who had been just out of their sight and hidden behind some large garbage bins and boxes since the moment they had heard the first gun shot.

"Gotcha!" One of the men yelled. But Jabari slammed the sharp end of his screwdriver into the man's arm and he howled in pain. Set's arms were pinned but he somehow got off a third shot straight down into the foot of the ridiculously strong man who was holding him. That guy yelled out in complete agony and instantly let go of Set, jumping around on one foot, and falling back up against one of the large trash cans he had been behind, while continuing to cry out in mind numbing pain, as both boys took off again at a run.

But they didn't get far. At the end of the alley down which they were running, four men appeared, two of them with guns out and ready for use. The boys stopped and turned to run back in the other direction, but there were three more men back there who had just run out from the warehouse, and at least one of them was also armed. A single thought occurred to Set. "I don't have enough bullets left."

The same thing occurred to Jabari at the same moment, and in these words: "Seven men there, three bullets and one screwdriver here. Not good."

16

A Future King's Ransom

Sometimes, you know what you need to do, without having any idea of exactly where you'll end up as a result, or what will meet you along the road. There's no real alternative. You just move forward.

The kingdom military truck was rumbling down the highway at nearly full speed. Walid said, "You know, they probably got a fifteen or twenty minute head-start." He spoke loudly through the open window between the truck's cab and the back area where he was seated.

"Yes, you're right," Hamid replied from the driver's seat. "But this truck may be faster than theirs. And we're not driving the first ten minutes in a sandstorm like they did."

"That's a good point," Walid conceded.

"Once we get into the city, what then?" Mafulla asked.

"I have to admit, I'm not sure," Hamid said. "But I'm thinking we go to the industrial side of town where all the big warehouses and old factories are located. If this is Ari Falma's doing, he has a history of using abandoned and empty buildings there."

"We can be on the lookout for their truck," Omari suggested. "And for any signs of activity that look suspicious. Hopefully, by now, the king will also have launched a search and rescue operation with more men and a better sense of possible locations. But we have to focus like it's just us."

"That makes sense," Walid said.

Hamid was driving as aggressively as he safely could manage. The truck was more powerful and faster than Walid had guessed, and they were making good time up the highway into the city. Not many other cars or trucks were on the road. There were a few, but they were passing more donkey carts and horses than motorized vehicles on their mad dash to town. Hamid had the rhythm down—honk and pass, honk and pass, hitting the brakes now and then before speeding around an obstacle. It was a good thing that, in the aftermath of the storm, the day was clear and visibility was perfect. When they came to one spot where goats were crossing the road in a big, spread out herd, he decided that, rather than waiting, they'd go off-road and around the bleating animals, to their rear. That was a very bouncy choice. And everyone had to hold on tight.

"Whoa!" Walid had to laugh at how hard one of the bumps had felt.

"Jeepers!" Mafulla exclaimed as he braced himself better. He looked over at Walid with eyebrows high and said, "I see some large bruises up ahead, very soon in your future, my friend."

The prince replied, "I think they'll more likely be behind me."

Mafulla laughed. "Good one. Ouch!"

"And it won't be the first time, for sure," Walid added.

"I hope that's the worst it gets today."

"Yeah. Really."

Then, at the end of their go-around maneuver, right before getting back on the highway beyond the group of animals, the truck hit some soft, deeper sand and the wheels spun a few times in a way that concerned them all. But Hamid gunned it and the truck jumped and bumped back onto the hard pavement and, after spinning its wheels for a moment again, it got going once more and soon resumed its previous speed far ahead of where it would have been if they had just waited.

At this point, they couldn't be more than a very few minutes behind the kidnappers. As they entered the outskirts of the city, Hamid kept taking the streets that would put them most quickly into the large warehouse district. His honking and passing tactic was still effective, although it seemed to anger several pedestrians and other drivers now and then. They had a few fists waved at them and words shouted in their direction. Although no one could actually make out what exactly the aggrieved parties were saying, it was clear enough that they were unhappy at this large truck careening down the street, passing a bit wildly, and taking corners at almost top speed.

Two city policemen on foot patrol waved and yelled at them to slow down, but Hamid was so focused that he wasn't even aware of them. Walid started to see a change in the street signs they were passing, and noted it with interest. Names like 'Rue de Montaigne,' 'Roman Way,' and 'Levant Lane' gave way to 'Avenue Industrial,' 'Storage Street,' 'Fabrication Boulevard,' and 'Container Lane.' Hamid had now slowed the truck considerably and the men were looking all around, up and down every side street, eyes sharp for the missing truck, the men, or the boys. Up ahead of them, Mafulla, who had also been noticing the names of the surrounding roads, saw a street sign that struck him as interestingly out of place: 'Rue de L'Or.'

"Hey, wait." Mafulla said. Hamid hit the breaks as he pointed and continued, "That sign up ahead: 'Rue de L'Or' means 'Street of Gold' doesn't it?"

"Yes, it does," Hamid answered.

"That could also be 'The Golden Street,' though, right?"

"Sure, depending on how you translate it, that's equally good."

"I have a feeling. Could you turn down it, please, to the right?"

Hamid accelerated again and turned the corner onto The

Golden Street. Mafulla squinted at the buildings. "We're in the 1100 block. We have to get to higher numbers. See if there's a 1600 block."

Walid raised his eyebrows now. "Good call," he said. "I think."

Mafulla looked over at him and said, "Maybe."

"But why here?"

"I have no idea. But with all the Golden Ratio stuff in the palace and wherever things are strange, I'm just suspicious." Then he watched the address numbers go by: 1151, 1155, and then 1157.

"A little faster," Mafulla said. They entered the 1200 block, then the 1300 block. The 1400 numbers passed as Hamid accelerated a bit more, and then the sign on the next building said 1501. "I think we should maybe park in the middle of this block and go on by foot, if that's Ok."

Omari looked at Hamid, and the older man nodded his agreement. Still, there was nothing much to be seen. Since the beginning of the 1400 block, nearly a third of the buildings looked empty or locked up. There was likely very little gold to be found or made on this street at the present time—unless, of course, it was brought in by means other than those of legitimate manufacturing, warehousing, or wholesaling. Hamid parked the truck and all four passengers got out, not even fully closing their doors for fear of the noise they would make.

"What's our destination?" Hamid quietly asked Mafulla.

"If there's a 1618 address across the street, then that's where we're going," he said.

There was still some traffic up and down the street. It wasn't much, but enough that the men didn't totally stand out as obvious interlopers. Suddenly, a sound of horseshoes clopping down the street behind them grabbed their attention. A large wagon heaped with something in sacks was being pulled toward them by two gray horses, moving in the direction they were also walking. Hamid motioned to the others to follow him. They walked out into the street beside the wagon. The driver looked down at them with what seemed to be an expression of disapproval mixed with curiosity, until Hamid held up his index finger to his lips, while showing him an otherwise hidden weapon. The driver then turned to look again at the street in front of them and continued on.

They walked beside the wagon up the block, across the intersection, and into the next cluster of buildings. The wagon was sheltering and almost completely hiding them from the view of anyone on the even numbered side of the street. Omari could see around the corner of the wagon. 1610 gave way to 1612, and 1614, numbers he called out to Hamid in a loud, rough whisper.

"Now, we cross over," Hamid said as he held up his hand and stopped in his tracks, as the others then did also, letting the wagon pass. He ducked down and rushed around the back of it and up against the side of the old yellow brick building whose address was 1616, and he was followed closely by his companions. "Look around. What do you see?"

Walid said, "There's a car in front of what has to be 1618. I think it's the one Harvey Kinkaid uses when he's in town. It sure looks like it."

"Ok, then, we're at the right place," Hamid concluded.

"There's no one out front and no one across the street," Omari said, as he looked in that direction.

"Let's get closer," Hamid directed them, as he slipped out of the alley and walked along the street, suddenly comporting himself like he was simply out for a stroll in the fresh air. The others followed his lead.

Mafulla had a big grin on his face as he turned to Walid, and said, "In case someone's watching us, I'm smiling like an idiot so that no one will suspect that we're on a serious mission."

Walid grinned back and made a motion as if he were laughing. Hamid turned left into the alleyway next to their target building. He then picked up the pace, moving quickly to get behind the same large trash cans and boxes that had, minutes before, concealed some of Idi Falma's men from the view of Set and Jabari.

"There's blood here on the alley." Hamid said. "Not a lot, but it's fresh. We're in the right place, I think. We should check for any doors in the back."

At that same moment, Set and Jabari were being led roughly down a hallway and into a large open area on the first floor of the building.

A man came up to them quickly with a threatening, ugly look on his face. "You shot my brother! I should kill you!"

"Back off," the man holding Set demanded. "This is more important than a little hole in your brother's leg."

"What are you saying to me?"

"I'm saying that it's the price of doing business in The Big Time. These guys are our future. Some of us get hurt. So what? We'll get paid really well as a result, but only if we deliver these two in good shape." The angry man just glared at them and spit on the floor, and he looked like he could kill them on the spot.

Set and Jabari had no expressions on their faces. Their gun had been taken away. The screwdriver had of course also been confiscated. And a short, fat man held the backpack that contained the now squirming monkey who was tied in it too tightly to be able to launch into any of his now normal heroics for the boys.

"What are you doing with us?" Set said. "This is no way to interview a prince for a story on tourism."

Jabari couldn't help but smile, despite all his fear. He thought, "Wow."

"Shut up! You're the ticket, the two tickets, to a lot of money," the man who had been holding Set replied, as he shoved the boy toward the wall a few feet away. "You're going to bring us a really big payday. Now, sit! Sit down, both of you! And shut up!"

They did as commanded and then Set said, "The problem is that I can't answer your interview questions if I shut up."

"What are you talking about? What interview questions?"

"The newspaper guy said I was going to be interviewed for a story. Do you want some photos first, before we start?"

"I'm warning you one last time," the man said.

"Good, I hate repeated warnings," Set replied. "It gets old. It's annoying. Plus, you're going to all this trouble for the wrong guys. It would be a shame to waste any more warnings … or effort of any kind, on the wrong guys."

"What are you saying, wrong guys? Tell me, then shut up."

Set looked at the five men who now stood in the room with him and Jabari. He said nothing.

"I asked you a question."

"Oh, sorry. It was the shut up part that grabbed my attention. I got distracted. But, so: Good! The interview begins. Let me first say that my name is Set—as in, major setback for you. I'm a normal kid. And this is my almost as normal friend, Jabari. I'm not the prince. And he's not the best friend of the prince. And in that sack is not a royal monkey. So I have no idea how you think you're going to get a fortune from us or for us. No one we know has a fortune, except of course, the real prince, who is not me, and whom you guys left at Memphis with his actual best friend and the rest of our class."

"You're lying!"

"I know you wish I was. But, I'm afraid this is the sad truth. You've grabbed the wrong guys. We're actually not worth very much. You'd be lucky to get enough for us to pay your medical bills."

"You think you're so funny. You joke around now just fine. But if we didn't have orders, strict orders, I'd knock the attitude out of you where you sit, Prince Walid."

"You can call me the King of England if you want, but that won't make it true. Get somebody in here who knows what he's doing—someone who's actually seen the prince, anyone—and he can tell you that I'm speaking the truth."

"Shut up. Just shut your mouth. You think I'm going to believe you and say 'Oh, Ok, it's a big mistake and I'm sorry we took you and inconvenienced you,' and then just open the door and let you leave now? And, oh yeah, 'Please send the real prince if you don't mind.' I'm no fool. You are the real prince."

"Oh? How do you know that?"

"Shaaban told me—he's the pretend reporter who brought you here. He saw the troops salute you. He heard people call you the prince, and saw you respond to the title."

"Well, he's not much of a pretend reporter, then. When you work for a newspaper, you have to do more than report what you see and hear. You have to investigate to see what's true. Shaaban is a very sloppy pretend reporter. You should pretend to fire him. The truth is that the real prince, Walid, and his best friend Mafulla offered to trade places with me and my friend Jabari here for a day, just for fun, as a game, so we could see what it was like to walk in their shoes. It was all a silly game. And so far, up until the unexpected truck ride and all this resulting unpleasantness, it was pretty nice. This part of it, though, I could actually do without. It's not as much fun as I had hoped."

The man who had been speaking to Set just stared at him for a moment and then looked over at one of his associates. "Bring in the boss."

"Yeah, Ok, I'll be right back. But he's not gonna like it."

"For this, you boys get blindfolded." The man reached down with two pieces of black cloth and wrapped one around each boy's eyes and head. Within thirty seconds, they could hear more people enter the open space, where sound echoed up to what had looked like a second floor loft, or a floored space partially overlooking the open part of the warehouse they were in.

"You idiots!" Set and Jabari heard a man say loudly. "You morons! That's not the prince. And this is not his friend."

"We're actually pretty friendly, the real prince and I," Jabari said in reply, and mostly for Set's enjoyment.

"Shut up!" Someone jerked on Jabari's arm.

"These are not the right boys!"

"What do you mean?"

"I mean, I know the prince, I've seen him a few feet from me. I almost did away with him once at close range. That's not him! And that's not the Adi boy with him. I've talked to him in person before. How could you be so stupid? A commoner is not a prince!" The man was now yelling. His voice was a bit high pitched and almost gurgling with fury.

"But."

"You're complete and blathering morons!"

"But Idi!"

"Don't ... say my ... don't say that word, you fool!"

The same voice, but now directed away from them then said, "Are you two geniuses the ones who grabbed these boys?"

"Yeah, it was us. We did it." Set and Jabari could hear the voice that they recognized as belonging to the cameraman.

"How could you get the wrong ones?"

"We didn't know. Everybody was calling the tall one here the prince, and the soldiers were saluting him and everything."

"Like I told you, it was a game," Set spoke up and said.

"What?" Idi said. "What do you mean? What kind of game?"

"It was a switching identity game we were all playing. I told the prince that I'd love to be him for a day, and he said, 'Ok let's do it,' and everyone else agreed to play along. It was just a fun game with our classmates, and the adults joined in as well. And your brilliant kidnappers didn't know. So the real Walid and Mafulla are back in Memphis wondering where we are, right about now."

"I can't believe this is happening!" Idi yelled. "Because of a stupid game?"

In the next moment, the boys heard approaching footsteps and then a British accent say, "Oh, my. Oh, no. What a disaster. It's a travesty! These are not the boys—no, no, no, not the boys at all. I can't give you anything for these two. Sorry, chaps. You've wasted a truly golden opportunity and ended up with a mess."

"But, sir!"

"No. I'm terribly disappointed, actually, quite terribly disappointed, indeed, and I should be off. There will be serious repercussions for this." The footsteps reversed and their sound began to fade as they moved across the open space in the opposite direction.

"Wait!" They heard the voice of Idi again and additional, quick footsteps. "Wait, please ... Wait! There's an old saying we have—'When life hands you kumquats, make kumquat jam!' Surely, there's something here that we can do!"

More faintly now, they could hear the distinctive accent once more say, "Yes, you can certainly do something quite useful. You can dispose of the evidence and forget we ever talked about this!"

Those words brought a shot of adrenalin into the bodies of both boys. The men had forgotten to tie their hands or feet, or just had not gotten to that detail yet in all the confusion, so Set ripped off his blindfold and began to stand up. The men were all momentarily distracted, looking away from them in total shock at Kinkaid and their boss, Idi Falma, now some distance across the open space. They were at that second just standing as if frozen in place, completely flustered and perplexed to the point of empty-headedness, and without any clue about what was going to happen next.

Set moved quickly and jerked the backpack away from the man who had been holding it. Just as quickly, in nearly the same movement, he undid the knot holding the bag shut and released an overly agitated Manni, throwing him into the man's face. And, as if he knew what to do at this point, the monkey nearly flew into the man, all claws and teeth and high pitched, unmuted, mind numbing screeches that filled the entire space where they stood. In almost a reenactment of what had happened on the train, the man whirled about, clawing at this frenetic monster on his head, and doubled over in pain and panic, he was shouting and twisting as he fell to the ground. Another man, standing right next to him, after a moment of sheer, unthinking shock, bent down and began trying to pry the wildly aggressive primate off him, without even considering for a split second how it had happened. The monkey just drew blood from him as well, and he jerked back with his hand feeling like it was on fire.

Hearing Manni on the attack, Jabari had ripped off his blindfold and, inspired by what he had seen Walid and Mafulla do on the train, he now kicked as hard as he possibly could into the gut of the man who was down already with Manni on his head. The kick expelled all the air from the man's lungs, as Set at about the same time grabbed a gun away from the other guy who was bending down with a bleeding hand to try once more to help his fallen colleague. And the taller boy hit him squarely on the back of the head with the gun's barrel, taking him down instantly. Jabari then grabbed Manni, Set grabbed Jabari and, running for the door nearest to them, he fired the new gun wildly in the general direction of all the men—one shot and then a second shot rang out and echoed through the space. The criminals dove for cover for just the seconds that it took the boys to clear the room and enter the hallway outside it at a full run, making for the exterior door they could see at a distance. Set would later wish he had shot just one time, which would probably have done the job, and not used an additional bullet right then, but he was at the time operating on pure adrenalin and desperation.

That very moment, two men rushed into the building from the door just up in front of them. Set instantly slowed down and raised the gun with what happened to be its one remaining bullet, as his finger began the first twitch toward pulling the trigger. But then somehow he focused better and recognized Hamid and Omari, as his heart leapt into his throat.

"They're all behind us! In there!" Set yelled out, gesturing. The two boys then ran around Hamid and out the door, practically crashing head on into Walid and Mafulla, who were still outside.

"You guys!"

"Whoa! Set! Jabari! Are you Ok?" Walid grabbed his taller classmate by the shoulders.

"Barely!"

"You have a gun!"

"Yeah, but just one bullet left. They were going to kill us!"

"Here!" Walid handed Set another pistol that he had just pulled from his belt, and Mafulla gave Jabari one that he also had in his possession as a reserve. "Set, give your old gun to Jabari, too, and come with us. Jabari, stay here for a few minutes, guard the door, and protect us, and Manni. You have at least six bullets or more." The monkey was jerking around and making a strange noise of excitement, but was no longer screeching.

"Ok," Jabari said. "The bad guys are in there—at least seven." He pointed.

Walid and Mafulla now ran into the hallway, guns raised, followed by Set, as they saw the backs of Hamid and Omari farther down the hall, almost at the inner doorway to the larger space. The first two men to come through the door at a run in hot pursuit of the boys got the surprise of their lives when they almost smashed head-on into Hamid and Omari, who took them down in a split second and were then instantly ready for the next adversaries who would appear. Walid and Mafulla were practically on them at that point, but stayed a few feet back in order to give the older Phi all the room they might need in which to operate. Walid bent down and separated the two now unconscious men from their weapons, sliding the firearms far down the hallway. It wasn't a full second before another man emerged from the door at a run, and then another one. The first man through didn't go down right away from Omari's fierce spinning kick, but instead hit the wall with a loud thud and a grunt, and then went into a fighting crouch, his own gun now loose near his feet and just out of his reach.

"Good recovery," Omari said with a bit of admiration in his voice and added, "but sorry, no time for that now," as he whipped out a revolver and shot the man at close range and dropped him to the floor. Glancing back for a second to see who had shot whom, Hamid was attacked by an unusually large assailant holding a knife. But he spun quickly and blocked the main force of the man's lunge, while tripping him and grabbing and twisting his arm. The big guy let out a yell and first fell into his own knife and then onto Hamid, and dropped to the floor. When he attempted to get up, Walid was there to stop him, with one fierce blow to the side of his head, as Hamid had already turned toward the main room.

Now, Hamid, Omari, Walid, and then Mafulla rushed through the door into the large open area, with Hamid leading the way, to see the backs of five other men across the building, moving quickly toward the front door. One of them turned and shot in their direction. Omari lifted his gun toward the men closest to the door, but Hamid reached back and put his hand on Omari's arm just as he saw the front door explode inward and Masoon appear in the breech, followed by what seemed in the initial confusion like a small army of men who filled the room so fast that the fleeing criminals couldn't even react before being set upon and taken down. The kidnappers and their cohorts at this point were not able to get off a single shot in that instant of confusion and immediate action on the part of the elite rescue team. They were separated from their weapons, and in most cases their conscious awareness, before they could even begin to respond.

Far across the large open room, away from all this action, one figure suddenly appeared from another interior doorway, armed with a rifle that was raised and pointed right at Prince Walid. A thunderous cluster of deafening shots rang out. The lone gunman, Idi Falma, collapsed on the floor of the warehouse, lying in a rapidly growing pool of his own blood, instantly dead where he had stood.

Masoon turned away from Falma and quickly looked over toward the boys and his good friend Hamid, who was at that moment, to his great surprise and momentary shock, also covered in blood and dropping slowly to his knees.

17

Urgent Connections

Throughout the kingdom a moment earlier, every single active Phi had suddenly stopped whatever he or she was doing. Some paused in mid conversation and became inexplicably silent. A few looked around them in that silence. Others put down a shovel or a rake or a hammer, one a fountain pen, and another even a piece of bread. Many different activities were put on hold. Three men and one woman in separate parts of the kingdom, going in different directions for different reasons and in widely varying circumstances, two of them alone, and two with companions, stopped walking and stood still and listened. Or at least, that's the best word available for what they did. In a strange way that cannot be fully understood, each of them turned up their senses like they would the volume control on a radio. One man pulled a car over to the side of the road and shut off the engine and got out and held on to the door, looking about and listening, poised for something that he could not identify.

Twelve miles from the edge of the capital city, Hamid's son, Malik, at that same instant felt a wave of nausea and a twinge of alertness, mixed with a measure of alarm that in its suddenness and urgency made no sense to him. Hoda saw the expression on his face just as she had a similar unexpected set of sensations, and then turned to look at the other students who were sitting around on the edge of what had been their campground. They had already by now cleaned all the sand off the tents, picked them up, taken them apart, folded and rolled them, and stored them neatly. She saw Kissa and Hasina turn to each other with no expressions at all.

"If I can have everyone's attention," Hoda said, loudly, "I'd like to ask you to join in one more brief period of meditative quiet, as we decide our course for the rest of the day. And if you don't mind, I'd like to put you together in small groups for this."

She began to walk toward the boys. "Bafur, I want you and Haji and Malik together. Would you come over here and sit together right now?" Her words seemed to wake Malik out of something like a spell. She then moved over toward the girls. "Ara, Kit, Bakat, I want the three of you together over here. Cabar and Khata, would you sit together here?" She pointed to a place in the sand. And she turned. "Kissa and Hasina: Please, come over here and join me."

She now addressed all of them again. "I would ask you to sit quietly for five minutes or so. I'll try to judge how long we need. But it shouldn't be much longer than that. Please sit in quiet meditative openness. Relax your body and rest any racing thoughts that may now be in your minds. Put aside any worry for our friends who are not here among us and allow yourself, for these few minutes, just to be. In the stillness and silence, some of us may be given hints of guidance or insight that we all can use."

As the students sat down in their groups, Hoda, still standing, looked over at the men and said, "Khalid, Reela, would you have the other men who are with us, our guards, do the same, and would you also join them? I understand that we should have at least two guards on duty who are alert to the perceptions of the outer senses while we go within. But if you both could sit with the others, I think we can prepare ourselves best for whatever is next."

"Yes, certainly. I think it's a good idea," Reela said, and Khalid nodded his agreement as well. Turning around, Khalid walked toward the trucks where their armed guards were gathered. As he grew close, he began to speak to them, and all were nodding their understanding. Two of the soldiers, both rather young, followed him back to the edge of the groups that were already in position, and they sat down with him and Reela.

"There is a classroom beyond words, in a territory beneath and behind all discursive thought," Hoda said to the students. "Let's now all enter its doorway and wait in rapt attention to hear whatever lessons might be shared with us." With that, she herself sat down in the sand and became quite still.

What separated Hasina from that classroom of which Hoda had just spoken was a wall thinner than the most fragile shell of a well-boiled egg. The least bit of silence and stillness was just the tool to crack it and peel it all back. Within seconds, she began to feel the sensations that were often precursors of unexpectedly vivid visions. It was as if her mind could that easily be tuned to frequencies that most know nothing about, and yet she was open and ready to receive signals from those sources at almost any time. She had not understood this in her early and middle childhood, but now that she had been identified as Phi and was being educated and trained in cultivating her abilities, it finally all made sense.

She occasionally had feelings of regret that she had not acted on the many visions that had come to her earlier in life, or at least told someone about them at the time. Maybe if she had, accidents and injuries to others could have been avoided, lives and enterprises could have been saved, grief would not have been experienced, and a few people she loved could have had many more good things come to them. But she didn't know then what powerful and demanding gifts these quick visions were. She didn't realize she was seeing things that were happening at a distance, or that would soon come about in the immediate future—at least, if no one intervened. She was one of the few people positioned in this way to know and do, if only she had realized the nature of her experience and what it allowed.

She now knew that she couldn't live in regret for paths not taken and things not done when she was younger. The past was what it was. A child is not expected to understand everything that impinges on consciousness. Those years are a whirl of sensations, thoughts, and experiences that are all new and strange and yet familiar at the same time. At a very young age, you often don't even know enough to recognize what's distinctively new or different or odd. And that's because, in another sense, everything is new and different and odd. But everything is also one, as well, with a unity amid the constant play of diversity. There's a cosmic continuity beneath the changing kaleidoscopic surface in the incipient experience of the infant, and the toddler, and the very young child. The ordinary is the extraordinary, which is the mundane, and the magically sacred, all at once. The newness is the sameness of the everyday.

When she thought about it, Hasina realized now that, in those earlier years, she would not have been able to handle the responsibilities of knowing and doing that were weighty enough now, at her present age. It would have been overwhelming for her to understand too much too soon. She should just choose to be grateful now for the innocence of those years and to be thankful for the support and knowledge and deeper wisdom that she had been so lavishly given, and was still growing into, at present.

Kissa's Phi abilities overlapped a lot with Hasina's. But where Hasina had an apparently superior pristine openness to knowledge across distances of space and time, Kissa was extraordinary in a way that Hasina had not manifested quite as clearly—in knowing people to their deepest souls, penetrating through their walls and deceptions, and effortlessly pulling off many masks of personality and pretense that the pretenders themselves were not aware they had fabricated to manipulate those around them. It was a talent extremely useful for an attractive young girl to have.

That's why she had never trusted Sir Harvey Kinkaid. Her dad seemed to enjoy talking with Kinkaid about Oxford, and England in general, and also about Sir Harvey's son, Lyle, who was Khalid's old roommate from years ago—along with any news about Lyle's current endeavors in philosophy at Cambridge. But Kissa kept her distance as well as she could from the man. He seemed to have a dark and twisted soul beneath his elegant and engaging manners. In his presence, she was chilled, and she had to put on an inner armor not to feel actually harmed by what was within him, a force of sorts that always posed a threat of emanating outward, invisibly polluting and entangling the souls that were closest around him. It had already happened to poor Patrick O'Connor, his assistant at Rolls Royce. Just being in Kinkaid's presence over an extended period of time had subtly and insidiously twisted his sensibilities and judgments, from those of a person with normal ethical concerns, to a man now willing to do almost anything for power, money, or status among the equally or more corrupted souls of the world.

Of course, it wasn't just recognized Phi who had the ability to receive insight and guidance through meditative stillness and an open heart of willingness. All human beings, as King Ali had taught Walid, represent a royalty of the spirit who have come into this exotically strange, terrible, and wonderful world with a birthright that they rarely acknowledge, understand, or assert. And yet still, there are times when a man or a woman, or even, and perhaps more often, a boy or a girl, will be struck with a message from beyond the visible, tangible world of the senses, just out of the blue and with no preparation, anticipation, or warning.

This actually happens to all of us at some points in our earliest years, but we often later lose our memories of these experiences, as they're not reinforced for us by the surrounding culture. We're rarely encouraged to become all that we can be in the full range of our capacities, or to do all that we can do. And so, some of our innate abilities, a crucial part of our royal inheritance, will atrophy and grow weak over time. They will never completely disappear. They can't be utterly extinguished. That would mean the annihilation of the soul itself. But they can be hobbled and starved and buried under the debris of triviality and those worldly pressures that we too often refer to as the practical demands of life—as if life has any demands greater and more practical than that we be the best of who we are. We too easily and commonly adapt ourselves to the lowest ways of the kingdom of this world. We conform to patterns of activity and thought that are sometimes in themselves unproblematic, but only as long as they don't eclipse what's higher. And yet, we too often allow them to make us forget the royal palace of the spirit and the aligned rights, duties, and privileges that exist in connection with it deep within us, even though it is precisely these things that most essentially define at our core who we are.

Despite all this, those of us who do understand our nature should never be too quick to divide the world between the top royalty of the mind, epitomized by Phi—who seek to partake of everything within the spirit that's available to us—on the one hand, and on the other side, the great swath of human beings who seem to live as exiles from their own royalty, and act as if they are mere commoners of the spirit. There is, instead, a vast spectrum of openness and experience represented in the world. The spiritually powerful exist, certainly, at one end of the sweep, with the most sadly dimmed and brutish personalities at the far terminus. An ordinary person, who's never as ordinary as he or she might seem to superficial appearances, is capable of more depth and breadth than any casual acquaintance, or sometimes even a good friend, might expect. There are depths behind depths, and layers beneath layers and, if we could only see all the people around us through eyes that know and remember this, the world would look so different, and more like it indeed most fundamentally is.

And at this moment, that might explain Khata. Within four or five minutes of meditative sitting, she began to tune out the sand under her, the girls around her, the warm air of Memphis enfolding her, and the events and worries of the day that until now had held her captive in the urgency of their troubling appearances. She began to go deep. She didn't even understand what she was doing, but she was doing it, nonetheless. And that's how most worthwhile and important things happen in this world. Understanding is a wonderful and mighty gift, but action must often proceed without its full presence. No one person's state of insight, or lack of it, can ever define what's happening in the world, or even what's going on in her own mind.

Tears began streaming down Khata's face. She was receiving a form of knowledge beyond our normal categories and explanations and, along with it, a very rare sort of experience of the most complete empathy possible. She was feeling the rush of fear that Set and Jabari had felt when they kicked the truck doors open and Set had to pull the trigger that filled their ears with such a deafening sound. She sensed the keen ambivalence of exuberance and shock and grief that were intermingled in Set's heart when he saw that he had shot a man who intended him great harm. She also felt the shot, close up, through that other man's foot—with a mixture of the injured man's sharp anguish and Set's own confused distress blended with the thrill of possible escape. The panic inside Jabari as he shoved the screwdriver through another man's flesh caught in her throat. The jubilation of their release seized her heart, and the adrenaline that rushed through the boys as they had run coursed through her soul. And then the sharp, almost paralyzing terror that had iced them from gut to throat when they were captured took her almost beyond her ability to bear what she was sensing.

There's no good way to describe from the outside what Khata was experiencing. She was not exactly seeing an inner motion picture of these things. She couldn't have described as a witness all that had happened to the boys, blow by blow. She was just accessing somehow the swirl of feelings and thoughts that had touched these friends of hers who had been involved in those things, and it was now becoming too much for her to feel and bear, as her silent tears turned to quiet sobs.

Cabar was worried and even a little scared at seeing and hearing this. She reached over to Khata and said, "What is it? What's wrong?" The other three girls in their little group a few feet away turned and looked over at Cabar, and then Khata.

"I, I, can't … I … don't … know," Khata gasped. "But the boys are going through, I think, a lot." She sobbed more openly.

"I know, I know, but why are you crying right now? What made you break down just now?"

"I don't know. I sort of felt it all—what they're going through, I think. I felt it, and it was hard, and I just couldn't take any more, and … I just can't."

Then, in the next moment, Hoda was bending down beside her, and she touched her. And with that touch, a good strange warmth filled the girl and made the cold inside her go away. "Are you Ok, Khata?"

"Yeah," she blubbered. "I think so."

"What happened?"

"I felt it all, I think. I felt what Set and Jabari had been feeling, and some other men as well, the ones who have them now. There was fear and excitement and dread and exhilaration and pain and stuff I don't know names for, and I think they've been going through a lot."

"Are they Ok?"

"I think maybe they're Ok, but they've just been through a lot—too much, way too much." She gasped a deep and jerky breath. "They shouldn't have to go through so much."

"Are any of our friends with them?"

"Yes. They are now."

"Is everyone Ok?"

"I don't know. One of the others has just gone through a lot and I don't understand, and it confuses me."

"Do the boys have full protection now?"

"Yes. I mean, I think so. But there's still danger. Or, at least, it feels like danger."

"How do you know?"

"I don't know. I just think so, but I don't know why I think so."

"You just do?"

"Yeah. Yeah. I just do." She broke down again, crying loudly at this point, and she bent over, covering her face with her hands.

"It's Ok. It's fine. You've done something important."

Hasina and Kissa came over and sat down beside her. Most of the boys and men sitting nearby were looking over at them at this point with a feeling of concern. Hoda held up her arm and said more loudly, "Everything's all right over here. All will be fine. Please try to continue your sitting. Put us out of mind. Turn your backs on us physically if you must, and try to continue. Please."

The men did as she asked, and she put her hand on Khata's arm. "A good cry is healthy. It's your way of cleansing your spirit and clearing out the emotional clutter. It's a way of releasing the energy that came into you during your experience just now. Don't feel bad about it. Just let it go. Let it flow through you and then simply give it up. Let it go."

As Hoda spoke, Khata's crying began to calm a bit and then, for moments, to stop. And she took a deep breath. "I'm sorry," she said.

"There's no need to apologize."

"But."

"You just had quite a remarkable experience, and such things can easily push us to a limit and beyond. We grow through being pushed, but it's not always pleasant at the time. And to allow the feelings to flow through you like this is healthy and good."

"Ok."

"There is something you can do at this point that may be of help to the boys, and any of the men with them, if you'd like."

"Yeah, sure, what is it?"

"Concentrate all your mental and emotional energy on them, right now, wherever they are, and whatever's going on, and ask for a shield of protection around them to keep the danger in check that may exist for them. Ask for them, and send them, any healing they need, and success in their challenge. Believe that your noble request for them will be honored. Imagine strong protection and support all around them. Contribute in this small but powerful way to its reality."

"I can do that?"

"Yes. There's a power greater than you that touched you just now, and from that power, you have received. Now, through the same power, you can give. Every path can be taken in two directions. Send them what they need, on the path from here to there. And Kissa and Hasina with the other girls will join me and seek to do it alongside you. Hoda took Khata's hand. "Ten seconds to ask for them and send them protection and healing and success," she said. The girls were all quiet. They all concentrated and did as Hoda had suggested.

The seconds passed in silence, and then their teacher again spoke. "There. It's done."

"Really? Just like that?"

"Yes. Just like that."

"But how?"

"You're specially connected to the boys today and their situation. We're all linked with them, but you're joined with them in a special way right now. Your experiences and emotions have shown me that. And I know such connections. I have some history with them. I know that you've helped the boys and our men in the only way any of us can right now. You can feel better because of it. They will be better and feel better as a result. You're now allowed to feel positive and confident for them."

"Ok. Ok. Thanks, Hoda."

Hoda touched her head with a silent blessing. Kissa then leaned forward and hugged Khata. Cabar scrunched up close to her and put her arm around her, and Kit patted her lightly on the back. Ara and Hasina and Bakat reached in and touched her as well. Khata gave them all a weak smile and said, simply, "Sisterhood?"

"Yeah, sisterhood," Kit repeated.

"That's right," Bakat added.

Hasina put her hand lightly on Hoda's arm and whispered, "Can I talk to you for a minute?"

Hoda nodded and said, "Sure, let's walk a few feet over there." She first turned back to Khata. "You're Ok?"

Khata nodded her head and said, "I am, now. Thanks." Hasina got up, and so did Kissa. But, before they walked away, Hasina bent down and kissed Khata on the head. Then she joined Hoda and Kissa several feet away.

Hasina spoke in a low voice. "Something bad has happened in town—something very bad. It's one of the men. It's not Walid or Mafulla, or Set or Jabari."

"Yes. I think it may be Hamid," Hoda replied.

"I think you're right," Kissa said. "I mean, as soon as you said it, I got a feeling. Did you see something or sense something, too?"

"I felt something a few minutes ago, before I asked everyone to sit. And I saw a look on Malik's face," Hoda explained.

"I felt something, too. But I didn't know exactly what," Kissa said.

"Yeah. Me, too," Hasina added. "For me, it was almost like a second cousin to a bad, deep pain. And I just became very alert and aware for a couple of seconds." She sort of screwed up her face as she tried to articulate what she had experienced.

Hoda took a breath and said, "Well, there's no way to find out what's happened, unless one of us has a full, clear vision of it and, so far, that isn't happening, is it?"

"No," Hasina said, a bit perplexed.

"Not for me." Kissa agreed.

"Ok, I think I know what we need to do. Let me consult the group."

Hoda walked over and stood where she could speak to everyone at one time. "Excuse me! Everyone! If I could have your attention: First, I thank you all for these moments of meditative awareness. Please allow yourselves to come back to your normal consciousness, if you're not already there. I hope you feel a bit rested from the time of inner stillness. And if anyone has a word to pass on to me or the rest of us from the abundance of your quietness, you can speak it now."

She stood, waiting. The girls and boys and men looked at her, from their various, still seated positions. Strangely, right in that moment, it occurred to every single one of them anew how beautiful this woman was, and poised, glowing with grace and kindness, in addition to the physical attributes that so dramatically set her apart. She was a work of art, inside and out. Plato was right. Beauty can reach us like nothing else can, and when rightly received and appreciated, it can lead us to truth and goodness and the spiritual connectedness, or sense of unity, that we all long to experience. Not everyone looking at her in this moment was thinking all that, of course, but they were each having experiences of her distinctiveness.

Hoda was the embodiment, an incarnation or clear manifestation of something so far beyond the norm that it inevitably led the hearts and minds of well-disposed observers into something like a spiritual territory that they might not otherwise have visited. And her kindness was itself a thing of beauty, thoroughly consonant with her physical presence. She commanded attention in a most powerful way and, yet also, in the gentlest way. It was hard for anyone, man or woman, boy or girl, to look on her at certain times and not require a second or two just to take it all in, register it, and then return to whatever normal, ordinary state of consciousness had been put on hold for the experience, in order to be able again to act, or think, or talk in a way appropriate to the situation.

Khalid was the first to speak. Of everyone there, he had the highest and fullest appreciation of his wife's beauty, inside and out. He was in a sense the most impressed by it, because of how thoroughly he had known it, but he also knew how to experience it in an ongoing way and still function normally, at least, most of the time. And he was in that regard, as in a few others, nearly unique among men. So he was the first to come back to normal thought in the situation, and to be able to say something in response to her words and her request.

"I think we need to go back to the palace right away, and complete our trip later, at some future opportunity." He looked around.

"I agree," Reela said, surprised at the certainty behind his words.

Hoda looked across the group. "Everyone who also agrees, please raise your hand."

Each individual there raised a hand, including her. Several of the students felt an inner wave of keen disappointment that they'd miss Giza, and especially the fun of the barge trip down the Nile that they had so anticipated, but they all understood the seriousness of the situation and couldn't continue on with what they had planned while their friends were in such danger.

She spoke again. "Ok, at this point, I'm sure we're right to curtail the trip and plan on doing the rest of it as soon as we can. We still want to learn more about Memphis, and visit Giza as a combined class. And I think I'm not alone in my eagerness for some time on the Nile, returning home on the water as certain personages of the past so famously have done."

There was a lot of nodding going on among many in the group, and various comments of agreement could be heard all around.

Just the acknowledgment from Hoda about her own eagerness for what now would be missed helped validate their feelings and renew their hope for having, at some point, the other experiences they had looked forward to sharing.

"But for now, let's pack up quickly, and take the trucks back into town. I sense that we'll all have a safe and uneventful return, so there's no need for anyone to experience any anxiety about our travel today. The many challenges of getting here and being here over the past however many hours are all behind us now. It's certainly seemed like an exceptionally long and full two days already, and a good part of this day is still left."

"It's true," Khalid added.

Hoda smiled. "So, everyone, to work! Let's prepare to leave!" She said this in a very positive tone of voice, and then turned her attention to what needed to be done next. The first thing was actually to go over to Malik, who had stood up and walked a few feet away from his friends Haji and Bafur, and was now by himself.

"Malik, I saw a look on your face before we sat down. Are you Ok?"

"I don't know. I'm not sure. I feel kind of weird. You must have seen me a second after I felt a rush of something, something almost painful and then scary, and it was an inner jolt that put me on total alert, like my eyes and ears and sense of touch and everything were all being magnified five times normal. But I had no idea why. I felt something bad and then I didn't know what I felt. I'm maybe worried about dad and I hope he's Ok."

"Well, I think the men and boys in town must have had some action going on that many of us felt. We have some here who are very intuitive, and several of us, like you, have sensed something challenging, but no one has had any vision or clear sense of anything that we know to be extreme … or even … transitional—at least, not yet. So, maybe we can go about our business of getting the trucks packed without undue worry or concern. I know your dad is with a group of very strong and capable people that he can depend on, and he could be about the strongest and most capable of them all."

"I hope Masoon's there, too" Malik said. "Masoon's a rock."

Hoda paused for a couple of seconds and said, with a very slow and deliberate tone, "Yes. Now that you mention him, I think that Masoon is there with them all."

Malik just looked at her with an odd mixture of surprise and yet full acceptance, trailed by a sense of reassurance that was at the same time muted by perplexity and a still serious concern. Hoda thought to herself how young he was, and yet, how mature in the circumstances. She understood what he was going through, much better than he did, and she reached over to him and gave him a quick hug that brought with it a surge of warmth coursing through him, a deeper comfort and a reassurance that, whatever was happening, he could deal with it and accept it and be all right, regardless of what it was.

On the battleground of the warehouse in Cairo, where everything had been silent for the longest single second in the history of the world, Omari had just taken off to run toward the downed shooter, weapon out and ready for any next threat. He hadn't even seen Hamid.

Near the other side of the big open space, Masoon had leapt forward over the inert body of a fallen criminal and was dashing full speed across the large room toward his best friend, the one and only medical doctor on the scene—the sole individual there who was capable of dealing with the most serious and traumatic wounds of war. And this good, strong, and expertly trained physician had just fallen to his knees, on the verge of further collapse and covered in blood, in front of the prince he had been so determined to save.

At that very moment, in so far as true simultaneity is at all possible in our world, while time itself had appeared to slow down to allow for whatever should come to be, a third group of men rushed into the room through the door that Masoon had broken down. Instantly, Amon and two other men who were closest to the door turned in a defensive position, weapons aimed and ready to fire. But at the front of the group was Walid's father, Rumi Shabeezar, physician to the king and director of health and medicine for the entire kingdom. He and another man behind him were both holding medical kits and were followed by several others. What he saw as he entered the room brought a rush of what felt like the coldest possible ice water into his veins which, in the next split second, filled his whole body and mind.

No matter what the visceral reaction of the body is to a sight that stuns and evokes the sudden potential of a horrific turn of events, the well trained mind can fight back and ascend to its proper position and retake control, sometimes as soon as the very next moment. As Rumi moved faster to cross the big room, his mind experienced everything more slowly. And the rest of the warehouse disappeared in a foggy mist at the edge of his peripheral consciousness. It wasn't only the awful appearance of Hamid just now, in the past moment, fully fallen to the floor with Masoon bent over him, but the look on Walid's face, a few feet behind them, as he gazed in shock at his own left hand, now clearly covered in his own dark red blood.

18

The Cost of Honor

Whenever the stakes are high, waiting while not knowing requires a special kind of strength. Walid's mother, Bhati, was with the king in his private sitting room. She stood at the window and said, "I certainly hope Rumi's particular skills are not needed in this situation today, but also of course that if he is needed, he can be as effective as possible."

The king knew that his skills would be desperately needed. But he remained at peace about that insight and just said, "Those are good things to hope." He was also wishing for the best, but he realized that the best today would be something far less than could be desired.

"Has Naqid or anyone located Kinkaid?"

"Well, in a sense. We now know that he's staying at the Grand Hotel, as we suspected. But we've not been able to locate him physically in the last hour. Our men are in plain clothes at the hotel, waiting to take him into custody for questioning. But there's a chance he may come here voluntarily."

"Why in the world would he do that?"

"We had Darwishi send him a message that some advice is needed for a special car log, a perspective that only he can provide, and we know him to be intensely interested in the car logs."

"Oh?"

"Yes. And if he assumes we have no idea of his possible involvement in the events of today, then he may indeed be bold enough to drop by and answer Dar's question. Arrogance often sets people up for their own downfall. As you know, the Greeks frequently wrote about it. And if he comes here, he won't leave until we've had a chance to talk with him at length—if he in fact leaves at all."

"I'm just so sorry that Walid and Mafulla had to be caught up in this. They're too young to be fighting kidnappers to save their friends!"

"I know how you feel, and I partially can agree, but I can also assure you that they are, at this point, better trained in many of the best fighting techniques than most in our military."

"But they're so young."

"Yes, they are. And yet they're in great shape for such a day as this, both physically and mentally."

"Still."

"They're actually in peak condition. And it's been only a few months that Masoon's been working with them. But the work has been intense and productive. They're talented, quick learners, and he's the best possible guide."

"I do appreciate your asking him to do that. It's so important for a prince to be able to protect himself, if the need should arise."

"Yes, it is," the king agreed.

"But as a mother, I can't help but be concerned."

"I understand. But you should remember that those who are with the boys would never put them into harm's way unnecessarily. They'll have plenty of protection and support around them.

"Yes. I know. You're right." Bhati let out a deep breath.

Ali said, "I keep close tabs on such things, and know well both the strengths and boundaries that the boys have at present."

"I understand. But let me ask you something that just came to mind."

"Certainly."

"Should we let Mafulla's parents know what's going on?"

"Not yet, I feel. There's no reason I can think of to alarm them at present. Mafulla is most likely safe, as much as is possible in such a situation, and I would hate to cause his parents undue worry. He can share the story with them soon enough when he's back."

"You're right again, I'm sure. Mothers just think we want to know everything, but everything is not always good to know. If we had perfect control of our emotions, it would be different. But we don't."

"You mothers have perfectly natural emotions and attitudes. You typically have a sensitivity that we men would do well to share." The king smiled as he said this.

"Well, the truth is usually better than a lack of truth."

"You're absolutely right, I must say. But in this instance, where we don't yet have the full truth, there's really no need to share something partial that might cause unnecessary anxiety, or even anguish."

"Yes, I suppose I almost reluctantly agree. But I do agree. I enjoy the privilege of living in the palace and having you as my brother-in-law. I'm the mother of the prince. The many good aspects of all that tend to counter-balance the serious responsibility that goes with the territory. I understand how fraught our days sometimes can be. I get to know everything, and then to worry freely!"

The king laughed and said, "If any of us truly knew everything, we would never worry at all."

Bhati sighed. "I'm sure you're right, on a very deep level. Wasn't it the philosopher Francis Bacon who said, 'A little knowledge is a dangerous thing?'"

"He did express that sort of sentiment, whether in those exact words or not. If I recall it correctly, Bacon's famous statement on a related and important matter was that, 'A little philosophy inclineth man's mind to atheism; but depth in philosophy bringeth men's minds about to religion.' And that conveys, in the most fundamental domain of human reason, and on a particular ultimate issue of the utmost value, basically the same idea."

"I see the parallel."

"But, actually, I believe it was another Brit, Alexander Pope, who originally uttered the more closely worded sentiment that, 'A little learning is a dangerous thing.' He was, however, later misquoted by a man with exactly that amount of learning and the phrase, 'A little knowledge is a dangerous thing' has ever since been widely attributed to Pope, whenever it's not ascribed to Bacon. Whatever its true origin, it does capture a real insight."

"How in the world do you know all these things?"

"Far too many idle hours before ascending to my current schedule of far too few."

"Ah, yes. A little monarchy is a dangerous thing."

The king laughed. "To be sure."

"When will we know exactly what's going on with the rescue operation?"

"It shouldn't be much longer. I sent two groups of men into the situation, with instructions to the second group that someone needs to return with a report as soon as something concrete is known and it's safe to leave the scene to bring us word. I want intelligence as quickly as I can get it, of course, but I didn't want anyone leaving a sensitive situation in such a way as to compromise anyone else who's there."

"I understand completely. That's a wise way to proceed."

Kular came to the door and stuck his head in. "Your Majesty, the school group that initially remained in Memphis has just now returned on the trucks. The students will be entertained in the first-floor sitting rooms, and the adults, other than the soldiers, of course, will be coming to see you momentarily."

"Good. Please show them in as soon as they arrive."

"Yes, Your Majesty. It will be my pleasure."

"I'm glad they're back," Bhati said. I'm eager to hear first hand what happened in Memphis."

The king remarked, "I'll have Kular bring in some tea and cookies for everyone."

"None for me, I'm afraid. I'll be too distracted until Walid returns."

Ali nodded, and walked over to the door to open it. He said, "Kular, could you bring me some tea and assorted cookies? Enough for perhaps three or four adults."

"Yes, Majesty. Right away," Kular responded. And then he said, "Oh! Here they are, now."

Khalid came into Kular's reception room first and said, "I've never been more glad in my life to walk into the palace."

The head royal butler responded, "We're also glad you're here, and the king's expecting you. Please go right in, Khalid and Hoda, and Mr. Adi. I'll have some refreshments for you in a moment."

"Thanks," Khalid said as he held open the inner door for Hoda and Reela to precede him into the king's quarters.

"There you are, friends. Please come in and sit," the king said.

"We've had quite a day and a half," Khalid responded, "but of course, not the ordeal today that some of our students and other friends are having. Do you know what's going on?"

"We know a good bit. Here, sit."

"What can you tell us, Your Majesty?"

"Less than I would wish."

"Well, we're eager to hear anything."

The king replied, "We figured out that the Falma operation might be behind all this, so I sent a rescue team into the warehouse district where he's hidden out and operated before. You know how habit is."

"Yes."

"Masoon is leading the first team. Then it occurred to me to send a second squad to back them up. Rumi is helping to lead that group. I've instructed the second wave to send word of news as soon as they safely can."

"Good, but there's nothing yet?"

"No, nothing yet. I'd be surprised, though, if we have to wait much longer," the king said.

Khalid replied, "As I'm sure you know, Your Majesty, Hamid, Omari, Walid, and Mafulla volunteered to chase the kidnappers in one of the trucks and follow them into town. I hope the teams all find each other, but more than that, I certainly hope someone can find Set and Jabari quickly and retrieve them unharmed!"

Bhati said, "Ali told me about Walid and Mafulla. And you know how a mother worries."

"They were eager to go out in pursuit," Reela told her, adding, "Hamid and Omari assured me that they would all stay together and be safe."

"Yes. Despite my natural concern, I trust that things will work out as they should."

The king said, "I have a feeling that, with the individuals who are on the teams, the kidnappers will not be able to evade our rescue effort and that, quite soon, it will prove fruitful. But of course, there's nothing like news from the front to assure us all."

Just then, they could all hear a loud voice outside, saying, "I have urgent news for the king! Yes, thank you." The door flew open and a young man of about twenty-one stood before them, slightly out of breath. "Your Majesty!"

The king rose up from his chair. "What news do you bring us?"

"We found them! We've rescued the boys! It was Idi Falma and his gang. He's Ari Falma's brother. We had to gun him down. He shot at the prince, and Hamid put his body in the way."

"What?" Bhati exclaimed.

The king asked, "How is Hamid?"

"I believe he took the bullet."

"Meant for my son?

Before the messenger could answer, Ali said, "How badly is he injured?"

"I had to leave before finding out the seriousness of his wound. But he looked pretty bad. Rumi's with him and Masoon's there with him."

"Is everyone else Ok?"

"The prince may have been shot, as well."

"No!" Bhati said, with a look of complete shock. She put her hand on the edge of the table next to her and gripped it.

The soldier said, "I'm so sorry. I'm not sure of that, but I think that maybe he was. But he was still standing when I left, and he was bent over a bit, unlike Hamid, who had collapsed on the floor, covered in blood."

"Oh, no."

The king touched Bhati's arm and said in a tone of kindness, "Be strong. We'll prevail."

"But."

"There are no more details?"

The messenger explained. "I left the moment we saw these things happen, understanding that you would want to know, as quickly as possible. I dared not wait for more outcomes, thinking you might want to go to the place as soon as you could. And I can take you."

"Do so. Take us now, please," Bhati said.

"Yes. Immediately," the man replied. The king took Bhati's arm and led the way out the door, with everyone following. He quickly turned to Hoda and said, "Someone needs to stay with the students, to keep them from worrying. Could you?"

"Yes, Your Majesty. I'll be glad to. Just be careful."

As they walked through the anteroom and into the hallway, Bhati asked the messenger, "Did my son look all right?"

He replied, "Well, as I said, the prince was standing when I saw him, but he was bent over. He had some blood on him, but not a lot, and he was still upright. I think he had fought bravely for his friends."

"We have to get to him, quickly." Bhati said in a low and serious voice. "How far away are they?"

"Ten minutes or so by fast car or truck," the man explained.

As they passed two palace guards down the hall, the king said, "Come with us now."

"Yes, Your Majesty, as you wish," one of them replied.

Hoda split off from the group at this point and went to rejoin the students downstairs where they were waiting. She had a strange mix of feelings that she didn't quite understand. Something dramatic and perhaps decisive was going on at this very moment.

Masoon was a good medic with a great deal of field experience, but he was not a trained doctor like Hamid. He was so focused on his friend that he hadn't seen Rumi come into the warehouse. But just at that moment, Rumi said to him, "More help is here," and dropped his bag next to Masoon, handing the warrior a small pouch. "Put this in Hamid's hand or in his pocket. I'll be right with you to help deal with the problem. And keep the blood flow under control as you can."

"He took a bullet meant for Walid, I think," Masoon said quickly.

The younger man who had entered with Rumi, carrying a second medical bag, now bent down to Hamid, as the head doctor took two more steps to the prince, who was, indeed, still standing. "Son, what happened?"

"I … don't … know. I felt a sting in my side, and reached down, and now, there's this blood." He held his hand up to his father.

"Let me see." Rumi glanced at the hand and then looked at Walid's side, where there was more blood.

"And I feel strange," The prince said. "I'm a little dizzy."

"Sit down, my boy." Rumi helped him to the floor, just as Mafulla came up.

He said, "What happened? Is Walid Ok?"

"Just a second, Mafulla," Rumi replied. "Just give me a second to figure this out." He pulled at some wet, blood-soaked cloth that was stuck to Walid's skin.

"Ouch!"

"I'll be very careful. Let me look at your side." He cut the fabric away and quickly examined the wound.

Walid grimaced and said, "Ow. Ow. Ow."

"Oh, my."

"What?" Mafulla said. What is it?"

"This is very good. A bullet only grazed you, it seems. It broke the skin and caused some bleeding, but it's done no bad internal damage. Here, hold this cloth on it. I have to get to Hamid, who, I believe, took the main force of the bullet for you and saved your life."

"Is he Ok?"

"I can't tell yet."

Rumi turned to where Masoon was bent down over Hamid. The general was saying, "My friend, can you speak? Can you speak to me? Hamid!"

"Where … the … prince?" Hamid formed the words with the only faint sound he could muster.

"He's fine," Rumi said. "I hear you saved him. He was slightly grazed by the bullet you diverted. I need to see your wounds."

Masoon had already begun cutting some of Hamid's clothing off him to expose where the entry wound might be. Rumi now said, half to Masoon, and half to Hamid, "There's too much blood, my friend. Far too much."

"Not all … mine," Hamid nearly whispered. Masoon then moved aside more so that Rumi could examine the injury. The doctor bent over and split the cloth more that was in the way.

"Ah, I see. Ok, Ok, then. But where did the? Oh, yes, there it is. There it is." Rumi took a deep breath and expelled it. "My good man, you took a very serious hit from a high caliber bullet.

It apparently passed all the way through you with such force, it was able to lightly wound Walid behind you. But I think it hit no crucial organs in your body. And you kept it from almost certainly killing my son. You deflected and slowed the round. And your body was clearly in the perfect position and angled just right so that the round wasn't fatal for you. You're a major hero today, as you have been on many days before." Rumi was saying this as he was digging through the medical bag, removing supplies, and going to work on his friend.

Masoon smiled at hearing this. "You're one tough and lucky Phi, as most people would say."

"I feel lucky … today," Hamid croaked out. "Where can I … place a bet? Or apply for a different job?" Masoon just shook his head.

"Stop talking," Rumi instructed him. "Save your strength."

He turned and said, "Masoon, where's the little pouch I gave you?"

"In his pocket."

"Good. It belongs to him for the time being. It's his. Make sure it stays with him."

"I'm glad you brought it."

Yes, it's good to have it and use it."

"So he's going to be Ok?"

"Yes, he is. I'm pleased to say that I can deal with this—with the help of our legendary stone." Rumi began to tear off some gauze and, looking at his patient, said, "Hamid, my friend, the good news is that you won't die. Well, not at least, from this. But, one day, as we say. The bad news is that today, and for a few more days, you'll feel a lot of pain. Any bullet that goes all the way through you will do some bad damage, but as I said, it seems that, remarkably, there are no vital organs involved in a serious way, and I'm confident that what can be repaired will be repaired, and the damage will heal."

"Good."

"You'll just have another couple of impressive scars to take their proper place within your overall collection."

"Those are my trophies," Hamid croaked out.

"Yes, and they should be seen that way. I'm just surprised that you're not unconscious from the force and shock of it all, but that's a senior Phi for you," Rumi said, as he continued to work. He was chattering on partly from his own nervous energy, with the great relief he felt, and partly to soothe his friend, who must have had quite an intense experience, thanks to the late Idi Falma.

"The guy, the gun," Hamid said.

The second medic, the one who had arrived with Rumi, had made his own quick inquiry and now said, "The guy's dead, Idi Falma, and the gun's in our possession." He then added, "It was a high powered sniper rifle."

Rumi said, "Then you indeed were in the right place at exactly the right time, and your body was in the best possible position for what you were trying to do, as well as for keeping the cost of your honor from being far too high today, or we would not be having this chat with each other right now. The price of your amazing action is still great, as you'll feel for some time to come, but I'd wager that your investment here will have great returns for many years in the future."

A couple of minutes earlier, Set had walked up to Walid and bent over and said, "Prince! I'm so, so, sorry."

"Hey man. Don't worry. I'm going to be Ok."

"Good."

"I'm just glad you are, too."

"Yeah, thanks to you guys. But what happened?"

"Dad said I was just grazed. Hamid got into the line of fire and took the main force of the bullet for me."

"Oh man!"

"This whole thing could have turned out way differently, and much, much worse."

"Yeah. But how's Hamid?"

"It looks like he's going to be Ok, too. Badly injured, for sure, but basically Ok—as in, alive. I could hear most of what Dad's been saying to him. He's got no major internal organ damage."

"Good. That's a relief."

"He saved my life."

"For sure, and you all saved mine, and Jabari's."

"Where is Jabari?" Walid looked around.

"I don't know," Set said. "Probably sitting with Manni somewhere, maybe in the hallway, trying to calm him down. I think the monkey freaked out even more than the rest of us when those guns all went off at about the same time. He leaped all the way from jungle jitters to primate pandemonium in less than half a second, for sure."

Walid smiled and took a deep breath to help manage the stinging pain of the gash in his side. And Set was right. Jabari was sitting out in the hallway by himself with Manni, stroking the little guy's fur and saying "Good monkey, good monkey." Neither of them saw the man with a gun silently slip around the corner behind them and point it at Jabari's head until he said, "You just took away my future, so I'm taking away yours."

"Oh!" Jabari yelled out. There was a sharp pop as he fell to his left and Manni screeched again. Unknown to their anonymous assailant, Jabari, who was stroking his pet monkey with his left hand, still had a revolver in his right hand that, as he rolled over, came into view, and there was another loud bang that dropped the man where he stood. The last bullet in the gun suddenly had become surprisingly useful, and of especially high value.

Set, Paki, and Amon were the first through the door and into the hall where they saw the aftermath of this scene. Manni was running around in small, tight circles and doing a low volume screech while Jabari lay on his side with a bullet hole in the wall right behind him, about exactly where his head had been, moments earlier.

"Jabari! Are you all right?" Set yelled, as Paki and Amon held their guns on the assailant, now lying motionless.

"Oh my goodness, my goodness, my goodness," Jabari said. "I didn't expect that—not for one second, no, not that. But yes, yes, thank you, I think I'm fine, because of that gun you gave me." He suddenly laughed out loud. "It was the one that had only one bullet in it. I'd put down the full gun, the one from Mafulla, and was holding the almost empty one, just sitting here and feeling what we had been through today. The guy appeared out of nowhere and said we had taken away his future and he was going to take away mine, and as soon as he said it, I rolled left toward Manni and pulled up the gun and, for the first time in my entire life, I pulled a trigger."

"Good shot," Set said.

"Thanks. Beginner's luck."

"It couldn't have come at a better time."

"It was a better time to begin than to end."

"Yeah. That's for sure."

By now, almost everyone but Walid, Hamid, Masoon, and Rumi was standing in the hall with the boys and the two Phi guards, Paki and Amon, who were now talking about what had just happened. Paki had checked on the assailant and retrieved his gun, and knew that he was no longer a threat.

But again, there was suddenly the sound of numerous loud footsteps approaching, and the door down the back hallway swung open. And both Phi present with Jabari, along with everyone else holding a weapon, wheeled around and prepared to let loose with a barrage that would end the possibility of any more harm to the side of the good on this day. But the first one through the door was Ali, and everyone immediately breathed a sigh of relief and lowered their weapons and bowed at his presence. Following him were Bhati, Khalid, Reela, and three palace guards with guns drawn.

"It's all clear," Omari called out.

"Where's Walid?" Bhati said.

"He's fine and just inside," Paki replied and motioned the way.

She ran down the hall, through the door, and into the big open space where Walid was still sitting on the floor. "Oh, my son! Are you all right? Were you shot?" She bent down and kissed him and put her arms around his shoulders, but was afraid to hug him, not knowing the location of his wounds.

"I'm fine, mother. I'm fine."

"What happened?"

"I just have a surface graze wound in my left side, thanks to the heroics of Hamid, who saved me from a high caliber bullet that could have taken my life in an instant."

"Oh! He's such a good man!" She gasped and began silently to cry. With a tear streaming down each cheek, she asked, "Where is he?"

Walid pointed and said, "Right behind you. Right there, with Dad and Masoon."

"Oh! I didn't see anything but you and the men who are attending to him. Let me thank him. I'll be right back," she said to Walid. She moved over to the fallen warrior, and bent down over him. His eyes were open and he was already looking much better than when Masoon had first seen him. "Hamid, you wonderful, good, strong, and courageous man! Thank you from the bottom of my heart for saving my son—our son, and the future king! We all love you and honor you, and appreciate you!"

"I'm glad I could help," Hamid said slowly. "He's a good one, the best prince we could have. He deserves a long life."

"Who did this?" she asked.

"He's over there. Dead and gone," Masoon said. "Idi Falma's his name. He'll no longer bother anyone in this world."

"Oh, I must go to see him," she said.

"Are you sure?"

"Yes. He tried to kill my son." She walked across the open area, straight over to the body and looked down, with a strange mixture of grief, anger, and compassion for a life that was lost in so many ways.

She spoke aloud, but softly. "God bless your soul. You were overcome by evil. But may it be so no more. May you be changed into the spirit you could have been. May you be embraced and forgiven and transformed beyond the delusions and corruptions that held you in chains. May perfect love now take you and remake your soul." Those were her only words as she stood and looked over the body for a few more seconds, and then walked away.

One nearby soldier picking weapons up off the floor had paused and overheard her, and he marveled at her words. Something strange and holy had just happened in that place.

The king was talking to Omari, Paki, and Amon out in the hallway, and then turned and walked through the door into the main part of the warehouse where the brief battle had taken place. He surveyed it all and then walked over to Walid. He said, "There's nothing quite like a field trip to liven up the week, is there?"

"Don't make me laugh!" Walid replied, while bouncing with a suppressed chuckle and holding his side. "That hurts!"

"Everything that hurts us can teach us," the king replied with a smile.

"Yes."

And then the wise man said, "I'm very, very proud of you and of what you've done today. You were brave and acted honorably."

"Thank you, Your Majesty. I'm sorry you missed the excitement," Walid responded.

"I am, as well."

"Thanks for coming."

"Yes. How's Hamid?" The king asked, as he glanced toward the Phi doctor lying on the floor, under the ongoing care of Rumi and Masoon.

"I think he'll be fine. He's badly hurt with a bullet wound that went straight through him, but dad says he's going to heal, and that he saved my life by his heroic action of getting between me and the gunman who was determined to kill me when his plan went wrong. He was also going to kill Set and Jabari. These were bad people."

"They were certainly people who allowed themselves to do many bad things. Most of them have been sent to their ultimate judgment and final opportunity," the king said, as he took Walid's hand. "The men whose lifeless bodies lie here today will no longer threaten the people and the life here that they could never understand or properly embrace."

"Yes. It's sad; and yet, that result is good."

"But my friend, I must ask you one thing, and it's urgently important."

"What is it, Uncle? Ask anything."

"Do you think that Kinkaid was involved in this?"

19

Tying Up Loose Ends

Sir Harvey Kinkaid had left the Falma warehouse no more than a minute or two before the rescue operation had begun. He got into his car in a serious funk of disappointment and irritation and just drove away—unaware of what was going on back inside the building that he had hoped would hold a quick key to the next stage of his plans. This had all seemed like such a sure thing. But anything worth doing is typically going to be harder than we might wish, he thought to himself with a twinge of disgust as he accelerated down the street and made a turn. So, now, he would go to the next step in his original strategy.

He had received a message earlier, right before he left the hotel, that the king's chief driver had a question about the Rolls Royce car logs, and it involved a matter that was sensitive enough for him to go in person to deal with it. The logs were now again crucial to his strategy, since the episode in Memphis had not worked out as he had hoped.

His drive around the block and down another street in the district took him toward the palace by a route different from the one being driven by the king's assault teams. He had skipped lunch today and was feeling the consequences, and so decided, before the next errand, to stop into a café near the palace for a quick bite. He pulled the car over, parked, and found a table at the popular spot. Without even looking at a menu, he ordered and had a small lunch before he continued on to the palace. He had no idea what the full consequences of his little break would be.

When he arrived at the palace gate and was admitted quickly onto the grounds as someone expected at the garages, he went straight up the drive to Darwishi's office. Three palace guards dressed as maintenance men saw him approach. The back gate had already sent word to the other gate guard stands that a lockdown was now in effect. No one was to leave by car or foot until Naqid gave the order. Unaware of all this, he parked outside the garages and sat for a second, thinking of how he might gain some extra information today.

Kinkaid then got out of his car and walked up to the door of the head driver's small office. He knocked and on hearing the muffled words "Come in," he opened the door to see Darwishi and another man going over some paperwork.

"Greetings, my good fellow," Kinkaid said, as he stuck his head through the doorway. "I just got your note a while ago, and my schedule allowed me to stop by and offer any help you may need."

"Oh, good. I'm glad you could come. There are some very important questions we knew you could help resolve."

"I'm always glad to be of assistance," Kinkaid replied.

"Please come in and sit down." Darwishi flashed a quick smile and gestured toward the chair next to his desk.

"Thank you."

"Are you continuing to enjoy the town throughout your current visit?"

"Why, yes, indeed I am. I'm discovering a few watering holes I didn't know about previously, and a lively place for evening entertainment."

"Good! There's so much in the city to discover. Is that young fellow O'Connor with you on this visit?"

"Yes, he is. He's back at the hotel now, working on some plans for one of our ventures. The young squire has become quite a city boy, but he also puts in long hours. I don't know what I'd do without him."

"I know what you mean. We all need help. And as the years pass, it becomes increasingly important."

"Indeed. And now, speaking of help, I believe the message I received at the hotel mentioned your need for some guidance on the car logs."

"Oh, yes, I needed to summon you here, and that seemed the best way to get your attention and insure that you might stop by today."

"I'm sorry. Excuse me?"

"We do need to ask you some questions."

"About the logs?"

"It's about what may be a related issue. But I'm not good at this sort of thing, so let me have a colleague come in for a moment, if you don't mind." Kinkaid was seriously perplexed by this enigmatic remark and didn't know what to say in reply. Darwishi rose out of his chair and walked to the door, cracked it open just a bit, and said, "Naqid, would you care to join us now?"

The head of the palace guards came into the office, followed by two other men. He said, "Thanks, Dar. If you'd like to take a break, we've had your visitor's car moved into the garage for an inspection."

"What?" Kinkaid could make no sense of what was being said. "What's going on here?"

Naqid continued to speak to the head driver. "You might want to supervise that. And be completely thorough."

"Good idea," Darwishi said, and left the room.

"Now, wait. What's this all about? I must protest," Kinkaid said as he began to stand up.

But one of the guards with Naqid put a hand firmly on the man's shoulder and, in a voice of cold intimidation that was not masked at all by the formal courtesy of his language, said, "Please, we must insist that you remain comfortably seated."

Naqid pulled Darwishi's desk chair out and arranged it so that he could sit facing Kinkaid, about four feet away from him. At first, he sat silently, just staring at Sir Harvey, as if examining him.

"What do you want with me?"

Naqid continued to be silent, unmoved, and intense in his focus now on Kinkaid's eyes. Kinkaid spoke again, "Oh. All right, I see. Interrogation Technique Number One. Surprise me. Make me uncomfortable. Create a tension in the room that will lead me to break the silence, such as I'm doing now—the theory being that, once I'm talking to fill the void, I'll lose a bit of control over what I say, and you can more easily manipulate me into giving you the information that it might be in my best interest to withhold."

"Impressive," Naqid said. "As I would have expected."

"I have many years of training in this, sir—decades, in fact."

"Good. I actually prefer to deal with a seasoned professional who understands the various stages that a lack of cooperation will lead us through. It's much more efficient. It saves my time and yours. And it often helps us avoid any degrading twists and turns and otherwise unpleasant developments that neither of us would welcome."

"Then we'll play no time-consuming games. What do you want from me?"

"I want to know what your involvement has been in the events of this day, stretching from Memphis to here in the city."

Kinkaid was inwardly surprised, and a touch nervous. He said, "I have no idea what you're talking about."

"Yes, you do."

"Now, you're wasting your own time as well as mine, I'm afraid."

"Not according to the testimony of a couple of direct witnesses, who've already told us plenty."

"What do you mean? What witnesses?"

"The prince himself saw your car outside 1618 Rue de L'Or today in the warehouse district. And there was no activity at that address except for an unfortunate and desperate criminal act of kidnapping in progress."

"The prince?" Kinkaid showed surprise, and then recovered and said, "Whatever was seen, it wasn't my car. As you know, I drive a quite common model of automobile when I'm in town."

"Is that model and color also driven by other Brits here in the city?"

"What? How would I know? I have no idea. Why do you ask?"

"Because another witness heard a British accent, and apparently your voice in that building, speaking about the kidnapping. He actually heard you identity two boys as not being the kidnap victims you had intended and requested. And he clearly heard you make the sadly unfortunate suggestion that they be … eliminated. It sounded to him like you were in charge of the entire operation and had become quite frustrated at the unexpected turn it had taken."

"My voice." Kinkaid laughed and said, "Every citizen of the crown from my part of the world sounds alike to many in yours who lack a certain sort of auditory discernment. I'm sorry that one of my fellow Brits was perhaps involved in a crime like kidnapping in your fair city, but I can assure you that it was not I."

"What have you been doing today?"

"Just normal things. Errands. Some paperwork."

"Do you have witnesses who could place you somewhere else than at 1618 Rue de L'Or within the past couple of hours?"

"I'm sure there are many witnesses to my whereabouts, but I've been on the move and focused on my own purposes and would not be able to name any individuals, other than my assistant O'Connor, who was with me earlier today, through most of the hours."

"Well, I'm not at all surprised that the only alibi you can provide involves your own assistant, since we have three witnesses who clearly saw you at the address on Rue de L'Or. You see, as you know, there was a large criminal gang operating there today, and I'm afraid most of them are no longer with us, having been—what was your word? Oh, yes, eliminated. But there were a few who managed to survive the events of the day and, under questioning, it seems that three of them have confirmed the other witnesses and identified you as the mastermind behind the entire operation."

"Rubbish. Absurd. A ridiculous tale."

"Or, perhaps I should be more precise. It seems that you suggested the operation, hired the late Idi Falma to undertake it, and were very disappointed when the wrong boys were captured."

"The late Idi Falma? I have no idea what you mean."

"Yes you do. And he committed his last crime today, I'm pleased to report."

"Oh. Well. I've heard the name somewhere."

"I know you have, often. Idi Falma and Harvey Kinkaid operating as partners. Who would have guessed?"

"I, sir, am a knighted British citizen and the top representative of the magnificent Rolls Royce in this region, and I would thank you not to mention common criminals in association with my good name."

"I think our interview, for now, is over. These gentlemen will take you to your new home, which should be sufficiently unpleasant for you."

"What are you talking about? This is outrageous!"

"You'll have plenty of time in our palace jail, and later in a less civilized alternative location, to reconsider your life choices and recent allegiances. In any case, you'll need something to occupy you for the many years, or in fact perhaps decades, that you'll be staying in these new quarters, depending on your general health and your ability to slog on in rather Spartan and less than desirable conditions. Contemplating alternative life scenarios may take up at least some of the otherwise endless and agonizing hours you have coming up there. And of course, we'll notify your employer of your change of address and circumstances. Thank you for your time."

Kinkaid sat in an angry and nearly panicked silence. He fought for mental clarity. There were three of them. One was big. And they were all armed. He noticed the sort of holster one of the guards was wearing, and the make of his sidearm in it. The right sort of sudden action might gain him access.

"Oh, I almost forgot," Naqid said, as he stepped between Kinkaid and the guard whose gun he had been studying. "And, you should pay close attention to what I'm about to tell you." Kinkaid was surprised and looked up. "If you should decide to come clean about all this and implicate any other individuals involved in your recent mischief, and especially if you'd be so kind as to save us a lot of time and energy and explain to us any broader plan within which you've been working, then we might be able to improve your future living circumstances considerably. And the sooner you choose to cooperate, the better those conditions might be. A continued lack of candor in these matters will lead, I'm afraid, to very disappointing results for you."

The man being addressed was now silent. Naqid looked up at the door and said in a loud voice, "Enter!" Three more guards came in. He then looked again at Kinkaid and said to the men, "Take him away, in suitable restraints."

Ari Falma sat in his own office going over some reports, three blocks from the warehouse on Golden Street. A man came up to the door. He knocked on the doorframe and said, "Boss, you want me to go check on Idi and the men and see how things are going over there?"

"Yeah. Thanks for reminding me. I need to talk to my brother for a few minutes, if you could get him for me. Send him here and you can stay there at the warehouse until he gets back, and watch to see if anyone tries to leave while he's gone."

"Ok, I can do that."

"And if anyone does leave, have one of our inner circle follow up at a distance, and report back where he goes."

"Will do."

"Good. Run down there and tell Idi I need to see him now. We've got to do just a little more planning on our sting operation, and I want his thoughts on how we can best bring Anwar in on this. He knows the guy better than I do. It's important that we find the leak we have, and I want those viper and storm guys off the street and out of our hair for good."

"Sure."

"Oh, one more thing."

"What?"

"Bring back some food. Idi always has food around. Get enough for me and you and the other guys here at the office. I haven't had time for lunch today and at this stage I'm starting to feel the results, and that puts me in a mood. I wouldn't want needless deaths to occur."

The man laughed. "You're funny, boss. When you starve, other people die. I get it. I'll go over there and be back as soon as I can."

Masoon had already left with Rumi to take Hamid to the university hospital where he could be treated further for his injury. The king had gathered all the other men and the boys. Three captives had been bound and gagged after a quick and intensive interview that had provided just the information that was needed, and word had been sent back to the palace for Naqid.

The king then explained that he wanted everyone out of the building as quickly as possible, and in their trucks away from the location, except for a few men to be stationed across the street, well hidden, to watch for any comings and goings throughout the rest of the day. These few were not to stop or detain anyone, just observe and follow any visitor, whenever he left the building. The rest of the group would return to the palace with their prisoners.

There was work to be done back there, and fellow students who would want to know that everyone is safe. Walid would be treated and bandaged again in the palace infirmary and then would be free to go about his day.

They were to leave everything as it was, until the observation team had been able to gather more information or determine that there was no more to be had. Everyone quickly left the building and got into the waiting trucks and drove off, leaving a team of three soldiers nearby to watch the place. And they had barely gotten set up in another abandoned building across the street, up on the second floor with a good view of 1618, when they saw Ari Falma's man walking briskly down the road and toward the warehouse. They watched him enter the front door and not more than a minute later, they saw him walk quickly back out and then jog, headed back down the street, looking over his shoulder, left and right as he nearly broke into a run.

One member of the observation team had at that point already made his way back down to the first floor where he concealed himself near the door with a view of 1618. When he saw the man flee the building, he quietly crept out from his hiding place and, at a proper distance, followed him, once he had turned a corner and disappeared from the street. Falma's man had slowed back down now and was again just walking fast, and yet was in such a total panic that he had no idea he was being followed. After initially glancing around him when he left the warehouse to make sure he was not in imminent danger, he just took off to get out of there and get to Ari with the horrible news as soon as he could. He was at this point looking straight ahead, as if to make it impossible to see anything else but where he was heading.

Falma was counting out some money in a box when the man came in, breathlessly exclaiming, "They're dead! They're dead! They're all dead!"

"What?"

"Your brother is dead in a pool of blood! His men are dead in the warehouse!"

"What are you saying?"

"Idi was shot many times. Many times. All over."

"What?"

"Idi's dead! And other men were shot. One was stabbed. Others were killed in different ways, I think. I don't know, but everyone I saw was dead." The man was out of breath and frightened beyond words. At that point, he bent over to catch his breath and said, "It was terrible."

Falma had jumped up from his chair. "Who could have done this?"

"I don't know. I don't know. It's the worst thing I've ever seen."

Falma felt a wave of fear course through his body. "Farouk, Farouk did such a thing to my men before, but he's nowhere near here. He's out of the kingdom, and he'd know nothing about our business now. It can't have been that animal Farouk—but then, who? Who?"

"I tell you, I don't know!"

"Was there any evidence?"

"Nothing. Nothing. Just blood everywhere, and one knife on the floor, and two guns and, two pieces of dark cloth that could have been blindfolds or masks or something."

"Masks? You said masks?"

"Yes, they could have been masks, but they were just lying on the floor close together."

"There were masks on the floor?"

"Yes, I think. Two of them."

"Masked men! Oh. No! The Viper and the Storm!"

"What?"

"They know we're trying to capture them! They somehow know! They've struck first! They've killed my brother and everyone else!"

"But they've never killed before."

"How do we know that? We don't know that. We have no idea who they are or what they do or how they do it, or why they do it. They're a mystery. And now they've killed my brother and my men. We know nothing else about them!" The words tumbled out of Ari's mouth.

"No, boss, we don't. You're right."

"You said it yourself, they left masks on the floor."

"Yeah, they did. There were those masks on the floor and they wear masks, and who else does that in a warehouse full of dead men?"

"The Viper and the Storm have decided not just to stop our robberies, but to eliminate us altogether, as we had planned to eliminate them!"

"We're next! I'm sure we're next. We have to be next. They wouldn't leave unfinished business."

"Get the others now. We have to tell them."

"But is that a good idea? Is it safe now, to be all together in one room, like Idi's men were all together in one place?"

"No, you're right. You're right. But then, what should we do?"

"I have no idea, boss. You're the one with the brains. You decide." At this point the man was frantically pacing around, while Falma stood in place, almost unable to move. He slapped his hand on the desk in front of him.

"We had a beautiful plan! We had many great plans! Now we have to abandon all the plans to protect our own miserable skin!"

"We need to get out of here!"

"Yes. We need to get out of this wretched, cursed place! I hate this place! Who are these masked men? Where are they?"

"I have no idea, but they may be close. They were three blocks away! Three blocks! They found Idi. They can find us! They may already have found us. We should leave and go to your house. We can't be here. They have to be nearby. If we have a leak that lets them know when and where we're going to strike, that person can tell them everything! They'll know about this office!"

"They what?"

"They'll know about this office. I'm sure they will."

"This is awful! You're right. We have no protection here. The reason we chose this place is that there are no police around, and now we of all people, masters of crime, haters of the police—we need police protection. It's just so stupid. It's evil."

"Yeah, it's crazy. But we should stop talking about it and get out of here."

Falma was almost in a trance. He said, "It's absurd. And the leak could be anyone! It could be you!"

"It's not me! I'm helping you! I'm the one telling you!"

"Ok, Ok. You're right. But we can't trust anyone else."

"That's true."

"Forget everyone else who's in the building. Forget any men who weren't killed today. One of them is the leak, the traitor. Just you and me, we gotta go now."

Falma and his lackey left as quickly as they could, yelling out to some other men in the far back of the building that they'd be back soon. They were convinced that more than half of their entire organization had just been eliminated by the two masked crime fighters they had targeted, men who had themselves now clearly crossed a line and become killers of the killers who were to be crucial links in the chain that was supposed to be able to pull everything together. Shock and fear were clouding the thoughts of these two, but still, their frantic reasoning made sense.

One problem that Ari Falma was experiencing in his reaction to this completely unexpected situation is that we all tend to interpret the world through what's already on our minds. The Viper and the Storm had been weighing on his mind. He'd been obsessing about them. They'd become a major distraction and had haunted his thoughts at all hours.

The thing is that we always approach the unknown through the known, or at least through what we believe we know. We mold and seek to shape the unfamiliar with the familiar. We try our best, at a subconscious level, to use our ordinary categories to deal with unsettling and extraordinary situations. It's completely natural and often can be helpful to operate in such a way. But there are many occasions where this automatic tendency can actually keep us from understanding the reality that we in fact confront, and it leads us in a direction that's unconnected to the true course of events.

Falma and his one trusted associate jumped into a car and sped away as fast as possible, without drawing any undue attention to themselves. They were headed to Ari's rented house, and had no idea what they'd do when they arrived there. Should they plan to counter-attack? But how could they do so? Would it be better to pack up and run again? Falma had no clear sense of what should be done next. He was in a complete panic and terrified for his life.

The king's man saw Falma and his associate drive off. He couldn't follow their car, but returned to the observation post as quickly as he could to report the location of the building from which they had emerged. And at that point, he made a field decision that they should enter the building and find out what could be learned there, and then report back to the king.

The three soldiers who had been assigned observation duty were well armed, since they had all initially been part of the assault teams on the building at 1618 Gold. But they still considered themselves at this point to be on a fact-finding mission, rather than acting as a military assault unit. So when their colleague returned and reported on what he had seen, they left their position and followed him with the idea in mind that they would approach the second building with great stealth.

One man went around to observe the back of the structure and any rear or side entrances. Another carefully watched the front. The third tried a few ground floor windows, first to see what he could glimpse through them, and second to determine whether any of them was open, or at least unlocked. He found one near the back that was large and unlocked and that opened into a room that seemed empty. He signaled to his colleagues, and they slowly and quietly slipped into the building through the same window.

They had no idea what would result from their nearly silent entry. But they were prepared for almost anything.

20

A Big Reunion

Hoda had just walked into the large room. Her students were gathered there with all of Khalid's who weren't otherwise occupied with the harsh and unexpected lessons that come from being in harm's way. Several of the students looked at her expectantly.

"Good news. The king has just learned that our friends successfully found and rescued Set and Jabari, who are unharmed and fine, and all our men and classmates are on their way back from the mission."

Several of the students cheered or applauded. Hoda added, "More detail should be available soon." She had chosen her words carefully, deliberately deciding to withhold for the moment what else she had heard, in case it was inaccurate or premature, and knowing it was at least incomplete information that would do no one in the room any good at this point to hear. If there would indeed be some bad news along with the good, it would come soon enough. She continued by saying, "Our job now is to try to relax and prepare to enjoy the food that Kular will be sending down for us momentarily."

"So, we don't know anything else at all?" Malik said.

"We know that everyone is on the way back. But we should know more in a little bit," Hoda replied evasively, and with great love in her heart for this boy, along with a strong desire for his good on this difficult day. "The initial report was very quick and limited, but quite encouraging." She then looked over at the door and said, "Here's Kular's gift for us, now!"

Five waiters came into the large room bearing trays of food and drink, fruit, cheeses, meats, vegetables, sauces, breads, and juices of many kinds. The aromas permeating the air immediately announced to everyone that a good experience was about to be had. The trays were put down on every available surface, on tables of all sorts around the room, and Hoda invited the students to help themselves, while the head waiter assured her also that there was plenty more to be had, should more be needed.

The girls were all sitting together, talking, and Bafur was on the periphery of their group, listening and making comments of his own. At least he was until the snacks appeared, and then he was the first to visit the nearest tray and load a small plate with a large serving of goodies. "Excellent! This looks so nice!" he exclaimed, with enthusiastic gusto in his voice. But those were the last words he uttered for at least a few minutes as he dug into the food on his plate, relishing every bite with various muffled sounds of high approval.

"The cheese plate seems to have whetted our friend's appetite," Hasina said.

"Mine too," Ara responded, as she also got up from a sofa to go snag some of the food for own enjoyment.

Khata turned to Kit and said, "Before the boys devour it all, we'd better serve ourselves, too."

"Good idea," Kit replied.

Within a few minutes, everyone was eating and drinking and savoring everything that Kular and the kitchen had sent them. They were still sitting around in groups discussing the events of the day and speculating on the hows and whys of it all, probably forty-five minutes later when, suddenly, Set and Jabari walked through the door.

"Hey!" Someone yelled. "They're back! It's the long lost prince and his best friend Mafulla!"

At that, everyone looked up, saw the tall boy along with the shortest boy in the class, and cheered and laughed, putting down their food plates to clap and clap and clap. "Bravo!" Someone else shouted out.

"A royal speech!" Someone else yelled above the applause and whistles.

Set held up his hand and said: "No, no, thank you! Thank you all very much! But no more royal prince and Mafulla roles for us! We've decided to retire from those exalted positions and allow the real items to be themselves. So, Ladies, and any true Gentlemen who might be in the room, though I'm not quite sure I see one, may I now present: The Real Prince Walid Shabeezar and the authentic Mafulla Adi, live and in person!" At that, Set turned with a dramatic gesture, and the real Walid and Mafulla did indeed walk into the room, to ongoing cheers, and each took a small bow, though Walid's made him grimace through his smile.

Malik shouted out over the noise, "Is everybody Ok?"

"Yes, yes, we all are," Walid said. "Malik, your dad saved my life today with some quick, dramatic action, and he got pretty banged up in the process, but my dad examined him and says he'll be just fine. I've got a bandage on my side, as well, but thanks to Hamid, I'm fine, too." There was more applause mingled with words of concern from everyone in the room now. Malik looked relieved, and yet still a little worried.

As everyone now again started chattering and talking among themselves and to the new arrivals, Walid walked over toward Malik, as he was also making his way to the prince, and when they were close, Walid now said in a much lower voice, "I think you'll be able to see him in a little while. Hamid was the hero of the day, for sure."

"What happened?"

"Idi Falma, one of the worst criminals in the kingdom, the guy who ordered the kidnapping today, tried to shoot and kill me, and your dad made sure it didn't happen."

"Did he get shot?"

Walid touched Malik's shoulder. "Don't worry. The answer is yes, but in a completely miraculous way that didn't damage any vital organs or mess up his appearance or anything. He's at the hospital now getting a little patch-up and cleansing done, along with some medication, and my dad says he'll be absolutely fine. But he'll be in some pain for a few days."

"But, he's going to be Ok?"

"For sure. My dad predicts a complete recovery, one-hundred percent."

"Good. I'm relieved."

"We were all worried for a couple of minutes, but it worked out in the end as well as it possibly could."

"So, you didn't get shot?"

"I got grazed and there was a little blood, but I'm Ok, thanks to your dad."

Malik let out a big breath and said again, "Good. That's good."

Walid said, "Hamid jumped in front of the bullet, man. He's as brave and focused as a person can possibly be. You can be really proud of what he did today."

"I'm sorry he got hurt, but I'm glad he could help."

"Malik, I really mean it, he was the total in-charge hero of heroes in the mess we walked into at an old warehouse. Idi Falma's dead and so are most of the men who worked for him. The others are already in jail and are in pretty bad shape. Your dad led the entire operation and stopped some bad, bad guys in the process."

Malik took in a deep breath again and let it out with great relief. And then he even managed a weak smile. "Thanks, Walid.

You're The Man. I appreciate your breaking it to me so well. I was worried, really bad." Walid patted him on the back and gave his arm a little squeeze.

"No cause for worry now, so you can relax."

"Definitely," Malik said, "But, hey, get some of this awesome food. You deserve it!"

"Thanks, man. Good idea," Walid replied.

And the prince, now feeling the utter exhaustion of his condition, turned to go get a plate of treats, but Kissa appeared with one, as if out of thin air, and handed it to him. "Hey," she said.

"Hey. And thanks for this."

"Are you Ok?"

"Yeah, basically."

"You said you've got a bandage on your side?"

"Yeah."

"What happened?"

"I got shot."

"No!"

"Just a little."

"How do you get shot just a little?"

"The bullet grazed me. It hurt, but Hamid took it full on and deflected it so that I'm here, still living and breathing."

"Oh, my goodness! That's terrible. Is he Ok?"

"Yeah, it was like a miracle, and he's going to be in pain for several days, but will return to full health soon."

"Good! That's good. Where can I hug you?"

"High up, just not around my waist."

She wrapped her arms around Walid's shoulders and squeezed. "I'm so glad you're Ok."

"Thanks. Me, too."

"How did you find the kidnappers?"

"Hamid had some ideas, and Mafulla helped with some spooky intuition stuff."

"What was going on when you got there?"

"A lot. We showed up barely in time. The kidnappers had just found out they had the wrong guys—they had meant to take me and Mafulla, of course—and it sounded like they were getting ready to kill Set and Jabari."

"Oh, no."

"Yeah. It was bad. But S&J gave them some serious trouble."

"Really?"

"Set shot a couple of the guys, I think, and I know Jabari shot one. He also stabbed a guy with a screwdriver."

"Ouch."

"And Manni did his thing again, messing up one guy pretty good."

"Honestly?"

"Yeah. And then that evil, Semi-Head-Jerk Idi Falma got desperate and tried to shoot me. And that's when Hamid got in the way and took the bullet. And it went right through him and just grazed me. And there was a lot of blood for a while, but I'm really fine and Hamid's going to be fine, too, dad says. And there likely won't even be a scar—on me, I mean—but I'm hoping at least for a fine line to remain so that I'll have some evidence, and people will believe my wild stories one day in the future."

"Oh, my."

"What? You're against a small tiny scar? I mean, just a fine line? It won't be anything ugly, just impressive enough to confirm my tale of wild woe."

"No, no, you silly. I'm just shocked at what you guys all went through."

"It was pretty crazy."

"How's Mafulla?"

Walid smiled. "I see he's already talking to Hasina over there. He's good. No injury that I know of. He sure did his part today, right in the middle of the action. He was so focused. I was really glad to have him beside me during it all. We're true partners."

Set and Jabari were in the middle of the room, telling their side of the story, the whole adventure from the windstorm to the firestorm. The other students were eating it up and saying all the right things to punctuate the narration: "Wow." "Ouch!" "No way." "Unbelievable!" And as the minutes passed, there was a strange thing happening. Both Set and Jabari began to feel that they were regaining, and in an authentic way, some of the status they thought they had lost when they gave up the pretend roles of the prince and best friend of the prince. They had now earned a respect and real admiration for what they both had gone through, and what they had done in response to it—a level of respect that all of us want and too few of us feel.

Khalid then walked into the room, and Omari joined them as well. Various students waved to them or came over to talk, but this was clearly a session focused on their fellow students. The older men would not have wanted it any other way. They enjoyed seeing all the positive attention that Set and Jabari were getting, along with Manni, of course, who was extremely well behaved now that he could feel he was also a center of attention and admiration once more—and, of course, now that tasty snacks abounded, many of them monkey friendly.

Across town, Ari Falma stopped his car outside a place he knew to have a telephone and quickly told his associate what he was going to do. He got out of the car, went in, and asked the proprietor if he could use his phone in private. This was a man who knew and feared Falma, and so he immediately agreed. Ari told the operator to connect him with *The Kingdom Daily News*, and when someone answered, he asked to be put through to a top reporter, saying he had the scoop of the year for the paper. Within thirty seconds, he heard a voice say, "Hello, City Desk."

Ari said, "I'm calling with the biggest story you've had all year."

"Yeah? Who are you, and what is it?"

"I can't tell you my name, but I'm a major figure of organized crime."

"You're what?"

"A major figure of organized crime. I'm a crime boss. And I have a story for you that needs to be told."

"Well, this is different. What's the story?"

"I had a big robbery planned recently on a luxury goods store where there was a lot of money in the safe. Then two masked crime fighters named The Golden Viper and Windstorm showed up just as the job was going down, and they stopped it. They broke it up."

"Sure, I remember that. You were involved in that?"

"It was my idea. I planned it. It was my heist. And it was my money, or it was supposed to end up as my money. But that's not the story. That's old news."

"So, what's the new story?"

"I was really mad about having my job interrupted. So I planned an elaborate deception to catch these two crime fighters, the Viper and the Storm. It was going to happen soon."

"Ok. So?"

"I'm getting to it."

"I'm pretty busy."

"You'll want to hear this. I promise you."

"Ok, what is it?"

"I know I have a leak in my organization, a traitor, and that's the only way those mysterious guys could have known about the luxury store heist."

"Ok. And?"

"And this leak must have told them about my plan to catch them and eliminate them."

"Eliminate?"

"I was going to get rid of them, a short time from now. Ok?"

"Are you serious?"

"Dead serious. I had a whole thing planned to lure them out, and to take them out of the picture here for good."

"Who is this? What's your name?"

"I'm not telling you that, idiot. I'm telling you only that The Golden Viper and Windstorm found out about my plans to do them in, from a traitor in my organization, whoever it is, and then they showed up at one of our places of operation today and killed everybody there, including my brother. And I'm afraid I'm next."

"They killed people?"

"Yeah. They killed a lot of my men. And my brother."

"The Golden Viper and Wind Storm?"

"Yes."

"How do you know?"

"Well, listen, I discovered a few minutes ago that lots of my men are dead. When one of my guys went to get my brother for a meeting, he found all of them dead, They had been murdered, and the only evidence of who did it that he could see was two masks on the floor in the abandoned warehouse where my guys were. Two masks. And I want to ask you something: Who fights crime in our city, who stops criminals from doing what they're doing and would wear masks inside, in a warehouse, in the daytime?"

"I don't know—Who?"

"What do you mean you don't know? There are only two guys in the history of our city who've ever fought crime while wearing masks, the guys who call themselves The Golden Viper and Windstorm. And they were the guys I was planning to kill. And, now, lots of my men just get put down right before I was going to take out these masked men, and where my guys are lying dead, there are two masks on the floor. It doesn't take a genius like me to figure out that these famous crime fighters have become crime committers and have crossed the line into the land of mass murder."

"Are you sure?"

"What does it sound like to you? Go to 1618 Rue de L'Or in the warehouse district and look for yourself. You'll see everything I'm describing. The evidence there is enough by itself, but when you add in the fact that I was planning to set up these guys in a sting operation to catch both them, and the leak in my gang who was feeding them information, and that I was going to eliminate the leak and them, you have the proof that what I'm saying is right. Your favorite crime fighter super heroes that you love so much are nothing but super villains who take the law into their own hands and kill anyone that it's convenient for them to get rid of."

"But you were going to do that. You were going to get rid of them."

"I'm a criminal and I admit it. These guys pretend to be heroes."

"Well."

"They put on this pose as great guardians of the city. And you praise what they do in your newspaper. I've read it. But the real news is that they're just like me. That's the story. They're just like me—and maybe even worse. They're mass killers. And they're on the loose."

There was a momentary silence. Then the editor replied, "If what you say is true, then this is a really big story."

"I told you. And it is true. Check it out. You'll find my brother dead in a pool of his own blood, and lots of other men dead, thanks to the Viper and the Storm. You'll see their gruesome handiwork, and you'll now for once know that these so-called saviors of the city are hard-nosed killers. The proof is at 1618 Rue de L'Or. And I've got to go and hide, or I know I'll be next."

With that, Ari Falma hung up the phone, satisfied that he had done the first thing he could to get even with these mystery men. Now, their names would be dirt, and everybody would be looking for them and trying to capture them and throw them in jail and get them out of his way for good. He would put them on the run and get this first form of revenge for what they'd done to him. Even though he still had no idea what his next move should be, this alone made him feel a little better. Maybe the police would get them before they could get him.

Right after the phone call ended, the reporter left his desk and the building in a hurry with a photographer. They got a car and went straight to 1618 Rue de L'Or. And when they got there, they were of course completely horrified by what they found—dead men, carnage, blood, and the two dark masks the mysterious caller had mentioned. The reporter went back straight to his office and wrote the headline story for the next day's paper: "Masked Crime Fighters Cross the Line." The photo he decided to run showed the two masks on the floor next to a gun and a pool of blood. He swore everyone around him to complete secrecy and sent the article to be set and printed for tomorrow's paper, with a big headline, extra large, front page, and a story that would cover all the prime news real estate above the fold.

Ari Falma walked back to his car after the call and was starting the engine when he suddenly realized that he had left a bundle of very sensitive and incriminating papers in the office that he had been in such a hurry to leave. They contained details about his operation and his finances that no one else could be allowed to see.

He let out a deep breath and a curse. "I can't believe it!" he said to his associate and to himself, as he pounded the steering wheel.

"What?"

"We have to go back to the office."

"Why? What do you mean?"

"I just realized that I've left papers there that will implicate us in all sorts of illegal activity, evidence that can get many of our contacts arrested and that could put us both away for life. It would also guide the Viper and the Storm to even more of our network. They could kill everybody. I've got to go right back for a minute and, if it's safe, get those papers out of there."

"But it's too dangerous to go back."

"It's too dangerous not to try."

"I guess, if we do it fast, then we're maybe Ok."

"Yeah, as long as we're fast," Falma said. He started the car, turned it around, and drove quickly back to the place they had just left in such a hurry. He parked out front and left the motor running. "Wait here," he said. "There's a gun in the glove box, if you need it. I'll be back in less than a minute."

He walked briskly through the front door and on his way to his office toward the back he saw, to his terrified shock, the men he had left behind—all shot and dead on the floor in various places. The smell of a gun battle was still in the air. He froze in place, turned, and frantically ran back to the car, jumped inside, turned it around, and raced off, gunning the engine.

"What's wrong? Where's the paperwork? What are you doing?"

"They're all dead."

"What?"

"They're all dead, the guys we left here."

"Who?"

"Badri, Shad, Farghali, and the new one. They're all dead on the floor."

"How could it be?"

He glanced in the rear view mirror, and said, "The Viper and the Storm got here since we left and they killed the guys. They found us. We got out just in time! We were almost dead, too. We just missed them, by minutes, or seconds. We have to get away from here fast. They're right behind us! I can feel it. They know our location. They know our moves. They're everywhere."

"This can't be!"

"Yes it can be, and it is."

"But."

"I mean it. You were right. Whoever's feeding them information has fed them everything. They have to know where my house is. We can't go there now."

"What should we do?"

"I have no idea. But I need to make one more call." He quickly drove back to the same shop and rushed in again and used the man's phone one more time. There were three rings. And then, at

The Kingdom Daily News, someone answered and said, "The City Desk. Assistant Editor."

Falma said, "Are you the guy I talked with a little while ago about the Viper and the Storm?"

"No, it was my boss."

"Let me talk to him!"

"He's not here right now. He's out working on the story."

"There's more than he knows, more than I told him!"

"What more?"

"Something I discovered just minutes ago."

"What is it?"

"Listen! The Viper and The Storm just showed up at my office, three blocks away from the warehouse at 1618 Rue de L'Or, and they also killed the guys who worked for me there! They're still killing! Just a few minutes ago."

"They did? I mean, they are?"

"Yeah. They killed more men! I barely missed them or I wouldn't be phoning you now. They're completely out of control, meting out their own version of vindictive punishment, regardless of all kingdom laws. And I'm afraid, I mean, I know, that I'm next. Do you hear me?"

"Have you called the police?"

"I'm a criminal. I don't call the police."

"Maybe you should."

"You're a funny man or a moron. And I'm in no mood to laugh."

"So you say that more men have been killed?"

"Yes! Several more. These guys are mass murderers, I'm telling you, and they won't stop until they've killed us all!

"What's the location of the new murders?"

Falma told him and said, "This is my last call. Do something about this."

"There's going to be a front page piece tomorrow. I'm sure of it."

"Add this extra information to it. This has to be known—all of it. The Viper and the Storm are the worst mass murderers in the history of the city and they won't let up until somebody stops them."

21

The King's Sitting Room

The leader of the three-man observation team had just completed his report to the king.

"You did the right thing." The king spoke with a tone of kind reassurance.

"I was hoping you'd think so, Your Majesty. The way they attacked us when they first saw us, it was all we could do. We had no other options."

"I understand completely. You did as I would have done. It was indeed terribly unfortunate but, in the circumstances, necessary."

"I hope it was also Ok that we left the scene as we had at the warehouse. Except, we emptied two drawers in a desk, the only drawers that contained papers, and brought them all with us."

"Yes, I commend you for getting that evidence. Masoon will go over the papers for anything of importance they might contain. And, as to leaving the human toll of the event where it took place, I also approve of your decision."

"Good. That's a relief."

"As you know, there are two schools of thought on this. One group says that you should always leave the scene as it is for the carnage to frighten any confederates who visit later on and see it, to their complete shock. The other viewpoint suggests that you should instead totally clean up and remove all traces of the events, so that any colleagues of the victims who come by later will just see no one there, and will always wonder where they went and what happened to them. This leaves more room for speculation and theories of betrayal. I prefer the straightforward approach myself, as it has a more immediate and visceral impact. Plus, it gets you out of the situation more quickly, which can be a safety issue."

"That's what we thought. So the bodies are still there."

"We'll give it a day or two and then send a team to do what needs to be done. I appreciate your report. Please tell the others how grateful I am for your work."

"Thanks, Your Majesty. I'll do exactly that." The man rose, bowed, and walked out just as Kular was showing Walid and Mafulla into the room. He did a quick bow to the prince as he passed. And the young man smiled and nodded in response.

"Come in, come in."

"Hi, Uncle, Your Majesty."

"Yeah. Hi, Your Majesty."

"Greetings to you both! Please, sit. What a day you've had!"

The boys flopped down on a big sofa. Walid let out a long breath of relief.

Mafulla said, "Well, field trips can end up being more interesting than you would ever expect."

"Yeah, I could write a book about what happened on this one," Walid remarked.

The king replied, "What amazes me is that you had, actually, five major events in two days. Omari and Reela filled me in on the attempted train robbery, which apparently had nothing to do with any of the usual suspects. Then you had the sand storm, and then the abduction, the chase, and the rescue operation. You both must be completely exhausted."

Mafulla said, "Yes we are, Your Majesty. But up until now, we've been running on adrenalin and the excitement of all the action. I'm starting to crash, big time, and I know Walid must feel lots worse with his impressive scratch."

"Hey. It's a lot more than a scratch. It's a respectable flesh wound."

"Ok, your almost grievous skin wound that's not at all a very serious scratch, but so much more."

"Funny. I'm glad it's not any worse. It doesn't hurt that much at this point. It's just sore and it still stings."

"I'm happy you weren't more badly hurt," the king said. "We all are."

"Yeah, really," Mafulla said. "And it was a great idea for you to have Walid's dad give Hamid The Stone of Giza."

"Well, it worked so effectively for Kular, and I thought, in case someone needs it, I should put it into Rumi's safekeeping. I'm glad he had it for Hamid. From what I've heard, things initially looked very bad for our friend."

Walid said, "Yes, sir, he was covered with blood, but a good amount of it was from the men who had attacked him earlier. And it's not anything you ever expect to see—Hamid taken down like that. We were really worried for a few minutes."

"I'm just glad I got off a shot at that guy," Mafulla said.

"What guy?" Walid turned to his friend.

"The evil little guy who tried to shoot you and instead hit Hamid, that Idi Falma."

"You got off a shot?"

"Yeah, I was one of the ones who plugged him when I saw he was going to shoot you."

"You were?"

"Yeah, and otherwise, I hadn't felt like I was being much help in the whole situation."

"What do you mean?"

"I didn't get to do much."

"You did a lot."

"Well, thanks. I'd taken down one guy by myself, earlier. I don't think you saw him. But for most of the time, it was like I was three seconds and ten feet behind the main action."

"Hey, danger was coming at us from all sides."

"That's for sure."

"I'm glad you were where you were, and that you did what you did. The fact that you were there gave me a lot more confidence in what was a massively dangerous situation."

"Really?"

"Yeah, for sure. I think you were a hugely important part of the team."

"Ok. Good. I feel better."

The king said, "Have you two emotionally processed the day yet?"

"I'm not sure I understand what you're asking," Walid answered with a look of puzzlement.

"In the pitch of battle, you do what you have to do, but afterwards, you can't predict the feelings you'll have about it all."

"Ok. I get what you're saying, Your Majesty," Mafulla replied. "I was glad I could help stop Falma, but then, right after it, I felt really sorry that he had to be killed to keep him from killing. It's kind of sadly ironic. You wish you could reform a guy like that, not have to take him out of the world. That's sort of hard to accept."

Walid looked over at his friend and said, "I know exactly what you mean. Where there's life, there's hope. Even for a guy like him, I guess."

"Yeah, I guess that's right."

The king said, "You two haven't heard this yet, because I just found out myself, but the observation team that I left on the street in that building across from 1618 saw a man enter the scene of the struggle shortly after you left. When he came back out just a minute later, one of our men followed him to a location three blocks away. He watched the building, and in a few more minutes, two men left. The description of one of them matches that of Ari Falma. Our man then returned to get his team. They all went back to the building and quietly entered to find out who or what was there, and they were seen and attacked."

"Oh, man. Are they Ok?"

"Yes, but they had to put down all the attackers, four other men who were there at the time. They had no other option. And that's always sad. Because of greed and improper ambition, along with a bent toward violence, there was a terrible human toll today."

"I'm really sorry to hear that," Walid said.

"Me, too," Mafulla added.

"Yes. We all deeply regret it, while yet realizing its unfortunate necessity in the situation. Our men also brought back some boxes of papers, and Masoon's now going through them. They may be the key to stopping Falma and any remaining men from whatever his further plans may be."

"Oh, that's good news, for sure," Walid commented.

"It seems that the only good Falma is a thwarted Falma," Mafulla added."

"Yes," Walid smiled at Mafulla and repeated the word he had used, "thwarted," but in a tone of respectful amusement.

The king commented, "It does indeed seem that way. They appear to have made no plans that aren't despicable ones. I'm glad there are only two brothers, or at least that we know of."

"That's for sure," Mafulla said.

The king continued. "More Falmas would just mean more problems, it seems. And, oh, by the way, we have Kinkaid in jail."

"You do?" Walid said, looking surprised.

"Yes, he took some bait that we waved at him."

"What happened?"

"He came to talk to Darwishi about the car logs after Dar left a note at the Grand Hotel saying there was a problem and his presence was needed to help solve it."

"Oh! So you used the car logs against him."

"Yes. And right before Kinkaid arrived at Dar's office, Naqid got the first intelligence from the warehouse that his car had been spotted there, by you, I believe, and also what several witnesses had said about him."

"Good."

"Naqid talked with him briefly and then took him into custody. So, we've eliminated two of our worries today, Idi Falma, and Harvey Kinkaid. We also nabbed Kinkaid's assistant in his room at the hotel, who has now also been relocated to a much smaller accommodation, but he was a smaller part of the picture."

"This is all good news," Walid said.

The king took a deep breath and replied, "I have to admit, though, that I'm more than a little ambivalent about having snagged Kinkaid."

"Why?" Mafulla asked. "He's a really bad guy and deserves a long stay in jail, if anybody does."

"Yes, indeed, there's no doubt about it. But he seems at least initially reticent to tell us what he's been up to, on a broader scale, in the big picture of things."

"Oh."

"And if he had been able to continue on, we could have had a chance to follow him and let him show us what he was doing. We might have been able to gather a lot more information about the ultimate threats that face us, presumably from the direction of Farouk al-Khoum and his brother, Faraj—and possibly, in other ways. But, in the end, I'm sure things will still play out well for us. And I'm also sure that this is enough talk for today." The king looked at his watch. "It's still early in the evening, but I'd imagine that you boys would like to bathe and change and just relax awhile before you try to sleep. You've had quite a day."

"Yeah, thanks, Uncle Ali, I really need some down time," Walid said.

"Me too, Your Majesty. Total down time," Mafulla replied.

"Well, please then, be off, sleep well, and heal in every way from the trauma of the day. You both showed your great character and your strong Phi skills throughout the events that transpired, in full service to others, and I'm very proud of you."

"Thanks, Your Majesty. We'll see you later," Walid said, as he rose and turned toward the door.

"Yeah, thanks, Your Majesty," Mafulla echoed his sentiments. "See you tomorrow." The boys walked out, said goodnight to Kular, and went straight to the task of bathing and changing. Each of their rooms opened into its own very nice and spacious bathroom area. Hot water never felt so good, or at least not since right after they had originally met, when they had both actually been the victims of another kidnapping scheme. The developments of the day brought back memories of that time, not so very long ago by real chronology, but in another way, it seemed to be far in the distant past.

When Mafulla had dried off and changed clothes, he just sat for a few minutes alone in his room, almost in a trance. The events of the past two days had indeed taken a toll on him. How could so much fit into such a short time? It seemed unreal when he looked back over the hours since his early rise time yesterday, the car trip to the train station, and everything that had followed. That was like a crazy week's worth of adventures, or a month's worth, but in two days. It was amazing—and completely exhausting. But, as much as he wanted to, Mafulla couldn't just roll over and go to sleep. Something got him back on his feet, took him out into the hallway, and pushed him down to Walid's room. He knocked on the door.

"Yes. Enter," said a very tired voice.

Mafulla opened the door, stuck his head through, and said in an unreal, super-cheerful voice, "Hey, what's up? The night's yet young! What should we do? Want to put on a mask and hit the streets for a little patrol time?"

"Hardee har, har," Walid said in reply, adding, "And the real answer is: Hardly. But you can come in and tell me how brave I was today, and yesterday, and since you first met me, if you want to go back that far and don't mind my drifting off to the sound of your recollections."

That made Mafulla laugh, and he said, "You were and have long been … Captain Courageous, Billy Braveheart, The Man With Nerves of Steel, and even The Utterly Flinchless Phi." He walked into the room while saying all this, and sat down on the floor. "I, on the other hand, by stark contrast, was The Craven Coward Who Carried On."

"Ha!" Walid said, "You were no coward, for sure! You were the opposite of that."

"Well, I felt surges of real fear quite a few times both yesterday and today," the younger boy admitted.

"Sure you did. I did too. We'd have just been stupid idiots not to realize what we were up against on the train, outside the train, in the storm, and in the fight at 1618."

"I was totally cool in the storm," Mafulla corrected his friend. "Completely cool."

"Oh. Ok. Me too, actually, but just because I had been through one before."

"Yeah, I picked up on your confidence and made it my own."

"That's good."

"Yeah, it can actually work, that business about borrowing someone else's comfort, or confidence, or even hope, I think."

"We do affect each other in a lot of ways."

"Mostly positive."

"Maybe even all positive," Walid ventured to say.

"Maybe so," Mafulla agreed. "I mean, since you've been around me, I can see many improvements. For example, you're much more limber, and I can tell your vocabulary's getting better."

"Incrementally," Walid admitted.

"Good. See there? Nice word for it. And for that word, and so many others, I can only say: You're welcome."

"I'm also funnier as a result," Walid added.

"Perhaps, incrementally," Mafulla conceded. "But let's not get too carried away. You are, though, definitely more attuned to my own special, subtle, high brow form of humor." And he, of course, raised his eyebrows as he said that.

"Ha! Ouch! Oh, my side."

"You see? I'm side-splittingly funny, even when exhausted. Clearly, I've expanded your merriment horizons a great deal. You're even willing to endure physical pain in order to react appropriately to my witticisms. And I take great satisfaction in that."

"Don't make me laugh any more. Seriously. My wound can't take it."

"Your graze."

"Ok, my graze, my very light wound."

"You're really sure it's not just an unusually impressive scratch?"

"Ok, Ok, maybe it's a serious scratch. But it's bigger and deeper than a normal scratch. And it bled a lot at first. It was a very scary scratch."

"Yeah, I know. I was worried about you. Can you believe our friend forever, Hamid?"

"It's pretty wild what he did, and how he did it in such a way that he's not dead."

"Phi stuff."

"Wow. I hadn't thought of that until this moment, until you just now said it, but I'm sure you're right. Phi stuff."

"He's pretty advanced. Maybe only the king and Masoon are more so."

"At least among the Phi that we know about," Walid said.

"True. We have no idea how many others there are, and maybe even some people we know."

"Yeah, maybe. It's a strange thing."

"Yeah, it is, but I understand the Need to Know Principle. I'm fine with it. I'm just glad we know all the Phi that we already do know."

"I was relieved to see Paki and Amon there today."

"Me, too. Nothing like getting blown up by a bomb and then getting back into action so soon."

"They're really strong guys."

"And they're totally devoted to duty."

"You got that right. Those kidnappers picked the wrong kids to nap."

"In more ways than one," Mafulla said.

"Yeah, that's for sure. In more ways than one."

"You think Set and Jabari are Ok?"

"I hope so." Walid ran his hand through his hair and thought for a second. "They looked fine. But they haven't been trained for a day like this like we have. I was really impressed with the way they reacted to everything. And when I heard the full story about what they did in the back of the truck and how they kicked out the doors, well, that was all pretty amazing."

"Yeah, when I heard the whole story, I was knocked out. They really handled themselves well with their initial two brief get-aways—you know, between the gun, the monkey, and the screw-driver."

"That could be the title of a book." Walid chuckled and held his side.

"What?"

"The Gun, The Monkey, and The Screwdriver."

Mafulla laughed. "Yeah, I guess it could. People might read it just to find out what in the heck the title means."

"And could you believe that Jabari had to shoot that guy when he thought everything was over, and he was just sitting there calming Manni down?"

"No, that was pretty incredible—and scary. We all sort of

thought that everything at that point was over. I was shocked when I heard the shot."

"That's one thing I learned today."

"What?"

"Danger isn't always over when you think it is. You need to keep your guard up and be vigilant. Like Uncle Ali has told us, over and over: Pay attention—always pay attention."

"Yeah, that's for sure," Mafulla agreed. "Eternal vigilance."

"Yep."

And then he said, "Oh, I meant to ask. Is Kissa all right?"

"Yeah, I think so," Walid answered. "But I got the feeling that she worried about us a lot today."

"Hasina too. When you like somebody, I mean really like them a lot, then you care about what happens to them in a deeper way, and your heart's sort of held hostage to fortune or destiny or whatever. I even worried pretty much about her when we left Memphis chasing the bad guys. I mean, the girls had soldiers protecting them, and Uncle Reela was there, but we had a car full of Phi."

"Yeah, I know what you mean," Walid agreed. "But then again, Hasina and Kissa and Hoda are also Phi and I think they may have lots more powers and skills than we know."

"You're right. I sort of forgot about that aspect of it—when I was worrying, I mean."

"Yeah, worry's like that. It fixates on one side of a situation and forgets the big picture. I do the same thing. I think the king manages to avoid doing it, and Masoon also."

"Yeah, so it seems."

"That's part of what being advanced Phi frees you from, I guess. You get rid of unnecessary, unhelpful emotions and attitudes and stuff."

"I suppose so. I can't wait to get more advanced. I didn't like the worry and the deep stabs of fear I felt today. It was bad. And it never accomplishes anything good."

"Yeah."

"I could really do without all that."

"Me, too. You're right that it never accomplishes anything good."

"And it feels terrible."

"I totally agree."

"Well, should we get to sleep? I mean, if you're absolutely sure you don't want to put on the masks and go out for a little late crime fighting action."

"I'm totally, one-hundred percent sure."

"Ok. You're probably right. Tomorrow's going to come soon enough, and you never know what it'll bring."

"True. So, I guess we should try to get some sleep."

"Yeah." Mafulla yawned.

Walid said, "I'm glad you came by, though, and that we got to talk some like this. And I'm glad we're having a combined class tomorrow. I think that was a good idea. Hoda and Khalid are doing a great job with us all this year, for sure."

"Yeah, they are. And I agree. There are some things I know we all need to talk through about today."

"Maybe they'll ask to see my wound."

"Scratch."

"Ok, scratch."

"Be humble about it. Refuse to embarrass yourself and me. Tell them that modesty forbids its display."

"Ha! Ouch! Ok. See you in the morning."

"Good night GV."

"Night, Stormie."

22

Learning Some Lessons

"Oh, man." Mafulla said this in a low voice, on first opening his eyes and seeing the light in the room. Then he sighed and mumbled, "I just hit the bed and totally passed out last night. What time is it?" Looking over at his Reverso on the bedside table, he stared at it for a second and then jumped out of bed. He threw on his clothes and nearly ran down the hall to the breakfast room where he always met Walid.

The prince was already in his regular chair, eating bread and cheese and sipping strong tea. At the first sight of his friend, he said, "I thought you were going to sleep in today."

"No, man. I was just completely out. I think my molecules merged with the mattress. I became one with the sheets. I was out cold for ten hours, straight. And then, boom, I just woke up, like somebody turned on a light switch. I even started talking to myself, out loud!"

"Oh yeah?"

"And, you know, I'm a pretty good conversationalist, so it could have gone on a while. But then I checked my watch and I thought, 'Whoa! I gotta get going!' And here I am, ready to roll. And, ready for a roll. That one on your plate looks good." At this, he did the double eyebrow jump and began to reach toward Walid's food.

"No, no. Roll around to the buffet table and get your own. Kular brought in plenty, even for your appetite."

"Ok. Keep yours, then. Enjoy it."

"Thanks."

"So, how did you sleep, my royal friend?"

"Pretty well. But not as well as you."

"Why not?"

"I woke up a few times with side pain and some flashbacks. But I'm good."

"Oh, yeah, the side. I almost forgot. How is it?"

"Still sore and stinging but not too bad."

"That's good. But you had flashbacks? Like in dreams?"

"No, before I fell asleep. I just had dreams that made no sense."

"I don't even think I dreamed at all. I was down deep," Mafulla said. "I'm actually glad I was able to wake up at all. It was like"—and, here, he did one of his dramatic voices—"The Bed of The Dead."

"Ok then, my formerly almost-dead, and by sleep nearly mummified friend, Good Old Mumfulla."

"Ha!"

"I'm glad you're back among the living, but you better quit joking around now and eat, so we can go."

"Tut, Tut—as in the Mummy King, of course—you know there's always time for a little Mumfoolery," Mafulla said this as he grabbed bread, cheese, apricots, and a cup of tea off the top of the buffet table against the wall.

Sitting down in his normal chair, he said, "Anything exciting going on this morning so far?"

"Nothing yet. But now that you're up, I'm sure that'll change."

"I do bring a certain, how do you say, outer edge of possibility to any new day."

"Yeah, I'd say."

"It's true that, in my presence, all things are open and a little more able to transpire."

"That's fine, as long as none of those things cause any of the rest of us to expire."

"Yes, that's an important qualification to the otherwise endless array of exotic possibilities and potentialities that flow forth around me."

At that stage in the completely serious conversation the boys were having, Kular brought in the usual stack of newspapers. "Excuse me, Prince Walid and Mafulla. Here are all the papers today. I haven't had a chance to look at any of them, but just brought them all in to you as soon as they hit my desk. There must be four or five here in the pile."

"Thanks, Kular," Walid said. "We don't have a lot of time this morning, but it's good to at least scan the headlines before we go off to class. Khalid often expects us to know what's going on in the world and around town. And, I guess we should."

"You're quite welcome, Prince. And yes, I'm sure you're right. Just let me know if you need anything else."

"Will do."

Kular left the room and Mafulla started to go through the papers. "Paris, Rome, London, New York, and here's our … Oh No!"

"What?"

"NO, NO, NO, NO!"

"What? What is it?" Walid asked with a look and voice of great concern.

Mafulla felt a sick queasiness in the pit of his stomach and a quick wave of dizziness momentarily unhinged his conscious awareness. He recovered and said, "Look! Look at the headline … at the top of the front page, above the fold, of all things!" He whipped the paper around so that Walid could see the front of the morning's *Kingdom Daily News.*

Walid read aloud the headline before he processed what it said:

> Masked Crime Fighters Cross the Line
> To Mass Murder

"What?" he exclaimed in a much louder voice.

"Read it! Keep reading out loud," Mafulla urged and leaned forward.

"Ok, but I can't believe this."

"Just read!"

"Today, the kingdom awakes to some of the worst news in our history. The mysterious masked crime fighters, The Golden Viper and Wind Storm, whose seemingly heroic actions have been featured in past issues of this paper, and who have been widely praised throughout the city for their dashing deeds in stopping crime, have now crossed every legal and moral line in their latest exploits and have left a terrible trail of brutally murdered victims in their path."

"What are they talking about? What do they even mean?" Mafulla couldn't help but interrupt.

"Wait, let me go on," Walid said. Then he continued reading.

"Just yesterday, these violent vigilantes swooped down on an old warehouse at 1618 Rue de L'Or and without mercy shot, slashed, and otherwise killed a number of the kingdom's most notorious criminals. The masked men had apparently disrupted the operations of this local gang of thugs at an earlier date and the leader of the group had hatched an elaborate plan for revenge, a scheme to catch these two well-publicized celebrity crime fighters and, in his words, 'eliminate them for good.' This man himself anonymously phoned in to the paper yesterday to report that a short time before his plan was able to unfold, to apprehend and put an end to the lives of these perpetrators of paramilitary policing, they somehow discovered his scheme and turned the tables, breaking in at one of his secret gathering spots and ruthlessly murdering most of his men. His voice, as he spoke of these things, showed his panicked fear of what would happen next. He even admitted he was afraid for his own life."

"How?" Mafulla couldn't believe what he was hearing. Walid could barely comprehend what he was reading. But he read on.

"This well positioned, first-hand source says that he was in an office in a nearby location at the time of the slaughter, and so managed to escape the carnage. But then, he reported that, later, when he left his safe haven for a few minutes, he came back to find that the masked murderers had been there as well, in the meantime, and had killed more of his men in this separate location. It was a bloodbath at both buildings. New paragraph."

"This is just so …"

"Wait." Walid put his finger on the paper where he had left off. And he continued.

"This reporter personally witnessed the carnage at the warehouse on Rue de L'Or and saw there on the floor the discarded dark masks of The Golden Viper and Wind Storm. We now realize that these two mystery men are no heroes at all. These vigilantes are not bulwarks against crime or righteous defenders of law and order, but are themselves heartless, vicious criminals with no real morals or concern for due process."

"But we didn't …"

"Of course not," Walid said. "Let me continue. More on page two. Ok." He then turned the page with a mouth so dry now that he could hardly speak, but he had to read on.

"We now have to ask whether what we've witnessed in the past was all just a game to them? Were these men merely stopping any crime that was not of their own making? Are they simply eliminating all the competition to their own personal ambitions to take over the domain of organized crime in the city and the kingdom? Whatever the true story might turn out to be, The Golden Viper and the Wind Storm as a pair have now been declared by the chief of police to be Public Enemy Number One, and they will be hunted down and locked away, given their day in court, and then punished appropriately and severely for this depraved and disgusting display of deadly violence against so many of our fellow human beings."

"What?"

"There's one more paragraph."

"Ok. Read it, read it!"

"We can grant that the hapless victims of these homicides were themselves petty criminals, but they were men and human beings, someone's sons and brothers and husbands and fathers. They didn't deserve to be put down like vicious wild animals without the basic opportunity for a fair trial or a measure of mercy. We join all right minded citizens in deploring these horrible actions, and we call on the monarchy for its full support in apprehending these wicked lawless men and bringing them to true justice." Walid looked up at his friend and said, "Oh, man."

Mafulla said, "This is bad. This is really, really bad."

"I can't believe it," Walid muttered. "This goes beyond anything I could even possibly have imagined."

Mafulla nodded his head and said, in a soft voice, "It's a nightmare."

"Yeah, an extremely bad nightmare, but here it is in the real world." Walid leaned over and put his head in his hands.

Mafulla took a deep breath and said, "What are we going to do?"

"I don't know. Should we write the paper or phone them, and give them the true story?"

"I guess we have to," Mafulla said.

And then Walid quickly added, "But we need to check with the king first and make sure what we can say."

"Oh, man. I wonder if the king has seen this yet." Mafulla looked worried.

"I wonder if our parents have seen it." Walid said. "I mean, my parents were part of it all yesterday and know what really happened, but your parents don't know anything about any of this, except that we're The Golden Viper and Windstorm."

"Oh, no. Oh, no. My mom's going to completely fall apart.

She's going to be totally hysterical. We need to get word to them right away that it's all false, it's all a misunderstanding, and that it'll be corrected quickly, all cleared up, fixed, retracted, and so on."

Walid said, "Let's stop at the communications room in just a minute on our way to class and ask Bancom to put in a call to the men watching your house, and Badar and Mumar also."

"But what exactly can we say without giving it away to Bancom and Badar and Mumar and the guards on my parents' street that we're the Viper and the Storm?"

"Oh, jeepers. Good point."

"We can't expand the circle that far. It's not right. It's not safe."

"Nothing's safe right now," Walid said and got up and started pacing around, back and forth. "The police are looking for us? This is just too crazy to imagine."

"Yeah."

Walid said, "Ok, Ok, let's be totally cool for a minute." He stopped in his tracks and advised his friend, "Take a deep breath, and relax. Shed the dread. Smile or something."

"Smile? Really?"

"Ok, too much. Just take a deep breath and calm the inner turmoil."

"All right. I can do that."

"We can't let appearances here roil our emotions."

"Oh. Roil. Very nice."

"Thanks."

"Yeah, I should flip the telescope around. I'm making this look too big."

"Me too. We should look through the other end of the telescope and shrink this thing. There will be a way through it, or around it."

"There always is."

Walid then turned toward the door and walked over and opened it and called out, down the hall, "Kular? Kular?"

"Yes, Prince?" The butler stepped into the hall from his open office door.

"Is the king in his rooms right now?"

"He's already gone to see Khalid and Hoda. He's going to participate in the big joint class today, at their invitation."

"Oh, Ok, thanks."

Walid turned back to Mafulla. "Wait. You decided to try the smile?"

"Yeah, after I took the deep breath. I figured, why not try?"

"Well, you can quit it now. It's not very convincing."

"You're right. What can I say? But it made me feel a little tiny better."

"Good."

"So … what are we going to do?"

"Well, let's see." Walid thought for a few seconds. "We could have Bancom send your parents a very general message, maybe something like: 'Please don't believe any words you read today in any context except this message, or anything you hear anyone else say about anything big, unless you first talk with the people you know best in the palace.' That might do the job."

Mafulla nodded his head and said, "That sounds good. It's really good. It's vague enough. And, I mean, this is the big story of the day, I guess, and it'll be on everyone's minds, and people will be talking about it, for sure, but there are also many other stories in the paper, and other things my parents could read other than the newspapers, and no one will likely know that what we're sending my parents is a message about the masked crime fighter stuff. And even if they guessed that, there's nothing to implicate us as being involved. So, Ok, I think we should send that. It may help. And then we have to tell Bancom that if my parents respond, someone should come and get me and let me know. I'm sure they'll want to talk to me."

"Great idea."

"Oh man, I hope they know not to worry. I hope they know we're Ok and that this will somehow all be Ok."

"Well, we'll make sure they know soon," Walid reassured him. "But let's write this down and get it to Bancom fast."

The king's men on the Adi's residential street didn't get an answer when they knocked on the door repeatedly, so they slipped the message under the door. At about the same time, Badar Sakat was bringing an identical note to the Adi shop in the marketplace. And he saw Shapur sweeping up right outside, which was normally his first job in the morning.

"Shapur?"

"Yes? Oh. Hi Badar. Good morning to you."

"Good morning to you as well, my friend. I have a message for you from the palace communications center. I'm supposed to deliver it in this envelope and immediately return to my shop, without waiting for you to open it or read it, if that's all right. Those are just my unusual instructions."

"Sure, that's fine. Is anything wrong?"

"No, I'm sure I would have been informed if there was a problem of any kind."

"Ok. Good. It's a bit mysterious and strange, but fine."

Badar laughed and said, "Well, not to worry—mystery's often my job! I just do as I'm told. That is, unless you ask my brother. He may have a different story."

Shapur laughed and said, "Thanks, Badar. I trust your words."

As Badar walked back across the street, Shapur opened the note and read it, and then mumbled aloud. "I wonder what in the world this means?" He took it into the shop where Shamilar was also helping for the morning and handed it to her, saying "Badar Sakat just delivered this from the palace and said he was supposed to give it to me and not stay around for me to open it or read it. I said, sure, Ok, and he handed it over and walked back to his shop. It's all very strange. What do you make of it?"

"What is it? Is Mafulla all right?" Shamilar asked before even looking at the note, and then she held it out almost at arm's length.

"I'm certain he is. The note is from Walid and Mafulla, from both of them. But it's an odd message."

She handed the note back and said, "Read it to me, please. I don't have my glasses on."

"Ok," Shapur agreed. "It just says: 'Please do not believe any words you read today in any context except this message, or anything you hear anyone else say about anything big, unless you first talk with the people you know best in the palace.' That's it. And then it's signed, 'Love from your oldest son and his best friend.' It's odd—very odd. What could they be referring to?"

Shamilar said, "I have no idea. Have you read anything today?"

Shapur thought for a second and said, "No, there was no time to look at the *Daily News* before we left home. It's still crammed into the box at the door, and we have some mail from yesterday that I haven't opened yet." He paused in thought for a second and then asked, "Are there any books or magazines, or fliers or anything else that he thinks we could have read already early this morning?"

"No, not that I can think of. Nothing, really."

"Ok, then, but we'll do as they say, for whatever reason, even though I have no clue what's going on. If we come across anything of interest in our reading today, or in anything we hear, we'll duly not believe it, and then we'll get in touch with them."

"Yes. I suppose so. It would be good to talk to Mafulla anyway. It's been several days—too long," Shamilar said.

"I agree, although I'm not sure now that I can believe what you just said, until first contacting the palace." Shapur looked keenly suspicious.

"This is where Mafulla gets all his foolishness, from you, his father."

"Hehehe."

Walid and Mafulla were jogging straight to class, still a bit in a daze and very agitated. Down the hall, across a public area, down another long hall, and, there it was, the door to the larger room where both classes were going to meet today. Walid grabbed Mafulla's arm and said, "Remember, don't say anything about GV and the Storm or the paper. We have to act normal."

"Right," Mafulla said. "Normal—as if that in itself won't make people seriously worry." They were the last two students to arrive.

"Well, well! Look who we have here, making a special appearance today, the Wonderful Walid, and the Magnificent Mafulla," Khalid said, with a smile. "Welcome, gentlemen. Please take a seat." There was scattered joking applause from around the room. The boys who were so introduced could see the king already sitting there in the back, and Mafulla saluted toward him, while Walid gave a small wave.

Khalid continued. "Now, we're going to spend some time today talking about what happened during our all too brief trip to Memphis. This is the first official meeting of both classes in something like a normal classroom setting, which I think is a great idea, and should become the norm, I would think, but that's another discussion. We also have a special guest today, the head of our nation, the king of our kingdom, the monarch we love—our great likable leader, His Majesty, King Ali."

At this fun, lighthearted introduction, the students all applauded, and there was a little light stomping and even some whistling as well. The king smiled and nodded to the class, as many turned around to look and smile at him.

"Thank you, my friends," he said.

Then Khalid spoke again. "The first topic we'd like to address today is, actually … The Great Identity Switch, involving Walid and Set, and Mafulla and Jabari. Two mornings ago, Set, if I recall correctly, you congratulated the prince on what he and Mafulla did to help stop the train robbers who had delayed us on our journey, and you expressed an interest in having the chance at some point to walk in his shoes for a day—to change places."

"Yeah. If I had only known!" Set said, to muted laughter from the class.

"But I did characterize your proposal correctly?" Khalid asked.

"That's right," Set said, looking first at Khalid and then around at all his fellow students. "Crazy and exciting things are always happening to Walid, it seems, and I thought it would be really cool to be in that position, even for just twenty-four hours." The prince nodded his agreement with this summary of events, as did Mafulla and Jabari.

"But the problem was that … we had no idea what we were getting into," Jabari said, to more light, general laughter around the room. He continued, "Neither did Manni, either. We ended up with one super surprised simian. Or two, if you choose to include me." For that, there were more laughs.

Khalid went on, now again looking at Set, "So, the two of you, or I mean, the four of you, for sport or fun, decided to exchange identities for a while—Walid and Set, and also your respective close friends, Mafulla and Jabari. And everyone played along, and as a result, the switch was surprisingly well done." Khalid paused and then added, "I imagine that many surprises resulted, in addition to the unfortunate one we all know about. So, I think it's important to ask at this point: What did you learn from the experience?"

Set spoke up right away. "I learned that being the prince is not all about feeling important, being treated as special, and just having great adventures. But that's, of course, all a part of it, too."

"Tell us more," Khalid encouraged him.

He thought for a second or two and then said, "Ok. Well, at first, I have to admit, I loved the special treatment. Just people calling me 'Prince' made me feel good. I mean: I knew it was only a game, but still it had an effect that surprised me. And then, when we got off the train and the army guys saluted me—that was amazing. Everyone, all of you guys, played along really well, and I totally appreciate that, so I got a feeling right away of what it's like to be Walid, and to feel like Walid ... except for the always itchy armpits, of course."

"Wait. What?" Walid objected with a puzzled look.

When Set said this, lots of the kids laughed. He quickly added, "Just kidding, Walid. I know you're actually one-hundred percent itch-free." Then he paused a second for more laughs and added, "Seriously, when I first had an itch to be you, I had no idea." More laughs. He paused again and grinned and said, "There's a lot of good stuff involved in being royalty, I have no hesitation to say. I'm sure you would agree, Real Prince?"

At that, Walid nodded his head and said, "Yeah, indeed. Lots of good stuff, even if you just ... scratch the surface." As he said this, he moved a hand back and forth on the side of his chest and said, "Ah, that's better," and got more chuckles from the group.

Set laughed in appreciation of how Walid was carrying on with his silly joke, and then he paused for a few seconds and got more serious and said, "I didn't realize how much being treated that way, in such a special way, would effect my emotions—my feelings about myself, and my overall attitude. I'm sure you get used to it, but at first it's a real rush. It's different." He looked over at Walid again and said, "Then, there's the other side."

"Yeah, the big, bad other side," Walid echoed.

"I'm sure there's a lot, lot more to the other side than I can even begin to realize, based on yesterday, but having serious enemies you don't even know and getting kidnapped and threatened is no fun at all. It's really scary. I have to admit that when I saw Walid's abilities, and Mafulla's, to handle the sudden threat on the train, I was a little envious of the preparation and the training I'm sure they get because of their positions in the palace, and that's what initially made me suggest the identity switch. I wanted to pretend like I had that sort of preparation, too, and could go into action like that. But, wow, it's really different being the targeted object of hostile intent—far different from anything I imagined. It's not just excitement. It's not at all what I thought. It's kind of a shock to the system. It gets to you, deep down."

Walid at this point spoke up, and said, "Well, I've heard what you did during the ride into town and before we got to you, I have to say that you reacted as well as any expertly trained military guy could have. You stayed calm and focused and used what you had. You used the power of thought and your physical abilities really well to stay alive and keep the bad guys off guard and scrambling. Mafulla and I truly admire what you and Jabari did. It was great."

At hearing his name in this context, Jabari's cheeks burned with a combination of embarrassment and pleasure and pride. He hung his head and thought what a good guy Walid is to have said such a thing. But then he knew what Walid was like, and this was just thoroughly consistent with his personality, and character. Jabari broke out of his pondering and then looked up and replied, "Hey, it was easy for me. Set was operating out of his own resources alone. But I had a wild monkey on my side." That brought more laughter into the room.

"Yeah, all I have is Mafulla," Walid joked, and laughter rang out again.

"I also need to say something else at this point, if it's Ok," Jabari added. He looked at Set and Walid and then at Khalid for approval.

Khalid said, "Certainly. We want to hear. Go ahead."

"Thanks. I just wanted to say that I also felt everything Set felt, and that's, in a way, even stranger. Set knew he wasn't really the prince. And I knew I wasn't really the best friend of the prince, although Walid and I are tight like glue," he said, holding his hands pressed together. There were a couple of laughs again.

"Like super sticky glue," Walid smiled and said.

"But, however artificially and temporarily, I was getting a

reflected fake glory and that was enough to make me feel different about myself. I mean, it seems silly, but I was really walking on air. I was special. And then, thinking about this last night, I realized two things. First, that everybody needs to feel special, and maybe we should be more aware of this, and go out of our way more often to show people how we respect and admire them just for who they are."

Jabari stopped for a moment as if to recall what he wanted to say next. And he looked around the room for a second and then went on. "But, also—and I know that, at first, this kind of sounds contradictory, and yet it's really not—I thought, maybe we ourselves, each and every one of us, shouldn't depend so much on other people for the way we feel about ourselves. Maybe most of our self-esteem should be solid and inside us, well rooted in our own hearts, regardless of what the people around us think or say. I mean, if other people like you and appreciate you, then great. But if they don't, or even if they just don't show it, then really, what difference should that make? Each of us knows who we are, deep down inside, or at least we should. We have things in us worth honoring and respecting. And we should really value ourselves. We should each feel our own special importance in the big picture, or the grand scheme of things." Many heads around the room were nodding in agreement with these words.

Walid spoke up and said, "Maybe this is a part of what the king often speaks of as the oasis within each of us—a special place of peace and power and goodness. Like a real oasis that's beautiful and calm, it shouldn't really matter what people say about it. Praise doesn't make it better. And people ignoring it won't take anything away from its intrinsic qualities. And we should realize that we're all like that."

"Good point, man. I totally agree," Jabari said and then he went on. "You're unique. I'm unique. Maybe if we more normally felt that way, it wouldn't turn our heads so much if other people happened to praise us or compliment us. And we wouldn't get so discouraged if others ignore us or criticize us. We'd just be happy to be who we are, and we'd feel fine, regardless. Ninety percent of self-esteem, maybe, I'm thinking, should come from within, from inside us, not from other people. And that's what I realized from all this, and I think it's huge."

At the conclusion of his remarks, everyone applauded. Jabari looked surprised and quickly said, "Oh, my! I thank you so much for your act of affirmation just now in your applause. And, of course, I suppose I shouldn't need it, but still: always feel free." Everyone again laughed.

He smiled at the laughs and said, "Thank you, thank you again. You're really putting me to the test today, but … I'm still who I am, even without the nice applause and the affirming laughter, but thank you very much, nonetheless. I appreciate you, even though, like me, you shouldn't need it." Then he added, "And if Manni were here right now, he would screech out his appreciation and high regard to each and every one of you. But, then again, who needs a monkey to tell you that you're great? You just are."

"Thanks, Jabari. Well said," commented Khalid, with a look of approval.

"I also appreciate your kind words, Khalid. Again, they're unrequired, utterly unnecessary, but gratefully valued."

Khalid laughed and said, "Yes, you've made your point quite well, my friend. Enough, already!" And he laughed again.

"Ok. But I will always be extremely grateful for the mere gesture of a … good grade, I should be quick to add. That can be part of the legitimate ten percent of self esteem that comes from outside me."

"Duly noted. A plus."

At that, Jabari grinned and did his best Mafulla double eyebrow jump, and everyone who saw him do it laughed again.

Khalid turned to the prince and said, "Walid and Mafulla, how did the identity switch affect you at all?"

Walid answered right away and said, "Well, I was actually at first sort of relieved a little bit, as if something real had been taken off my shoulders. I mean, I knew we were just goofing around, and it was a game we were all playing, but there was something surprising about being able to step aside and let somebody else take at least a part of the big role that I'm still so new in. For sure, I love representing my family and the great people of the kingdom, and being the prince and all, but I didn't realize how much relief I'd feel in letting someone else step into the spotlight even in a pretend way for a few hours. It was really great. In just the first few minutes, I got to relax in a whole new way. And that was something I hadn't expected at all."

Mafulla then spoke up and said, "My experience was totally different."

"How so?" Khalid asked.

"Well, right away, I sort of really missed my usual role, big time." As Mafulla admitted this, he held up his hands in a wide expansive gesture that generated some smiles and a couple of friendly chuckles. He then continued, "It's kind of embarrassing to say this, but, I mean, Walid's sort of the sun and I'm just the moon. You can call me … Moonfulla." With this, there was of course a big double eyebrow jump. Chuckles again. "My light, such as it is, is mostly just reflected—the public light, at least. I saw Jabari catching the bounce and I felt like, sigh, there it goes. And that's just crazy. But I guess it's a real proof of how powerful role-playing can be. With even the fake adopting of someone else's identity, we can so easily morph into the role and feel what we would feel, or might feel, or at least part of it, if the change was real. But of course, I don't mean to imply for a second that Jabari himself normally feels bad or jealous that I get a reflected experience or role of something like near-royalty—not at all. But, once you've had the special and, let's face it, totally unearned privilege that I've had, you really miss it, at least at first, if it's gone in even a pretend way. It's as if, when you know what it's like, you really come to feel a need for something most people never experience at all, and that's weird."

Set said, "Maybe there are some things you're almost better off not knowing."

"Yeah, maybe so," Jabari agreed.

"You might be right," Mafulla said. "But, ultimately, I guess, no piece of knowledge or understanding is in itself a bad thing. It can be a challenge, though, and like every other challenge, what matters most is how you handle it." At that statement, the other guys nodded their heads in full agreement.

"How did the rest of you feel when the pretend prince and his friend were kidnapped for real?" Khalid asked the entire class.

"Shocked. And scared," Ara said.

"Really scared," Khata added.

"Yeah," Bafur said, and glanced around the room as he continued with the words, "We'd feel terrible if something like that happened to Walid and Mafulla, but we all sort of assume that somehow they're ready, or prepared, or something, for a thing like that to happen, and it wouldn't be such a surprise or maybe affect them as much. And that's likely just baloney, which, I have to say is best when it's fried and served with mustard on very thin bread."

"Now, everyone's a comedian," Khalid said with a smile.

"Ok, well, what I mean is that, when you really think about it, such a thing would probably be just as rough for the real prince and the real Mafulla, but we too easily assume that the real ones are primed for stuff like that. And then, when it happens to one of us ordinary guys, or two of us, we totally freak out with worry. But it's likely just as bad, regardless of who might experience it."

"That's a wise perspective, Bafur," Hoda said. "Wise, indeed." Then she said to the group in general, "Do you think that the kidnapping affected the boys and the girls of our classes who weren't directly involved in different ways, or the same?"

"I bet it was basically the same," Cabar said. "I mean, we all have emotions and we all like Set and Jabari a lot, and so I'm guessing we were all equally worried about them."

Malik spoke up and said, "I really wanted to do something about it. I mean, when Hamid and Omari left with Walid and Mafulla to chase the kidnappers, I thought: Really? They get to go, but not the rest of us? It bummed me out a little at first, and then I remembered what Walid and Mafulla were able to do on the train and I thought, Ok, it's the preparation that Omari and Hamid know they have. That's the reason. And I felt more Ok about it, but I still itched to do something."

"We're a couple of itchy guys," Walid said, looking over at Malik, who smiled and nodded.

Then Haji spoke up and said, "I sort of felt the same way. I've watched my dad over the years work out and prepare for stuff like this, and I've heard all about the great things he's done in the past. And I feel like I need to be able to step up, too, and do something good when bad things happen. And so, yeah, I was worried for the guys, but that just built up energy in me to do something, and it also took me a while to be Ok with the fact that we had to stay behind. What helped me feel better about it, though, was remembering that we didn't really know what was going to happen next. And we had some soldiers with us in Memphis, but maybe they'd need help if there was another problem. And those of us guys who remained behind at the campsite, well maybe we were needed there to provide the possibility of that extra help."

"That makes sense. I wish I had thought of it like that," Malik said. "I guess, in a way, we were ... needed backup."

"You were," Hoda said. "You really were. Could you imagine how we would have felt if all you guys went off to the city in hot pursuit of the known criminals and left my entire class out in the middle of nowhere, facing the unknown without you? It would have been a lot scarier. It wouldn't have been enough to just have the soldiers with us. We wouldn't have felt the same. And then, what if another group of violent criminals had attacked us? We depended on you guys, Malik, Haji, and Bafur." She made it a point to add the third name, because she suspected that Bafur had rarely felt heroic, or that he was at all appreciated as a protector, and she wanted him to share this feeling.

The three boys instantly looked like they felt better, at hearing this. Bafur said, "Thanks, Hoda. That's good. I didn't realize I was being of any help at all. I wished I could do something, but felt sort of like I didn't have anything to offer in such a crazy situation, except maybe good thoughts and prayers for all our friends who were involved."

"Mom's right," Kissa said. "We needed you guys who stayed with us."

"Yeah, she is," Hasina spoke up and said. "We all tried to use our thoughts in positive ways to be supportive, but you guys just have a form of strength and ability that's not as normal for us ladies. We felt a lot better with you there to help keep us safe and calmer." Hasina knew just what to say.

"I agree," Ara said. "We all do." The other girls were nodding that they felt the same.

"Ok, good. That's good. I'm now glad we could be there, then," Malik said. "It's really helpful that we're having this little talk," he added, "because, otherwise, nobody knows what anyone else is thinking and feeling."

"Yeah, true," Malik said.

"That's absolutely right," Hoda added. "And, you know, maybe we have unearthed a bit of a difference between the way the students in the two classes reacted to the events. Everyone wished they could help, and wanted to. But the boys seem to have had more of a visceral urge to do something physical to help. The girls wanted to find another way to be supportive."

"That's interesting," Bafur said.

"Yeah, it is," Bakat agreed.

"Totally," Ara chimed in.

But just then, Walid's dad, Rumi, came into the room with something under his arm. He said, "I'm so sorry to interrupt, Khalid, Hoda, and everyone, but, Your Majesty, there's something that you need to see immediately."

23

The Stunning Headline

Rumi walked quickly toward the back of the room and handed the king a copy of the morning's edition of *The Kingdom Daily News*. He then looked over at Khalid and Hoda, who were both standing against the wall on the side of the room, and repeated his apology. "I'm really sorry about this. It's an urgent matter or I wouldn't have barged in on you in the middle of your class."

"It's not a problem. You're always welcome," Khalid said.

Rumi's use of the word 'urgent' got everyone's curiosity up, and a mild sense of anxiety enveloped the room. Various students shot glances at each other as they all sat in silence, waiting to find out what was going on. The king started reading silently at first, and then said aloud, "Well. This is a completely surprising turn of events. Khalid? Hoda? May I have the floor?"

"Yes, Your Majesty, certainly," Khalid said, surprised.

"Absolutely," Hoda replied.

"Rumi, please stay," the king requested.

The two teachers both moved toward seats, as did Rumi, and the king stood up to walk to the front of the room. Of course, knowing court etiquette, everyone else instantly started standing as well, and the king waved them all back down. "Sit, Sit, please. You honor me. I thank you."

He got to the front and turned to face everyone else, holding the newspaper in his hand. Walid's heart was racing. Mafulla's was about to break out of his chest. BaBoom, BaBoom, BaBoom, BaBoom. Each of the two boys swallowed hard. But no one else noticed their nervous and intense concern. All eyes were on the king, who looked around the room and asked, "Has anyone seen today's paper?"

Various people were shaking their heads no. Walid and Mafulla were afraid to open their mouths or even move in response to the king's question. Khalid said, "It was apparently running late this morning. It hadn't been delivered when it was time to leave the house and come to the palace, and it's usually there much earlier."

"Same here," Set said. "No paper this morning at my house either, at least when we left for school."

"Well, it's been delivered now, and there's a surprising headline at the top of the front page. Allow me to read it to you all."

Masked Crime Fighters Cross the Line
To Mass Murder

The king turned the paper briefly in their direction so that they could all see the very large and shocking headline. He then turned it back around and started to read. As he began and went on, he heard a couple of voices whisper, "What?" and "No way!" He glanced up, but kept on reading. When he got to the end, there was total silence in the room.

Kissa and Hasina looked at each other with a mixture of utter perplexity and yet alarm on their faces. They each wanted desperately to look at Walid and Mafulla, but dared not do so.

The king folded the paper and put it down on a desk. He looked around the room and remarked, "I believe that we're all going to get much more of an educational experience today than even the most hopeful of us had anticipated." He then looked over at Khalid and said, "If I remember correctly, the boys' class discussed the exploits of these mysterious masked marvels the day the news came out about their first public appearance, when they stopped a robbery in the marketplace and returned some personal and valuable items to a lady who had been knocked to the ground by a common thief."

"Your memory serves you well, Your Majesty," Khalid said.

"Good. And could any of the boys tell me what the drift of opinion was on that day in class? What did you think about these masked men?"

"That they're awesome," Jabari said.

"Yeah," Set agreed. "Most of us thought right away that they were doing great things for the city, things that needed to be more commonly done. If we had time, we'd probably have created a fan club for them, or something."

Khata said, "A lot of the girls have talked about them, too. We were excited that there were men like that out on the street stopping crime and protecting the rest of us in places where the police might not be."

"Then they broke up that luxury store robbery not long ago," Kit said. "My mom shops there, and what if she had been in the store when the thief showed up? It's dangerous now all over, and those guys have just been trying to make our city a little safer."

"But what about the newspaper and what it's saying?" The king asked.

"Well, we know it to be totally false, nothing but lies," Set said.

"How do we know that?"

"We were there! Those pieces of dark cloth on the floor that they're calling masks —the only pieces of cloth on the floor that I saw were the blindfolds those guys had put on me and Jabari."

"Yeah, we got them off and threw them down. They weren't masks at all," Jabari said, with real frustration in his voice.

"And, how did the unfortunate deaths happen yesterday?" The king continued his questions.

Walid answered, "Those guys tried to kill Set and Jabari and then all the rest of us, too, when we got there to rescue them. And we had to fight back and defend ourselves and, unfortunately, some of the bad guys went down. There was no other way they could be stopped. They were violent to the max, and vicious to the core. They wouldn't just quit and give up. And our guys were better shots."

"Yeah," Mafulla said, "it was the palace rescue teams that had to take down those guys, not two masked crime fighters. We were there. We saw it all happen."

The irony, of course, that just occurred to both Walid and Mafulla, in the course of making these remarks, was that there was a sense in which The Golden Viper and Windstorm had indeed been there and had been involved, not as costumed or masked characters, but as the people they really were, namely, Walid and Mafulla. And yet not, of course, in the way the paper was claiming, and that the anonymous caller was saying.

"How anonymous was that caller?" The king further asked.

"Well, he may have fooled the paper, but it was clearly Ari Falma," Walid said. "He talked about his brother being killed, and that guy, the guy who tried to shoot and kill me, was Idi Falma. And unless Idi had other crime lord brothers—which we have no evidence of at all—then, obviously the caller was his notorious brother Ari. And he even admitted to being the criminal in charge of the organization. Again, that's Ari Falma."

"Correct," the king said. He paused in thought for a moment and went on, concluding, "So, what the paper is reporting today as major front page headline news, is completely false." Everyone nodded.

"How could that happen?"

Jabari said, "They were told all this false stuff by that Falma guy, and they went to the site of the battle—I have to call it that because that's really what it was—and they saw just enough there that they could interpret as confirming his story. His account was already in their heads, and they looked and found what they expected to see. And they leaped way beyond what was actually there to believe what he wanted them to believe."

"That sounds right," the king replied.

"And it's all false," Jabari added.

The king nodded and said, "And now, what's happening as a result?"

"The public—all the readers of the paper who don't have the contrary, disproving evidence that we have—will turn against two innocent men and the police will misuse time, energy, and manpower trying to hunt them down," Malik said.

"Absolutely right, Malik, and well said. What, then, if anything, could the paper have done to avoid this major mistake on their part?"

"They could have called the police, and then the palace," Kit suggested.

"Yes. And while they may indeed have called the police, they did not call the palace or check with us at all," the king said. "They believed the word of a criminal enough to go searching for evidence to confirm his exciting and scandalous story, and then they took things at face value in a world where little should be taken in this way."

"But Your Majesty, may I ask a question?" Bakat spoke with a tone of hesitation.

"Certainly. Ask anything."

"Why do we say they should have called the palace? If they're going to report on a crime, it makes sense to call the police, because they deal with criminals all the time, but why do we think they should have even considered calling here at the palace for information about such a matter?"

"That's a good question. But there's an equally good answer.

For one thing, what they saw at the warehouse could have been the result of a palace guard operation, or a military operation, which it after all was, and the palace can always be consulted about such things. The scale of the unfortunate aftermath was beyond the results of normal criminal activity. The newspaper reporter should have at least done something to rule out the possibilities of palace guard or military action before accepting the word of a self-acknowledged criminal."

"Oh. Yes. That makes sense."

"I would be surprised if someone at the police station didn't at least suggest that they check in with us, just in case we were somehow involved. Perhaps they did offer such guidance, and the reporter chose not to take the time, under the press of a deadline. And, after all, it sounds like he persuaded his source at police headquarters to believe what he had already come to accept. But the people at the newspaper, like the police, should be more careful in such matters. Sound journalism requires great care. So does good police work."

Khalid spoke up. "An unreliable source put an idea in their heads that then became the organizing principle for everything they saw or heard."

"Yes, that's right. Now, why would the unreliable source, Ari Falma, have made that telephone call to the newspaper and told them all this false information in the first place?"

"Well," Mafulla said, "he must have found out that many of his men were dead, and maybe he was looking for a way to hide the fact that they died because of a kidnapping plot against the royal family."

"That's possible." The king nodded thoughtfully. "But why go public to cover up something that wasn't likely to be publicly known?"

"Good point. Maybe he made up the Viper and Storm story because of how they've stopped his criminal activity in the past, and he saw this as a great chance to get even. So he covered up the kidnapping and rescue scenario with a lie that would serve his purposes."

"Or, maybe he didn't know about the kidnapping plot at all," Walid said.

"How could he not know?" Set asked.

"Yeah, how could that be?" Jabari echoed his friend.

"Well, maybe this was something that his brother Idi was doing on his own, and Ari didn't know about it. It was Idi who was there. Ari himself admitted that his brother was there and he wasn't."

Mafulla said, "But, in the past, from what I know about them, and it surely isn't much, they both worked together. Why would one brother do something so big and not tell the other brother about it?"

Walid replied, "Sibling rivalry? I don't know. Maybe Idi, the younger of the two, was trying to do something to surprise and impress his brother and prove he could pull off a job on his own that was really big and produced a lot of money. I don't know."

"That's a stretch, but an interesting thought," Mafulla said.

"I just wonder whether Ari would have even thought to call the newspaper and make all these claims so quickly himself, right after the events that happened, if he wasn't really scared for his own life."

"Good point."

Walid continued. "The paper mentioned that he sounded panicked and afraid. I don't think he would have come across like that if he had just been making up a lie to get revenge on the crime fighter guys. It strikes me that he would have placed that call when he did and the way he did only if he really believed the story he was telling and was trying to get someone to stop the masked men."

"I see what you're saying," Mafulla replied. "That makes sense."

"Yeah. But I admit I'm struggling to figure out why he would have thought that, in particular, the Viper and the Storm had done those things, rather than someone else. If he didn't know about the kidnapping, it would never have occurred to him that his men could have been killed by a rescue team from the palace who were there to free some victims. The actual truth couldn't have crossed his mind. He wouldn't have known about any of that, and he would have been trying to come up with an explanation that could make some sense of what he found."

The king then said, "Some of you may remember that there was a hostage rescue operation months ago when Ari Falma had kidnapped Mafulla's mother and his two younger siblings. Palace rescue teams stormed the hiding place, and that successful operation also unfortunately resulted in a number of deaths, a consequence that could not have been avoided. Falma learned of the deaths, and we subsequently had reason to think that he wrongly attributed them to a mysterious individual for whom he had worked, a man who may have revolutionary aims—an individual named Farouk al-Khoum. Fearing that Farouk would do the same to him, Falma fled the kingdom for months. And then he came back, but with precisely what intent, we don't know. And yet, confidentially, we suspect that he's now in league with the former king, who, like Falma's previous boss, Farouk al-Khoum, has his own revolutionary intentions. And that puts Falma at odds in a new way with Farouk. But this is all highly sensitive information, and I would ask that you not share it with anyone outside this group." The room was totally quiet at this point, apart from the king's voice.

Ali continued: "Actually, we're confronted with the odd situation that there have been two pairs of brothers vying for similar and competing goals. Farouk has a brother Faraj, and they're helping each other with an ambition to rule our land, but are very competitive with each other. Ari Falma had as a brother, Idi, and we have reason to believe that there was also a great tension between them. Ari was older and smarter, and Idi, we think, must have resented being in his shadow. So he may indeed have launched this kidnapping effort without telling his brother, just to show that he could pull it off without Ari's help. And presumably, Harvey Kinkaid, working for Farouk and unaware of the Falma ambitions regarding the monarchy, was going to pay Idi a lot of money for the prince. So, Idi was going to do something for Kinkaid that would benefit Farouk, likely without knowing that latter fact, and Farouk was working against what Idi and Ari's new supporter, the previous king here, was helping them to help him achieve."

"Wow. That's complicated." Set said this out loud without even realizing he was doing so.

"There are too many bad guys involved," Mafulla said. "You almost need a chart, or a play book."

"Yes. You're both right," The king said. And he continued. "Then, as we know, the plan launched by Kinkaid went bad. Idi hired men who kidnapped the wrong people, and we found them and fought the kidnappers. Ari discovers his brother and their men dead. Who did this? Assuming now that Idi was indeed acting on his own and doing all this secretly, without his brother's knowledge, then Ari couldn't possibly know it was us, because he had no reason to think that we would be anywhere near that building on that day, or have any intentions toward him or his men that would have such a result. Who then could it be? He recently had a robbery planned, one that presumably he depended on for a large amount of money, that was stopped by these two masked men, The Golden Viper and Windstorm. He resented their interference and hated them for stopping the theft. He says he planned to catch and kill them. Then he sees his men caught and killed. So he leaps to a conclusion. He has the Viper and the Storm on his brain. They're what he's been thinking about recently, and even obsessing about. So, it's no surprise that they come to mind. He reasons that they must have found out about his plan and moved to stop him, pre-emptively killing his men, as he thought that other mystery man Farouk al-Khoum had recently done, as well. We always use the past to help us understand the present. It often works. But sometimes, it doesn't."

"That all makes sense, Your Majesty," Set said. And the king nodded toward him and continued his musings.

"Ari Falma thinks, 'Mystery men kill my men. It's happened before and it's happened now. Mystery men want to kill me.' So, he flees the scene and has no idea what to do or where to go to be safe. He has no way of fighting these unseen and unknown adversaries. So he gets the idea to enlist the paper and public opinion and the police in protecting him, the real lawless individual remaining at large here on the scene. And it works! He tells his story to the paper, and the editor goes to The Golden Street to check it out, and there are all these dead men, and two strips of cloth—the masks, in both their minds now—and as a result, we get this outrageously false story."

The king then paused and said, "The interesting thing about the current hypothesis we're considering is that, if it's right, then this man who lies about nearly everything, Ari Falma, was for once not lying when he called the paper. He was telling them what he sincerely believed to be the truth, if we're right in how we're now interpreting all this. And so the newspaper has today printed heinous falsehoods for everyone to read and believe—that is to say, everyone except us, of course, because we know the truth already. And as coming from the paper, these gross falsehoods aren't lies—because the reporters and editors there apparently believe that what they're saying is true. They're not seeking to deceive anyone. They've been careless, not mendacious. But the result is the same in that now most all their readers will have outrageously false beliefs about what's happened." The king let all of them think about what he had just said. He allowed them to hang on his words long enough to soak in the whole story.

Mafulla raised his hand, and the king nodded. "So," he broke the silence, "I guess, Your Majesty, that someone from the palace needs to talk to the paper and explain that the story is false, that those men were not murdered at all by two formerly upstanding but now allegedly lunatic, out-of-control vigilantes, known as The

Golden Viper and Windstorm. But instead, they were killed in self-defense by a palace assault force on a rescue operation. And the masked men who have just had their names trashed in the realm of public opinion are not at all the terrible criminals that they've now been falsely portrayed as being. Then the paper tomorrow could print a retraction and a correction, and everything would be set right."

"Yes!" the king said. "That would be a marvelous resolution. I just wish we could do it."

"What do you mean?" Walid asked with complete confusion on his face and in his voice. "Why can't we do it?"

"In order to be able to catch Ari Falma, who is still at large—and who, after all, is the real kingpin of most of the crime around here—in order to be able to stop him from doing much worse things than even those that his brother was attempting yesterday—evil deeds on a vastly larger scale, and damaging to many more people—we can't let him know too much about what's actually going on."

"I don't understand," Set spoke up and said.

"There's a reason we leave a crime scene and a rescue scene the way we left the warehouse yesterday, as well as the other building where some of Falma's men were discovered by our observation team. If other criminals show up and see it that way, it can strike a visceral fear into their hearts and they can also interpret it in whatever way is natural for them. And then this may get them to do things that will set them up for their own downfall. If everything is clear and tidy and easy to understand, then we lose some tactical and even strategic advantages."

"How does that work?" Set asked. He then added, "Is it Ok for me to ask this, Your Majesty?"

The king said, "Yes, certainly. You're asking a good question. Right now, Ari Falma is presumably still afraid of Farouk al-Khoum, thinking wrongly that he killed many of his men months ago. If he knew that it was our people in a rescue operation, he would fear only us. Now, though, he has double the fear. He naturally fears us as he would the police, but he also has this extra focus of concern. And so his attention is divided. He can't help but worry that the legitimate authorities will find out what he's up to and stop him, and likely imprison or execute him. And he now worries that this somewhat mysterious, unseen opponent, the man Farouk al-Khoum, will return at any time to finish the job he started, and kill the rest of his men and him. Plus, now, as of yesterday, he thinks he has even more deadly enemies, the apparently powerful, mysterious, and masked Viper and Storm. And they've struck now more recently and closer to him. He's probably terrified for his life. And that's when people like him make mistakes. Well, to be more precise, it's one of two conditions where people make big mistakes—when they're overconfident to the point of real arrogance, or when they're confused and worried to the point of great fear. We need for Falma to continue to be confused and misled and to be watching out in all the wrong ways. That's when he will do something that will make our jobs easier, and perhaps even destroy his own plans, whatever they might be."

The king paused for a second and then said, "If we clear it up for the newspaper, then they will clear it up for him, and we'll lose the tremendous strategic advantage we now have in his confusion, false beliefs, and fears. We can't afford to do that."

Bafur said, "But what about the poor guys—the Viper and the Storm?" Everybody's going to hate them for false reasons, and the police will be trying to catch or hurt them."

"Well, we can talk to the police chief privately and put a stop to the manhunt. The chief can keep his men from pursuing this and, if they ask why, he may even just say something like, 'The paper didn't get it at all right, and the king's men have chosen to deal with the situation.' Falma will probably not learn anything about the turnaround at police headquarters, but if he does and he even wrongly comes to think that it's because the chief wants these mystery men to continue to pursue and hunt him down, he'll likely be even more frightened. His ploy to get the police on his side in this crucial matter will have failed. And he'll be all alone to face his fears."

"But that still leaves the general public hating some good guys, because of the false claims."

"Yes, for a time, and that's indeed unfortunate. What mitigates the situation to some extent, however, is that the reputations that are being tarnished for a while are those associated with assumed identities rather than real ones."

"I hadn't thought of that."

"An identity that has been taken up can also be put aside for a time such as this, so that no other harm will come to the two innocent men. But the paper's allegations can't be corrected yet. Not at least by us, and not with the full story from the palace as to what really happened. We have to give this some time and trust that when these two masked men find out about what's going on, when they read or hear the story in the paper, they'll back off their normal activities and stay out of sight long enough to allow the entire storm to pass, so to speak. Or they may choose to take their own positive action. If they speak to the paper, they may be able to do something that might help clear their names. But of course they could tell the paper nothing of what actually happened." The king paused and said this again. "They couldn't tell the paper about what really took place. So our secrets would be preserved. They could only deny their own involvement and offer possible alternative hypotheses. But that's in their hands at this point, for sure, and not mine."

Walid shot a furtive glance at Mafulla, who made his own eye contact over this, but only for the briefest moment.

Set then spoke up. "But, Your Majesty, is it morally right for us to stand back and allow good people to have their reputations trashed, even in connection with assumed identities or roles, just because it temporarily serves our purposes? Or, to put it another way, can right really be served by wrong?"

"Your questions are good ones. Right is never properly served by wrong. But what in most circumstances would be wrong can, in particularly vexed situations, be not only permissible, but also required, and thus not only right in the minimal moral sense of allowable or justifiable, but in the stronger sense of being actually obligated."

"I'm not sure I follow."

"Jabari had to shoot someone yesterday. Ordinarily that would be a morally prohibited and wrong act. But in the circumstances, it wasn't just a forgivable wrong, or even a right act in only the minimal sense of morally permissible, but perhaps even, in the precise terrible circumstances, required. If that man had not been stopped at that moment, both Jabari and others could have been killed."

"I see what you're saying, Your Majesty."

"Wisdom is needed for understanding how our most basic principles are to be applied in specific conditions and circumstances. Some will say that it's never justified to act in self-defense as you and many of our friends had to act yesterday. And it's impossible to prove them wrong. Yet the voice of wisdom, in my view, guides us differently. The injuries or deaths inflicted in strict self-defense were, in my understanding, tragic necessities, given the circumstances that rapidly unfolded. Nothing different should have been done instead."

"That makes sense to me, and I see how it applies to my question," Set concluded. "Thanks for that."

"You're welcome. But I also need to issue a cautionary note," the king said. "We should always be much quicker to sacrifice ourselves and our own reputations, if needed, in order to stop great evil, than ever to endanger or sacrifice the health or reputation of another innocent person. But sometimes, difficult things are required of us. And yet, they should never be done without a real sense of the tragedy involved, a regrettable difficulty created and necessitated by the evil that has arisen. We do regret any loss that our actions cause, however good the end or purpose might be that those actions serve. But we do what we must. And we should feel no ongoing guilt about what is required."

"Well said, Your Majesty," Khalid commented.

"Thank you, my friend. It will be very interesting to see what happens next," the king replied.

Ara put up her hand and said, "I'm sorry, Your Majesty, but are there really revolutionaries out there, people seeking to overturn your rule and take over our kingdom?"

"Yes, always, throughout the entirety of human history, there have been people who were not in power and who wanted the power. Our time is no different."

"Does that worry you?"

"I wondered the same thing, Your Majesty," Khata said. And then she added, "Does that keep you up at night?"

"No—not at all. My job is to deal with every problem that comes our way. Worry doesn't help in this task. Care and consideration and courage do." The king smiled. "Are there any other questions?"

Another hand went up and the king nodded. Kit said, "So, Your Majesty, I want to make sure I'm clear on what you told Set just a minute ago. You said it's Ok to let another person believe something false and go on believing it when we could correct him, and we're morally justified in withholding the truth in order to help us with our own plans?"

"Nice way of summing it up," Set added.

"Thanks." Kit glanced at Set and then back at the king.

Ali smiled and said, "That's a very well articulated and perceptive follow up question. I'll try to answer every bit as carefully as I think you've posed the issue."

"I was hoping it would be Ok to ask."

"It is. And I'm glad you did. I believe that every human being needs truth. And I believe that we all have a natural obligation to provide the truth to others when we have it and reasonably believe that making it available will not result in great harm to innocent people. But if a certain truth would be used by a particular individual as a weapon to do great harm, or to help provide conditions in which he could continue to do great harm, then we have no obligation to put that weapon into that person's hands and thus act as his accomplice, however unintentionally. As things normally go, people deserve the truth, until they prove otherwise and disqualify themselves by the evil they would choose to do with it. I hope that makes sense." Kit nodded her head, with a very thoughtful look on her face.

At that moment, a messenger came through the door with a piece of paper in his hand and showed it to the king. He read it and looked up. "I'm terribly sorry, everyone, I have to take the prince and Mafulla to my chambers for a bit to help me with a situation that's developed. It's nothing to worry about, which as you know, I'd not encourage in any case, but it's just something they've been involved in helping me with. If you wouldn't mind?" He looked over at Khalid, who nodded, and then he gestured to the two boys. They got up from their chairs and sort of waved to everyone else, with a sheepish look on their faces. Rumi also rose from his chair.

Walid glanced over at Khalid and mouthed the word, "Sorry."

Khalid smiled and nodded again and motioned with his hand for them to leave freely. The king then said to all who were still in their seats, "Thank you for your time and attention today, class, and for the gracious invitation, Hoda and Khalid. I've enjoyed very much being with you. I trust that certain aspects of our conversations can stay confidential among us. It's been nice to see all of you and to hear your comments. You're a remarkable group of people and I am, as always, proud to know you and count you as friends. I hope we can do something like this again, soon. There's a lot more to philosophize about in the Falma interpretation of yesterday's events, as well as in the overall situation. I hope it can provide for more ongoing and fruitful discussion. Until next time!" He smiled, nodded, and walked out the door, accompanied by the two boys and applause from the students and teachers. Rumi said a quick word to Khalid and then gave the students a small wave of his hand and also left the room.

No one had a clue as to what would soon take place.

24

The Truth Can Set You Free

"Mafulla, my friend, you have two very concerned parents in my sitting room at this very moment."

"Oh man. I was so afraid of this."

"Let's go there together and ease their minds." The king spoke in a low voice as they walked down the hallway.

"Are they Ok, or totally distraught?"

"They're all right, the note from Kular says. They're just very concerned and … keen on speaking with you."

"They saw a paper?"

"They saw a paper. We need to assure them that we don't harbor any vicious criminals within our walls. We should tell them what I just told the class. But they'll need a bit more background, not having been with everyone throughout the day yesterday, and not having been briefed about it all in advance of seeing the article."

"Ok."

When the king and the boys walked through the door of the sitting room, Shamilar jumped up from her chair as Shapur rose slowly. She ran over to Mafulla, and said, "Oh! My son! My son! I don't believe it!"

"Mom, you shouldn't believe a word of it."

"And I don't, not for a second!" A tear ran down her face.

"Good."

"But, my precious boy, why did our paper say those terrible things?"

Before Mafulla could respond, the king said, "Please, sit, dear friends, and I'll explain everything that's happened, and what will take place next. And be assured that Mafulla and Walid are fine, and that they will be fine. The police won't pursue them for any reason at all. There won't be any trouble from these false charges. And there's, of course, no shred of truth in what the paper has said about them. By the time I finish filling you in on all the relevant facts, you'll be able to relax once more and experience an appropriate sense of peace about it all. I promise."

The king never had a more attentive audience for one of his explanations. Shamilar was literally on the edge of her seat. Her hands often came to her mouth in shock or worry at one or another part of the long backstory. Ali was very diplomatic and careful about what he said, but he was also as complete as he needed to be. Shapur sat well ensconced in his chair and nodded his understanding at various points in the king's remarks. "So, there you have it," the king concluded.

"Oh, my." Shamilar was pretty much without words at this point, but at least she was also without the tremendous worry and emotional tension that she had brought across town and into the room.

Shapur said, "Thank you, Your Majesty, for all this. What a life you must live! I had no idea. The boys are learning more about human nature from all these events than any number of books could show them, and in a visceral way that will last in their hearts and minds."

"Yes, indeed, palace life is an ongoing education for all of us in a great many ways."

"But is it safe?" Shamilar asked.

The king responded, "There are many dangers and threats in the world, things that we all face regardless of where we live and what we do. Palace life brings its own special mix of dangers and threats, but it also carries with it more defenses and protections than most people enjoy."

"But are the protections enough for boys their ages?"

"Yes. In balance, I firmly believe that the boys are both quite safe. And they're also positioned to do great good in their lives. Absolute safety is, of course, not an option anywhere in the world of the living. Where there's life, there's risk. But where there's life, there's hope. And we happen to be genuine experts in both risk management and robust hope around here."

He then added, "Where else could Mafulla have a top notch security guard detail, and one that involves a crazy monkey?" At that, everyone had to smile.

"I understand, Your Majesty. I understand," Shamilar said. "I just worry. Mothers worry."

"Yes. It's natural. You care deeply about your son. We all do. And you worry. But that just means the rest of us should do more to reassure you. And we'll try to be better about it."

"Oh, no, Your Majesty. You don't have to go to any trouble on account of me. You have a very big job as it is. I can't even imagine. But what you've done just now, the story you've told us, the time you've given us—well, that's a great gift I treasure. And I trust that everything will work out in this situation. Just hearing you tell us about it, I grew in my confidence that nothing here is out of control, that Mafulla is being cared for and that, in so many ways, he can already take care of himself. I almost forget that he's not five years old any more, or even eight. You know, every age he's grown through is still in my mind and in my heart. I often forget that even though the five-year-old and the eight-year-old are still inside him, there's also now much more to him, as well—in fact, a lot more. He's so grown and so much more developed into a capable young man. But it just takes a mother some time to adjust to that. You and Shapur are very generous in being so patient with me."

The king smiled at her warmly. "We've all benefited from the concern of a mother or a father, or someone else who took care of us when we were small. We understand the myriad little dangers that you have to become habituated to watching out for and helping us to avoid. And strong habits stay with you. I'm just glad you came to me with your concerns so quickly."

Kular stuck his head in the door, and said, "I'm so sorry to interrupt, Your Majesty, but I thought you might want to know that Naqid is here, as you requested."

"Good, thank you, Kular. Please invite him to have a seat in the reception area and I'll be with him shortly."

"Yes, Your Majesty."

"Oh, King Ali, we don't want to keep you from important business," Shamilar said. "I'm fine now. We're fine. You've been so helpful and kind about all this."

"It's my pleasure," the king said.

"We should go and let you get on with your day."

"My time is yours whenever you need it," the king replied and stood.

Everyone else rose, and Shapur said, "Thank you again, Your Majesty."

"You're quite welcome, my friend. And please, feel free to visit any time, even when the newspaper is behaving itself."

That got a laugh from Shapur and he said, "We will, whether that ever happens or not." Mafulla and Walid walked them out, as Naqid bowed his greeting and slipped into the king's room.

The boys spoke with Mafulla's parents in the hallway for a few more minutes, both apologizing profusely for the anxiety they had been put through, and expressing their own feelings about the whole ordeal. Then, after some hugs and kisses and firm handshakes, the two relieved parents turned to leave.

But a second later, one of them stopped and turned back to the boys. "Be careful in everything you do," Shamilar said to Mafulla. "And you too, young man—Your Highness," she said to Walid, and wagged her finger at him.

Across town, there was little relief to be felt. The two men sat in shadows inside the small apartment building that had been their refuge for the night. The man with the large bushy mustache said, "It was a good idea, coming to Badri's apartment."

"He certainly doesn't need it any more. And it's far away from my house," Ari Falma said. "It was better than a hotel. No record, no witnesses. And there was food available. The fact that he lived alone made it possible. Now, I just have to decide what we do next."

"Well, at least the newspaper came through for you today, and even better than we had hoped."

"Yes, it was quite well done. And the part about the police was a nice touch, an unexpected extra gift to us at a time when we need it."

"You really think it was those two guys—the Viper and the Storm?"

"Who else could it be? If Farouk was anywhere around, there would have been some warning. We've got eyes and ears all over town. Somebody would have told me something. And he has no idea what we're doing now, or even where we are."

"Unless the leak was also talking to him."

That brought Ari to silence. He let out a breath and said, "Oh, my friend, how could such a thing be? I have to admit that I hadn't imagined that possibility at all. But what event would have triggered Farouk to do what was done yesterday, on precisely that day? The Viper and the Storm had a specific reason. We were prepared to take them down, and right away. Our plan involved them, not Farouk. It was they who had cause then to do something dramatic to save their own lives."

"True, but if Farouk has been patient, and is always looking to get revenge on you, and he learned that all those men would be gathered in a confined space, for whatever reason, he could have chosen that moment to strike for precisely its convenience. How often have so many of us been in one place like that for an extended time?"

"I see what you're saying," Falma acknowledged. "It's altogether possible. I may have blundered badly. Farouk surely has men who could do that, and in an instant. It may actually be a bigger stretch to suppose that the two masked men did it, two men alone against so many. But they're obviously trained and expert in martial arts and weapons and have a much higher degree of military skill than is ordinary. That was proved at The Luxury Shop. And there have been rumors since then of other exploits, wild actions against many opponents where they prevailed. And you saw the masks."

"I saw what could have been masks, yes. And yet, we don't know for sure, and we don't have solid confirmation for any of those stories."

"No, no, we don't. But where there's smoke, there's fire."

"That's also true."

"There wouldn't be so many rumors flying around about these two men unless there was a great deal of reality and truth to it. There's an old example we have of what I mean."

"What's that?"

"Counterfeit money works only because of real money. There can be baseless rumors, but when we hear so many from such otherwise reliable sources on the street, you start to wonder who these guys really are, and what they're capable of. I still think we saw an answer to that question yesterday."

"You're most likely right. I just still think we should be on the lookout not only for them, but also Farouk."

"That's smart. And it's wise. We have many enemies who would bring us harm. We have no reason to think that Farouk is here in

Cairo, or even his men, but we should still be exceedingly watchful. And we may indeed need to relocate again and leave the kingdom once more to get far away from where this recent action took place, far from where we could so easily be found, in the vulnerable state we're now experiencing, without our closest men."

"That sounds good to me. In fact, it's hard to think of anything more sensible, at present. The men out in the broader network who were untouched by this can still put things aside for us, and keep your share safe while we're away. Business can in that sense proceed in our absence."

"Yes, it can—as long as we've not lost too much standing in their eyes, in virtue of having lost so many of our top men."

"They know our men were strong. They'll have to realize that there were extraordinary forces in play yesterday, whatever the real truth is. No one can withstand an overwhelming, hostile force of nature when it concentrates all its fury in one small place."

"That's true." Ari nodded his head. "Nature will have its way."

"So, what do we do?"

"For now, I think, we have to go. We get out of here quickly. We'll send word to the network later."

In the palace, outside the king's rooms, Mafulla lingered for a few seconds more and watched his parents as they walked down the hallway. "See you soon!"

His mother turned and said, "Not soon enough!" and smiled. As they continued their path to the big staircase that would take them down to the large front entrance of the palace, Mafulla turned to Walid.

"Well, I guess we should be getting back to …"

"Not yet," Walid interrupted and quickly said. "Come to my room." He grabbed his friend by the arm and led him down the hall in the opposite direction, at a fast pace.

As soon as they were inside his door, he closed it and said, "We have to contact the paper. Remember what the king said in front of us and everyone else. He said that if the Viper and the Storm contacted the paper and denied all involvement, it might do some good. He said that we, or they—well, we—couldn't tell what really happened, but that if they or we offered plausible alternative hypotheses, that might help. Falma can still believe what he believes. He would know that the Viper and the Storm would deny everything, if they were at all like him, which he thinks they are. So it won't affect him or the confusion in him that the king wants to encourage, but it will affect the public sentiment—or at least, it might."

"Ok. I'm sure you're right. But this won't be easy. What can we say?"

"I think we should write it out to get it straight and then call the paper and read it over the phone in a fake voice or something."

"But won't the operator know that the phone call is coming from the palace?"

"Good point."

"If the paper has sources in the phone company, we could be really compromised."

"Ok, Ok, let me think," Walid said. "I know. How about if we address a note to the palace guard and say it's for them and the newspaper, and ask Masoon to carry it over to the paper? It will be like someone just delivered it here, not that it originated here."

"Good. I like it. We could do that. But it would really be important that the letter be written just right, very convincingly."

Walid replied, "Of course, I'm a convincing guy."

"Ok, well, you've convinced me, at least. So, let's get started. Where's some paper?"

"It's in the chest over there."

"You want it at your desk?"

"Yeah."

Mafulla walked over, found what was needed and brought it to his buddy, who sat down at the desk to write. "Ok, then, so here's the paper and a pen. I'll step aside and let you do the first draft."

"Thank you, dear innocent crime-fighting friend." Walid grinned. "I do appreciate your great faith in me—especially since you're the known master in the vast realm of words."

"Well put," Mafulla said, "But my faith is in the authenticity of your sincerity."

"I'll be making up a story."

"Ok, then do so authentically and sincerely."

Walid then sat down and began to write. "To the Palace Guard and the Police and *The Kingdom Daily News*: We have disguised our identities and had this note dropped at the palace for the king's men, and then to be delivered to the paper and the police."

"That's good. Nice start."

"We are The Golden Viper and Windstorm. We did not do what the paper has alleged in its headline article this morning. We had no involvement in those tragic events."

"Well, we did, you know."

"Oh. Yeah. But it wasn't the masked men identities, and this is coming from them."

"Oh, Ok. I guess that's right. So, keep writing."

"We have been libeled by a well known criminal, Ari Falma, and by the newspaper itself, now that it has passed on his outrageously false and vituperative claims—which are all wild allegations that have completely misrepresented who we are and what we do."

"Oh, I like that. Vituperative—that's very nice. You've been a good student to me," Mafulla said, still looking over Walid's shoulder.

"Yeah, I threw that in for you, since this is coming from both of us."

"Ok. Now comes the crucial stuff. You can do it. I have faith in you."

"We cannot correct your story with an alternate, accurate description of what happened at that warehouse on the Street of Gold, largely because it was not the work of anyone wearing a mask. In our secret identities as The Golden Viper and Windstorm, we would never do such a thing. As everyone who has ever seen us knows, we do not wear dark masks in our work of crime fighting. We wear light colored masks in all our efforts to help the public. We always have. Second, we do not go around targeting people for execution or any form of serious bodily harm. We seek to break up robberies and assaults and other types of crime that blight our great city. We may indeed have stopped Ari Falma's gang from stealing a great sum of money at an earlier date. And now he apparently hates us for it and would do anything to get revenge on us. His phone call to the paper, with all his false claims, was itself merely an effort to destroy our reputations and harm us. We do not expect to be liked by criminals. But we refuse to be defamed by them in the kingdom's own top newspaper."

"I like that. Keep going."

"For future reference: The masks we use are always the ordinary white, ivory, tan, or khaki wind scarves that you see so commonly nowadays on the street, especially when there is sand blowing in the air. On one occasion, light yellow had to do the job. Whatever pieces of dark cloth may have been found on the floor of that warehouse where criminal activity was apparently underway, they were not our wind scarves or masks. We did not engage in what we have been accused of doing, and would never involve ourselves in any illegal act of that sort—or of any sort."

"Good. Well said."

"So then, you may wonder: What happened at the warehouse and at the other building that resulted in those numerous deaths? We can only speculate for you here on all the reasonable possibilities. Anyone who knows of his history could conjure up several such scenarios. Ari Falma has many enemies, some of them terrible criminals, as well. One of them, or several of them, could have picked that time and place for an unfortunate act of revenge on him. The perpetrator could have been a shadowy figure that Falma once worked for, a man Falma believes to have done precisely this sort of thing before, months ago, in a location of a similar nature. Or it could have been the work of one or more of his many double-crossed victims within the criminal world, out for their own distorted version of justice. It might have been the desperate action of other thieves who resent him or who would like to take over his territory. It could have been some intended future victims of his who turned the tables on those killers in his employment and defended themselves with deadly force. The real possibilities are nearly endless."

"You're doing a fantastic job. I couldn't do better."

"Our point, however, is simple. It was not The Golden Viper and Windstorm. We have never committed a crime. We have only helped to prevent or stop crimes. We believe in the people of this city and of this kingdom. We seek justice and safety for all of us. We act with honor, and not with the low and vicious motives that a dastardly criminal like Ari Falma would falsely attribute to us for his own purposes. He wants us out of his way so that his brand of crime can flourish in the city, bringing misery and poverty to others. We believe that the people of our kingdom want something very different from that. And we share the values of the best among us."

Mafulla interrupted and said, "By the way, 'dastardly' was also very nice. Kudos to you, my super-literate friend."

"Thanks. Let me go on."

"Yes, please."

Walid turned back to his writing. He paused and wrote, "We believe that our fellow law-abiding citizens want to live in a just and safe environment where their children can grow up healthy and unafraid, where their homes are secure, where the streets are friendly, and where neighbors will help watch out for each other and stop men like Falma from creating the lawless tyranny that he so desperately desires."

"Again, nice word choice: 'lawless tyranny' is much better than 'anarchy' as a description."

"Thanks."

"But I shouldn't keep interrupting. Go on."

"We pledge to our fair kingdom and great city our continued efforts for good. And we ask that you help us rid our beautiful region of vermin like Falma, not by violence, but by the due process of law. Capture and convict. Never condone or coddle. But never, ever cross the line that separates the likes of him from the rest of us. And never believe such a pathological liar when he spreads easy words of groundless and self-interested defamation about others."

"Excellent! A call to action like that is perfect."

"Thanks. Signed: The Golden Viper and Windstorm."

"Good! I like it! And they'll finally know how to spell Windstorm. I hope they pay attention and get it right from now on."

Walid smiled and said, "So, let's get this to Masoon and ask him to take it to the paper today, saying that it was delivered here, to him, for whatever reason."

"Good plan, GV."

"Thanks, Stormie."

"We may be able to do more good as the Viper and the Storm after all."

"Yeah, I think you're right."

The boys put the note in a plain envelope, took it downstairs where they managed to find Masoon, and explained the whole situation to him. He agreed to take it by the newspaper offices within the hour, and congratulated them on their quick action to do such a thing. He asked to read the letter first, and heartily approved of the contents, praising the job they had done and saying how impressed he was.

The newspaper retraction story came out the very next day. The large bold headline said:

Our Deepest Apologies to the Masked Men:
The Golden Viper and Windstorm Are Innocent!

On the front page, above the fold, as the lead news of the day, the newspaper explained that it had been terribly wrong in printing the previous day's story. It went on to say that the city editor who had written and placed it had been put on "unpaid administrative leave for the present," and that when he returned, he'd be "starting all over again at the bottom of the organization, and relearning all the jobs necessary for providing the most accurate news each day." Following that was an apology and a brief account of how they could have managed to get things so wrong. And then they reprinted the entire text of the letter that Walid had written, which continued inside on the second page of the paper.

When Mafulla saw the headline, he was tremendously relieved. And then he noticed its correct spelling of his secret identity name and he laughed and said, "Finally! There's hope for the press yet!" But neither he nor Walid had any idea of what would really result from this, which was probably, in the end, a bigger shock than even the previous day's initially false headline and story.

This day's edition of *The Kingdom Daily News* ended up being the most bought and the most read single day edition in the history of the city. People passed it around and even bought copies for friends, which necessitated extra printings. Mafulla's parents were thrilled with the results, and so was everyone else who knew the true identities of these masked crusaders for the good. Even the tone of the letter, people said, showed the sterling character of these masked men. They should be given some sort of medal.

Kissa and Hasina were as relieved as they ever had been about anything in their entire lives. When Set read the headline and the article, he pumped his fist over his head and yelled, "All Right!" Many people actually held Golden Viper and Windstorm parties over the next few days, in celebration of these heroes and the public clearing of their names. And on at least three occasions, three different pairs of men, friends or associates who were innocently walking through the marketplace on windy days and wearing lightly colored wind scarves over their faces, got salutes and even applause from bystanders. Criminal activity slowed down to almost nothing. There was peace on the streets. The newspaper now gave credit for almost everything good that happened in the capital to these newly praised heroes of the city, and of the entire kingdom.

Walid and Mafulla could only watch all this in complete amazement. The king had advised that they curtail the activities under their alternative identities for a while, and they readily complied with his wishes. But in the meantime, they marveled at the groundswell of public opinion in their favor. Restaurants even named specials after them. 'The Golden Viper' and 'Windstorm' became the two most popular sandwich names in town. Young boys played superhero crime stoppers, pretending to be them. And a month after the original newspaper headlines, the most popular radio station in town started broadcasting an ongoing serial drama called "The Adventures of The Viper and The Storm," written by some of the best fiction authors in the kingdom and voiced by the most popular actors of the day. It became, in one week, the most listened-to show in the kingdom.

As a result of the radio broadcasts and everything else, young boys everywhere began to draw pictures of the masked heroes, and in a short time, the newspaper even ran now and then a story told in pictures, to capture the imaginary exploits of The Viper and The Storm. No one knew it at the time, but these printed action stories would one day give rise to comic strips and books. There was even talk of a movie in the works.

Classes were taught on heroism and the nature of identity, along with issues of justice and social obligation. Such discussions also made their way into community meetings and civic gatherings. Never had so much good come from what had initially appeared to be so wrong, and even terrible.

The newspaper then actually reported on all these developments in a special edition, whose title was eye catching:

> From Reviled to Revered:
> The Saga of The Viper and The Storm

Walid and Mafulla first saw that headline one morning when the king, instead of Kular, brought in the day's papers with that one on top and a second copy below. When he put them down in front of the boys, they couldn't believe what they were seeing.

Ali said, "And I thought I was famous as the king. You two are the real celebrities in the palace now, and throughout the whole kingdom."

It's a good thing that Ari Falma missed it all. He had left the kingdom just hours before the retraction article came out, and had no direct contact with people in the city for at least a month and a half afterwards. He would have been astonished at the fact that his attempt to trash the reputations of the two masked men had completely backfired on him, and that as a result of what it had occasioned in response, his was the most despised name in the history of the kingdom, and the masked men were now the most praised and honored citizens of the realm. It was quite a turnaround.

Two made-up names had changed the course of almost everything in the city and the kingdom—at least for the time being. But big storms were brewing in locales far away. Greedy men were still plotting and planning and envisioning their rise. It's often been said that times of peace are mere interludes between periods of war. And as long as human nature remains imprisoned by false ideas and unworthy motives, the world will continue on in that way. But where the light of real wisdom can break through, things can change.

The kingdom was greatly blessed by the many bearers of light who now lived and worked in the palace in service to the king. And at the center of all these good people, the core group of Phi around

Ali was comprised of individuals who were busy making great things happen, and who would be the people he could depend on to resist the truly terrible things that would soon come their way.

But that's another story.

APPENDIX

The Diary of Walid Shabeezar

Golden Insights

Some things we learn by hearing, some by seeing, others by reading, and many by doing. As I continue my adventure in the palace with the king and Mafulla and other good friends, I rededicate myself now and then to writing in this journal, mostly at night, but even during the day when I can. I think it's important to record the lessons I've recently learned, and the new thoughts that have entered my mind.

∆ ∆ ∆

Bad things can prepare the way for good things. And they often do. But it's frequently up to us and how we respond.

Life unfolds in unexpected ways. There are unseen forces that open some doors, and close others. We do best when we pay attention. I need to pay attention well at all times.

Until you learn to focus, your life can be one long series of distractions. And distractions, by definition, rarely get you where you want to go.

False beliefs bring down more plans and people than any weapon. And inappropriate emotions can be just as bad.

Fear and greed are the worst long-term motivators. Faith and love are the best.

We sometimes have to work hard to uproot fear and worry from our lives.

The best people are the best friends to have. Great friends change everything.

Real friendship takes a lot of effort, and justifies the investment.

It's often easier to ask a question than to answer it. But sometimes, the hardest and most important thing is to ask the right question.

In this world, there will always be more questions than answers. We need to get comfortable with that. It's just the way of life in this world.

△ △ △

We're all living paradoxes. Inside each of us is a conundrum or two. The enigmas of life aren't all just out there in the world. Some of the deepest live within us.

Human power is great. Human limits are real. The trick is to appreciate each of these truths without discounting the other.

Perceived limits within our minds and bodies: We should seek to get around them, go over them, shove them aside, dig under them, or blow them up. But then, if we fail in every way, we just might be up against a real and ultimate limit. And that's to be respected with awe, and yet, maybe, we should still keep pushing away at it.

Dealing with apparent limits makes us strong. Remember to push at the walls of the cage.

Kissa told me about something the girls discussed in their class: Freedom and Order—an interesting pair of ideas. We want enough freedom to be able to create the right forms of order for our lives. And we want enough order of the right sort to provide for strong, healthy forms of freedom. Fixate on one and you lose the other. Balance both in the right ways, and you have the most basic conditions for a good and fulfilling life. But who's to say where that balance is at any given time? Wisdom alone can tell us. And the answer may be different for different lives. We can fail often in our effort to find it in our own. But that's Ok if we continue on, learning as we go.

Apparent opposites, creatively combined, can give rise to something great. Khalid said the German philosopher Hegel based his thought on something like that. Confronted with two extremes, there may be a middle way that's better than either of them. Most people lurch to one far side or the other. Wisdom finds a synthesis of the possibilities.

△ △ △

In your unconscious mind, you can know things that your conscious mind can't see. If you're basically a smart, sane, sensitive person, your instincts and intuitions can serve you well. Then, when you have a strong intuition, you can be bold to trust it, and I think you'll be right more often than not. But all those conditions are important.

There are many deep things going on in the world far beyond what we can see or hear or clearly know.

Some people try to fight against destiny. It's best to partner up with it. It won't lead you astray, but will help magnify who you are and what you can do.

It's good to be optimistic, even in difficult times. And it's in those times that your optimism can deepen and grow and prove its value.

It's also good to be realistic, while being optimistic. The optimist at least tries. The realist prepares for resistance and trouble.

Those who fear and resist their destiny tend to think of it as opposed to their free will. Nothing could be farther from the truth. Your des-

tiny depends in part on your choice. Much is offered, but more is required, and that's always up to you.

The full truth about anything is much larger than we can imagine. We're not called to be omniscient, but only to seek to be wise.

There's no need to fear people who act from bad motives. Wariness is enough. Despite any contrary appearances, corruption is weakness and eventually, in some way, will meet defeat.

Mafulla said something that keeps echoing in my head. A situation that can appear very bad and even scary on the surface, when it's thought through thoroughly, can look really different.

The power of the mind is to untangle confusion and find truth.

I had an insight from Uncle Ali. Age doesn't just eventually bring new wrinkles to your body, it can also bring new wrinkles to your thought, and these are good to have.

A perfectly smooth surface has no depth.

There's deep texture to even simple wisdom.

No path worth taking will be smooth and easy. The best are often rough and uphill.

Life is never perfectly smooth. Our thoughts shouldn't be, either.

There is a beauty to texture and depth.

If your body is going to show the magnitude of your experience, make sure your mind does, too.

The good wrinkles to have flow from experiences fully lived. Each is a talisman or touchstone of adventure.

△ △ △

A true friend will accept you for who you are. A false friend wants you to be what they need. Avoid false friends. Appreciate the true.

Beware of those who would cast you as an extra in the movie that's their life, while falsely promising you a starring role.

The most effective manipulators can seem to be your best supporters and fans. They flatter and praise in order to gain your trust and effort for their cause, despite what it might mean for you.

Honesty connects people. Dishonesty distances.

Truth is strong. Falsehood is weak. Seek strength, avoid weakness, and live well.

△ △ △

You never know what the next moment will bring. Act accordingly.

Be open. Be always and ever open. Life is about new things.

Surprise is the grammar of change.

Life can catch us unprepared, or meet our preparation unexpectedly.

The world's capacity for novel and new far exceeds our talent to guess what's next.

Anyone who is truly paying attention is both more and less likely to be surprised. That's a nice paradox, and a surprise of its own.

Inner strength means getting the job done, come what may.

Inner resilience is the royal road to outer results.

∆ ∆ ∆

Timing can be the razor's edge between success and failure.

Leaping forth before the right time appears, or holding back as the proper time passes, are good ways of going badly wrong.

Don't often dash or delay. It's rarely wise to hurry or hesitate. It's best to find your proper timing in all things.

Failure should educate and not discourage. Everyone has this teacher, and school is always in session.

I overheard an older person say something interesting. He said: At this point in my life, I live high atop a mountain of mistakes, and from this peak, the view I now have is called wisdom.

The best wisdom is hard earned. We get bruised to get better.

The best success is hard earned. We fall three times and get up four.

Nothing feels better deep down than helping a friend in need.

∆ ∆ ∆

Clever deceit will meet with defeat unless tethered to the highest values, and used only to save the innocent from great harm.

Power should serve a higher purpose. By itself, it can corrupt and destroy.

Statesmanship, not gamesmanship, should be the heart of politics.

Self-interest is the first interest in life. And it's natural, but to be healthy, it needs to be surrounded by many other interests that can guide it properly.

Self-interest is an urge in need of the truly urgent companion known as sagacity.

A successful monarchy puts itself out of a job. Democratic self-rule by a well-informed and enlightened electorate is the ideal of governance, at least in this world.

Each of us comes into life with a duty to help make the world a better place for others as well as ourselves. That's what citizenship is all about. When our community is better off, we're better off.

I need to give myself more often the gift of quietness within, to open myself to new insights and ideas. And only a measure of emptiness will accommodate the arrival of new things.

Emptying the mind now and then will make enough space for new thoughts.

Another paradox: A measure of emptiness allows for a fuller life. A true spirituality is all about emptiness and proper filling.

∆ ∆ ∆

The most spiritual place there is might just be the deepest place within each of us. Guard it. Go to it. Dwell in it.

You can't always tell from the way something starts how it's going to end. Good starts make good endings more likely, but there's never any guarantee. The same is true of bad starts. A turnaround is always possible. And I believe in turnarounds.

If you need help, it can come from the most surprising places. Never be afraid to ask. And when it appears, use it well.

Note to self: Avoid angry monkeys. Cultivate monkey friends.

△ △ △

Kissa told me something about a conversation she had with Hasina on the train. They both did something to help out during the bad stuff, something they didn't really understand, but they did it anyway, and it worked. She said that Hoda had often told her that, in life, what often comes before how. She knew what to do before she had any idea about how it worked. But that's Ok. I've got to remember this. Sometimes action properly precedes understanding.

Do what's right when it needs to be done, and figure it all out later.

We each have roles in life that give us opportunities, but they can also bring stress. Most of the stress is unnecessary. Maybe all of it is. When I recognize it, I can shed it, and enjoy my day much more.

Surface judgments rarely provide deep insights.

We can't know a place just by viewing it. We can't know a person just by seeing him. To get to really know anything or anyone with a depth of being, you have to be around it, or him, or her, for a while.

Understanding is always earned. Ignorance is easy and free—at first. But then, in the end, it carries a huge cost and hard consequences.

△△△

Sometimes, a bad problem hides a worse one. Peel the onion. Never stop too soon. Dealing with a symptom won't cure the underlying cause.

Experience can diminish fear. When you've been through a scary situation once, you'll never fear it exactly the same way again.

Much more is going on in our world than meets the eye. Try to remember that at all times.

There are many ways of knowing.

The soul sees more than the eyes. And it can hear more than the ears.

Often in life, you have to follow the breadcrumbs that mark the path forward, and not worry about who baked the bread or what kind it is. Pay attention to the clues you have, and pursue them to where they lead. You can ask all the other questions later.

△△△

Nothing's over until it's over. That sounds trivial, but it's crucial to remember. Sometimes, things seem to end, and we let down our guard and turn our attention elsewhere just before the biggest ending of all.

Stay ready. Stay alert. Stay flexible. Stay strong. That's the only way to have a chance to stay safe and flourish.

Sometimes, you can feel the support of people at a distance. You don't have to know how it works in order to benefit from it.

When you send love and support to someone other than yourself, you necessarily do some good in the world.

Focus matters.

When you finally let go, you can truly take charge and act well.

Δ Δ Δ

Everything that hurts can teach. Pain can lead to new levels of existence and awareness. Never regret what's difficult. Use it, instead.

Things can be not just different from what they seem, but the opposite of what they seem. Even events that appear terrible can open the door for something wonderful.

Trust with your whole heart only those who love you with theirs.

Do what you think is right, whatever the world might believe. This is the key, as long as you're humbly open to the deepest leadings there are.

Good will always last, and can grow in ways that will delight you.

Be ready for anything, accept what comes, and be thankful for all the magnificent wonders of life.

You never know what to expect from The Viper and The Storm.

However things may seem, the good will prevail in the end.

Acknowledgments

I'm thankful once more for the marvelous muse who spoke these characters and their stories into my head each day. As I've said before, it was like watching a movie and just writing down what I saw and heard. I never had to make up anything. I just tried to get it all down the best I could. And as strange as it may sound to say, I'm thankful for each good person in these stories, who have all become like personal friends in the kingdom of my mind and heart. I'm grateful for everything they've brought into my life. I love them as if they're real; and they are, in their own special way.

I'm also very appreciative of the many living, nonfictional people who have continued to encourage me and support me with their good cheer through every day of writing this book. Just like Walid and his friends, we need each other. Thanks, Don, Tony, Tom, Ed, Mary, and many of you who have given me words of encouragement along the way. Writing can be a solitary enterprise. You keep me going!

Ed Hearn, like always, provided me with the sharp eye of an expert editor, finding typos I would never have noticed on my own. In books as well as in life, I often see what should be there rather than what is there! Ed has saved me from many errors and long sentences. Bruce May also helped a great deal with wise editorial questions and suggestions. Sara Morris provided our cover design and Abigail Chiaramonte finished the book design, with interior and exterior matters. I thank you all!

I'm also nurtured each day by the beautiful place where I live, and by the great dogs I get to play with or take for walks whenever I need a break. The cats in the house are constant entertainment and support as well. Thanks as always to my family.

I can't wait to see what happens next. I hope you feel the same way.

Tom Morris
Wilmington, NC

Afterword

Beyond *The Viper and The Storm*

First, there was *The Oasis Within*, a short tale about a series of deep conversations and surprising events that took place as a group of men and camels crossed the desert in Egypt in 1934. Then there was *The Golden Palace,* the official Book One to a series of subsequent stories about these remarkable individuals, collectively entitled:

Walid and the Mysteries of Phi

Then came Book Two, *The Stone of Giza.* This is Book Three. If you've read the prologue to the series, *The Oasis Within,* or you've enjoyed *The Golden Palace* and *The Stone of Giza,* you'll likely love the entire series, which presents a sprawling epic account of action, adventure, and ideas set in and around a reimagined Cairo, Egypt in 1934 and 1935, with a few sojourns farther abroad. Its books contain captivating tales about life, death, meaning, love, friendship, the deepest secrets behind everyday events, and the extraordinary power of a well-focused mind. The events they relate will interact along the way with such classics as Plato's *Republic*, *The Epic of Gilgamesh*, *Beowulf*, *Frankenstein*, and *Moby Dick*, among many other seminal texts. With unexpected humor and continual intrigue, you'll gradually discover in these books the outlines of a powerful worldview and a profound philosophy of life.

To find out more, visit **www.TomVMorris.com/novels** or go to **www.TheOasisWithin.com.**

The prologue and companion book to the series, *The Oasis Within,* as well as any book in the series, will be available for large group purchases at special discounts. To find out more, contact the author through his oldest and most reliable email, **TomVMorris@aol.com** or through his website. Tom is also available to speak with book groups via email, Skype, or any other means that would help in the discussion of these stories. Make a request, and speak to the author.

About the Author

Tom Morris is one of the most active philosophers and public speakers in the world. A native of North Carolina, he's a graduate of The University of North Carolina (Chapel Hill), where he was a Morehead-Cain Scholar, and he holds a Ph.D. in both Philosophy and Religious Studies from Yale University. For fifteen years, he served as a Professor of Philosophy at the University of Notre Dame, where he was one of their most popular teachers. You can find him online now anytime at **www.TomVMorris.com.**

Tom has been honored with the University of North Carolina's Distinguished Young Alumnus Award, as well as with honorary doctorates in recognition of his work. He has been a George A. and Eliza Gardner Howard Foundation Fellow, through Brown University, and a Fellow with the National Endowment for the Humanities.

Tom is also the author of over twenty-two pioneering books. His twelfth book, *True Success: A New Philosophy of Excellence,* launched him into an ongoing adventure as a philosopher working and speaking throughout the world. His audiences have included a great many of the Fortune 500 companies and dozens of the largest national and international trade associations. His work has been mentioned, commented on, or covered by NBC, ABC, CNN, CNBC, NPR, and in most major newspapers and news magazines. He's also the author of the highly acclaimed books *If Aristotle Ran General Motors, Philosophy for Dummies, The Art of Achievement, The Stoic Art of Living, Twisdom, Superheroes and Philosophy,* and *If Harry Potter Ran General Electric: Leadership Wisdom from the World of the Wizards,* as well as many others. His most recent books include the philosophical prologue to the current series, *The Oasis Within,* and the subsequent novels, *The Golden Palace*, and *The Stone of Giza,* as well as the current book *The Viper and The Storm.* He just may be the world's happiest philosopher.

Φ

www.ingramcontent.com/pod-product-compliance
Lightning Source LLC
Chambersburg PA
CBHW030420310726
48979CB00009B/1543/J

* 9 7 8 0 9 9 6 7 1 2 3 8 5 *